A Writing Upon the Sand

A
Writing
Upon the
Sand

J.M. KIRKLEY

Conformed Image
PRESS

Acknowledgments

I'm grateful to Mr. Casey Edward Greene, Galveston Rosenberg Library Scholar who helped me sift through the inconsistencies of survivor stories and little known facts about the Great Storm, and staff Carol Wood, who helped with research.

Thanks to Doc Deason, my meteorologist son-in-law, who set up tours of the Alabama and Florida National Weather Bureaus, and to meteorologists John Purdy and Jon Rizzo for sharing their experiences and knowledge of hurricanes.

I'm grateful to Galveston First Baptist Church for providing church history records of the 1900 Storm and to Linda Groff and Darrell Marullo, for the 1900 orphan record of the Galveston Orphans Home.

A special thanks to my awesome advanced readers: Kay Autrey and Alissa Deason my first readers who read very rough drafts and offered feedback and encouragement, Tim Kirkley, Natalie O'Neill, Kristi Wolfe, Susie Deason, Nancy Kerr, Christie Lathrop, and Sylvia Alf. Your insights steered and strengthened my story. To Payton Ressen, my editor, who affirmed and provided constructive suggestions, to Pam Holzman, my eagle-eye Proofreader, who polished my grammar and time period accuracy. To Roseanna White Designs, who created the stellar cover design. I'm grateful to Brent, my spouse, who made treks to Galveston, toured the Bryan Museum with me, and hung out at Starbucks on the Strand while I did research at the Rosenberg Library.

"May your character be not a writing upon the sand,
but an inscription upon the rock....
May your whole life be so settled, fixed and established,
that all the blasts of hell and all the storms of earth
shall never be able to remove you."
-Charles Haddon Spurgeon

Prologue

Galveston Island, Texas, 1926

Only fools and those desperate for peace returned to the place that spawned their nightmares. Emily hadn't planned on ever coming back.

She curled her fingers around the sheets and tamped down the urge to flee. The old nightmare had returned, conjuring rising water, sharp with the taste of brine.

Throwing off the covers smothering her chest, she slipped on a satin robe and paced over to the window. Goosebumps crawled across her flesh as the air penetrated the wrap. She rubbed her arms, more to soothe the tingling in her limbs than to ward off any chill.

Emily parted the curtains and peered out from the fifth-story window at the Gulf of Mexico, searching the horizon. Twilight's purple haze shone on the water under a cloudless sky. Seeing it, she released a sigh into the room.

Her husband shifted on the mattress. In the gray light, she traced the outline of his body sprawled across the bed. A pillow muffled his soft snoring. Her gaze lingered on him while he settled and drifted deeper asleep.

His one request had been to celebrate their twenty-fifth wedding anniversary where their courtship began. The pleading in his eyes had silenced any protest. Emily agreed to come for no other reason: she loved him more than life.

Returning here was proof.

If only that made what she was about to do easier. Before she could talk herself out of it, Emily exchanged the robe for a yellow cotton shift. She scratched a note of where she was headed on the hotel notepad and propped it next to her husband's billfold. Careful not to rouse him, she lifted a wide-brimmed hat off the chair and tiptoed out of the room.

When she reached the curb, she glanced up and down Seawall Boulevard, noting the changes since the 1900 Storm. Hotels, restaurants, and homes faced the sea. To her right, the Crystal Palace's causeway stretched over the boulevard. Beyond it, Murdock's Bathhouse once more jutted out over the water, the waves lapping against the pilings.

The autumn breeze whiffled her bobbed hair, whipping a veil of copper waves in her eyes. She tucked the strands under her hat and peered back at the Hotel Galvez. Along the sweeping entrance, palm trees flapped in the breeze.

She hesitated. Pressure built in her ears as a Model T Ford clattered by.

You can do this. You must. Straightening, Emily faced the Gulf, the sea pulsing with an ancient rhythm. A whisper of the past beckoned her feet forward.

Her steps slowed as she neared the raised seawall, getting her first glimpse below. The long seam of concrete sutured the edges of land and sea, stitching closed the gaping wound dealt by the Great Storm. The barrier skirted the shoreline in both directions and buffered the island against further blows from wind and waves.

If only they'd built it sooner.

She bit back a sob. Tears pricked her eyes, threatening to pay tribute to the pain, to those lost. She batted her eyes dry. *Not here.*

The cadence of the surf pulled her gaze away. Beyond the seawall, the tide churned toward the shore. She took the stairs and descended to the sand below.

She paused to untie her low-heeled shoes and scoop them up by their straps. Her heels sank into the powdery sand as she approached the water's edge. The low tide washed smooth the shoreline, packing it firm beneath her feet.

Seeking solitude, she set out up the beach, facing the sunrise. Along the way, she gathered up scalloped shells the tide had deposited on the sand. She'd use them later.

Emily paused on an empty stretch of beach. The tide's ebb and flow mirrored the wariness pulling at her temples, flashing images of that fateful day long ago. *The tide surging in the streets. Debris flowing swiftly as arrows. The dark watery gloom.*

She blinked and blew out a breath, shaking off the scenes. No wonder she'd become vigilant at avoiding reminders of the Great Storm or its aftermath. At all times, she avoided closed-in spaces. Smells, however, caught her unaware. A whiff of something foul or burning made her heart race and her stomach revolt, proof she hadn't outrun the past or its stenches.

Though that dark time had flung a long shadow over the years, there were moments that glimmered at the edges. After all, in the end, the worst of times had brought her and her husband together.

For both their sakes, she longed to put right the past and rid herself of the terrible secret she had carried alone all these years. She hoped it wasn't too late.

Emily knew in her heart what she needed to do.

Gathering her courage, she peered out at the horizon. The rising sun burned through the mist, casting an amber beam upon the water.

Lord, give me grace.

The tide splashed and foamed near her feet as what lay buried deep within started bubbling up to the surface. Her breathing slowed as she allowed the memories to flow unfettered.

She'd kept the letter all this time, the one that changed everything.

Chapter 1

Emily stifled a yawn while creasing the ends of her boarding ticket into pleats. Anticipation over having to switch trains in Houston had kept her wired for much of the night.

An unsteady hand stilled her from fidgeting. "You'll do just fine." Grandpa Dunne squeezed her fingers to emphasize the point. "Estelle's pastor will meet you at the train in Houston. Now, if that doesn't ease your mind, I have it on good authority that angels ride the rails."

The wink he gave coaxed a smile from her.

He pulled out his watch and popped open the lid. Emily leaned in, noting the time. Half past seven. Her gaze slid to the portrait painted inside the cover. Her grandmother, Rebecca, dressed in yellow silk. Chestnut curls framed a heart-shaped face, but her eyes, as bright as morning glories, drew her in. Emily wished she'd known her. Grandpa touched her likeness for a moment, his gaze wistful. He closed the lid gently and tucked the watch into his waistcoat pocket over his heart.

He shuffled with his cane, edging closer. "You never did say how the folks took the news of your leaving. To hear Rosa tell it, you're going with her blessing. She even made it sound like Samuel agreed to the venture. A bit more to it than that, I suspect." He gave her a meaningful look.

Emily let out a huff. "I'll say. Pa dug in his heels." *Hotly.* "Wouldn't budge until Ma harped about the loan Uncle Clayton paid years ago when the hailstorm ruined the crops. Said Pa was in no position to refuse Aunt Estelle's request. And that sending me was the only way to repay kin for saving the farm." The tension in the room had left Emily breathless.

Grandpa scratched the stubble on his jaw. "Nothing like goading a man's pride to force his hand. The problem is nobody goads a bull without him charging. Those brown eyes tell me you caught the brunt of it."

She should have seen it coming. Pa had glared through a lock of rust-colored hair while his pride warred with indebtedness. His voice had dropped deceptively soft right before he delivered his parting blow.

"He ah…" Emily cleared her throat, "he said I wasn't allowed under his roof if I left the farm. That when I failed—and I'd surely fail—I'd have to scrape out a living or starve." The words had stung like the backhanded slap he meant them to be. He always had to gain the upper hand.

Grandpa grunted. "The way I see it, Estelle offered you a fine position. You'll do us proud."

As always, his encouragement lifted her spirits.

The whistle blared, and the conductor called all aboard. Folks on the platform murmured their goodbyes and leaned in for hugs before filing onto the train. It was time.

Saying goodbye threatened to splinter the veneer of her composure. She bit her lip, groping for words to convey a lifetime of thanks. How would she manage without having Grandpa nearby?

Her throat ached as she searched his eyes. "I'm glad you're the one seeing me off. You'll never know… I can never thank you enough for all you've done for me."

He dipped his chin, his stoic manner faltering. He appeared frail, his dark eyes watery. He squinted down the tracks to collect himself while stroking the ends of his silver mustache.

After a moment, he reached into his coat pocket and pulled out an envelope. "Here." He pressed it into her gloved hand. "It'll get you through a rainy day. Set it aside."

She hesitated despite the rush of gratitude.

"Take it," he urged. "When the hard times come, and Lord knows they do, you'll have something to fall back on."

Her fingers trembled. "This means more than I can say."

She dropped it into her drawstring pouch and pulled the strings closed.

"Now, when you settle in with Estelle, I want to hear from you. She'll look after you well."

Emotions flared high as he leaned heavily on his cane. Would this be the last time she saw him in this life? She pressed her hand to the ache in her chest.

Her chin wobbled. "I'll miss you."

Swallowing the tears that threatened to spill, she buried her face in the folds of his jacket. A tap on the shoulder from behind interrupted the moment.

"It's time, ma'am," the conductor said.

Grandpa patted her back. "Now you go on … find a seat."

Emily leaned in and kissed his stubbly cheek. She drew in his comfort, inhaling the cedar clinging to his clothes.

"Goodbye, Grandpa." Her voice cracked.

On shaking legs, she hefted her luggage and mounted the steps into the coach. Inside, the muggy June air smelled of leather and coal dust. Emily squeezed down the aisle lugging the suitcase and small trunk. Midway back, she sat next to the window and set the luggage by her knees. She sank on the cushion, pushed up the window, and breathed in the fresh air.

The conductor strolled down the aisle, gathering tickets. He hoisted her suitcase onto the brass rack above her seat, where she could keep an eye on it.

He reached for the small travel trunk, and she stilled his hand. "I'll keep it here." Less than two feet wide and a foot deep, the trunk took up more space than she cared to admit, but it held what she valued most.

He shrugged. "Suit yourself."

She'd stuffed all her belongings into those two pieces.

She glanced around at the folks dressed in hats and gloves, wearing their Sunday best. All the women, both young and old, rode with escorts. No wonder Aunt Estelle had arranged for her pastor to accompany Emily from Houston to Galveston. As it turned out, he had a meeting in Houston that day.

She opened her purse and counted the bills inside Grandpa's envelope. Ten dollars, bless him. Other than the train fare, she had no additional cash. She drew the drawstrings tight and wrapped them around her wrist.

Over the hiss of steam, the whistle wailed. The train belched cinders and lurched forward out of the depot. Emily peered through the wisps of steam at Grandpa, leaning on his cane beside the tracks. She thrust out a hand and waved goodbye. Her heart squeezed as he slowly shrank in size until he faded from view. Only then did she press her back into the cushion.

Had she been a fool to leave everything familiar to chase after a dream? Leaving Grandpa behind grew heavier as the train gathered speed and settled into a rhythmic sway, soon crossing the trestle over the Angelina River.

As the train chugged further southward, Emily stretched the muscles in her neck. Stiffness had set in after hours of gripping the handles while the train pitched and jerked through the Piney Woods.

She glanced up from her novel and rested her gaze out the window at the meadow dotted with black-eyed Susans and firewheels. There, a white cowbird perched on the back of a longhorn bull.

Her stomach rumbled. She consulted the watch pinned to the shawl collar. Quarter past twelve. She removed her gloves and dug into the pouch, pulling out letters from Aunt Estelle and leftovers from breakfast. Two buttermilk biscuits stuffed with ham and a jelly jar filled with sweet tea. She unscrewed the lid and took a sip before unfolding the waxed paper and munching on a biscuit Mary Ellen had prepared.

Sleeping on a pallet in her sister's cramped parlor had added to her stiffness. But watching her nieces fuss over Grandpa during breakfast comforted Emily, as did his decision to move in with Mary Ellen and Joe.

Her folks made no such fuss over her when she'd left the farm. Some farewell that turned out to be. Ma on the porch, her apron pressed into crisp pleats, her hair scraped into a bun as severe as the expression on her face. Pa headed away from Emily, his boots ringing through the dogtrot as he strode toward the pasture, his silence shouting his disapproval. Had she expected anything more?

Her brother's presence had steadied her. While Will loaded her luggage onto the wagon, Emily sat rigidly on the hardwood bench. She'd peered up at her mother's face, searching for any hint of sadness or goodwill toward her, finding none. Nothing but triumph gleamed in her eyes.

Proof that Rosa Cleburne hadn't stood up to Pa for Emily's sake. It hurt knowing she'd been nothing more than a pawn to the Queen in the match between her folks, valued the least, expendable. Emily might regret leaving if she mattered more to them.

Well, at least she mattered to Aunt Estelle.

She opened the letter that started her on this journey. The yellow rosebud stationery crinkled in her hands as she reread it one more time.

June 1, 1900

Dear Emily,
I hope this letter finds you well. The optimism of the new century fills us with fresh hope, despite our circumstances.
We've sought the latest treatment for Clayton. Although it's too early to tell, the pain in his chest and cough have eased somewhat.
Leisure moments are rare as hen's teeth, so I'll be brief. I'm

writing to make you an offer, one I trust you will seriously consider. Are you intrigued?

Most days, I'm pulled between nursing Clayton, helping the children with schoolwork, tending to Rachel, and managing a household. It's reached the point where I must hire additional help.

Then an idea came to me, one I believe was divinely inspired. Hiring a governess would lighten my load since Jake and Sarah have fallen behind in school. And who better to teach the children than kin? You'd be a perfect choice if you're willing to come.

Given Clayton's condition, it's impossible to say how long we'll need you.

We'll pay your train fare plus respectable wages if you accept my offer. We have a guest room, and Galveston has plenty of social events if that suits you.

East Texas has always been home for you, as it once was for me. But I've discovered that God brings certain people into our lives who become like family, and that makes all the difference no matter where we call home.

Although I felt prompted to write, you must affirm whether this is the right course for you. I'm eager to hear what you decide. Give everyone my love.

Best regards,
Aunt Estelle

Emily had leaped at the opportunity to be governess to her cousins after being forced to settle for occasional tutoring. Even leaving the farm had been beyond her reach. Until now.

Emily looked forward to meeting her aunt, though she felt as if she knew her already from the letters they exchanged through the years.

She slid the letter back into the envelope before reaching for the other biscuit and her aunt's latest letter. She skimmed it for the minister's description. *Our pastor, as you'll recall, is Colin Hensleigh. He's speaking at the pastor's conference and assured me the meeting would be over in plenty of time to meet your train. Look for a tall, distinguished gentleman with a lean physique and the loveliest accent. He said he'll be the one carrying a Bible.*

Her shoulders drooped. Chitchatting with strangers made her head throb. She dreaded the long pauses, the fishing for topics that held no interest to her. She pictured a white-haired gentleman with a deep voice that was more southern drawl than twang. With any luck, he'd soon tire of her company and opt to read the Psalms.

Emily washed down the biscuit with the tea and cleared off her lap, stowing everything in her purse. She brushed crumbs off the brown suit she'd sewn for the trip.

The brown twill cost what little she had saved from tutoring, but she needed to arrive looking presentable. The shawl collar lacked a braid for the trim, but the tailoring of the jacket and flounced skirt flattered her slim figure. She'd pulled the used brass buttons from the sewing box. From the fabric scrap, she'd made the drawstring pouch. She envisioned an embroidered design on the bag, but no time.

She'd found a strip of grosgrain ribbon to freshen her brimmed straw hat, which she wore over a bun knotted at the nape of her neck.

Sunlight streamed into the interior of the coach, warming her seat. She settled back onto the cushion and yawned. With her appetite satisfied, the train's rhythmic sway pulled at her eyelids, lulling them closed.

The bell and whistle blared, jerking Emily awake. She blinked and squinted, glancing about the coach.

The sunlight now slanted deep across the aisle. How long had she been asleep?

The conductor announced the Houston central depot. The other passengers began folding up newspapers and tucking away their belongings. Emily stowed her book away, thrust her hands into her gloves, and looped the cords on the drawstring pouch around her wrist, gripping it tight.

The brakes squealed as the train rumbled into the depot. Emily glanced out the window. A cloud of steam blocked her view of the station.

The moment the train stopped, the passengers swarmed into motion. Emily reached overhead for her suitcase.

A gentleman across the aisle stepped forward. "Allow me."

"Thank you kindly."

He pulled down the luggage and set it beside her. Hefting the bag and her small trunk, Emily lugged them down the aisle behind the others, eager to exit the train. The humidity weighed heavy and oppressive, draping her chest like wet wool. Moisture popped out on her forehead.

Her stomach fluttered in anticipation as she filed out of the coach. She dismounted the steps. Her gaze traveled up the imposing three-story brick building before panning the faces of the crowd gathered beside the tracks.

Emily reached up on tiptoe and searched for Mr. Hensleigh. "Tall, lean, toting a Bible," she murmured.

Smartly dressed men and women pressed close with the scent of lilac and pipe tobacco. They flashed smiles of recognition and clasped hands. Their voices pitched in greeting. Emily watched them hug and pick up the children in their arms.

One by one, the men lifted their chins and called out names, threading their way toward familiar faces.

Still, no one approached her. Her pulse kicked up. Her grip stiffened around the handles of her luggage, growing heavy, her fingers tingling. She stepped outside the huddle, needing room to breathe, to think. Where was he?

Porters were unloading trunks and baggage from the baggage car and toting them behind passengers toward the horse-drawn carriages lined up ahead, just off to the right.

Before long, the crowd began to thin out.

Emily swung around and fastened her gaze on the station door, willing the man fitting her aunt's description to emerge. The last passengers dispersed, their voices trailing off, leaving her alone.

Soon the carriages clattered down the road, the echo loud and grating. Still, no one strode through the doors.

The waning sun deepened the shadows in the station yard. It would be nightfall when the train pulled into Galveston.

Her insides quivered. Where was Mr. Hensleigh? Until that moment, she hadn't realized how much she depended on him to steer her right to the Edwards' doorstep.

But he had yet to come. Now what?

Emily's breathing thinned. She stood rigid beside the tracks, groping for direction. Having cast off all ties to home, she was set adrift with no compass to navigate an unfamiliar island.

Chapter 2

Emily made her way into the station on unsteady legs and slumped onto the nearest bench, plopping her luggage at her feet. Her pulse pounded at her eardrums.

She scanned the station, searching. Where could Mr. Hensleigh be? Had the conference lasted longer than he expected?

She glanced at the double-faced clock bracketing the brick wall. Five thirty-five. Less than thirty minutes before the train departed.

A whistle shrilled, and a bell clanged. Passengers blurred past her view in a flurry of tapping shoes.

Amid all the people, loneliness clawed at her chest.

Emily spotted a tall gentleman coming through the main entrance. He toted a leather-bound book. With a gust of relief, she sat up straight, poised to flag his attention. He veered over to a circle of men visiting near the ticket booth. Several of the others, she noted, carried leather-bound books. From a distance, she couldn't distinguish a novel from a Bible.

"So much for that setting him apart from the crowd," Emily muttered.

She shifted on the hard seat and propped her chin up with a fist. Had he been pulled aside after the meeting and lost track of time?

A ticket agent called for tickets to Galveston. She pinched the bridge of her nose. She'd have to board the train without him. What if no carriages were available after nightfall to take her to the Edwards' home? She had their address on the envelope but no directions. She pictured wandering alone down unlit streets, searching for Sealy Avenue.

If only the man had kept his word!

Enough waiting. Emily pulled open her drawstring pouch and dug out the coin purse, her lips tightened. With gloved fingers, she fumbled with the clasp, wincing at the sharp footfalls that quickened, growing louder. A strand of copper fell in her eyes. She batted it away.

A pair of polished wingtips came into view, halting in front of her. "Pardon me, miss."

A man cleared his throat. The British accent registered as she fished out dollar bills. Emily glared up at the intruder from under the brim of her hat.

"Are you Miss Cleburne?" The man sounded winded.

Emily tilted her head back and gazed at the gentleman towering over her. The muscles in her back stiffened. "I am."

"Right. Well," the man peered at her, his eyes earnest, "I confess I'm torn between introducing myself and begging your forgiveness. But if you're to forgive my delay, you must know whom to pardon." He tipped his derby, revealing a mass of walnut hair. "I'm Colin Hensleigh, and I'm dreadfully sorry I made you wait on me."

Taken aback, her gaze swept over his appearance. He was nothing like she pictured him to be. Possibly thirty years old. His impeccably tailored navy blue suit and striped tie set off a pair of fine eyes the same color. He snapped open his leather briefcase, slid his Bible in, and tucked it under his arm.

Emily exhaled through her nose. Clutching the ticket fare, she stood up. "Well, let's not waste any more time. We need tickets."

"Allow me." He motioned to her luggage.

Emily gestured with a wave of her hand and pivoted on her heel, marching toward the ticket booth.

She sank onto the cushioned seat and rolled her shoulders to relieve the stiffness. Lifting the lid on the trunk, Emily picked up the novel and set it on her lap. She turned her face to the coach window, needing a few minutes to collect herself.

Her traveling companion must have sensed this, for he hoisted her luggage onto the racks without saying a word. As he sat in the seat beside her, she detected traces of spicy bergamot and citrus.

Rubbing her neck, she peered out the window at the puffing dark steam that rained down soot over the cars. The smell of cinder smoke drifted in through the windows.

She cracked open the book to where she'd clipped the brass bookmark. Her pulse began to slow into its normal rhythm as she turned her mind to Emily Bronte's tale.

"Tickets," the conductor bellowed as he strode up the aisle, hefting luggage onto racks and collecting tickets.

The whistle shrilled, piercing the silence. As the train chuffed out of the station, Emily held the book to her chest and watched the buildings and fence posts slide past her view.

Over the locomotive rumble, Mr. Hensleigh cleared his throat and shifted on the seat. "Allow me to explain what happened."

His voice had a soothing melodic quality, not that she was in any frame of mind to hear his excuses. She begrudgingly set down the novel in her lap, folded her arms around her middle, and rested her head on the seat cushion.

He rubbed his fingertips along the white ridge of a scar above his left eyebrow. "I had every intention of being on time. Early, in fact. In my defense, it appears I was the brunt of a little ministerial humor."

Emily arched a brow, not amused.

"The prankster, a fellow minister, was unaware of my plans to meet you. I decided to stretch my legs and walk to the station. Not knowing my way around Houston, Edmund sent me on a wild goose chase in the opposite direction." He shook his head over his ignorance. "I must've walked six blocks before I became suspicious and asked for directions. Once pointed on the right course, I promise you I hurried to the station."

Her gaze fell to her lap. That Mr. Hensleigh witnessed her being upset chafed more than the silly prank.

Annoyance leaked into her tone. "Are you always so trusting?"

He tipped his head, regarding her. "Is it not better to err on the side of trust unless trust has been violated?"

Naïve man. Didn't he know that he'd pay dearly for trusting the wrong person?

"You might be less winded if you'd made your friend *earn* your trust rather than giving it freely."

Mr. Hensleigh chuckled. "Spoken like a true governess."

His smile faded, his expression turning thoughtful. He paused, as if remembering. "I know how unsettling it is to arrive in a strange place. I regret that you had to experience that alone."

Their eyes met. Without conscious thought, she said, "I was about to board the train alone."

He nodded at her candor. "I figured as much, though I find your honesty refreshing." She gave him a long look, and he lifted a shoulder. "In my profession, I find few folks are plainspoken around me. I'm just relieved I spotted you in time."

He reached into his leather bag and pulled out a paper sack. "Perhaps I can interest you in a peace offering."

She eyed the sack. "What's in it?"

"Leftovers from the meal the ladies prepared. They're wonderful cooks." He pulled out items wrapped in waxed paper and chuckled over the amount. "It appears they took it upon themselves to put meat on my bones. Please join me. There's more than enough."

The sweet and savory food made her mouth water. "I could eat."

He divided the food, and they dined on fried chicken, cornbread, and wedges of sweet potato pie.

Mr. Hensleigh brushed cornbread crumbs from his hands. "I've grown to appreciate Southern recipes very much."

"Well, it's obvious you're not from around these parts."

"So my accent gave it away, did it?" He wiped his mouth with a napkin. "I'm from Dover, England, but I grew up in Bermuda. Care to hear how I came to Galveston?"

Emily chewed and swallowed a thick, creamy bite of sweet potato pie. "Will it be shorter than a sermon?"

His mouth twitched. "Quite."

"Go on then. But first, tell me about Bermuda."

Setting the wrapping aside, he propped his elbows on his knees and steepled the tips of his fingers, tapping them against the cleft in his chin. His jaw firmed. "My parents were missionaries on the island until the epidemic of '89."

"Epidemic?"

"Yellow fever." His brows knit together. "They ... neither survived. They died three days apart. I was seventeen, so it fell on me to raise my sister."

"How old was she?"

"Gracie was five at the time, poor tyke."

Emily leaned back in her seat and tried to fathom shouldering the responsibility of caring for a sister after losing both parents. "How dreadful for y'all."

Colin nodded absently. "We soon headed home to England, where I completed seminary. Then, one evening while fishing, we met a lovely couple from Galveston. We discussed everything from the best shops to buy fish and chips to our mutual passion for helping orphans. As we visited, our conversation deepened, as between old friends. They shared their church's struggle to fill the shoes of their beloved pastor who died, and asked if I might be willing to consider coming. As it turned out, that year we boarded a vessel bound for Galveston." He paused with a sudden gleam in his eye. "That couple, by the way, was your aunt and uncle."

Emily's lips parted. "I had no idea."

"I count Clayton and Estelle as dear family." His expression softened. "And once again I'm near water. All my life I've been drawn to the sea, so how fitting that I now call Galveston home."

Emily rested her head on the cushion. What a story. "England, Bermuda, Galveston… You've seen so much."

"Indeed." Though sadness shadowed his eyes, he forced brightness into his tone. "Enough of my tale. Tell me about yourself. Where you were raised, about your family, your desire to teach."

"Compared to your life, mine's as dull as dusting chalkboards."

"I doubt that's true. We all have a story to call our own." The minister tipped his head and waited expectantly.

Emily picked up the waxed paper from her lap and started creasing wide pleats while she gathered her thoughts.

"Well, I grew up on a farm near Chireno, that's in East Texas. The Piney Woods is thick with forests and wild game. Our nearest neighbors are several miles down the road, so we didn't visit much except on Sundays."

How much to say about kin? "I'm the youngest of four. There's Kate, Will, Mary Ellen, and myself. My father grows crops, mostly corn and potatoes." *And discord—bumper crops of it.* "I grew up around ministers so I'm aware of your pranks." Mr. Hensleigh's eyes narrowed, and she held back a smile. "My grandpa is a minister."

He chuckled. "Right. Estelle speaks highly of him."

Emily settled back onto her cushion. "As for teaching, ever since I first entered the schoolhouse and eyed the letters and numbers written across the chalkboard, I wanted to unlock their meaning. I discovered…" she paused to clear the emotion from her voice, "that reading opened wide my narrow world. I wanted that for others. So I started helping the younger ones with their reading and sums after I finished my assignments. Grandpa encouraged my interest and paid my tuition to the Teacher's College in Nacogdoches." She clutched the pleated paper. *End it there.* She gave a stiff smile. "When Aunt Estelle needed a governess, she thought of me. So here I am."

"Right." His eyebrows furrowed as if he examined her story and found a piece or two missing from the jigsaw puzzle she presented. "Had you just completed your studies?"

Emily hesitated. Did he think she was younger than twenty or immature for her age? She rubbed her gloves down her skirt, smudging soot flecks on her new suit.

She pressed her lips together. "I did have one offer down in Pleasanton, but it … it didn't work out."

Pa saw to that. He forbade her from boarding near the schoolhouse, insisting that boarding with strangers wasn't safe. At the time, she suspected it had more to do with him needing a worker come harvest time. Not that he ever cared a fig about her dreams. His had hollowed out like a dried gourd, leaving only seeds rattling around inside a hardened shell.

Emily's traveling companion must have sensed her unease, for he amiably lightened the conversation. "You were fortunate to know what you wanted to do at such a young age and to have a grandfather who encouraged you. It took me a while to discern my path."

Then he switched topics and launched into tales about Indians and pirates that once inhabited Galveston, the swarm of immigrants that entered its port, and the Galveston Orphans Home. Given his story, she understood why he channeled his efforts toward helping orphans.

The train reached Galveston Bay as dusk deepened the night sky. Ahead, the bridge stretched out over the water.

As the train slowed to a crawl and rumbled over the bridge, she kept her gaze straight ahead. Her fingers dug into the armrests until her knuckles whitened. She tried not to think about how deep the water was beneath her.

"Miss Cleburne, do try to relax. It's just a few short miles, and we'll be on the island," he reassured her.

Like spilled ink, the water spread out and pooled around the island. Lights glittered in the distance, yet all she could think about was getting off the bridge and setting her feet on firm ground.

Darkness descended as the train sputtered to a stop at the Union Railroad Station.

Emily's legs shook as Colin escorted her through the station carrying the luggage, past the oblong rows of seating and exotic potted palm trees.

Stepping out of the station, Emily inhaled the sea air tinged with salt and fish.

Her eyes swept across the town, up the tall buildings lit with electricity. She gazed up at the night sky spangled with stars.

Mr. Hensleigh spoke. "I've arranged for a carriage to the Edwards' home.

It's not far. We mustn't linger, or a swarm of mosquitoes will be your welcoming committee. They can be most dreadful at night."

⟶⟵

The horse-drawn carriage swayed down 25th Street and turned onto Sealy Avenue. Emily peered out the window, noting the narrow gaps between houses, too close for her liking.

At last, the horse clomped up to a two-story Queen Anne home. Lamplight glowed in the downstairs parlor.

She had arrived. Her heart pounded in her chest.

Mr. Hensleigh offered his hand, and she climbed down the steps from the carriage. She entered through the creaking wrought iron gate while he toted the luggage. Together their feet pattered up the steep stairs leading to the front door.

He lifted the door knocker and let it fall. Standing shoulder to shoulder, they waited while a fragrance that smelled like home drifted on the breeze, perfuming the air.

Breathless, Emily tugged at the hem of her jacket and straightened her posture. Soon the padding of feet down the hall drew near, and the door opened.

Chapter 3

Aunt Estelle appeared on the threshold, bathed in the glow of the porch light. While she thanked her minister for his escort, Emily gazed at her aunt's face. She recalled the photograph taken years ago when Estelle announced her engagement to Clayton, but the pose was a silhouette.

Over the humming cicadas, Mr. Hensleigh bid them goodnight and trotted down the stairs to the waiting carriage.

Estelle turned to Emily with open arms, her relief lifting her finely shaped brows. "What a godsend to have you here, Emily."

Gathering her close, Emily returned the hug, breathing in the crisp scent of lemon verbena. The comfort of kinship calmed and steadied her pulse.

She pulled back and gazed into Estelle's face. Thick chestnut curls pulled into a frazzled bun framed a heart-shaped face, but her eyes, blue as morning glory blossoms, drew her in. It was like gazing at the miniature portrait of her grandmother, Rebecca.

The doorknob jiggled and rattled. Emily pried open her eyes and squinted at the door to her right.

She strained to hear Aunt Estelle say, "Rachel, let Miss Emily sleep. You will get to meet her soon enough. Run along and play. Sarah promised to teach you how to play hopscotch, remember?"

"But I want to meet Emmy," a tiny voice objected.

Her aunt's voice faded under the sound of footsteps down the stairs.

Upon arriving, Estelle had led her straight up to her room, insisting they postpone visiting until morning. After a sound sleep, Emily saw the wisdom in that decision.

She yawned and stretched her limbs, indulging in the rare luxury of lingering in bed. Her gaze traveled around the room. How unlike home were the painted blue walls, the lace curtains fluttering in the breeze, and the mahogany armoire opposite the bed polished to a soft luster. A nightstand to her left had shelves for her books. Grandpa gifted a new novel each year for her birthday. She treasured each one.

Sunlight filtered through the lace curtains fluttering at the window. A writing desk and chair were angled by the window, providing a view outdoors.

Crawling out of bed, she dug her toes into the braided rug and padded over to inspect the desk. She pulled down the slanted lid. Inside the drawer and cubbies, she found ink pens, sharpened pencils, postage stamps, and stationery. Tonight she would keep her word and write Grandpa.

Her delight bloomed as she pulled out the drawers beneath. A spelling book, scissors, a ruler, a pencil box filled with colored pencils, small slate chalkboards with chalk, and construction paper. How thoughtful of Aunt Estelle to supply what she couldn't initially afford.

Reaching over, she parted the curtains and peered out the window. A row of spiky pink oleander shrubs bordered the yard. Towards the front of the house, a live oak tree spread its green leaves. Along the back fence grew the honeysuckle vines that had scented the air upon her arrival.

Emily gazed at the dark gray house next door. A turret thrust skyward above the two-story pitched roof, covered with scalloped shingles that put her in mind of scales on a dragon's neck. A narrow balcony jutted out directly across from her window. An adjacent door went from the porch into a bedroom lined with windows; a distinctly masculine room, given the display of deer antlers, ducks, geese, and fish mounted on one visible wall.

She wondered who lived there. She would have to consider that later, for she had cousins to meet.

She dressed in her brown suit since her other dress needed pressing. She took extra care with grooming before trotting downstairs.

Freshly baked bread drew her up the hallway, past the parlor, study, and dining room, to the kitchen on her right. She noted a candlestick telephone set on a half-moon table below a mirror in the hallway. She paused at the door to the kitchen and peered inside. A woman stood at the back sink, scouring a cast iron skillet. Her gray hair quivered with each stroke.

To her left, Aunt Estelle's muffled voice came from inside the pantry. "We're low on cornmeal, grits, ginger snaps, and peanut butter."

"I'll add them to the list," the woman offered, drying her hand on a cup towel.

Her gaze landed on Emily. "You must be the niece. I'm Inez, the cook."

"Yes, ma'am. I'm Emily." She straightened her shawl collar, wishing her suit didn't smell like coal dust.

Estelle stepped out and shut the pantry door. "Inez is much more than our cook. I don't know how I'd manage without her."

Not one for accepting compliments, Inez brushed it off with a wave of her hand. She lumbered over to the work table in the center and jotted down the items on a list with a pencil.

Estelle joined Inez at the table and began slicing a loaf of bread with a serrated knife.

She glanced up at Emily. "How'd you sleep, dear?"

"Never better."

"Inez fixed you a plate of ham and grits. Help yourself to the bread."

Inez lifted the covered plate off the back stove, her tone crusty. "I set breakfast on the table at seven, sharp. I'll expect you then."

The cook clucked her tongue, eyeing Emily's slender figure. "Give me a few months, and you'll fill out that suit."

Without asking, Inez stacked two slices of bread onto the plate and thrust the food at her.

Emily's mouth tightened. Not her too? She had escaped her mother putting food on her plate, her constant nagging over Emily being thin as a rail.

"Enjoy your breakfast," Estelle said. She fluttered around the kitchen, steeping the tea, organizing the bed tray, and adding a serving of fresh plums. "Clayton likes a cup of tea with *The Daily News*."

Inez leaned on the work table, her brows drawn together. "Wouldn't hurt you to sit for a spell. Have a cup of tea with your niece."

Estelle hefted the tray and paused for a beat. "You're right. What a lovely idea."

She glanced at Emily. "I'll join you once I get Clayton comfortable." She carried the tray upstairs while Emily took her plate to the table in the dining room.

∞

Emily sat straight in the mahogany chair and examined her reflection in the mirror on the opposite wall. She patted her hair when a copper strand sprang loose from her bun, brushing her cheek. She tucked it behind her ear.

Against the far wall, sunlight streamed through the set of tall windows. It gleamed on the brass chandelier above the table and the blue and white oval platters displayed on the yellow walls.

She fingered the monogrammed E etched on the silver napkin ring, pulled out the linen square, and placed it on her lap. Such fancy things, when she was used to mismatched dishes.

She sampled the ham and buttered grits and nibbled on the edges of a slice of bread smeared with pear preserves.

Estelle entered the room carrying a teacup and sank onto the chair beside Emily. "At last, a free moment."

Emily licked the sweetness from her lips. "I found my desk well-stocked. I'm much obliged."

"Just some things I had delivered from our mercantile store. There are more supplies in the study. I'm anxious for you to put them to good use."

"Yes, ma'am."

While Estelle sipped the tea, Emily examined her aunt's features in the morning light. *The spitting image.*

Estelle peered at her over the rim of her cup and caught her staring.

Emily's ears heated. "I can't get over how much you favor Grandma."

A soft smile touched Estelle's lips as she lowered the cup. "I consider that high praise. I wish I were more like her in ways that count."

"How so?"

"Without a backward glance, she traded a privileged life for serving in ministry." Estelle rested her chin on her palm. "She learned to be content with having less, always setting another plate on the table whenever folks dropped by to talk with Papa. She lived generously, despite hard times, while I worried about doing without."

"I wish I'd known her," Emily put in.

"She would've been so proud that you're our governess."

Inez entered with a tea tray. Steam curled from the spout as she poured the hot liquid, setting the tray on the table before returning to the kitchen.

Estelle motioned to the teapot, the platters on the wall. "The china belonged to Mama. She used to say, 'They're just things. Things chip and fade. Better to bless others with what we have and enjoy their company, than to store up treasures in an empty house.'"

Emily's spoon clinked on the teacup as she stirred in a dollop of cream and two sugar cubes. She tried to imagine her mother growing up in the same household as Aunt Estelle, having folks who dished out encouragement around the supper table. Yet Ma turned out hardened and bitter. It was clear from overhearing her folks' arguments that she laid the blame for their misery squarely on Pa's shoulders. It all started at Oil Springs—whatever happened there.

"Clayton slept fitfully last night," Estelle broke into Emily's thoughts. "He's due a nap. We moved him into the front bedroom. The upper gallery has plenty of fresh air and sunshine. Both are critical for his recovery."

She took Emily's hand and gave it a gentle squeeze. "He's as grateful as I am that you're here. Sadly, tuberculosis prevents him from having visitors. Doctor's orders. Not even the children. He misses them terribly, especially going on outings to the beach." Estelle's tone held a wistful note as she gazed out the window.

An idea formed. "What if I were to take the children to the beach after school? Call it an incentive to get their homework done."

Estelle's face brightened. "What a fine idea."

Emily cradled the warm cup in her hands, feeling contentment spread as she sipped the tea. Most pupils simply needed motivation and individual tutoring to fill the learning gaps. Besides, they had all summer to buckle down and work.

The back door flew open at the end of the hallway. Estelle craned her neck. "That sounds like the children now."

Voices spilled through the doorway, sending a wave of insecurity rippling through Emily's composure.

"...down yet?"

"Ah, Rachel, are you going to ask me that again?"

"I just want to meet her."

In the doorway, the youngest girl clasped her fingers over her mouth. She turned to her brother and sister, wide-eyed. "Oh, she's here!"

Little Rachel's golden ringlets bounced on the gingham puffed sleeves. She walked straight over to Estelle, her siblings following. Poking her tongue at the inside of her cheek, she gazed up at Emily with blue eyes that dwarfed her face.

"I'm Rachel." She peered over her shoulder. "And that's Sarah and Jake."

Sarah was a petite version of Estelle, dressed dainty and prim in a matching gingham dress and pinafore. She hung back a step behind her brother as though she depended on him to take the lead. Her eyes flicked up from the floor and bounced down to examine her shoes. She seemed withdrawn for seven years old, or shy?

Jake's short pants and shirt hung on his lanky frame. His height made him look much older than Sarah, though only a year separated them in age. Sweat trickled down his temple. He wiped it with his forearm and squirmed, shifting his weight from one foot to the other.

With a start, Emily realized the children were as nervous as she was. Clearing her throat, she forced a smile. "It's nice to meet y'all. I've been counting the days."

Little Rachel chimed in. "Me too."

Jake snickered. "You can't count."

"Can so." Holding up her hand, Rachel pointed to each pudgy finger. "One, two, three. I'm three and a half years old. See?"

"Fine. You can count a little," Jake admitted.

"Almost forgot." Rachel held up a cloth doll for Emily's inspection. "This is Miss Riggles." The painted face held a smile. Her blue calico dress and bonnet appeared lovingly mended. Rachel cradled the doll like a real baby, her voice soft. "She's my best friend in the whole world."

Jake jerked his thumb at Miss Riggles. "She wags that doll everywhere she goes."

He fixed his gaze on Emily. His mouth pulled down at one corner. "Mama said we have to start school Monday. All my friends get the whole summer off. Why can't we?"

Jake's cap of sun-bleached hair and freckles revealed his love for being outdoors. His tone said he held Emily personally responsible for depriving him of the pleasure.

Estelle's brows lifted. "Jacob, we've discussed this. You must keep up with your friends in school."

"But why can't—"

"That will do." Estelle looked pointedly at him.

Jake cut his hazel eyes out the window. His face twisted into a pout.

Estelle peered at her son with a pained gaze. "Why don't you show Miss Emily your shells?"

Jake lifted a shoulder, unwilling to give in just yet.

Emily kept her tone casual. "Want to add to your collection?"

Jake's eyes slid on Emily, betraying a spark of interest.

Estelle reached over and smoothed down Jake's cowlick. "Miss Emily has offered to take y'all to the beach. *After* you finish your school work."

Little Rachel bounced on her toes. "Oh, can I go with Miss Emmy too?"

The nickname filled Emily with an unexpected rush of belonging.

Estelle glanced at Emily, a question in her eyes. Emily nodded her approval.

Estelle rubbed Rachel's back. "Of course you may."

Rachel clapped her hands, her smile broadening.

Emily glanced at Jake, who appeared to hold back his approval. "So … tell me about your shells."

Though he sounded less than enthused, Jake couldn't keep from puffing out his chest. "I've found ten whole sand dollars and several pairs of angel wings. Even have the shell of a crab."

"May I see them?"

"Oh, all right. Follow me."

Jake led the way upstairs to show off his treasures from the sea. The girls formed a line behind him, their dresses flowing in ruffles around their knees.

Emily blew out a breath and followed behind the children.

Her stomach churned. She had her work cut out for her. It didn't help that she lacked experience teaching multiple subjects, or that both cousins lagged in school. What if she failed to advance the children in their studies? Jake's attitude about summer school and Sarah's shyness did nothing to ease her jitters. Was she up to the challenge?

There's no turning back.

Failure to succeed brought stiff consequences, more dreaded than any "F" marked in red pencil. Emily tugged at the hem of her jacket. Good thing she was no quitter.

Lord, guide my steps.

Despite the challenges before her, her insides tingled with anticipation. At last, she stood on the threshold of fulfilling her dream. Like a swallowtail breaking free from its chrysalis, she stretched her wings, testing them. She wondered if the butterfly felt the same trepidation when it flapped its wings and lifted from the perch, taking flight.

Chapter 4

Emily trailed behind Estelle and the children toward a horse-drawn carriage watching their fine clothes swish in the breeze.

In the sunlight, her calico dress appeared faded and puckered, but she had nothing else to wear. Her one suit hung damp from laundering. The strands of envy threatened to choke her earlier contentment. She released a sigh. She might as well be content with what little she had.

The carriage dipped as she climbed the step and settled beside little Rachel. The girl held Miss Riggles snugly in the crook of her arm.

The driver gripped the reins with large, weathered hands. Though silver threaded his cropped hair, he had an air of vitality about him, as though he preferred being on the move over sitting in one spot. Dressed in his Sunday best, his gold-rimmed spectacles slid low on his nose, his brown skin glowing in the sunlight.

Estelle shifted sideways in her seat, facing him. "Jasper, I'd like you to meet my niece Emily, our new governess. Jasper is our deliveryman for the store. He's kind enough to take us to church on his way to join his family for services."

"Now, Miss Estelle, you know I'm blessed to do it." He pushed his spectacles onto the bridge of his nose and dipped his chin at Emily. "Pleasure, ma'am. You ring the store anytime, and I'll deliver whatever you need that very day."

"I'll bear that in mind." Though Emily doubted she'd be ordering anything soon from the family's mercantile store. Not without spare cash.

The carriage swayed and rolled forward. The horse clopped down avenues with live oak trees and rows of colorfully painted houses. Emily admired the intricate latticework trimming the upper and lower porches and the gables and turrets under pitched roofs covered with slate shingles.

In the yards, palm trees were rustling in the breeze. Yellow roses climbed along wrought iron fences near hitching posts. Everywhere she turned, oleander bushes bloomed in pink and white blossoms.

The carriage rumbled through intersections with the grid of streets laid out in an orderly fashion. Soon it pulled up to a church with a soaring steeple.

One by one, they stepped down from the carriage and joined the flow of people streaming into the sanctuary. At the entrance, Estelle pulled everyone aside to speak with a family.

"Emily," Estelle led out, "these are our dear friends, Peter and Lena Kesler, and their children, Andrew and Lacey."

As they exchanged greetings, Emily noticed the Kesler children were similar in age to her cousins and favored their mother, whom the ruddy-cheeked husband looked upon with affection. With dark hair and eyes like onyx studs, Lena was striking.

Tiny as a china doll, Emily mused. Emily stood a half foot taller than Estelle's friend. She hated comparing herself to others, for she never measured up. Meeting Mrs. Kesler proved no exception.

Lavender wafted from the folds of her muslin dress as Lena shifted closer. "I know Estelle must head home once services are over, but you and the children are welcome to join us for a picnic at the beach. I've made enough food to feed an entire pew!"

Emily bit the inside of her cheek. "That's … mighty kind of you to offer, but I—I don't—"

"You *must* come. We can visit while the children play. "Truth is," Lena lowered her voice and whispered conspiratorially, "I'm starving for grown-up conversation after listening to children prattle all week."

Put on the spot, Emily glanced at her cousins. Their heads bobbed up and down, their eyes pleading with her to agree.

Despite her reservations, she caved. "Alright, I reckon we can go."

The strains of the doxology piped from the organ, drawing them indoors. Emily entered the sanctuary, grander than her country church back home. She panned the broad center aisle, the pointed arches, and the light streaming through the stained glass windows. Seeing the familiar hymnals and the paddle fans tucked in the pew racks brought an unexpected lump to her throat. *This* she knew.

Taking a seat beside little Rachel, she glanced around at the women dressed in pastel frocks, with their hats piled high in rows of braided lace and silk rosettes tied with bows.

Emily's gaze fell to her lap, eyeing the homespun calico. She clutched her gloved hands together, sorely aware of being out of step with the times. Her cheeks heated beneath the brim of her hat. She reached for a paddle fan and swept it in front of her face, stirring the air while staring straight ahead at the crimson and gold stained glass cross above the pulpit.

Few women in the country had the luxury of being preoccupied with the latest fashions. Life revolved around crops and cattle and endless chores. Folks drew comfort from simple pleasures and in their faith.

Not that belief had come easy for her. On the contrary, what it took to survive in the Cleburne household had whittled away at childlike trust. A family where harsh words were scattered like chicken feed and failure to live up to her folks' rules brought the sting of a switch and stone-cold silence around the table. No wonder she'd resisted the tug at her heart whenever Grandpa spoke on God's great love. Hearing that He paid the debt that she owed for breaking His laws seemed too good to be true. That the Lord submitted to brutal lashes and death on a cross had robbed her of sleep. Again the words, "For God so loved…" wooed her. It had always been the crux of the matter, His terrible love. But how could she turn away from the thing she craved most? With trembling hands, she'd grabbed hold of the gift of grace, allowing peace to flood her soul.

Voices swelled in harmony around her. Emily blinked against the moisture building in her eyes. She lifted her voice and joined in singing Amazing Grace. The words filled her with wonder still.

The roar of the surf mingled with the banter of the Keslers and Emily's cousins. Overhead, seagulls squawked as they trekked through the sand toward the shoreline. Despite Emily's reservations, the conversation had flowed easily between her and Lena on the ride over from church.

Her feet stilled as she neared the shore. Sunlight threw crystal chips on the water, shimmering light flecks that pulsed on the waves. She counted seven rows cresting and foaming toward shore. The scent of salt air tasted strong. Her skin was already coated with a moist film despite the steady breeze gusting strands of hair loose from her bun. Without a hat pin, her straw hat would sail off. She gazed out where the water touched the sky. How could something so vast and deep, so formidable, open her chest with a warm rush of awe?

Lena grabbed her arm. "Mesmerizing, isn't it? Let's set out the food and eat."

They spread a quilt out on the sand, and Peter lowered the picnic basket in the middle. They ate thick cheese sandwiches on rye bread, dill pickles,

German potato salad, vanilla wafers, apple strudel from the Kesler's bakery, and sipped on tea.

With their stomachs filled, they removed their shoes and headed to the water. The powdery sand sifted through Emily's toes. She stepped over a rope of dried seaweed onto firmly packed sand that the tide had washed smooth. She hugged the water's edge, going no further. Soon an oncoming wave frothed and washed over her feet, chilling her, though the water was warm as bathwater.

The children weren't content to stay nearby. They skipped along the shore while Jake bent over inspecting shells.

After a while, Peter clasped Lena's hand. "Come with me. Time to turn them around."

Lena called over her shoulder to Emily. "Be right back." The couple trotted down the beach after the youngsters.

Looking past the surf, Emily spied a sailboat drifting along, the sails bending toward the water.

Glancing sideways, she recognized Colin Hensleigh meandering along the beach, his hands stuffed in his trousers, his walnut hair tousled in the breeze. Upon reaching her, he turned to see what had captured her attention.

"Have you ever sailed, Miss Cleburne?"

"No. And from the looks of that boat tilting over, I reckon I'll stay on land."

Amusement tugged at his mouth. "That boat has a rudder in the hull, which keeps it upright in the trade winds unless a strong gale blows through. I assure you, the vessel is sturdier than it looks."

She arched an eyebrow, skeptical.

"I've sailed all my life and haven't capsized yet."

"But what if a storm were to blow in unexpectedly?"

"There's an old saying that I heed. Red sky at night, sailor's delight. Red sky at morning, sailor's warning."

"So you watch the sky and sail accordingly?"

"That, and read the weather forecast. When the weather is fair, there's nothing more glorious than sailing in the evening when the water mirrors a fiery sky. Perhaps you'll learn to enjoy sailing while you're here."

Emily folded her arms over her stomach and let out a huff. Sail in a tiny boat over water? Was he mad?

"I cannot imagine what might entice me. You may be drawn to the sea, but I'll stick to the view from shore."

He peered at the whipped clouds piling up over the water and shrugged. "From either vantage point, nature feeds my soul. I ponder what heaven must be like if the earth and its splendor is God's footstool."

Not wishing to detain him, Emily said, "Well, ponder away while you enjoy your walk. I'll not keep you."

That evening in the parlor, Estelle and Emily settled onto the soft-cushioned armchairs facing the sofa and gathered their needlework.

A candy dish filled with lemon drops lay on the coffee table within Emily's reach. Tempting. Her mother deemed eating penny candy a frivolous waste of cash.

Estelle noticed her eyeing the dish. "Help yourself. Inez keeps us supplied with lemon drops. They're Clayton's favorite."

Emily reached for a piece of candy and sucked on the sweet, lemony tartness while her gaze traveled around the room. The glow from the lamps shone on the hardwood floors and bathed the parlor in honeyed tones. A plush, gold ivory rug anchored the gold brocade sofa and matching armchairs. She admired the English cottage painting with a rose arbor and hollyhocks that hung above the mantle where the clock ticked a gentle rhythm. From floor-to-ceiling, cream swag curtains and lace panels draped the windows on the front wall. The scent of honeysuckle drifted through the opened windows. Pressed tin covered the ten-foot-high ceiling.

Emily fingered the nubby center of a daisy she had begun embroidering on her drawstring purse. Across Estelle's lap draped a section of a nine-patch quilt.

"So," Estelle began, "did you enjoy your outing?"

Emily closed her eyes. "I had a nice time."

"The beach engulfs the senses, doesn't it? It encourages me to meditate while I soak up the view."

"Mr. Hensleigh said something similar. We talked briefly during his walk."

"He regularly takes long walks on the beach. And Lena… Did you enjoy her company?"

"I did." Emily found herself smiling.

"You seem surprised."

"I figured it'd be awkward, not knowing her at all. But Lena put me at ease. We plan to meet again this week so the kids can play."

"I predict y'all will become fast friends."

Emily threaded the yellow floss through the needle, considering this. "She's as pretty as a Gibson Girl, though not the least bit vain."

"In that way, she reminds me of you."

Emily drew back. "Me? I'm tall and gangly as a newborn colt."

Estelle shook her head, chuckling. "Your height distinguishes you. It's part of what makes you unique."

"But you're the spitting image of Grandma. Who wouldn't want to look like her?"

"At your age, it didn't stop me from comparing myself to the girls I admired and wanting to be like them. I didn't appreciate then that we're all unique with our own strengths."

"Well, mine's a mighty short list."

Estelle tipped her head. "Think so? Then you're overlooking what others see in you."

Emily had difficulty meeting Estelle's gaze.

"You're bright and determined; qualities that will make for a fine governess. You have Rosa's delicate skin and Papa's high cheekbones. And that hair! What thick copper waves. The color suits you, I think."

Emily warmed under her aunt's praise. She fingered a lock of hair. "I've always considered the color more curse than blessing."

Estelle regarded her, her eyes softening. "All you need is a little encouragement to bring out your best features. And I've got just the thing in mind."

Emily's eyes widened, her interest piqued.

"How about I advance your first month's salary and we go shopping? A new outfit or two does wonders to boost a girl's confidence. If you're interested, I'll check with Inez about watching the children on Saturday. We'll go during Clayton's afternoon nap."

"Well, if you're offering … I accept. The only decent thing I have to wear is my suit. On the farm, it didn't matter." Feeling self-conscious, Emily's eyes fell to the French knot she just sewed in the center of a daisy.

"There are plenty of apparel shops. Or if you'd prefer, you may use my sewing machine. Our store has the best selection of fabric on the island."

"I'd like that, but I could use a hand sorting through fabric and patterns."

"I'd be happy to help. And anything you buy at the store is sold at a discount."

Emily blew out a breath and relaxed her shoulders, settling into the cushion. "I appreciate this more than I can say."

"It's a small gesture compared to your moving here. Besides, getting out will do us both good."

With that settled, Estelle returned to plying her needle.

Emily's eyes rested on her aunt's profile. The regret of not knowing her grandma loosened and eased somewhat, for the very image of Rebecca sat beside her. Emily treasured the ease of their growing companionship and her aunt's guidance.

Later that evening, a puddle of lamplight shone on her notes. She sucked on a lemon drop and jotted down her plan in preparation for her first day of teaching. Tomorrow she would assess each pupil and see where they fared according to their grade levels.

She rubbed her tight shoulder muscles. She needed a diversion before crawling into bed. As she reached for *Jane Eyre* set on top of the desk, she heard a clicking noise from outside.

Curious, Emily turned and peered through the gap in the lace curtain. The full moon peeked above the treetops, silvering the landscape. From the balcony next door came another click, click. Then a tiny flame caught and flared. Her neighbor held a pocket lamp and lit a cigar. The glow from the flame illuminated the angular planes of his face, revealing a square chin, the shadows hollowing grooves in his cheeks. Strands of hair shielded his eyes from view.

He puffed on the cigar until the end glowed red and a whiff of the sweet fragrance drifted in through the window. A plume of smoke swirled and curled upward.

Satisfied, he turned and began pacing on the porch, his shoulders hunched. He paused midstride and dropped his chin, rubbing the back of his neck. Emily wondered what weighed on his mind that set him to pacing.

She brushed back the curtain and leaned closer to the screen. The tangy candy melted on her tongue. After a beat, the man puffed on the cigar and resumed his steps.

Not long ago, she'd paced the farmhouse porch clutching Aunt Estelle's letter. Perhaps the man had decisions of his own that he mulled over. She let out a huff and shook her head. What did she know of what weighed on his mind?

Just then, he pivoted on his heel. Turning, he swung his head sideways.

His body went still. Wraiths of smoke snaked around his face as he stared in the moonlight straight at her.

Emily sucked in a breath and dropped the curtain. Flicking off the desk lamp, she plunged the room into shadows.

Chapter 5

"It rhymes with blue," Emily prompted, resisting the urge to tap her foot.

Jake's cheeks puffed out as he blew out a breath. "In something something two, Columbus sailed the ocean blue." He shrugged his shoulders. "The year is all that's fuzzy."

Emily lifted her brows. "The *year* is part of what you need to know."

The boy's face scrunched up. "Can't seem to recall it."

His gaze wandered out the study window. For the ninth time that hour, he peered at the lower branches of the live oak tree. Emily pressed her lips together. What would it take to hold his attention? A trained monkey perched on her shoulder?

Enough!

She swiped a frazzled strand of hair out of her eyes and pushed back the chair. The Turkish rug muffled the scraping of the chair legs. She rose from the long table, planted her palms on the surface, and leaned forward. She counted up to thirteen while an ineffective breeze leaked in through the window, barely stirring the sticky, afternoon heat.

At last, the silence gained Jake's attention. Seeing her loom over him, he drew back in his seat.

"The year was 1492," she drew out each syllable. "'In fourteen hundred ninety-two, Columbus sailed the ocean blue.' I expect you to *know* this by the third grade. I need you to apply yourself to learning *something* about America's history. Do you reckon you can do that?"

His eyes widened at her change in tone. "Yes, ma'am."

Her eyelid twitched, betraying the tension building behind her eyes. She shouldn't have gotten so frustrated, but she passed the point of keeping it in check. The boy saw no relevance in history, no interest in books, and lacked the motivation to master multiplication. Given the sacrifices she made to get an education, she failed to understand his attitude one bit.

Emily peered beside him at Sarah, who rubbed her eyes while appearing to study the buttercups she'd doodled down the side of the practice sheet she used for penmanship. The girl fared no better. She scribbled in large letters, lagged a grade behind in reading, and her spelling fell below the second-grade level. She hadn't grasped even simple addition.

All the basics, Emily frowned. Where to start?

Leather-bound books lined the study from floor to ceiling, but neither child cared to crack open one of them. Were they oblivious to their privilege or just plain ungrateful?

⚬⚬⚬

Emily sat hunched over the desk in her room, her head cradled in her hands. She'd begged off joining Estelle in the parlor after picking at the bowl of oyster stew for supper. What remained of the peppermint tea she'd brewed to settle her stomach set tepid by her elbow.

What am I to do?

She massaged her temples with the heels of her hands. The children were so far behind; more than needing basic concepts explained. Far more than she had anticipated. But that wasn't the worst of it. Their disinterest stumped her completely. She wasn't sure where to begin, much less how to conquer it. Her eyes glazed over, blurring her vision.

A ball of tension knotted in her stomach. What if Jake and Sarah didn't make progress? Tears pricked behind her eyelids. She squeezed them shut.

She was in way over her head. She'd never taught multiple subjects, much less held her pupils' attention throughout the day. What made her think she could succeed when other teachers, more experienced teachers, had failed to advance the children?

Emily opened her eyes and heaved a sigh into the room. If only she could talk things over with Grandpa. In his unhurried way, he always listened until she got things off her chest and sorted through whatever bothered her. Then he'd point her toward doing the right thing. Often the hard thing. He'd tell her that anything worthwhile usually came at a cost. That she'd succeed if she persisted. She could almost hear his gravelly drawl. *But first, you've got to understand what you're up against, Sweet Pea. Get understanding. Get wisdom. They're bookends that hold everything else in place.*

She drew in a shaky breath. *Lord, what's the matter with the kids? Give me wisdom so that I can help them.*

She blinked the moisture from her eyes and grew still. Time lapsed as she stared at the braided rug beside her bed, her gaze tracing the oval pattern of blue and brown interwoven with hints of red and tan.

Something Colin Hensleigh said came to mind. *Pirates—there were pirates here. Pirates and Indians.*

With a sniff, Emily sat up straight. Reaching for a fresh sheet of paper and a pencil, she tapped the pencil against the desktop. What if she exposed Jake to local history? It couldn't hurt. She jotted that down.

An owl hooted off in the distance. The evening breeze ruffled the lacey curtains.

She leaned back in the chair. What to read? She'd spied a copy of *Treasure Island* on the library shelf. Jake had probably never read the pirate's tale. What boy could resist buried treasure? But would a dainty girl like Sarah care for it? If not, maybe *The Swiss Family Robinson*. She scratched down reading aloud a chapter per day.

Sarah needed practice with penmanship and spelling. She yawned, considering a writing assignment for tomorrow.

After muddling through their first week of lessons, Emily watched Jake trudge into the library behind Sarah. He slumped onto the cushioned chair beside his sister.

They had no more than started off the day with prayer and the pledge of allegiance when Jake turned his gaze outdoors.

Emily considered closing the muslin curtains but chose the direct approach. "What's on your mind, Jake?"

"Huh?" His eyes flicked on her. At length, he shrugged. His mouth pulled down at one corner. "My dad, I guess. Just wondering about him."

Her expression softened as a gleam of understanding flashed. "In that case, for your writing assignment today, you may each make a greeting card for your father. Draw a design or decorate the cover however you like. Then write your message inside."

"Can I glue seashells on mine?" Jake asked.

"Of course." Seeing the children perk up, she added, "Go find your decorations while I pull out the supplies."

The children scuttled out of the room. Emily opened the table's middle drawer and dug out construction paper, scissors, glue, and freshly sharpened pencils.

From the kitchen, she heard Inez rattling and clinking bowls. Later, the oven door creaked open. Before long, baked peanut butter cookies sweetened the house. The promise of a cold glass of milk and cookies after school lifted her spirits.

Jake and Sarah returned carrying their decorations. After giving them instructions, the children folded thick sheets of construction paper and set to work. Sarah glued pressed leaves and honeysuckle in the center of her card and edged it with a blue ribbon, while Jake created a design out of scalloped shells. When they finished decorating the covers, they took their time printing their messages inside.

Emily eyed their work. Finally, a bit of traction.

She rubbed her chin, noticing Sarah's printing. "Why such big letters, Sarah?"

Sarah shrugged, rubbing her eyes. "Fills up the card, I guess."

"Hmm…" Acting on a hunch, Emily held up Jake's finished message and stepped back several feet. "Can you read this?"

Sarah squinted at the letters.

That evening Emily and Estelle settled into the chairs in the parlor with their needlework. Estelle brought a tea tray with a pot of lavender tea sweetened with honey. While she poured the purplish-colored tea into cups, Emily set a basket at her feet.

Emily accepted the cup and saucer. "Has Sarah ever had her eyes examined?"

Estelle paused. "Not that I recall. Why do you ask?" She lifted the cup to her lips.

"She has trouble reading words at a distance. I checked."

Estelle's cup clacked against the saucer, her shoulders sagging. "But how … how did her teachers overlook such a thing? How could I?"

"Sarah probably compensated and sat near the blackboard. Abby, a girl I tutored, was in the third grade before anyone noticed her poor eyesight. She sat in the front row and volunteered to clean the chalkboards after every lesson. And you—you're one person doing the work of two."

Estelle angled toward the lamp and threaded the needle. "I suppose that explains why Sarah is doing poorly. I'll ring for an appointment tomorrow."

"Good. That's good." Emily drank the fragrant brew, needing its calming effect. She crossed her legs and uncrossed them. How to say the rest gently? "It seems … it may be one reason."

"One?" Estelle lowered her needle, her face pinched.

"Well, it's … you see, both children are a bit distracted."

"I won't have them disrespecting you, Emily."

"It's not that."

"You must insist they apply themselves."

"Of course. But what if the problem is something else?"

"What *now*?" Estelle's tone said she'd reached her fill of problems.

Emily cleared her throat and added carefully, "I asked Jake what he had on his mind. He said his dad. Reckon they're worried about his health?"

Estelle rubbed her forehead. "Who could blame them, poor dears? Clayton's tuberculosis is worrisome. We all feel the strain of it, especially around the table and at bedtime."

Emily reached down into the basket and lifted the cards. "I had Jake and Sarah make these for him." She handed them to Estelle.

"Oh, my," Estelle murmured, touching the glued shells and the pressed flowers. Her eyes grew moist. "I'll put these on Clayton's breakfast tray. He'll cherish them." Estelle gently set the cards on the side table.

Emily let out a slow breath. "Jake and Sarah put a lot of work into making those cards. Enough that I'll have them write him weekly. Do you think he could jot a few lines in return? If he feels up to it, that is?"

"What a fine idea." Estelle reached over and briefly squeezed her hand. "This affirms how desperately we needed you."

Emily's cheeks warmed under her aunt's approval. She ducked her head and focused on threading the needle with white embroidery floss. She stitched the petals of a daisy onto the face of her purse.

"On a lighter note," Emily switched subjects, "do you know of any old-timers who remember when pirates and Indians lived here? On the train, Mr. Hensleigh shared some island history."

"Perhaps. Why?"

"I'd like the children, particularly Jake, to hear some local stories. He needs a taste of history, something more than endless dates and facts."

Estelle tapped her chin with a forefinger. "Jasper's father is well into his eighties. As I recall, Mosey and Iris came on the slave ship. Let's look for Jasper on Saturday. He'll be in and out of the store making deliveries."

The bell jingled behind them as Emily and Estelle entered the mercantile store. Emily caught a whiff of coffee beans, tobacco, cinnamon, and beeswax candles. In every square foot of the deep, narrow store, shelves were stocked from floor to ceiling with everything from canned goods, soaps, medicines, and blue mason jars, to jars of penny candy. Above, lanterns, pails, and horse harnesses hung from the ceiling. Along the back wall, bolts of fabric were a field of colors and prints.

First, they selected sewing patterns for a skirt, shirtwaist, and dress, proving her aunt had an eye for style.

With that task done, Emily ran her palms over the silky bolts, lingering on the yellow satin. She lacked the courage to wear it. Her mother had insisted that dark, muted colors were more suitable. The colors made Emily feel plain. Yellow, however, was sunshine and daffodils.

Rebecca Dunne had worn yellow silk in Grandpa's miniature portrait of her. Emily wondered where Rosa had formed such ideas. Certainly not from her own mother. The sharp contrast between mother and daughter puzzled her.

Estelle sorted through bolts of material, lifting the ends of the fabric for inspection. She recommended a cream muslin print for a shirtwaist and tan broadcloth for a skirt that could be worn with her brown suit jacket.

Emily peered sideways at Estelle. "I'd never manage this without you."

Estelle's eyes sparkled. "We're not through yet." She pointed to the dotted Swiss. "Lavender or yellow for the dress?"

"Yellow?"

"Either would complement your coloring."

"I've never fancied myself wearing such colors." Fingering the nubby dotted fabric, Emily dared to break free from the restrictive mold set by her mother. "But then, it's high time I tried something different."

She put the yellow bolt on the stack. They picked out notions while they had the fabric cut. Emily added a pair of cream-colored gloves. The total left her four dollars to spare.

The bell jingling over the door announced Jasper's arrival. He spotted them and came over. "Howdy, ladies."

Emily introduced the subject of the children visiting with his father about early Galveston. Jasper flashed a smile. "He'd be proud to talk with you but plan on sitting a spell. Daddy tends to pull folks in with his stories. Just let me know when, and I'll bring all y'all over to the house."

"Thank you kindly, Jasper," Emily threw over her shoulder. She gathered up the sacks and followed Estelle out the door.

Outside, Emily filled her lungs with the tang of sea air. The aroma of meat roasting from a nearby restaurant teased her nose. The sun warmed her back as she and Estelle fell in step with the flow of shoppers along the sidewalk. The downtown Strand teemed with folks bustling in and out of the shops. Her gaze roved up the ornate metropolitan buildings and peered through windows gleaming with crystal goblets, silver tea sets, and French china. Strange-sounding languages tickled her ears as if she were on some foreign shore rather than off the coast of Texas.

Strolling by a millinery shop, a straw turban in the display window caught her eye. Cream rosettes and silk trimmed the brim. Seeing her interest, Estelle nudged her inside.

Emily removed the hatpin from her plain hat and set it on the counter. She gained a sense of poise the instant the turban rested on her loosely tied bun. Stepping before a mirror, she blinked at her reflection. The style set off her brown eyes and softened the copper wisps framing her face.

Aunt Estelle sensed the change in her. "A lovely hat for a lovely lady."

With no reservations, Emily purchased the turban, leaving her a half-dollar to spare.

The following week, Emily reached into the candy dish on her desk. She popped a lemon drop in her mouth. Sucking on hard candy broke the monotony of grading papers. Inez had set the candy dish there. Who knew the crusty cook had a soft—

Shouts erupted from next door. Startled, Emily jerked and swiveled on the seat. The papers at her elbow scattered. Ignoring them, she peered out through the screen. The voices came from her neighbor's bedroom.

Digging her elbows into her knees, she leaned forward and listened.

Chapter 6

"…bet I did!" A stout man, broad as a boxcar, jabbed his forefinger in the young man's face. "I've got plans for you."

"I have my plans. A *respectable* career."

"Your plans mean nothing to me, boy. I won't abide handing my business over to outsiders. Pity you're my only heir," he spat.

The son jerked off his tie and collar and tossed them on top of the dresser. "I should've known Harvard and Europe came with strings attached."

The father's laugh boomed with a harsh edge. "Only fools expect a free ride. It's high time you set aside your ambition. Step up and do your duty. Or you'll force me to become … unpleasant."

Though the son towered over his father in height and had a muscular frame, the threat stilled his movements. "You are nothing if not malicious."

"Mark my words: you haven't seen malice yet. These things have a way of trickling down on those beneath us. Pity, that. Rather unnecessary, wouldn't you say?"

The son thrust out his chin with his mouth clamped shut.

"You have till you turn twenty-five," the father announced. "Get on board, or we'll see how long you last sleeping on your sailboat and eating sardines out of tins."

Having had the last word, the father spun on his heel and stalked out of the room.

The room fell silent. Then what sounded like muttered cursing. Moments later, the balcony door slammed shut, ringing through the air.

Emily shot to her feet and stepped behind the curtain. Remaining hidden, she peeked over at her neighbor.

He leaned his elbows on the railing. Emily rolled the lemon drop on her tongue and took in his unguarded appearance.

Her first glimpse of him in the moonlight had hinted at angular features. The sunlight polished the dimples carving into his cheeks, the strong chin and jaw now shadowed with evening stubble.

Below his mustache, his mouth pressed in a grim line. Emily doubted he would comply with his father's demands.

No wonder the man paced the porch in the dark. He must resent threats to coerce him into taking over his father's business when he had other plans, his dreams.

A lock of crisp, sand-colored hair blew in his eyes. He plowed his fingers through the strands, pushing them back. Those soulful eyes, tossed with defiance, were fixed on some unseen point past the street.

Like the spring moon pulling on the tides, those eyes tugged at something within her.

Careful. You know nothing about him.

And what little she did know gave her pause. Being good-looking may have turned her head, but he was at odds with a father who didn't bat an eye over threatening to oust him unless he lived up to his family's demands.

Hitting too close to home, Emily tore her gaze off the play of emotions puckering the neighbor's brow and back onto the papers strewn on the desk. She straightened them into a tidy stack and resumed grading papers.

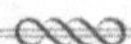

Emily clapped shut the pages of the book.

"Ah, Miss Emily," Jake whined, "what's inside Billy Bones' chest?"

He's hooked!

After days of luring him in, Emily couldn't resist a bit of gloating. "So … I take it you want to keep on reading. That was our agreement. At the end of chapter three, we'd decide whether to finish the story or switch to another."

Emily peered across the table at Sarah. "What about you?"

Despite the prim set of her mouth, Emily suspected that the story had reeled Sarah in, too.

Jake's head whipped toward his sister, his cowlick sticking out in tufts at the crown. "You want to keep going, right?"

The girl lifted a shoulder attempting to belie her interest in the grisly old seaman's tale. "Well … if that's what *you* want to do."

Emily stifled a smile. "Then it's settled." She patted the leathery cover of *Treasure Island.* "We'll continue reading chapter four tomorrow."

Jake's face scrunched into a frown. "But what if the next part doesn't tell us what's inside the chest?"

"Patience, Jake. Half the pleasure of reading books is wondering what comes next."

She motioned toward the library door. "Time for recess."

The children needed no further encouragement. They bolted from the room. Emily rose, following them down the hall and out the back door.

Emily stepped out into the rising heat. On the porch, Sarah squatted by little Rachel, who sat cross-legged, bouncing a ball and swiping at a jack and missed. Her bottom lip quivered over the failed attempt.

Sarah sat down beside her. "Let me show you again. Like this."

Emily caught a flash of movement before Jake disappeared between the houses. She moved off the porch and peered around the corner.

Jake hiked a leg up on the low branch of the live oak tree and hoisted himself up. He reached for the next limb above his head, climbing higher and higher.

"Be careful," Emily called out.

Without looking down, Jake scaled up the tree.

Fifteen feet off the ground, he grabbed hold of an upper branch and swung out onto the limb, swaying. He let go with one hand and hung by his arm, scratching his armpit and screeching, "Hey, look at me! I'm a monkey. Ooh, ooh, ooh!"

"Jake, don't—"

His one-handed grip loosened.

The breath froze in Emily's lungs. Her gaze riveted on his fingers, watching them slip. He fell, landing with a thud. His body sprawled onto the ground—in the neighbor's yard.

"Jake!"

She dashed on shaky legs, pushing through the oleanders over into the other yard. She knelt on the ground. Jake lay motionless.

Behind her, a rustling stirred the shrubs, and Rachel and Sarah appeared. They hovered over their brother, their faces pinched with worry.

"Is he all right?" Sarah's panting fanned Emily's face.

Jake blinked and let loose a groan, lifting his head off the ground.

"Lie still." Emily pressed her palm on his shoulder, keeping him from moving. Putting up no resistance, the boy lowered his head. "Are you hurt anywhere?" She scanned his body, checking for signs of injury.

"Had the wind knocked out of me, is all."

"You sure?"

"Yep. Need to catch my breath."

Swamped with relief, Emily heaved a sigh.

She peered at Sarah and Rachel from under her brows. "Give him a minute. He'll be fine. Go on and play."

"Go on." Jake flapped his wrist, shoeing away his audience.

"You rest, okay?" Sarah cooed. She clasped little Rachel's hand and tugged at it. "Come on. He'll be all right."

The girls cut through the oleanders, meandering away.

After a few minutes, Jake eased himself up on his elbow. As he did so, crushed leaves released their fragrance into the air. Peppermint?

Only then did Emily take in the foliage where he landed.

"Oh no," she muttered. "Looks like you fared better than the plants."

His foot had snapped the stalks off several foxgloves. His weight had crushed the yarrow and daisy arnica, along with small clumps of thyme, sage, and the spreading peppermint. Herbs. Jake had landed in the middle of the neighbor's herb garden.

Her cheeks heated. She should have insisted that Jake come down from that tree. Now, this.

"You could've broken your neck," her voice pitched. "As it is, your horseplay ruined their garden."

Jake gulped. "I didn't mean to kill the flowers. Honest."

She wagged a finger at him. "That may be so, but regret doesn't patch things up. You're going to march right over and apologize to your neighbor."

"Ah, Miss Emily, don't make me do it. I'm sorry."

"I'm not the one who needs to hear it."

A shadow fell across Jake's body.

"Hello," a man drawled. "I'm your neighbor."

Emily craned her neck and squinted up. Her palms broke out in a sweat. The young man from the balcony loomed over her, dressed in a crisp white oxford shirt, tan waistcoat, and trousers.

Emily wiped her hands down the sides of her brown skirt, grateful she'd paired it with the new shirtwaist she had sewn.

Amusement tugged at the corners of his mouth. He appeared to have witnessed the scolding.

Emily pushed up from the ground and pulled Jake to his feet, brushing off leaves and smashed flower petals stuck to the back of his shirt and legs.

She placed her hands on her hips. "Well, Jacob. What do you have to say for yourself?"

"I'm sorry, mister."

"Chambers, Nathan Chambers," the neighbor supplied.

"That would be *Mr.* Chambers to you." Emily wasn't through with him yet. "Now tell Mr. Chambers why you're sorry."

"I, um, I'm sorry I squashed your flowers. See, I was horsing around up in the tree. Well, more like monkeying around, and my hand just slipped."

The neighbor's mouth twitched. "Apology accepted, son, though I don't relish breaking the news to Mother about losing her homegrown remedies."

Emily lifted her chin. "He'll pay for the damages."

Jake's mouth popped open.

"Oh, that won't be necessary, Miss—"

"Cleburne. I—I'm Emily Cleburne, his governess. And if I have a say, he'll cover the cost of replacing those plants."

Jake gulped, his eyes widening. "How will I pay for them?"

"I suppose by doing chores around the house."

Mr. Chambers scratched his ear. "I could use an errand boy from time to time."

Jake's face brightened. "Can I?"

"May I," she corrected. "Let me talk it over with your ma. She'll decide. Now go on and play."

Jake hung his head. "Yes, ma'am." He sounded glum but eager to end the discussion.

Emily watched him trot to the backyard. "Hey Sarah, Rachel. Want to play catch?"

The girls came into view and joined him in the middle of the yard, tossing the ball.

Emily faced her neighbor and caught him staring. Astute green eyes raked over her appearance, missing nothing. He chuckled. He plucked something from behind her ear, his thumb grazing her earlobe. With a start, she drew back. He spun the pink oleander blossom between his thumb and forefinger.

Mercy! How must I look?

Emily patted her braided hair self-consciously. She felt as put together as the snapped foxgloves dangling at her feet.

She cleared her throat. "Jake must learn to be more careful. I'd be obliged if you'll let me know the cost of replacing those plants, and I'll talk with my aunt about the chores."

"Fair enough."

Nathan paused, running his hand over his mustache. "Say, are you planning to attend the July 4th celebration tomorrow? Perhaps I'll see you there. You can let me know what Mrs. Edwards decides."

"Of course. I'll be taking the children."

"Along with Mrs. Edwards?"

Emily shook her head. "She's not able to get away."

Nathan frowned. "You're not planning on corralling them by yourself, are you? I suspect there'll be quite a crowd."

Did he think her incapable of supervising three children because Jake fell from a silly tree?

"Mis-ter Chambers," Emily set her hands on her hips, her voice clipped and tight, "I assure you I can manage *just* fine. I am their governess after all, and the children need to learn something about our—"

"Whoa," Nathan held up his hand in surrender. "Didn't mean to imply you weren't up to the challenge. Just thought you might like a hand, is all."

Emily blinked, feeling her ears burn. She couldn't think straight with his eyes roaming over her face.

"Let's start over, shall we?" Laugh lines deepened around his mouth as he played with the watch chain draped from his waistcoat pocket, the sun winking off the gold. "May I escort you and the children to the festivities? I'll be reporting the event for the newspaper, but I reckon we could squeeze in a little fun while we're planning Jake's penance."

Emily huffed. "It's not penance. It's consequences for what he's ruined."

"Are you dodging my invitation?"

"No. Just clarifying my point."

"Is it always this hard to get a straight answer from you, or do you presume me too forward?"

In truth, his offer spun her into a tangled heap.

"I'm—" She let out a gust of air. "I presume nothing. We just met."

"Good. Then let me put your mind at ease. If you're concerned about proprieties, I assure you that half of Galveston will be present."

She considered his invitation, searching his eyes. They sparked with humor and issued a challenge.

"All right then," she heard herself say. What was she doing?

They agreed on a time.

"Until tomorrow." He gave a slight bow and handed her the oleander blossom.

Whistling, the neighbor turned and strode across the yard, up the stairs, and through the front door.

Emily fingered the smooth sprig, examining the blossom's pink papery folds. The flower smelled like a light dusting of talcum powder. Fragrant yet poisonous, she'd heard.

What had possessed her to accept an invitation, one that included the children no less, from a total stranger?

Emily went very still. How was she going to explain any of this to Aunt Estelle?

Chapter 7

Estelle briskly plied the needle to a row of stitches. "Jake caused no small mischief if our neighbor became involved." Her mouth twitched despite her calm tone, alerting Emily of her displeasure.

Seated beside her in the parlor chairs, Emily steadied her hand and finished threading yellow floss through the needle while she took the time to gather her wits.

Following the recess, the children had spewed the news about Jake's tree mishap over a glass of milk and graham crackers. Estelle's initial relief soon faded when she heard of the ruined plants, Jake's apology, and the offer to run errands for Mr. Chambers as compensation. Estelle had dropped the matter. Until now.

The rich crab croquettes and potato salad Emily had eaten for supper sat heavily on her stomach, making her feel a bit queasy.

If only she'd made Jake come down out of that tree!

Emily cleared her throat. "I, um, I felt that Jake needed to apologize on the spot and pay for damages. I hope I didn't overstep my place. Mr. Chambers, h-he merely suggested that Jake run errands. With your permission, of course."

Estelle arched a brow. "I agree that Jake must pay for replacing the plants, and I'm not opposed to his running errands as part of his chores. But I must say that it seemed rather forward of Mr. Chambers to approach you without a proper introduction."

"Wouldn't you agree the situation merited it? The way I see it, Mr. Chambers was guilty of curiosity over what we were doing in his yard."

Estelle let out a sigh. "I suppose."

With stiff fingers, Emily wound the silky floss around the needle, forming a French knot. She poked it through the center of the daisy, completing the design on her purse.

Her pulse hitched up a notch. "About Mr. Chambers … what do you know of him?"

Estelle peered up, studying her. "Why do you ask?"

Emily shifted on the cushion. "H—he offered to escort us to the parade tomorrow."

Estelle's fingers stilled, the needle hovering over the quilt. "What did you say?"

"Why, I hesitated. We'd only just met. But Mr. Chambers seemed nice enough, and he insisted half the island would be there, so … I accepted."

Estelle's brows squeezed together. "He shouldn't have put you on the spot. He gave you no opportunity to decide whether spending time with him would please you or not."

"I'm sure he was just being neighborly. He only offered after he learned I'd be taking the children alone."

"He may have had the best intentions, but he still took liberties. Though it's my place to be your chaperone, I can't leave Clayton that long." Estelle stitched a row and looked up from her work. "Lena mentioned taking the children to the parade. I'll arrange for her to go in my place."

Emily stared at her lap. "I didn't mean… I'm sorry I caused more work for you."

Estelle gave her hand a warm squeeze. "Your welfare is no inconvenience for me."

Emily lifted her gaze, her stomach fluttering. "How would you feel if I were to accept other invitations from him?"

Estelle pressed her lips together. The ticking clock filled the lengthening silence. When she spoke, she appeared to measure her words with care. "Mr. Chambers doesn't come from the most respectable family, regardless of their wealth."

"What about them?"

"Hayden Chambers owns a string of saloons on the island and Houston. On the rare occasions when he's home, his shouts drift from next door. Mrs. Chambers has shunned my attempts to visit her. From what I gather, she stays in and receives no callers."

Given her folks, the news didn't put Emily off. "What can you tell me about their son?"

"I haven't spoken with him since he returned from abroad. I recall him being quite the sportsman and seaman. Always polite, though distant. To his credit, he's worked hard to live down his father's reputation. He hasn't sowed any wild oats that have become public knowledge. Granted, he may have lacked a proper upbringing, but one might hope that Harvard instilled a stronger sense of decorum in him."

She was far more concerned about his integrity than whether he behaved with impeccable manners. Didn't it take fortitude to rise above his father's reputation and resist being bullied into running saloons?

"Surely you don't fault him because of his kin."

"No, but neither does it silence my reservations." Estelle hesitated. "It pains me to say this… I mean no disrespect toward your father, but I owe it to Rosa to speak my piece."

Her father? What did Pa have to do with this?

Seeing her confusion, Estelle explained. "Nathan Chambers reminds me of Samuel in his younger days."

"How so?"

"Samuel was just as handsome and dapper, with enough charisma to charm land out from underneath a squatter. He also came from a troubled home, as does Mr. Chambers."

Emily set down her embroidery. "Tell me more, please."

"Samuel was full of schemes but careful to win favor by doing what others expected of him. He made it a point to sit beside us on the pew every Sunday. And he spoke words that Rosa longed to hear. They blinded her to his restlessness, his shortcomings. She knew next to nothing about him and even less about his family. He saw to that."

Other questions piled up, one foremost in her mind. "I've never understood how Ma turned out so bitter. Has she always been that way?"

"No. Rosa used to be good-natured but far too impressionable. Samuel took advantage of her disposition. He charmed her away from sensibility and sober judgment. She didn't question him. Nor did she pause to seek counsel or consider Papa's reluctance to bless their courtship.

"Only after he convinced her to elope did Rosa see him in a different light. They no sooner exchanged vows when he stopped attending family gatherings and church altogether. Rosa made excuses for him. Until Oil Springs."

Emily scooted to the edge of her seat. The oil boom of '77 had been a hot source of conflict in the home. "What happened there?"

"According to Rosa, your father left the farm for quick cash, drilling oil and building the pipeline into Nacogdoches. While he camped with the men on the project, he began playing poker to pass the time. One night stakes got out of hand. He later confessed that he wagered your mother's entire dowry on a full house and lost to four of a kind. Her portion of the family's land inheritance—gone."

Emily's stomach soured. An entire dowry. No wonder there was so much strife between her folks. Pa made matters worse every time he rode out into the night with cash in his pocket. How much had he gambled away through the years? No wonder they had no savings.

"Well, that certainly explains Ma's resentment," Emily said, her mind whirling.

Regret laced Estelle's tone. "Sadly, I watched Rosa retreat into a hardened shell. She went to the other extreme, as folks do. Becoming rigid in her beliefs and fearing her daughters would make the same mistakes she did. I share this because I want what's best for you."

Emily chewed on the inside of her cheek as other questions pushed to the surface. "What can you tell me about Pa's kin?" She'd received a sharp scolding for asking about them and never misstepped again.

"It's rather tragic," Estelle confessed. "Are you sure you want to hear it?"

Her palms dampened. "I have a right to know about my kin."

Estelle released a long sigh. "Your grandfather, Joseph, got into a dispute with a man named Owen Grigsby over cattle. Mr. Grigsby presented enough cause for the sheriff to arrest Joseph for stealing his livestock. When the lawman came to make the arrest, Joseph shot him through the heart."

Emily let out a gasp. "Why did he do such a thing?"

"It turned out that Joseph had indeed robbed the man. As soon as Grigsby's kin caught wind of the shooting, they banded together and took the law into their own hands. They followed Joseph into San Augustine. Gunned him down on the town square."

Stunned speechless, Emily pressed her fingertips over her lips and sank back onto the cushion. She stared unseeing at the cottage painting above the mantle until the stalks of hollyhocks blurred into ochre blobs.

What a black mark upon the family. No wonder folks threw them wary looks when they heard the name Cleburne. Shame burned in her chest, hot and searing.

Estelle must have sensed her shift in mood. She added, "Don't allow the actions of others to discredit your good name. You make your own choices in this life."

Emily nodded absently and straightened. She cleared her throat. "Thanks for telling me." The news proved harder to hear than she thought possible, though it answered questions that had puzzled her for years. "I think I'll turn in early. Get some sleep."

"Rest well, dear," Estelle murmured, though her expression suggested she doubted sleep would come any time soon.

"Goodnight."

Emily gathered her embroidery and left the parlor. She trudged up the stairs, her limbs heavy.

Some legacy! What a jolt to have gambling, stealing, and murder carved upon her family tree.

She planned on spending the rest of the evening immersed in the pages of *Jane Eyre*. Better to turn her mind toward Jane coming to terms with the aftermath of Rochester's insane first wife being hidden upstairs in Thornfield Hall than her own reality.

The following day, the crowd swelled along the parade route, lining both sides of the street. Emily had never seen so many people congregated together in one place. The noise overstimulated her senses.

Nathan Chambers stood close, his body pressed against her side. While he scratched notes on a small notepad, he'd glance over to gauge her reaction to the parade, or his proximity, she wasn't sure which.

Lena Kesler's presence to her right grounded her. In front of them, the children rose on tiptoes watching the marching band. The crowd erupted in cheers when "Stars and Stripes Forever" rang out.

Perched on Emily's hip, little Rachel wiggled to see the end of the procession. She covered her ears, muffling the sound of the pounding drums and blaring tubas.

The music trailed off. Folks began to thin out and head for refreshments. Corn popping in an outdoor popcorn furnace scented the air.

Nathan asked, "Care for popcorn or lemonade?"

Emily's throat was parched. "Lemonade, please."

He motioned with an index finger at Jake and Andrew. "You two young men, I need a hand bringing drinks for the ladies. Jake, consider this your first errand."

"Yes, sir," Jake lifted his chin and stood tall beside Andrew. Together they strode off with Nathan.

Lena touched Emily's elbow. "I've spotted a friend. Mind if I catch Adelle before she leaves?"

"Go. I'll stay with the girls."

Emily set little Rachel down beside Sarah and Lacey. She pushed her knuckles into the small of her back and eased the low ache from holding the child.

Emily watched Nathan stroll toward the lemonade stand. He looked smart in his linen sack suit and Panama hat.

A well-preened debutante paraded in front of him. She peered over her shoulder at Nathan, her gaze lingering. Apparently, not every female overlooked him due to his father.

Emily respected Aunt Estelle's advice, but Nathan had nothing to gain if he were to pursue her. Being a governess gave her no status in the community.

She stifled a yawn. She had read well into the night, finishing the last of *Jane Eyre*. At least most novels ended on a happy note for the heroine.

Having no dowry, Emily had no similar hope. Broaching that subject with Pa had proved disastrous. "Count your blessings," he'd mocked. "You've got your health and straight teeth, don't you?" Her cheeks had flared hot with humiliation over having no more worth in his eyes than a plow horse, where the buyer checked the animal's mouth before agreeing to the purchase.

Hearing the shocking news last night about her kin left Emily feeling numb and vulnerable. However nonsensical, she couldn't shake the impression that she had the word "Unsuitable" branded across her forehead. She resisted the urge to tug down on the brim of her turban until it covered her eyebrows.

Emily doubted Nathan would look down his nose at her because of her kin, given they both had disreputable family members.

Nathan turned and caught her eye and winked. She could not deny that his attentiveness flattered her more than she let on. Perhaps he considered her pretty or at least novel.

Wearing fashionable clothes boosted her confidence. Emily ran a glove over the dotted swiss fabric. She admired the yellow satin sash at the waist and the lace trimming the collar, bodice, and ruffled sleeves.

At least now she understood why Ma had dressed her in drab, plain clothes. She did it to protect her from falling prey to the wrong sort of men. It was new, this pity for Rosa. Not that Emily condoned her mother's poor choices, but she pitied the pain of blind trust. She refused to become like her mother, ever.

A tug on the arm pulled Emily from her musing.

Sarah peered up at her. "What does patriot mean?"

"A patriot is a person loyal to a cause, like our heroes who fought against England so that we might become a free nation."

"They put up a heroes statue of a lady on Broadway."

"Yes, the new Texas Heroes Monument. It honors the men who fought in the war with Mexico."

Sarah tilted her head. "But why put a lady on top of it?"

"She's Lady Victory."

"She has a circle of leaves in her hand."

"You mean a laurel wreath."

"Laurel?" Sarah lifted her brows.

"A long time ago in Greece," Emily explained, "the winner of a race wore a victory crown: a wreath made of laurel leaves. Lady Victory is holding out a wreath as if to say, 'You won!'"

"But leaves?" Sarah screwed up her face. "You'd think they'd get more than leaves for winning a war." She turned her nose up. "I would give them a gold crown."

Emily's stifled a chuckle.

A familiar voice caught her attention. "Hello, ladies."

She turned and spotted Colin Hensleigh approaching.

He tipped his derby. "You look the picture of summertime in that yellow dress, Miss Cleburne."

"Thank you kindly."

The sleeves rustled in the breeze around her elbows.

The minister leaned down and tweaked little Rachel's pigtail. "And how are Miss Rachel and Miss Riggles today?"

The girl giggled and squeezed her doll. "Fine. We saw a parade but the band hurt my ears."

A female voice broke in. "Colin, there you are!"

Emily turned and peered at the pert young lady who called the minister by his given name. She reached for his hand as her mouth sagged into a pout.

"Sorry," Colin murmured. "I'm afraid I lost sight of you when Miss Pickering pulled me aside."

"Well, no wonder," the girl's eyes rolled dramatically. "No one escapes that biddy's clutches without hearing an earful. I swear she dines on gossip like a glutton then dishes out the news in prayer requests." She huffed in annoyance. "I suppose I have no choice but to forgive you for deserting me—this time."

Colin gave her a tolerant smile. "Gracie, this is Miss Cleburne, the Edwards' niece. Miss Cleburne, meet my sister, Grace, who strives to live up to her name."

Grace pulled a face and gazed at Emily, her blue eyes flaring with curiosity.

Her British accent lilted light and breezy. "From what my brother has told me, it's a wonder you made it to Galveston the way he left *you* stranded, too. It seems we share that in common."

Colin's neck reddened. "Gracie," his tone warned, "it's not nice to dredge up my shortcomings when Miss Cleburne was kind enough to overlook them."

Nathan appeared at Emily's elbow. "Your lemonade, Miss Cleburne," he drawled, peering sidelong at the minister, taking his measure.

Chapter 8

Emily stumbled through introductions, explaining, "Mr. Hensleigh is our family's pastor."

She sipped the lemonade to cover her awkwardness. The tartness puckered her mouth.

Lena came alongside Emily as they passed out the beverages. Nearby the children ceased their chattering and slurped their drinks.

With casual ease, Colin extended his hand to Emily's escort. "A pleasure to meet you, Mr. Chambers. Allow me to invite you to join us on Sunday."

Nathan clasped his hand and glanced at Emily, his gaze sharpened. "I trust there'll be an available seat beside Miss Cleburne."

Emily's cheeks flushed. "Why, of course, you're welcome to join us."

Nathan flashed a smile, appearing pleased. "I'll be there. And since fair winds are forecasted, may I interest y'all in going sailing this evening?" He glanced around the group before his gaze settled upon Emily.

Sailing? A tremor of alarm rippled into her stomach.

Grace clapped her hands together. "Oh, I adore sailing!" She turned to Colin. "May we go?"

He grinned at her eagerness. "Of course, if it pleases you."

Lena caught Emily's attention. "I'm afraid I can't. I promised my neighbor, Millie, that I would watch her kids while she shops for her mother."

Emily pounced on the excuse, grateful for it. "I understand, truly." She gave Nathan a shrug. "I reckon that settles it. I must bow out as well."

Grace nudged Colin with her elbow. "Surely, a minister and an old maid would make fine chaperones."

Colin raised an eyebrow, chuckling. "Don't be daft. Sixteen years hardly qualifies you as old, much less a chaperone." He peered at Emily, searching her face. "But I'd be honored to stand in for Mrs. Kesler. That is if you'd care to go."

"Excellent." Nathan rubbed his hands together as though he considered the matter settled. "I'll clean the boat."

Satisfied by the turn of events, an easy smile slid across his face. He gazed at Emily.

They all did, expectantly.

She threw them a stiff smile. Seeing no graceful way out, she clutched the sweating glass to keep from wringing her hands.

"It's kind of you to offer, really, but I'm partial to staying dry—on land." The excuse sounded flimsy, but she stubbornly clung to it.

Nathan pushed his hands into the pockets of his trousers, his eyes never straying from her face. "Although you allowed me to sit beside you in church, I'm beginning to wonder if you enjoy making me work for your company. Fair enough. Know this—I'm an experienced sailor. You won't get wet. I guarantee you'll have a good time, like the rest of us."

Emily's voice tightened. "Let me assure you, I'm not being coy."

The minister tipped his head, regarding her. "Upon my word, Miss Cleburne's lack of enthusiasm is genuine." Their eyes locked. "You'd be quite safe, and the weather is ideal for sailing, especially for a novice out to test the waters. Should you consider joining us, perhaps you'll discover the thrill of the sea. Although, I daresay that requires a parting company with land to experience it."

She bit back a groan. The minister had only her best interest at heart. It's what made him so annoyingly persuasive.

Everyone peered at her, waiting. Would they think her weak-kneed or timid if she refused to go? Might Nathan think less of her?

Folding her arms around her waist, she faced him, feigning nonchalance. "Well, I'll admit my idea of a thrill isn't tipping in a boat, but then I've shot at wolves and faced panthers preying on our pigs and chickens, so what's sailing compared to that?"

Nathan's eyes crinkled with amusement, even admiration. It spurred her on.

She lifted her chin. "Count me in."

Emily regretted her bravado. She ducked as Nathan hauled the tiller for a long reach into the wind. It sent her heart racing in time with the speed of the twenty-two-foot sailboat.

Grace, who sat on the board seat beside Colin, squealed with delight. Her excitement grated on Emily. What was so thrilling about being scared witless?

At least she had the good sense to change into something practical. The salty spray spattered her calico dress and her half boots. So much for staying dry.

She glared across at the minister, who appeared the picture of composure, peaceful and serene.

The mainsail billowed with a wind gust and sent the boat heeling. The horizon slanted. Emily leaned toward the foaming water, her stomach rising in her throat. She gripped the handholds hard and leaned away.

She couldn't shake the sensation of plunging into the water, the current dragging her under until her lungs burned and her arms hung lifeless, dangling like limp strands of seaweed. A shiver crawled over her flesh despite the sun warming her shoulders.

Once the boat was on a more even keel, Nathan sat on the seat of the stern. He lashed the tiller. He had been so focused on hoisting the sails and steering the boat out of the harbor that he'd failed to notice her gaze fixed straight ahead, her body rigid with tension.

Emily sensed his gaze assessing her unease. "Try to relax a little, Miss Cleburne."

"Maybe I could *do* that if my stomach wasn't flopping like a landed fish." She winced at the edge in her tone.

"I chose the calmer waters of the Bay rather than sailing the Gulf. You're perfectly safe."

Safe? Hardly. Not when the water was over her head.

Emily heaved a sigh. "It doesn't help that I can't swim," she confessed.

Nathan frowned. "Well, no wonder you're tense. I've got something that will put your mind at ease."

Nathan had Colin man the tiller while he went below in the cabin. Colin took the helm with a practiced hand.

Emily rubbed at her stiff neck. "How can you be so calm?"

Colin looked about. "The weather's fair. Mr. Chambers is a capable sailor, as am I." He lifted a shoulder. "Beyond that, I trust my life into God's hands."

That struck a nerve. "So did Jonah, yet he didn't fare well at sea," Emily quipped. Trusting her soul into God's keeping was one thing, but trusting her life proved far harder.

Colin chuckled. "Right."

Nathan clomped up the steps carrying a canvas vest and handed it to Emily. "Here. Let's get this on you. In the unlikely event that the boat capsizes, you'll stay afloat."

"What is it?"

"A life jacket. The material makes one float in water."

She mustered a weak smile as he slid the vest over her shoulders and strapped it on snugly.

"Look—over the bow!" Grace pointed, her walnut braids whipping like ropes around her shoulders.

A slick, gray creature with a curved fin leaped out of the water. Emily's startled cry turned to fascination as the mammal dipped and weaved in the current beside the boat.

She gave a nervous laugh. "It seems friendly."

Colin eased back on the seat. "I've heard tales of dolphins rescuing shipwrecked seamen by pulling them to shore. Consider him your guide, Miss Cleburne."

She drew comfort from the story as her frolicking friend stayed alongside the boat all the way into the harbor.

After docking, Nathan gave Emily a hand up out of the boat. She wobbled on the wooden pier, unsteady on her feet.

"Easy," he murmured.

Emily gripped his hand until she gained her balance. She wasted no time walking off the pier. Relief coursed through her so strong that she fought the urge to drop to her knees and kiss the ground. Unlike water, the land steadied her. It was solid. Safe.

The following Monday, Emily snapped open the *Galveston Daily News*, inhaling a whiff of paper and ink. She began the history lesson by reading Nathan's article about the Fourth of July parade.

She finished the last line and folded the paper on its vertical crease, setting it on the library table before her.

"Since your father couldn't attend the 4th of July celebration, I'd like you to write about that day. Share with him anything you learned or enjoyed."

Sarah pushed her new gold-rimmed glasses up on her nose, her eyes appearing less strained. "I liked the marching band. I'll draw a picture of drums to go with my story."

"Excellent." Emily peered at Jake. "What about you?"

"Hmm?" He frowned, shaking his head. "Those heroes... I wonder if I'd be brave like them if I had to fight a war." He searched Emily's eyes. "Weren't they scared?"

"Being brave doesn't mean you're not scared, Jake. But fear didn't stop our heroes from fighting for liberty."

"But what if … what if they froze and couldn't move, couldn't fire back?" He shuddered in his seat.

"Would that make them any less brave for facing their foes?"

Jake shook his head. "It's not the same. They'd be killed, sure as the world."

"But isn't it honorable when one tries with all his might, win or lose? Even if he were to die, his headstone would read, 'Here lies a hero, brave and true.'"

Jake scratched below his shirt band, a struggle marring his boyish features. "No offense Miss Emily, but I'd rather mine says, 'Here lies Jacob Edwards, who lived a mighty long life.'"

He lifted his shoulders, content with being no hero.

Emily stifled a chuckle. At least he applied something of history to his young life.

A rap on the front door drew her attention. With Inez out running errands and Estelle upstairs, she stood up.

"Pull out paper and get started," she instructed.

Emily strode out of the study and up the hall. She pulled open the door and drew up short.

A woman dressed in black tilted her head at an angle like a curious crow. Behind spectacles perched on the bridge of a beaklike nose, her eyes raked over Emily's appearance.

"Oh," she twittered. "I was expecting Inez or Estelle. But of course, you're Emily, the governess, Estelle's niece from Chireno. I spotted you yesterday with that young man, Nathan Chambers. I'm here to speak with Estelle."

The caller gave no introduction but examined her as though she were about to dissect a worm—Emily being the worm.

Emily narrowed her eyes, wary. "I—I'm sorry, and you are?"

"Gracious. Where are my manners? I'm Wilhelmina Pickering."

Ah, the town gossip. Emily drew back as her wariness doubled.

Make this short. "Mrs. Pickering, Aunt Estelle is nursing Uncle Clayton, but you're welcome to wait in the parlor."

"It's Miss Pickering, and I'll just leave my card."

The woman drew a calling card from her purse and clutched it between her boney fingers. Emily stared at the thorny rosebuds encircling the card, eager to end the woman's scrutiny.

Miss Pickering had other plans. "I must say … I'm concerned about your young man, Mr. Chambers. To grow up in a home built on debauchery. Now he's at church, with you." The pause forced Emily to look up. "I trust your interest in him is … shall we say … purely spiritual in nature."

Emily gaped at her, then let out a huff, sputtering, "Excuse me!" Plucking the card, she thrust the door shut.

∞

At the close of the school day, Emily plodded behind the children into the kitchen. The chicken and dumplings bubbling on the stove made her mouth water.

Little Rachel stood on tiptoes at the center table, watching Inez knead bread dough on the flour-dusted surface. A bit of white smudged her chin.

Rachel joined Jake and Sarah at the cookie jar. They grabbed fistfuls of gingersnaps and glasses of milk before their chatter flowed out the back door.

Estelle looked up from steeping a pot of tea. "You look like you could use a cup."

Emily's mouth tightened. "I'm beyond tea reviving me."

She handed her aunt the calling card.

Estelle met her gaze. "I see Miss Pickering has made her usual impression."

Inez scowled. "She butts into folks' business as if the Almighty needs a helping hand."

"There's no arguing she's a mess," Estelle agreed.

Her aunt pulled down china cups and saucers from the wooden server, filled a teacup for Emily, and handed it to her.

Emily stirred in cream and sugar and took a sip before recounting the gist of the conversation. "I've never been more flabbergasted in my life. We'd just met, and she had the gall to lecture me about Mr. Chambers. The woman is outrageous!"

Estelle shook her head. "At least she didn't prod you into saying something you'd later regret."

"I slammed the door in the woman's face," Emily barked a laugh, covering her warm cheeks with her palms.

"There are times when silence is an apt reply, dear."

Inez clucked her tongue while turning the dough ball into a greased pan. "Although most folks take what Wilhelmina says with a grain of salt, it doesn't do a lady's reputation any good to be the topic of gossip. Mark my word, Wilhelmina will stir the pot till you nip that young man's designs for you, good and proper." She gave her head a firm nod to drive home her point.

Emily clacked the cup against the saucer. "I'll not bow to Miss Pickering. If she's so obnoxious, why doesn't someone put a stop to her prying? Like Mr. Hensleigh. Surely he doesn't approve."

"Of course not," Estelle insisted. "But change requires a deeper work in our hearts as God refines us. That can be a drawn-out process, like baking the loaves." Estelle touched the covered pan, where the smell of yeast permeated the cloth.

Emily's mouth pulled inward. "I see your point," she admitted begrudgingly.

She reached into the fragrant cookie jar for a gingersnap, mulling over her growing fantasy of Nathan Chambers pursuing her in courtship, despite the possibility of Miss Pickering's interference. She knew the wisdom of guarding her heart until she knew him better. Yet there was no denying the way her stomach fluttered when he slid beside her on the pew yesterday, shoulders touching. He followed it up with a promise to join her next week.

She let out a sigh and dunked the cookie in the cooling tea. She bit off a chunk, tasting the subtle bite of ginger.

Admittedly, she knew nothing about love or passion. But whatever she felt for Nathan, she hoped Miss Pickering didn't stir up trouble.

Chapter 9

The following week, Emily and Lena reclined on a quilt watching the children dig a moat in the sand around their sandcastle. The splashing breakers rushed closer and breached one corner of their handiwork.

Lacey walked to the water's edge, bent down, and washed the sand from her hands. She picked up a piece of driftwood and stilled, staring intently at something.

Over her shoulder, she called out, "Mama, what's this? Is it a jellyfish?"

"Wait! Don't touch it." Lena scrambled to her feet and trotted over. "Let me have a look."

With the sandcastle forgotten, the other children circled Lacey, who poked at the thing with the wood.

Lena stooped down to eye level, capturing their full attention. "Don't get too close to things that sting."

Lena's lecture was drowned out by the seagulls squealing and hovering twenty feet away, where a man tossed bread chunks into the air.

At day's end, folks crowded onto the beach seeking relief from the heat, their voices a steady rumble over the surf. Among them, Colin Hensleigh strolled over to Emily. He had loosened the tie around his neck and rolled his shirtsleeves over his forearms.

He removed his derby and held it in his hand while the breeze ruffled his walnut hair. "Good evening. It appears the dog days of summer have driven everyone to the beach."

He glanced up and down the shoreline where hundreds waded in the surf in knee-length swimsuits.

Emily shielded her eyes from the sun's glare and peered at him. "We're coming later in the day. Any earlier, and we bake." Even at this hour, a film of moisture coated her skin.

"Right. It makes me long for the cooler hours after twilight." He paused and cleared his throat. "I noticed Mr. Chambers joined us for services again. He seems quite attentive."

Emily stiffened. "Does that surprise you?"

Colin tilted his head and regarded her with an openness that held nothing but genuine interest.

Emily let out a sigh. "It's just that Aunt Estelle has reservations about his father. Then there's Miss Pickering," she clenched her jaw, "who Inez says will keep tongues wagging as long as Mr. Chambers looks in my direction. I suspect you've heard an earful from our resident gossip."

One look at his mouth pressed in a flat line confirmed as much.

Fresh irritation shot through her, searing her words with heat. "I trust you're doing your utmost to quell her tongue."

"Rest assured, Miss Cleburne, I don't condone gossip."

Satisfied with his answer, she pressed on. "I suppose you've got something to add about Mr. Chambers. Go ahead, say it."

Emily winced at the tartness of her tone. He didn't deserve it.

Appearing to take no offense, he met her gaze. "Only that there's wisdom in learning more before keeping close company with him."

"I'd hardly call a bit of socializing close company. Sailing and attending church together. I should think you'd encourage such things."

The minister lowered his brows. "Do bear in mind there can be a thin line between encouraging someone in their faith and trifling with his affection. I have seen where that leads."

He watched the hollow tumbling of the wave as it rushed toward the shore. His gaze remained fixed as he spoke in a faraway tone. "Better to allow things to unfold gently so you know where you stand."

Were his words for her benefit or his own? "Is that why you've never married?"

Though Colin's expression was unreadable, his right eye twitched. "I've chosen to devote myself to ministry and raising Grace."

A shadow flitted across his face. He appeared to shake off whatever memory had stirred in him.

A twinkle glinted in his eyes. "Before I go, you must tell me if we converted you into being a true sailing enthusiast."

Emily pulled a face. "You know water scares me stiff. At least the dolphin redeemed 'discovering the thrill of the sea' as you call sailing." A trace of a smile tugged at her lips. "What an amazing creature."

The minister nodded with satisfaction as he put on his derby and turned to go. "Then it appears there's hope yet." She tipped her head, waiting for him to continue. "Perhaps one day your love may grow to match my own."

Emily's brows lowered. She shot him a puzzled look.

He threw over his shoulder, "With the sea, Miss Cleburne, with the sea."

∞

That third Saturday in July, Jasper pulled the delivery wagon carrying Emily, Jake, and Sarah up to his father's cottage. From two blocks away, Emily heard the roar of the surf. Clouds scudded gray and billowy, gusting in from the Gulf, carrying the smell of wet sand.

Emily and the children had just climbed down from the wagon when fat raindrops splatted the ground. They hurried behind Jasper through the gate, the shower pelting them in earnest as they scrambled up the steps. After crossing the threshold, the sound drummed on the tin roof above them.

The fragrance of ham hocks and red beans simmering on the wood-burning stove filled the one-room cottage. Emily brushed off water from her face and neck. She waited a moment while her eyes adjusted to the dimness in the room before taking in the shiplap walls and the tidy furnishings.

She saw a man hunched on the corner rocker flanking the stove. His spine bowed from years of bending and stooping, his eyes behind his gold-rimmed spectacles fixed out the window. A book lay open on his lap.

Jasper raised his voice. "Daddy, these folks come to hear your story. This here's Miss Emily, Sarah, and Jake."

Having been reminded of the purpose of the visit, Mosey Pitts dipped his chin in greeting. He puffed on his pipe until smoke curled around his gray head.

The sweet scent of tobacco drew Emily over. "Thanks for agreeing to visit with us. The children and I have looked forward to hearing your early memories of Galveston."

Up close, his umber-colored skin appeared leathery from exposure to the sun and sea air.

Jasper motioned for the children to sit. They settled in and crossed their legs on the braided rug in front of the rocker.

The delivery man hauled over a ladder back chair for Emily.

The heat from the stove felt pleasant and began to dry the dampness from her shirtwaist and twill shirt.

Jasper stirred the pot of beans, then opened the ice box and started chipping ice. He spoke over the chunks chinking in the glasses. "Y'all go ahead. Ask him what he saw, but speak up so he can hear you."

Emily motioned for Jake to take the lead.

"Well sir," the boy's voice squeaked, and he cleared his throat. "Were there really Indians and pirates here when you were a kid? Jasper said so."

"Called them Weepers." His slow cadence was rich and deep.

"Pirates?" Jake's mouth slackened. "They wouldn't be caught crying."

"I know that's right," Mosey chuckled. "Meant the Karankawa. When one of them lost a child, the whole tribe would go to weeping all year long. Morning, noon, and night, as though they'd lost one of their own. To their way of thinking, I reckon they did."

Pondering this, he rubbed the stubble on his chin with his index finger.

Jake scooted closer. "Ever see one?"

"Came upon a Karankawa once while fishing. Tall as a reed, with round blue spots tattooed on his cheeks, looking like two sets of eyes staring at me, a cane poked through his lip. The strangest sight I ever saw."

Jake licked his lips. "What'd you do?"

"I tore out of there. Left my fishing pole, it spooked me so."

Mosey put the book onto the lamp table beside him while Jasper passed around the iced tea.

Emily reached for the cold glass. "Thank you, Jasper."

The children murmured thanks as Jasper set a tin plate of vanilla wafers on the rug between them. They crunched on cookies while Emily sipped the strong, sweet tea.

Jake spoke around a mouthful of the cookie. "Were you here when the pirates came?"

"Lafitte and his men took over the harbor before he brought Maw and me here. So many of us were pouring off the ship that day."

Jake sat up straight. "So you saw him, Lafitte? Was he mean and ugly, with an eye patch?"

Mosey's eyebrows rose. "No, sir. Handsome as a sly fox. Conniving as one, too. Saw him up close the day it all cut loose." He tipped back the glass with a shaky hand and swallowed the tea. "Summer was nigh past when we got off the ship, then that big blow hit."

Sarah pushed her glasses up on her nose. "Big blow?"

"1818 hurricane," Jasper explained. "Go on, Daddy."

"It rained something fierce. Lafitte rounded up the women folk to higher ground near the bay, to his place by the fort. I hid under Maw's skirt. Packed us in a room so tight we could barely breathe. It was black as pitch, the wind shrieking something awful.

"During the night, a—a cannon came barreling through the wall. Landed on…" He paused and worked his throat. When he continued, his voice sounded small. "Missed me, but Maw… I hung onto her till she slipped away. They had to pry me off her." Mosey stared off, his dark eyes glistening in the flickering light.

Sarah blinked back tears. "How old were you when you lost your mama?"

He sniffled and wiped his nose with the back of his sleeve. "Don't rightly know. Five. Maybe six."

The children exchanged glances, their faces filled with compassion. Emily sensed the moment they put themselves in young Mosey's place. They imagined the tale through the eyes of the young Mosey, not much different in age than themselves.

Mosey drew on his pipe, appearing in no hurry to break the silence. He waited until his voice gained strength.

"The next day, we ventured outside. It heaped on the agony. Dead bodies strewn everywhere. Not near enough food or water to go around. When I heard Lafitte was fixing to round us up like cattle and ship us off to New Orleans, I high-tailed it to the end of the island. I took my chances with the rattlers. Weren't any worse than pirates, no sir." He arched an brow for emphasis.

Sarah gasped. "You were all by yourself with *snakes*?"

"Didn't call it Snake Island back then for nothing."

Mosey drew on his pipe. "Once the ship sailed, this old woman took pity on me. She took me in. She needed a hand with chores. Suited us both."

Jake scratched his cheek. "Ever hear of pirates burying treasure on the island?"

Sarah's mouth pulled sideways in a smirk. "Buried treasure is just in story books, Jake."

"Truth is," Mosey divided a look between the two, "folks have been digging around Three Trees for a coon's age searching for treasure. None has turned up yet, but it doesn't stop folks from saying that grove of oaks is where Lafitte buried his gold."

Emily traced the rim of the glass with her finger. "Is there any proof there's real gold?" she wondered aloud.

"Some say one of Lafitte's men, old crazy Ben, paid with gold doubloons after Lafitte left for good."

Jake's eyes gleamed. "Where is Three Trees?"

"Well, now, it's a fair piece down the island. Said to be near the old Indian camp."

The wagon wheels crunched on the shell road as Emily and the children rode back to the Edwards' home.

The evening air had turned balmy after the shower. The clouds appeared lit with a golden glow.

The visit had far exceeded her expectations. Mosey had spun a tale rich in local history. The wonder and empathy on the children's faces had been its reward.

A broad smile spread across her lips as she listened to the children talk about pirates with hidden gold doubloons and weeping Indians. She savored the moment, filled to the brim.

Too elated to sleep, Emily crawled out of bed well past midnight. The floorboards creaked as she moved over to the window and peered out into the night. The scent of honeysuckle permeated through the screen. Overhead, the full moon peeked from behind the drifting clouds, casting shadows around the houses and under the trees. Light pooled under the string of streetlights lining Sealy Avenue.

A whippoorwill called a plaintive cry from somewhere near.

Her eyes roamed over to the Chambers' house. Inside, the rooms appeared dark as a crypt.

Out on the balcony, a flicker of movement caught her eye. She squinted at a slanting shadow. Someone was creeping to the handrail.

Had Nathan come out to smoke? She waited for the torch lighter to flare, for the cigar tip to glow red.

Instead, Nathan glanced over his shoulder. Her breath caught in her throat as he hoisted himself over the railing. Nathan gripped the trellis alongside the house and quickly lowered himself to the ground below.

Being careful to stay hidden in the shadows, he skulked away into the night.

Chapter 10

Emily stared after him, slack-jawed. Expelling a shaky breath, she splayed her fingers on her collarbone.

Where was he going at this hour?

A midnight swim, perhaps? Her cheeks flushed. Lena had mentioned something about men and women swimming together in the moonlit surf without a stitch of clothes. But why sneak out? Surely a family who ran saloons didn't object to skinny dipping.

She fingered the holes in the eyelet collar on her nightgown. What if Nathan had headed to a brothel or gambling hall?

Wherever he went, it didn't sit well that he snuck out of his own house. Memories churned of watching her father ride out after dark to whereabouts unknown. Emily rubbed the grit from her eyes and pushed those times aside. It didn't help that Aunt Estelle compared Nathan to Pa. But didn't Nathan deserve the benefit of the doubt? She'd give him a chance to explain his whereabouts.

Emily yawned, her mind becoming clouded by fatigue. She longed for a soft breeze to stir the muggy air.

The last thing she heard as she crawled between the sheets was the call of the whippoorwill retreating, its lonesome cry echoing in the distance.

◇◇◇

"Miss Cleburne, are you feeling unwell?"

Emily cut her eyes at Nathan as they strolled out of the sanctuary.

"Forgive me for saying so," he continued, his gaze raking over her appearance, "but you look a bit pale."

She pressed her lips together. *Might it be the ill effects of watching you slink off into the night?*

Twinges of a headache brewed behind her eyes.

She moved out from the stream of folks greeting Colin on their way out the double doors, the scent of jasmine and musk rising sharp and cloying.

On the steps, Emily squinted up at Nathan from under the brim of her straw turban, the glare of the sun harsh.

Sleep had been fitful, leaving her out of sorts and edgy. Though annoyance simmered behind her chilled expression, she managed to restrain her tongue.

Almost.

"Didn't sleep worth a hoot last night." She managed to keep her tone even. Peering sideways, she baited him. "You?"

Nathan narrowed his eyes. "Slept like a babe."

Emily's neck stiffened, her senses set on high alert. True. Babes were up half the night, disturbing other folks' sleep.

She stepped away from the flow of people mingling in knots on the church steps. Their voices drifted on the breeze over the rattling of the palm tree fronds lining the street.

A dull ache pulsed along her forehead. She searched Nathan's face for a hint of guilt, seeing none.

"Well," she sniffed, "at least one of us is hale and hearty."

Had she really expected an explanation about last night on the church steps, with an audience?

"If you'll excuse me," Emily angled away, "I promised my aunt I'd stock the orphanage pantry for her."

"Allow me to assist. Lunch at Ritter's with the guys from work can't compete with your company."

She waved her hand. "No need. Jasper will unload the staples for me."

Nathan cupped her elbow and turned her to face him. She peered up from under lowered eyebrows.

He lowered his voice to a soft timber. "As always, it's my pleasure to spend time with you."

She stepped away from his touch. "Some other time, perhaps."

Before he could say another word, Emily flew down the steps and caught up with Aunt Estelle and the children.

Slept like a babe, indeed! Had she learned nothing from living under the Cleburne roof? Better to take a step back now before being made a fool later. That would never do.

⌬⌬⌬

Emily stood back in the narrow pantry and inspected her work. She drew in a whiff of cinnamon and cloves from the spice cabinet and eyed the bags of oats, flour, and grits in neat, compact rows on the shelves.

She massaged the muscles in her lower back. It felt good to channel her frustration into a task. Humming with energy, she made short work of organizing the monthly donations from the Edwards' mercantile store.

Jasper hauled a burlap sack full of saltwater taffy. He flashed a grin. "Reckon the kids would like a treat?"

Recalling the bleak stares when she and Jasper arrived at the orphanage, Emily wondered if even taffy would bring a smile to the children's faces. "Let's pass it out and see."

"Fine by me."

Emily reached into the sack for several pieces. Removing a wrapper, she popped a peppermint-flavored candy into her mouth. The taffy stuck to her teeth and melted on her tongue, satisfying her sudden craving for something sweet.

Jasper led the way through the dining room and up the hallway into the expansive central reception hall. He pointed them out through the front double doors and onto the shaded portico.

As they treaded midway down the steps, they passed a small child seated there, hugging his knees. He peered up at them, his eyes observant in a way that spoke of intelligence and curiosity.

"Red lady," he spoke up.

Red? Emily glanced at her brown suit, pausing on the lower step to where she was at eye level with him. He reached and fingered a copper wave streaming down her shoulder.

"Beautiful."

"Thank you kindly."

She smiled and offered him a piece of taffy. "I'm Miss Emily. Tell me your name."

"Chai Lin."

The boy took the taffy and peeled off the wrapper.

At closer inspection, Chai Lin's appearance stood out among the other fair-haired children, with his sallow skin and hair so dark the strands looked dipped in an ink pot. She knew firsthand the insults hurled at kids who stood out as different. Her heart went out to him.

She guessed he was about five years old. "Have you started school yet?"

"No, but I will soon." Pride and determination dimpled his cheeks.

Laughter erupted nearby. Emily glanced towards the middle of the fenced yard, where a ring of orphans hovered around a gentleman wearing a bowler hat. Like baby chicks, they pecked for the man's attention.

A lanky snaggletooth lad peered over the heads of the younger ones and caught sight of the sack. He poked a finger. "Hey, y'all. Look what I spy!"

The group turned to see what had caught the boy's attention. Colin Hensleigh pivoted in their midst.

"Ah, Miss Cleburne, Jasper," he called, waving them over. "Come meet the children."

Emily offered Chai Lin her hand. He clasped hold and pushed up to his bare feet, his grip firm. They crunched through the sand up to the group, and the circle parted.

Colin's face softened. "I see you've already met Chai Lin. That young man will set the bar high as the most eager to learn." Chai Lin beamed up at the minister.

Colin put his arm around a scrawny tyke, tousling his unruly hair. "Meet Aaron, or Scoot as he's aptly named." The child resembled a scruffy mascot. "He came to us about a year ago, always underfoot, thus earning his nickname from the cook, who shooed him from the kitchen. He scooted swifter than a fox, chased by a hound." Snickers rippled around the ring. "To this day, he's still the fastest boy here." Scoot scuffed his sand-coated feet. His mouth pulled sideways into a smirk.

The minister went around the circle telling stories that distinguished each boy and girl. No wonder they're huddled around him so. He took their pleas for attention and turned them into strengths.

As Colin spoke, Emily studied the children's grave expressions, seeing a soul-deep hunger to matter to someone else. A look she recognized whenever she gazed at her reflection in the mirror.

Had that blinded her from seeing weaknesses in Nathan's character? The question disturbed her more than watching him sneak out into the night. She refused to offer blind trust as her mother did. One way or another, she would get to the truth. She had to.

"Miss Cleburne," Mr. Hensleigh interrupted her musing. "May I have a word with you while Jasper passes out the treats?"

Emily blinked at him. "Of course."

Jasper opened the sack and chortled like Santa. He scooped out candy, dispensing fistfuls into eager palms.

Emily squeezed Chai Lin's hand and let go.

The minister tipped his head toward the far side of the yard. Emily gathered her wits about her and fell into step beside him. When they gained a distance from earshot, he paused until she turned and faced him.

"I noticed during my sermon," he began, clearing his throat, "and just now, that you were … how shall I put it?"

"Looking pale," Emily supplied, feeling the heat climb the back of her neck.

His navy eyes took in her expression. His tone softened. "At first glance, you appeared merely distracted. But it's more than that. You look distressed."

The man was too discerning by half. Emily stared off at the wrought iron fence facing 21st Street. To her chagrin, the posts started blurring. She batted away the moisture building behind her eyelids.

"Forgive me," his voice broke in. "I didn't mean to add to your discomfort. I've learned that problems have less weight when we don't shoulder them alone."

She folded her arms and hugged her middle, letting the silence stretch until Colin shifted his weight.

"Well," he cleared his throat, "I merely wanted to offer a listening ear. Should you ever need—"

"I saw him slip out into the night," she murmured.

"Pardon?"

"Nathan—Mr. Chambers. He left his house sometime around midnight."

"I feared as much."

Emily's eyes widened. "You knew? How?"

"Shortly after, I spotted him crossing Fat Alley."

"Fat Alley…?"

"One of the seedier sections of town."

"What were you doing in such a place?"

"Rescuing a runaway. The girl telephoned, begging me to get her away from the variety show where she worked. I happened upon Mr. Chambers along the way."

"Did you see where he went?" Emily narrowed her eyes and studied him, seeing his hesitation. "You know, don't you?"

She pinned him with a stare.

Colin rubbed the back of his neck. "I hate being the bearer of bad tidings, or offend or embarrass you—"

"I promise I won't shoot the messenger," she reassured him. Regardless, her clipped tone said she was losing patience with being perceived as a female with delicate sensibilities.

His mouth pressed into a grim line. "He headed into the area with saloons, brothels, variety shows."

She pounced on the last. "Variety shows … you mean like vaudeville?"

"Not in the least. From what little I glimpsed last night, the place bulged with men downing beer while ogling skimpily-clad dancers on stage."

"Just because he headed that way doesn't prove anything." Maybe Nathan had a reason for being in that part of town.

The minister looked away, his brows drawn together.

"There's more, isn't there?" Emily sensed it.

He let out a sigh and met her gaze. An apology flashed in his eyes. "I saw Mr. Chambers duck out of sight when my carriage passed by. Whatever his errand, it appeared that he intended to keep it secretive."

Secretive. Hadn't Emily endured enough secrets with kin?

The gate creaked on its hinges behind them, and a group of women entered the yard and headed inside the Gothic-style home.

Colin pulled out his pocket watch attached to a silver chain and noted the time. He let out a sigh. "I have a meeting with the Board of Lady Managers that's due to begin on the hour. Will you be all right?"

Emily nodded absently, feeling a bit lightheaded though she refused to admit it.

She watched Colin walk past the boys playing kickball in the sand. He climbed the front steps. Her gaze traveled up the arched windows above the front porch. Above the pitched roof, a soaring cupola speared the sky. The afternoon heat had bleached that sky as pale as the home's cream-colored bricks.

She swayed slightly on her feet. Saloons, brothels, variety shows. Didn't Nathan realize that he gambled on his reputation just by entering that part of town? And if Colin had spotted him, who else might have?

Her stomach soured. Had she misjudged Nathan because he refused to run saloons? What if he had vices hidden from the townsfolk, from her?

Emily set her jaw. She refused to be kept in the dark, in the shadow of more secrets. Before she'd allow Nathan to pursue her, she first intended to find out why he kept his whereabouts of last night hidden.

Chapter 11

"I have a surprise for y'all," Emily announced, mustering a smile for the children's sake. "After you finish."

Jake and Sarah peered up from their writing about Mosey Pitts. Emily tapped two envelopes on the surface of the library table, hoping the surprise might end their dawdling. The heat made them all sluggish.

Sarah leaned forward in her chair. "What's in it?"

"Finish," Emily repeated, "and you may open yours."

Sarah took up the challenge. She bent her head over the paper, jotting with quick strokes while being careful to stay within the lines.

Jake cut his eyes at her writing and scribbled to finish first.

Emily reined in her impatience. "Neatly, Jake. You want your father to be able to read what you write."

Her gaze strayed out the window at the Chambers' house. *Nathan.* She had thought of little else since yesterday. She always erred on the side of caution with folks. Why had she made an exception with him?

Emily picked up a sheet of paper and fanned her face. What Colin Hensleigh had divulged made her stomach churn. She'd prided herself on being a good judge of character. But now—

"Finished!" Sarah's mouth tipped in a smug little smile, setting the pencil down.

Emily turned to Jake. His tongue stuck out the side of his mouth as he wrote.

"Hurry up, Jake," Sarah whined.

"Give me a minute. I'm telling Daddy about the gold buried at Three Trees."

"Remember," Emily stressed, "Mr. Pitts talked about a legend; a tale of buried treasure. Thus far, no one has found any gold."

"Yeah, but like Miss Inez always says, where there's smoke, there's fire. So," he lifted a shoulder as if it was a foregone conclusion, "it's got to be true."

"Oh, brother," Sarah muttered. "Just finish, will you?"

The oatmeal raisin cookies baking in the oven reached Emily's nose.

"Done." Jake leaned back. "What's my surprise?"

Emily turned over the envelopes. "You have mail."

The children glanced at each other before reading their names printed on the front and reaching for theirs.

"Who's it from?" Sarah examined the penmanship, her eyes widening. "Papa!"

"That's right," Emily confirmed.

Sarah slid her index finger under the flap and broke the waxed seal. Emily peered at Jake, who remained strangely silent as he stared at the envelope, his brows puckered.

"Open it," she prompted.

Sudden tears stood in his eyes. He threw down the paper and shot to his feet. "Writing him was a *sorry* idea," he bawled. "I wished you'd never made me do it!"

He fled out of the room and slammed the back door.

Emily puffed out a breath, stunned. What happened?

Sarah peered up from the letter.

"Go ahead and read yours," Emily instructed. "I'll be back."

Emily got up and followed Jake outdoors. She found him sitting with his legs dangling off the porch, facing away. Hearing the door slap shut, he glanced over his shoulder. He sniffed and wiped his nose on his shirt sleeve.

She walked over and squatted beside him, her skirt bunching around her knees. She took in his wet spiky lashes, the anger brewing behind his red-rimmed eyes.

Where did I go wrong? Tears were the last thing she'd expected.

"I … I'm sorry the letter upset you."

"Nothing's been the same since Daddy got sick," Jake scowled. "I can't even see him. Mama won't let me."

Emily laid a hand on his shoulder. He shrugged it away.

Over a stack of pancakes and cane syrup at breakfast, her aunt had mentioned Uncle Clayton's doctor visit scheduled for later today. Did that cause Jake's outburst?

Emily softened her tone. "She's just following the doctor's orders."

"What does he know?"

Emily worried her lower lip between her teeth. "You must miss your pa terribly, and I'm sure he misses you too. I bet he gets pretty lonesome being in bed all day. Imagine if you couldn't play with your sisters or be with your folks."

Jake thrust out his chin. "I'd sneak out of my room. No doctor would make me stay by myself!"

Emily pressed her lips together, switching tactics. "I'd hoped your letter might cheer him up a bit … and you, too."

Jake fell silent and chewed his thumbnail.

Moisture popped out on Emily's forehead. She was about to push up to her feet when he peered sideways.

"Reckon it did any good?" His voice sounded small but hopeful.

"Only one way to find out."

A frown creased his forehead. "It's still not the same," he insisted.

New insight struck her. *Jake misses the comfort of being together as a family as much as he misses his pa.*

"You're right. It's not the same. But we must make the best of the situation until you all can be together again. In the meantime, maybe your letters will bring him a smile."

Jake sniffled, considering this. "Reckon the shells on my card reminded him of our picnics at the beach?"

Emily tipped her head toward the door. "How about we go inside and see." She nudged him with her shoulder. "Maybe you can sweet-talk Inez out of a plate of those oatmeal cookies."

"Oh … all right." He scrambled to his feet.

Emily unfolded her stiff legs, feeling the burn in her thighs. *Please let Uncle Clayton's letter be something cheerful.* At this point, they could both use a dose of cheerfulness.

The back porch swing creaked as Emily plopped down onto the seat. She brought along the novel her aunt had recommended from the library. As she pushed off with her toes, the rhythmic sway stirred the sultry air, lulling her senses. Her mind drifted to the events of the day.

Jake's outburst had thrown her off-kilter, though watching the children reread their letters from their father eased the pang of witnessing Jake's tears.

Pots clanged from inside the kitchen, competing with the pulsing buzz from the cicadas in the trees.

At this hour, the chicken frying made her stomach rumble. Inez was hot on the warpath over the doctor arriving later than expected. His visit delayed supper by more than an hour. Red-faced, the cook had brushed off offers to help.

Emily fingered her brass bookmark where she had left off and opened *Sense and Sensibility*. She inhaled the faint scent of leather and began reading.

After a few paragraphs, she paused, unable to concentrate. Despite her best effort, she could not follow the sensible point Elinor Dashwood made with her sister, let alone follow the plot.

She heaved a sigh. It was no use. Neither the rhythmic sway nor her favorite pastime emptied her mind of what troubled her.

Not when the word *secretive* dared her to solve its riddles. What was Nathan doing prowling around that part of town at that hour? Where had he gone? It made no—

A rustling came from the oleanders alongside the house. She cut her eyes and squinted as the object of her musing stepped onto the porch.

Emily snapped the book shut on her lap. "Oh, you startled me!"

She touched her throat, feeling her pulse leap under her fingertips.

Nathan leaned against the railing and crossed his ankles, his body silhouetted in the fading light. He drew on a cigar and blew out a ring of smoke.

"Evening," he drawled.

She forced steadiness into her voice. "Didn't your mama teach you it's not polite to sneak up on a gal?"

Nathan had the nerve to chuckle. "I suspect it takes more than the element of surprise to spook one who shoots at wolves and panthers. Besides, after the way you loped away from me on the church steps, the element of surprise seemed the best approach. It works to my advantage when I'm tracking deer."

She straightened her spine. Did Nathan consider this a game of sport? Had she only imagined that spark of interest, or did he thrive on the chase? The hunt?

"You'd do well to remember I'm no one's prey," she asserted, though his sudden appearance left her feeling exposed.

"Oh, I've yet to see a doe as alluring as you in my sights."

She ignored the flattery and let the silence stretch. Above the rooftops, streaks of red and orange clouds flamed the sky. She became aware of the darkness hovering at the edges of twilight, the seclusion of the fence, and the six feet separating them.

Was Inez listening at the kitchen window? Unease expanded in her chest.

Swallowing, Emily glanced at the door. "It's late." She gripped her book and got up.

"There you go … running off again," he murmured.

Nathan pushed off from the rail. His long strides ate up the distance between them.

He blocked her path. "Have I done something to offend you?"

"You mean besides taking liberties?"

"Surely nothing that's caused you to avoid me."

She huffed out a breath.

Nathan leaned in. She took in the unbuttoned collar on his oxford shirt, the lack of a jacket, waistcoat, and tie, and the scent of sweet tobacco tinged with ash.

"It's apparent you have a bee under your bonnet," his voice dipped low. "Tell me what I've done so I can make amends."

She folded her arms, pressing the book to her chest. "You treat me with familiarity, yet what do I know about you?"

He spread his hands in a candid gesture. "What do you want to know? Ask."

That drew her up short. Did Nathan have nothing to hide?

"All right." She licked her dry lips. "Let's start with what you do for pleasure … where you spend your evenings."

He tucked in his chin, his expression curious. "I never turn down an invitation to the Artillery Club or an oyster roast, and I'm rather fond of the theatre, music concerts, and dancing." Amusement laced his tone. "Anything else?"

"What about late-night activities?"

His body stiffened. "That's rather cryptic." His voice took on an edge.

Emily's mouth tightened. "This, coming from a man who leaves the house by way of the trellis."

She sensed his body go stone-still, his eyes hooded. His silence ate up her resolve. Behind him, the fiery clouds had faded to cinders.

"Oh, never mind," she snapped. "I should know better than to expect an honest answer."

Emily turned and skirted around him.

Nathan grasped hold of her wrist. "Wait," he insisted.

Emily hesitated before she jerked free. She pushed open the door and yanked it shut behind her. In the shadowy hallway, her body trembled.

"Emily. Miss Cleburne," he called, his voice sounding muffled through the door.

Hush! Emily winced, hoping no one heard him. She pressed an ear to the door, listening. The soles of his shoes thudded on the wooden porch.

Go away!

Behind the kitchen door, Inez was beating the fire out of the mashed potatoes. She'd set supper on the table soon.

Upstairs she heard the water running. The children were washing up for supper. They'd be down any minute.

She hugged the novel to her chest as her heart hammered against her ribcage. She strained to hear sounds through the door.

Her fingers fidgeted along the spine of the book.

At last, the clomping faded into silence.

Emily sagged against the door. She closed her eyes and blew out a slow breath.

He'd hidden things from her. What kind of a man did that?

Jake's remark rang in her ears. *"Where there's smoke, there's fire."*

Wisdom dictated that she keep her distance to avoid getting scorched.

The family would expect her to join them around the table. How would she choke down mashed potatoes and gravy and fried chicken while the children talked about their letters from Uncle Clayton? Aunt Estelle would see right through her shattered composure. She couldn't tolerate the scrutiny, not tonight.

She had no time to waste. Emily fled up the hallway and mounted the stairs, her legs wooden. She would make excuses for missing supper. Why bother eating when her appetite, like her confidence in her judgment, had dulled?

Chapter 12

"How long before Jim and Long John Silver get to the island? They'll find the treasure, right?" Jake licked his lips, his eyebrows raised.

Emily's posture slumped in the chair as her gaze slid over the top of the page at him.

"Right?" The boy was nothing if not persistent. Today that persistence chafed at Emily's last nerve.

She bookmarked the end of the chapter. "Hold your horses, Jake. They just came on board the ship."

She laid *Treasure Island* down on the study table with a thud. She needed morning recess. Recess and caramel-coated popcorn with peanuts, though she doubted an entire box of Cracker Jack would suffice.

"Can't we read another chapter?" he pressed. "Please, please? I want to see where they go next."

Sarah peered up at Emily with concern filling her blue eyes. "One chapter at a time, Jake. It's the rules," she lisped in her most prissy tone.

Much to Emily's chagrin, Jake's fascination with pirate gold had taken on a life of its own. She wished he held the same interest in their next subject. She took a moment to gather her flagging resolve.

If only the children would buckle down and try harder.

Emily understood the reason for their inattention. But their lack of progress in arithmetic ate away at her confidence. She'd tried every angle she knew to break down the steps. Yet Sarah and Jake looked at numbers on the chalkboard with the same blank stares as calves eyeing a new gate. How often did she have to repeat the same thing before it stuck in their brains?

Emily drummed her fingers on the table. The morning breeze rustled the muslin curtains as an idea formed. "Before your exam, let's review again."

She pulled out a broken piece of chalk from the desk drawer, feeling the dry dust already coat her fingers. She drew three sets of twelve circles on the small chalkboard. "Jake, let's say you found three rows of twelve gold doubloons washed ashore on the beach. How many gold pieces would that be?"

Jake shifted forward in his chair, his gaze scanning the rows with new interest.

Using pirate gold just might work. *Please let it sink in.*

As Emily waited for his answer, she started drawing two rows of coins for Sarah to add.

<hr>

The clock chimed two o'clock while the children fidgeted in their chairs, awaiting their test scores.

Emily gritted her teeth and stood up, pausing until Jake quit doodling and peered up at her.

She gripped her wrist behind her back. "Neither of you passed the test."

Jake drew back in his chair. "How do you figure?"

Emily let out a huff. "That's my point! You didn't figure correctly. And don't think for a minute that I'll tolerate failure from either of you."

Sarah blanched pale. She tugged at her ear and stared at the surface of the table.

Murmurs drifted from the parlor. The orphanage committee. There were guests present.

Emily lowered her voice. "After recess, we'll review every problem you missed until you both get them right."

"But mine are harder," Jake whined.

Emily planted her palms flat on the table and leaned forward, spearing him with a look that brooked no argument. "And you're older, so I expect more from you. Understood?"

Jake swallowed. "Yes, ma'am."

"Now, go play," Emily waved her hand in dismissal.

The children scrambled to their feet and escaped out the back door.

Emily pinched the bridge of her nose. So much for pirate gold solving the mystery of arithmetic. Calculating numbers in her head had always come easy for her. All that drilling. How was it possible that neither child passed the test? What would it take to get through to them?

She glanced over at the newspaper on the table, scanning the headlines. *Carrie Nations Wields Ax at Saloon.* The crusader was at it again. She lifted the paper on her way out of the study.

She stopped in the kitchen and pulled a handful of fig newtons from the pantry. She popped one in her mouth before she hit the back door. If she kept devouring sweets at this rate, she'd soon be letting out her skirts.

As she stepped outside, the sunlight glared bright, flooding the porch. The muggy heat dampened her skin. Emily sank onto the swing, sending it swaying. She squinted at the children dashing around the yard, playing tag.

Last night's porch scene proved every bit as oppressive as the heat. She couldn't help but wonder what might have happened if she had remained on the porch and waited out Nathan's silence. Would he have explained? She might have given him half a chance had she seen a hint of openness in his expression. In that split second before she bolted, she'd caught a glimpse of panic in his eyes. As if frantic to contain what she'd witnessed, the way one frantically tries to plug a hole in the side of a paint pail before whitewash spills and spreads everywhere.

She'd been a fool to hold out hope that he had nothing to hide. She never did abide foolishness, least of all in herself.

Disappointment over Nathan stung, but no more so than her naivety. If only she hadn't dismissed Aunt Estelle's reservations so easily. What she needed now was to gain perspective and stay on guard.

At least Inez hadn't overheard him calling her name through the door. She dodged having to explain—

Raised voices burst through the window from next door. Emily sprang to her feet and scooted to the edge of the porch, straining to listen.

"…out of your mind to write such a thing!"

"Mother, don't start."

"I swear you'll be the death of me yet."

"I'm just doing my job."

"Who do you think you're kidding? Don't you see?" her voice shrilled. "Your father won't tolerate such a slap in the face. His pride won't allow it."

"Then let the chips fall where they may."

"You'd rather bear the brunt of his rage?"

"I'm a grown man. Let him try."

"Well, don't think it won't trickle down onto me!"

"If he so much as lays a hand—"

"No," she pleaded. "For all our sakes, promise me you won't rock the boat."

"I'm through cowering to him."

"Please … if anything were to happen. Whatever would I do? I couldn't bear it," she wailed, bursting into sobs. The sobs trailed off, growing faint before a door slammed.

From the yard, little Rachel squealed, "Tag, you're it!"

Emily glanced over her shoulder at the newspaper. What had Nathan written? She stuffed another cookie into her mouth and strode over. Emily scooped up the paper. The sharp scent of ink wafted upward as she held it close and read the print.

There. Under the lead story, the reporter's name. *Nathan Chambers.* How did she miss it?

The gooey fig filling thickened in her mouth as she chewed.

She read on. So the prohibitionist had taken up a hatchet this time instead of smashing saloons with rocks. The tone of the story depicted a heroine fighting for a just cause.

She massaged her brow. What might public reaction be, given that the son of a saloon owner wrote the article? Some would say it took backbone to write it. Emily sniffed. How might their opinion change if it became public knowledge that the saloon owner's son led a secretive life?

She folded and creased the newspaper, fanning at the dampness beading along her hairline.

The back door creaked open, and Lena stepped onto the porch, her hand lingering on the doorknob. "There you are." Emily brightened, seeing her friendly face. "Reverend Hensleigh is asking that you join us."

"Me? Whatever for?"

Lena lifted a shoulder. "Not quite sure."

Emily glanced at the watch pinned to her shirtwaist. "Can't it wait till after your meeting?"

"I don't think so."

Emily blew out a breath. "All right, then."

Lena paused before heading inside. "There's a concert tonight at the Garten Verein. Join us, won't you? We're having a picnic on the grounds. Bring Sarah and Jake. The music is divine."

Emily had heard of the German garden club, and the idea of spending an evening with Lena eased the tension pinching between her shoulders. "Sounds delightful."

Emily tossed the newspaper onto the swing and followed after her friend.

They entered the parlor, and the hum of voices quieted. Colin set down the china cup with a soft chink and rose from the armchair. Across from him on the sofa sat his sister, Grace, who stopped speaking mid-sentence. She turned from Estelle, who sat beside her, pouring coffee, and watched. Seated in the matching chair, Miss Pickering peered at Emily over the rim of her cup.

"Ah, Miss Cleburne," Colin stepped forward. "How good of you to join us."

Estelle lifted the steaming pot from the coffee table. "Have time for coffee, dear?"

The aroma tempted her. "No, ma'am." Emily glanced at the ticking mantle clock.

"In that case," Colin said, "I shall get straight to the point. Several of our committee members have taken leave due to family matters. Though it cannot be helped, the timing has put us in quite a bind, with the upcoming school year approaching. You see, each year our church donates school supplies for all the orphans."

Colin rubbed his chin, hesitating. "I know this is quite a lot to ask on top of your teaching duties, but would you consider helping us get things in order for the school year? It would mean working on Saturdays."

Emily crossed her arms, focusing. "Doing what, exactly?"

"Before we can purchase supplies, we must inventory and organize the current materials. I trust your expertise would make short work of compiling a list. Of course," he added, "we will assist you every way possible."

Colin straightened his tie. An apology flitted through his eyes, telling her he understood if she refused. Yet, his vote of confidence boosted her sagging spirits.

She pictured the orphans, one in particular. Chai Lin had no parents who cared whether he succeeded, but that didn't hinder his eagerness to learn. If Jake and Sarah had half his determination, they'd have passed their math test. Didn't Chai Lin deserve the same chance as her cousins?

She met his gaze. "I'll do what I can."

"Splendid," Colin flashed a relieved grin.

Miss Pickering spoke up. "Pastor, I don't suppose you've seen the jumbled heap in that supply closet."

He glanced sidelong at Miss Pickering. "No, I have not."

"Well, let me tell you, it's piled from floor to ceiling with odds and ends of every sort." She tapped a boney finger to her chin. "I'll make certain it's cleared out before Miss Cleburne and I begin inventory."

Miss Cleburne and I? Oh, no! Volunteering did not include her being in confined spaces with Miss Pickering. The back door banged open as Emily cast around for a graceful way out of having to work with the woman. Feet pattered up the hall.

Jake barged into the parlor, waving an envelope. He flapped it above his head like a white flag. Looking hopeful that his errand might put him back in his teacher's good graces, he thrust the small square at her.

"Look who has mail this time," he grinned in a singsong voice.

"Son," Estelle murmured, "you're interrupting. You may give it to Miss Emily when we're through."

Jake spun and faced his mother. "But Mr. Chambers made me promise I'd give it to her right away. You told me I could run errands for him, remember?"

Mr. Chambers. Emily froze. *Not now!*

She schooled her features and snatched the envelope from Jake. "Much obliged. Now do as your—"

"But Mr. Chambers said," Jake stressed, "this answers your question from last night … whatever that means. He said you'd know. You do, right?"

The boy tipped up his head at her expectantly.

Miss Pickering clucked her tongue.

Adrenaline shot through Emily's veins, swift and tingly, the sudden jolt weakening her knees.

Her eyes flitted around the room, touching Miss Pickering's narrowed gaze, Colin's furrowed brow, on Grace's mischievous smile. Emily wanted to wipe that smile off her face, but seeing Aunt Estelle's eyes glitter with disappointment pulled her up short.

The mantle clock ticked the seconds as silence sucked the air from the room, from her lungs.

It was too much.

She longed to flee the prying eyes of those who were privy to her failing a test far weightier than arithmetic.

She glanced at the pressed tin ceiling and tossed a fervent plea heavenward, but saw no hope of escape.

Chapter *13*

"She'd better tear that up straightway," Miss Pickering pointed at the envelope, "and quit giving that young man encouragement, or bear the consequences."

"Wilhelmina, please," Estelle warned.

Emily's face flamed with heat. She felt Lena's fingers curl around her hand and gently squeeze.

Miss Pickering stared pointedly at Estelle. "It's your place to teach her."

"More coffee?" Estelle arched an eyebrow.

"She's losing her way and you say nothing?"

"There's a time to speak and a time to be silent."

"So speak! Tell her to steer clear of temptation."

"This is neither the time nor—"

"Mark my words—he'll tarnish her reputation. Then what will become of her?"

Grace leaned in, her eyes pinging back and forth, clearly relishing her front-row seat to the sparring match.

Seeing her glee, something inside Emily snapped. She glared at Miss Pickering and blurted, "I'll thank you to stay out—"

"Well, Miss Cleburne," Colin's clipped voice broke in, "we've taken up enough of your time. On behalf of the committee, I cannot thank you enough for your willingness to come to our aid."

Grace's head swiveled toward her brother, her brows squished together. Then her gaze sharpened and landed on Emily while she worried at her bottom lip between her teeth.

Colin cleared his throat and faced Miss Pickering, who blinked like a hoot owl, her feathers ruffled over the abrupt halt to her prying.

"And with you at the helm," he assured the woman, "I'm certain we'll have things running in tip-top shape come the first day of school."

The puckered lines around Miss Pickering's mouth softened as she preened under the minister's recognition.

Miss Pickering stroked her cheek. "Yes, well … I'll see that someone clears out the closet."

Emily clenched the envelope, her face pinched. Efficient as ever, Colin had shifted the scrutiny off of her. She should be grateful, but at the moment, it left her itching to give Miss Pickering a tongue-lashing.

Emily turned from the scene and whispered to Lena, "See you tonight." She spun on her heel and marched out of the room and up the stairs.

"What a colossal mess," she muttered under her breath.

The envelope she clutched dashed any hope of avoiding a talk with Aunt Estelle about what happened with Nathan on the porch.

Needing a moment to calm her jangled nerves, Emily slipped into the bathroom and shut the door. Her breathing sounded loud in the still room.

Her fingers trembled as she opened the flap and pulled out the thick, square card. She turned toward the window light and read the message.

Two words slanted in bold print: *Trust Me.*

She snorted, incredulous. "I'd sooner sprout wings and fly to the moon before that happens."

She refused to be gullible, much less offer him her unearned trust.

Emily stretched her legs on the cotton quilt beside Lena and Peter. She listened to the string quartet playing Schubert's Serenade.

Around them, clusters of people sprawled out on the lawn behind the dance pavilion at the Garten Verein. The octagon-shaped building glowed like an ornamental lamp, spilling light through the expansive wall of windows and open doorways. Above it, the setting sun tinted the wispy clouds a golden pink.

Her gaze drifted over her shoulder to the north end of the park. The water fountain splashed and glistened, lit by glowing lights circling its three tiers.

Around the fountain, couples strolled arm in arm down the walkways under the full moon rising. Emily ignored the pang of envy as they leaned close and spoke in hushed tones.

Her thoughts drifted to Nathan. His note had opened her up to more than Miss Pickering's prying. A tingling rose on the back of her neck and flushed her face, heating behind her eyelids. For someone who took pride in being cautious, how had she allowed things to get so out of hand?

It pained her to see Estelle's disappointment, knowing she had caused it. First thing tomorrow, she'd tell her aunt nothing untoward happened on the porch, that she'd be more careful about appearances. Somehow she'd prove herself trustworthy. She had to. Being the children's governess depended on it.

Bach's *Air* swelled from the outdoor bandstand, pulling her from her musing. A bead of moisture trickled between her shoulder blades, but she barely noticed it dampening her yellow dress.

Her eyes drifted shut as she leaned back on her palms and focused on each languid note. Like a yearning, its melancholy tone resonated deep, strumming her heartstrings. The intertwining harmony and melody flowed on for long moments before it changed, becoming buoyant, springing with hope. Its beauty released her unrest into the air. She felt light, as if floating above the troubles of the day. If only it were possible to stay in that transported place where the world's cares had no foothold. But all too soon, the musicians held the last note.

Emily opened her eyes as the applause erupted. When the clapping ebbed, the chatter of people hummed while they got up and began to move around.

She spotted the children weaving through the crowd. They flopped down on the quilt and dove into the picnic basket for the shortbread tin while Lena poured them glasses of lemonade. Emily reached for a small square and bit into the rich, buttery cookie.

Sarah's face brightened with excitement. "Miss Emily, you should see the animals in the little zoo. I got to pet a baby lamb. He's so soft and fluffy."

Emily smiled over the child's delight.

"Come watch us bowl," Jake spoke around the cookie in his mouth.

"In a little bit," Lena put in. "Go play. We'll meet you later on the playground."

The children polished off their drinks and dug for more cookies before scampering off to play.

Lena touched Emily's arm. "Walk with me?"

Emily brushed crumbs from her lap and got up off the quilt.

Her friend whispered something in Peter's ear.

Emily's stomach clenched. After the fiasco with Miss Pickering, did Lena have second thoughts about their friendship?

When Lena gained her feet, they strolled along the walkway that led under the live oak trees.

"About Miss Pickering," Lena began.

Here we go. "Thanks for standing by my side."

"Silly goose, that's what friends do. We stick together." Lena peered sideways. "You look surprised."

"I reckon I am. I wouldn't blame you if you kept your distance to avoid gossip."

"I don't allow Wilhelmina to dictate who my friends are, and neither should you. That includes Mr. Chambers."

"I don't know… Maybe I should discourage his attention."

"I see him sitting beside you in church. I thought you liked him."

"I do, even still." And wasn't that the crux of the matter?

Lena motioned to a wooden bench along the path. "Shall we?"

They sat side by side, and Emily caught the faint scent of lavender as Lena faced her with a crinkled brow. "Has he acted … improperly towards you in any way?"

Emily shifted on the bench. "No, nothing like that. It's just that I know so little about him, and what I know puzzles me. I can thank my father for chasing away any suitors." Her mouth pulled into a wry twist. "That leaves me venturing into uncharted territory with no compass." She couldn't afford to make a mistake that could affect her livelihood. She turned up a palm. "How did you find your way with Peter?"

"I had to learn in a hurry."

"Why is that?"

"We married less than two months after we met."

Emily's mouth gaped open. "What possessed you to marry a man you barely knew?"

Lena shook her head and chuckled. "I was young—all of sixteen, and drawn to him. Mama and I had just arrived from Germany."

"You don't look German to me."

"Half German. Mama was from Spain."

That explained her lovely dark hair and eyes.

Lena's smile faded. "Anyway, I'd arrived here badly shaken, and Peter's steadiness comforted me." She swallowed hard. "You see, we, um … we'd lost Papa during the voyage."

"How awful." Emily didn't know what else to say.

Lena stared off into the night. "His heart failed him on the voyage. To make matters worse, we barely had two nickels to rub together. Mama kept saying, 'God will provide a way,' yet I worried about finding work. At the time, I knew very little English. However," she added with a gleam in her eye, "I had perfected Papa's apple strudel recipe."

"So you found Peter's bakery and asked for work?"

"As it turned out, Peter found me." Her voice held a touch of wonder.

"He met us on the docks when we got off the boat. He'd come that evening led by an inner prompting, he later confided. He heard us speaking German and introduced himself. After he learned we were from Frankfurt and that I could bake, he hired me right then."

Goosebumps prickled up Emily's arms. "That's amazing!"

Lena gave a slow nod. "Peter took us to a family in the church that took in boarders and came by every evening once he closed the bakery."

"But to marry him so soon," Emily shook her head. "How did you know he was right for you?"

Lena touched a finger to her lips, a soft smile forming. "His blue eyes told me everything I needed to know."

"His blue eyes?" Emily peered at her, dubious.

"They were gentle, honest." Lena shrugged. "They mirrored his decency, his compassion when he gave out day-old bread to the needy, only kindness and respect for Mama. And when I'd catch him staring while I was kneading dough, those warm looks left no room for doubting his intentions. I felt cherished. Secure. So when he asked for my hand in marriage, I said yes."

"Well, he does adore you," Emily agreed.

"I am blessed to have a partner who's also my best friend."

In the gathering dusk, fireflies winked on the lawn.

Lena nudged Emily's side. "Now, back to our Mr. Chambers." Their eyes met. "I'm confident you'll figure out the riddles of men. You'll know if Mr. Chambers is right for you—in time."

Andrew came lumbering toward them, holding his stomach. He slumped on the bench beside Lena.

"I don't feel so good," he moaned.

Lena brushed aside his dark hair, matted with sweat, and pressed her palm to his forehead. "Hmm. No fever. You probably ate too many cookies and raced around after Jake. There are no half-measures with you two. Let me take you to Papa."

"But Jake needs me," Andrew pouted. "We're going to beat the girls in lawn bowling."

"I've never played, but I can take your place," Emily offered against her better judgment.

His eyebrows lowered over his dark eyes with a look that said her offer spelled defeat. Still, he managed politely, "Yes, ma'am."

Lena glanced at Emily. "I'll catch up with you."

"Follow that path," Andrew gestured with his chin to the one forking right. Then he laid his head down on his mother's belly.

<hr>

On the lit bowling green, the air was sticky and warm with the lingering scent of freshly mowed grass. Players rolled their bowls, aiming at the white ball centered near the end of the parallel lane.

Jake had explained the game to Emily, spitting out a string of terms and rules that left her befuddled. It didn't help that they called the white ball a jack, whereas the pointy metal pieces were jacks in the game of jacks. Or that the grapefruit-sized bowling balls they called bowls. The game made no sense.

On the next rink over, a group of men shook hands, congratulating the winners. She stifled the urge to scowl at the victors.

Ignore them. Just concentrate on your swing.

Emily swiped wisps of damp hair away from her eyes. She wished she'd worn her hair up off her neck instead of tying it loosely with a ribbon. Wiping her sweaty palm down the front of her dress, she held the bowl in her right hand.

"It's easy," Jake assured her. "Just remember to aim to the right of the jack with a forehand draw, and it'll curve to the left on its own."

"What…?" Emily scrunched up her face. "Who makes balls that don't roll in the right direction," she muttered.

She had about as much chance of scoring a point as the children had of calculating numbers in their heads. *Ah. So this is what math is like for them.* From now on, she vowed to be more patient.

Emily released a breath and focused on the white jack at the end of the rink. She swung her arm down and backward and felt her grip loosening, the ball slip from her fingers. The bowl flew and landed with a thud—behind her.

"Oh no," Jake groaned, smacking his forehead. "Ah, Miss Emily, that's worse than when you rolled the bowl into the neighbor's rink! I said pull your arm back a little way, not let go of the bowl."

Puffing out her heated cheeks, Emily moved back and scooped up the ball near the sand ditch.

"She didn't do it on purpose, Jake," Sarah chided.

Straightening her spine, Emily shot a glance at the next rink over. A ruddy-faced fellow jerked his gaze away, his shoulders trembling with laughter.

The tips of her ears burned hot.

Great, an audience.

So what if she played pitifully? She was no quitter. Emily squared her shoulders and stepped up to try again.

Jake came over. "Here, let me show you one more time."

She caught a whiff of cigar smoke and spice. From behind her, a familiar voice drawled, "Step aside, Jake. Allow me."

Chapter 14

Before Emily could react, Nathan removed his seersucker jacket and handed it to Jake. His sudden nearness threw her off guard as he adjusted the wooden bowl in her hand for a proper grip. With gentle pressure, Nathan cupped her elbow with one hand while his fingers encircled her wrist.

"Let's turn the tables, shall we?" he murmured in her ear.

Like a puppeteer pulling on the strings of a marionette, Nathan guided her arm in a fluid swing, sending the bowl rolling forward. It plowed down the green and clacked against the wooden bowls, knocking them out of the way before coming to rest within inches of the jack.

"Well, I'll be," Jake beamed. "That beats all I've ever seen!"

The girls' mouths popped open. Sarah and Lacey looked at each other and then back at the jack, frowning over the upset in their lead.

Glancing sideways, Emily watched a smug grin broaden on Nathan's face. Seeing it shattered the short-lived sway he held over her.

Gathering her wits, she pushed with her elbows and untangled herself from his arms. She needed room to breathe, to think.

She peered at Jake. "Next time, just—just … fill in for me."

The boy's shoulders slumped. "Oh, all right."

Emily whirled around and marched off the bowling green.

Hearing Nathan's footsteps, she turned toward him and snipped, "How did you—? What are you doing here?"

"Showing you the finer points of lawn bowling," he pointed out, slipping on his jacket. "And if you'll pardon my saying so, it appears I arrived not a moment too soon. We may salvage this game yet."

He acted as if last evening had never happened. As if he didn't speak his last words to her through a door shut in his face.

She folded her arms over her waist. "Well, you can take your fancy moves elsewhere and leave me alone."

Nathan's eyes lit with a challenge. "Not this time."

"I beg your pardon. Who are you to ignore my wishes?"

"It's rather unladylike for you to storm off."

What gall, him lecturing her on how to behave. "Don't confuse disapproval with lack of patience."

"Whoa." Nathan held up a hand. "What do you think I've done that merits your disapproval?"

"Let's just say ... I know you're not out taking midnight swims in the Gulf."

Nathan's eyes gleamed in the moonlight as he leaned closer and dropped his voice. "Disappointed? Were you hoping to catch a peak at me skinny dipping?"

Heat flooded her face. "You're doing nothing so innocent."

The muscle under his right eye twitched. "Oh? You followed me?"

"Hardly!"

Nathan flashed a grin that carved dimples into his cheeks. "What if I were to tell you that I followed you here tonight? Would you be flattered?"

She would not be distracted. "You may charm folks with that smile, but you haven't pulled the wool over my eyes. And don't think for a minute that I'll abide whatever it is you're doing while you're out *prowling* around Galveston in the dead of night!"

"Keep your voice down," Nathan warned in a quiet tone.

Nearby on the green, a gentleman leaning on a cane turned and regarded them.

Just then, Lena came strolling at a distance along the pathway. Nathan glanced over his shoulder, following Emily's gaze.

He clenched his jaw. "Not another word."

Emily pressed her lips together and waited until her friend came alongside her.

"Mrs. Kesler, good evening," Nathan voiced a stilted greeting while Emily forced a smile.

"Hello. How's the game coming along?" Lena divided a look between them.

"Sarah and Lacey were ahead by a country mile," Emily told her, "until Mr. Chambers showed me how to swipe their balls away from the jack."

"It's harder than it looks." Lena studied Emily with keen eyes, missing nothing.

"Oh, I'll figure out the game." Emily flicked a glance at Nathan.

In the pavilion, the string quartet began warming up for dancing.

Nathan lifted an eyebrow and extended his hand. "May I have the first dance, Miss Cleburne?"

Emily hesitated. The last thing she needed was having his arms wrapped around her, but maybe she could worm some answers out of him.

"I'll step in for you," Lena offered. "That is … if you'd like."

Emily threw her a grateful look. "Thank you kindly."

Nathan tipped his head toward the pavilion. "Shall we?"

Emily smoothed the wrinkles from her yellow dress and slipped her hand into the crook of his arm. Together, they wended their way along the path toward the pavilion.

As they passed by the clubhouse, bursts of laughter flowed from around the tables on the lit porch. The waiter with a thick mustache and bushy eyebrows bustled among the diners carrying a glass pitcher brimming with frothy root beer.

The scent of German sausage mixed with a familiar odor. Emily's steps faltered. It reminded her of her father's stale breath after he'd been out all night. Her gaze touched the steins lifted around the tables and on the foaming pitcher. *Ale.*

At home, tension had risen to a fever pitch after Ma attended the prohibition rally in Nacogdoches. Emily shuddered to think of her mother's reaction to her being in a place that served beer.

Nathan noticed her lagging steps. "You do know how to dance, don't you?"

"Of course," she said in a crisp tone, resuming her pace.

She had Will to thank for dragging her into the barn on Saturdays so he could practice his dance steps. Her brother did it to avoid embarrassing himself on the dance floor with Corine, but no matter. Knowing the basic steps now gave her a measure of confidence.

They entered the pavilion, the air feeling close and sultry despite the open doors. They moved past the outer railing around the dance floor. In the center, couples glided to the Brahms Waltz. Overhead, the ceiling domed like a lit umbrella above the upstairs galleries.

Nathan led her onto the edge of the dance floor and put his arm about her waist, pulling her close. Close enough for Emily to notice the golden flecks in his green eyes. She set her hand on his shoulder, feeling the crisp crinkled fabric of his jacket. He lifted their joined hands outward, and they fell into step with the music.

Nathan expertly guided her around the dance floor, his fancy footwork unlike her brother's slow, careful steps. Emily focused on the waltz's rise, fall, and sway, determined not to trip over his feet.

"The way your mind works," Nathan lowered his voice and picked up the conversation where they'd left off, "you leap to conclusions with little or no facts in evidence."

Her eyebrows squeezed together. "And whose fault is that? You're rather tight-lipped about providing me with facts."

Nathan leaned closer. "Smile, so that old bird next to us will quit staring."

"Why stare at us?"

"At you," he corrected as he swept her in circles. "Quit scowling at me. It's drawing attention."

On the next turn, Emily spotted the matron with the double chin twirling nearby, her puffy eyes landing on Emily with undisguised curiosity.

Emily lifted the corners of her mouth and peered into Nathan's face. The smile felt stiff but convincing enough that the woman's gaze veered elsewhere.

Emily refocused her attention on Nathan. "Without the facts, I'm left to speculate on your whereabouts, none of which casts you in a good light. You can remedy that right now. Tell me where you went when you climbed down the trellis."

Nathan fell silent as the melody intensified and gained momentum, climbing higher. He spun her in double twirls, past the darkened wall of windows and the whirling blur of white and pastel-colored gowns. Notes of gardenia, sandalwood, and jasmine swirled around her, potent and cloying.

Emily felt the floor suddenly dip and sway. She tightened her grip on Nathan, willing the wave of dizziness to pass. She lifted her gaze. Nathan's eyes darkened with a shuttered look of surprise.

A soft smile played across his lips. "A man could get whiplash from your sudden shift in moods. First, you march away, and now you're clinging to me for dear life. I much prefer the latter."

She peered over his shoulder as they glided past the railing, though her flushed cheeks betrayed her lack of composure. "All this spinning made me light-headed, is all."

Emily attempted to lean back to a proper distance, but his arm held her snugly.

"I'll not have this conversation above a whisper, so quit squirming." His shoulder tensed. "Did Jake deliver my message?"

"Oh, like a herald. He barged in right as I was visiting with the orphanage committee, including my aunt and the town gossip. After he'd gained everyone's attention, he thrust the envelope at me and announced who sent it."

Nathan winced. "Unfortunate timing."

"I'll say. I expected more than two words for the trouble you caused me."

"Trust me," he repeated with conviction.

"You give me no reason, even now."

"Do you always judge so hastily?"

"Only fools overlook questionable character, and I'm no fool." Nor would this man turn her into one. If she wanted to spare herself from falling into the trap, she needed to keep that aim foremost in her mind.

"I'd never take you for one," he murmured. "Your guardedness is part of your charm."

Emily lifted her chin, satisfied, though she didn't like how his remark disarmed her. She pushed it aside and shored up her resolve.

"If I've learned one thing from being a reporter," he went on, "it's that things aren't always as they appear."

"Neither are people. Some folks go to great lengths to cover up whatever might soil their precious reputations."

His jaw hardened. "So you judge and convict me without a fair hearing. What next, a lynching?"

Despite herself, a faint smile tugged at her mouth. She had evidence that could make him squirm.

Emily kept her voice even. "You want a fair hearing? Fine. Answer one question."

Nathan tightened his hand around her waist. "Go on," he prompted, his expression unreadable.

"When you left the house that night… What were you doing entering Fat Alley?"

Nathan's eyes widened as he misstepped on the spin. Their feet tangled. He trampled her toes before he righted himself. Pain shot up her foot, and she dug her fingers into his shoulder, wincing.

Their gazes locked. Nathan's body quaked with alarm. Her question did more than make him squirm: it shook him to the core.

Abruptly, Nathan tugged on her hand. "Come," he ordered in a tone that left no room for argument.

He led her past the railing, out the back door, and down the steps. Goosebumps crawled up her flesh as a surge of adrenaline kicked up her pulse. She hadn't expected to stun him.

With a backward glance, Emily realized that being among the crowd had encouraged her to press him for answers. Now without a room full of witnesses, her confidence was seeping out of her with every step.

Nathan hauled her down the path away from the brightly lit pavilion. There in the moonlight, she scanned the emptied lawn and benches. Her stomach fluttered when she saw the direction he led them. The park's north end appeared deserted now that dancing had enticed the couples indoors. Palm trees and live oaks threw shadows on the walkway as their footfalls echoed in the night.

Coming upon the spurting fountain, she swallowed and glanced around. What was she doing alone with Nathan, again? Had she learned nothing from last evening?

Nathan released her hand and spun around. Looming over her, he stood with his hands planted on his hips. His gaze bore into hers, his expression unyielding as chiseled granite.

Chapter 15

"What makes you think I'd be in that part of town?" he demanded, his tone tight and low.

She drew back a step, her heart pounding. "You deny it?"

"No respectable lady goes anywhere near there."

"I didn't!"

His mouth curled in a smirk. "Then I'd say your imagination has sorely run amuck."

"A witness says otherwise," she countered.

The smug lines around his mouth faded. "Is that so? Who's been filling your pretty little head with lies?"

"He wouldn't."

"Who," he pressed, moving closer.

Emily clamped her lips together and held her tongue.

"You failed to mention a suitor."

She chuffed out a breath. "You're way off the mark."

"Am I? What *gentleman*," his voice dripped with sarcasm, "takes a lady into his confidence without intentions of courting her?"

"My word! He's a man of…"

"A preacher?" His eyebrows shot up, and he scowled. "What sort of designs does Hensleigh have on you, anyway?"

"That's absurd! My aunt and uncle are like kin to him. If anything, he feels obliged to watch over me for their sake."

"And he shared this *hearsay* with you in private. Does your aunt know he's sharing confidences with you? Sounds rather cozy, just the two of you, hmm?"

He made it sound too familiar, too intimate. "Our *cozy chat* took place a stone's throw from a ring of orphans, and I assure you I had to pry out of him what he'd witnessed."

His nostrils flared. "Did it ever occur to you to ask the good Reverend what he was doing in that part of town?"

"Helping a runaway. Not that it's any of your concern."

"And yet it's yours? Just how close are you two?"

Was there no limit to his brashness? What happened to her having him on the witness stand?

"I'll not dignify that with a single remark." She turned her back on him.

Folding her arms, Emily gazed into the water cascading down the tiers, splashing into the large basin below.

The very idea, that she had more than a friendly acquaintance with Colin Hensleigh. Besides, she and Nathan had no understanding between them. So why play the jealous suitor … unless he did it to throw her off his scent.

She turned and faced him squarely. "It hasn't escaped my notice that you have yet to answer my question. Now the longer you skirt around it, the less inclined I am to believe anything you have to say."

He stared down at her, his eyes narrowed.

Emily lifted her chin. "We both know where you were that night. I want to know why. Now either you gain my trust by telling me the truth, or I'll have nothing more to do with you. On this, I will not waver."

He clenched his jaw. The silence thickened as he appeared to consider his next move.

His gaze raked over the vacant park before he leaned forward, carefully pitching his voice lower. "I needed information."

She caught her breath. "What about?"

He rubbed the back of his neck. "I can't divulge that."

She glared up at him. "This is how you gain my trust?"

"All right," he muttered, gripping her shoulders. "But first, swear to me that you'll tell no one. *No one*."

"I'll do nothing of the kind until I know what this is about!"

"Stop being bull-headed," Nathan hissed. "It'll all be splashed across the front page soon enough, but if word leaks out beforehand…"

Emily stumbled back out of his grip, wide-eyed. The front page? Was he talking about *news*?

Like sending out a Morse code, a cricket chirped its high pitch call. The constant noise grated on her.

Feeling weak-kneed, Emily sank onto the basin's rim, still warm from the afternoon heat. She gazed down at her silvery reflection rippling on the water's surface. All this sneaking around, being closemouthed, for a *story*? Still, why sneak out? Why would his folks care where he went?

The twinkling lights illuminated an orange goldfish. Reaching down, she dragged a fingertip along the cool surface and watched the fish meander in the wake of the trail.

Nathan lowered himself and sat by her side. She flicked water off her finger and peered into his eyes, wanting to believe what Lena said was true. That Nathan's eyes would tell her what she needed to know.

"So," she ventured, "all this is about an article … for your newspaper?"

His mouth pulled in a flat line. "A bit closer to home than that."

Must he be so cryptic? "If I vow not to breathe a word, will you tell me everything?"

Nathan leaned in, his warm breath puffing in the shell of her ear. "I can't. It's too tangled. But I'll give you this much: it involves my father's illegal activity, the kind that'd make a decent gal as you cringe."

Emily drew back, needing to read his eyes. She caught the sincerity there, the touch of vulnerability.

"Writing about your kin could cost you dearly."

Nathan gave a mirthless chuckle. "I refuse to overlook corruption that preys on the weaker sex, regardless of what it costs me. Not when I have the power to blow the whistle." He plowed his fingers through his hair. "For years, I've watched the man run over everyone in his path. No one is above the law; not even him. I've said all that I dare."

Her body grew limp with relief while the gurgling fountain soothed her. Rather than involving himself in anything indecent, Nathan planned to do the decent thing and expose the twisted ways of his father. How had she misjudged his motives so completely?

She gave her head a little shake. "It's high time I quit jumping to conclusions without the benefit of all the facts." She peered sheepishly at him through her lashes. "Forgive me?"

Nathan's look softened. "If you'll quit avoiding me." His voice held a hint of playfulness.

"Fair enough. And you—in the future, kindly show more discretion when getting messages to me."

His mouth twitched. "I can do that."

Emily nodded with satisfaction. "I'm curious … with so much at stake, why tell me?"

His eyes fastened on her, darkening with intensity. "I had to remove every obstacle."

He inched nearer.

"What are you saying?" Her pulse thrummed in her ears.

Her throat went dry as he cupped the back of her neck and pressed his mouth to hers. Stunned, she tensed when he deepened the kiss, his fingers weaving through the hair gathered at the nape of her neck.

She pulled back, breathless. Heat stole into her cheeks. "You presume too much, Mr. Chambers."

Emily shifted on the ledge, putting some distance between them.

She caught the glint in his eyes as he reached for her hand and rubbed his thumb over her knuckles. "It's only a matter of time. You must know by now that I've set my sights on you."

Emily pulled her hand free. "If you remember your manners, sir, that's for me to decide."

She wished her voice sounded firmer, that his words didn't send a flutter of anticipation coursing through her stomach. How was she going to guard her heart now?

⸛

Emily and the children entered the front door of the Edwards' home, shutting it with a soft snick. A light shone downstairs. Given the late hour, no creaking floorboards disturbed the silence.

She put her finger to her lips, whispering, "Y'all be quiet as little mice. Now hurry on up to bed."

Jake led the way up the stairs.

Her foot touched the bottom step when she heard her aunt clear her throat. The sound came from the parlor.

"Emily, please join me for a cup of tea."

Although her aunt's tone sounded cordial, it was no request.

Emily shut her eyes. *Not now.* Any hope she had of putting off their talk until tomorrow vanished.

She peered over her shoulder. Estelle sat poised on the sofa, a tray set on the coffee table, her expression unreadable.

Emily licked her dry lips. She caught a glimpse of her reflection in the mirror above the half-moon table in the entryway. Her warm skin appeared flushed, her eyes too bright. She smoothed back the loose strands Nathan had pulled from the yellow ribbon.

What if her aunt saw right through her? What then?

She had no use for hypocrites. Nevertheless, the moment called for more composure than she possessed. Breathing in a steadying breath, she plastered a smile and treaded into the parlor.

Emily chose the armchair opposite Aunt Estelle and lowered herself onto the cushion. As she did, a copper strand fell into her eyes. She tucked it behind her ear and watched her aunt pour chamomile tea into the teacups.

Beside the tray, a *Good Housekeeping* magazine lay open with a white paper poking out from within the folds. In the dim light, she took in the latest Gibson Girl drawing. A couple was kissing on a secluded shoreline, the turning tide swirling over their laps, their hats floating away, forgotten.

Sucking on her bottom lip, Emily recalled her first kiss. The firm pressure of Nathan's mouth…

"Want some sugar?"

"Huh?" Emily's gaze bounced off the page onto her aunt, who motioned toward the sugar bowl.

Emily cleared her throat. "Ah … no, ma'am."

Estelle handed her the tea. "I gather you had an exciting evening."

Cradling the saucer, Emily sensed her aunt's eyes roaming over her appearance. Her fingers tightened around the plate.

She coaxed a smile in place and met her aunt's gaze. "I've never heard such heavenly music. Then Jake tried to teach me how to bowl, bless his heart." She forced a chuckle. "The way I played, he must think I'm a lost cause."

A faint smile touched Estelle's lips as she raised the cup and sipped the tea, allowing the conversation to trail off while the mantle clock ticked off the time.

Emily rubbed her thumb over the saucer's rim and stared into the golden liquid.

Estelle cleared her throat. "About last night…"

Emily blinked and glanced up. Though her aunt's tone sounded casual, her eyes brimmed with motherly concern.

Watch your step.

Emily felt a band of pressure tighten around her forehead. To buy time, she lifted the cup and sipped. The brew had turned tepid. She drank it down anyway.

"I … I sat on the porch and watched the sunset," she said. "What glorious—"

"Alone?"

Jake's words ran through her mind like ticker tape. *"But Mr. Chambers said this answers your question from last night."*

Emily's stomach churned. "At first. But then Mr. Chambers, he dropped by—just for a minute."

"What did y'all talk about?" Estelle kept her tone even.

Emily reached for a lemon drop from the candy dish and sucked off the dusting of sugar. "We talked about … hunting. As you know, he's quite the hunter." Hardly the gist of the conversation, but it served its purpose.

"That he is." Estelle's gaze lingered on Emily. "What else?"

Emily wedged the lemon drop into her cheek, aware of her pulse galloping ahead of her thoughts. "Nothing much, really."

Well, he hadn't divulged much. So much had changed since last night.

Estelle let out a sigh. "Did he say anything to upset you, dear?"

"W-why do you ask?"

"The door slammed on your way in."

Did she hear that from upstairs? "Hmm … maybe the breeze caught it?"

Estelle's pointed look made Emily squirm on the brocade cushion. "Mr. Chambers called to you through the door."

Inez. The cook must have told her.

"Did he? I felt poorly, so I said goodnight and went to lie down."

The lines creasing Estelle's forehead deepened. "Did the note Jake brought in have anything to do with you feeling poorly? So poorly you missed supper?"

Emily's gaze fell to her lap. She hid behind a thick wave of unruly hair draping her cheek. "I regret that Miss Pickering had to witness that."

"Wilhelmina is the least of my concerns."

Emily glanced up at Estelle. Disappointment shadowed her blue eyes for the second time that day. That look pinned Emily to the chair. She had to make this right.

Emily scooted to the edge of the cushion and set down the tea. The cup rattled the saucer. "I assure you that nothing inappropriate happened last night. Nor will it."

Estelle pressed her lips together and peered down at the Gibson Girl scene between them, her gaze pensive. She reached for the white paper in the magazine and set it on her lap. A letter-sized envelope.

"You needn't worry about me," Emily insisted, her gaze flicking on the envelope. Was that her name written with uneven strokes?

Estelle studied her hands, rubbing her thumb over a torn cuticle. "When I took Clayton his supper, he noticed I was preoccupied. These days I try not to burden him with too much, but this time I felt the need to share what bothered me."

She handed Emily the envelope. "From Clayton. Even from his sickbed, he cares for those in his household."

Estelle rose from the couch and came around, and gave Emily's shoulder a gentle squeeze. Her skirt swished as she headed upstairs, the scent of lemon verbena lingering in the room.

With cold fingers, Emily clutched the envelope. Two in one day did not bode well.

Chapter 16

The room grew silent aside from the ticking on the mantle.

Emily blew out a breath. With clammy fingers, she pulled out a single sheet of thick vellum with the bold letter E inscribed at the top center of the page. She leaned toward the lamplight and read.

> *My Dear Emily,*
>
> *Estelle and I thank God for sending you to us. In this short time, your work with the children has exceeded our hopes.*
>
> *Therefore, it pains me to address your acquaintance with our neighbor, Nathan Chambers. I share Estelle's concern over his behavior toward you.*
>
> *I do not presume to know his motives. Regardless, it does not sit well with me that he takes your standing in the community so lightly as to raise speculation with members of the orphanage committee. I insist that you discourage any further attention from him.*
>
> *Love protects, and I must protect not only you but the children. I must spare them undue hurt or confusion.*
>
> *I trust you'll heed my counsel and not veer from the firm path you've always chosen. I hope nothing jeopardizes your role as the children's governess, for you have proven vital in the lives of those I hold dear.*
>
> *Warmest regards,*
> *Uncle Clayton*

She stared hard at the bottom of the page where his signature waned. "He can't be serious," she muttered, her body stiffening.

She had reached her fill of folks meddling in her life as if she had no say in who courted her. Leaving home gained her that right. She hadn't escaped Pa's highhandedness to have Uncle Clayton interfere, regardless of how well-meaning his intentions.

Still, her throat thickened. Her uncle insisted on protecting her from further scrutiny. That was more than Pa ever did.

Perhaps her family's attitude would soften toward Nathan when the news hit the headlines. In the meantime, she needed to avoid further speculation. Let the dust settle. She hated tiptoeing around her aunt's questions, but what other choice did she have? Besides, she was privy to information that no one else knew.

Emily sniffed and sat up straight. Tucking the letter in the envelope, she got up from the chair and left the room.

In the hallway, Emily caught sight of her reflection in the mirror. Her feet stilled. Red blotches bloomed up her neck like a rash. Her brow furrowed as she peered closer, noting the tension pinching the skin under her eyes. A vein pulsed up the middle of her forehead, building into a headache.

It'll only be for a little while.

She raked her teeth over her lower lip. "You're a Cleburne. You'll manage," she muttered to the image peering back at her. "Keeping things private should be no strain."

An eyebrow crept high. *You criticize others for keeping secrets. Now you're doing the same thing.*

Her mouth twisted into a scowl. She'd had enough musing for one day. Without a backward glance, she pivoted on her heel and marched up the stairs.

⌘

The mid-August heat turned the orphanage closet into a boiler room. Emily's calico dress stuck to her skin from being drenched in sweat. She longed to slide chin deep into a tub with lavender-scented water. The image alone coaxed a smile.

Emily climbed the stepstool and swiped a dampened cloth along the wall's upper shelves. Dust tickled the back of her throat.

A dirt dauber had made a nest of hollowed-out mud tubes wedged in the corner crease. She detested things that flew at her and stung.

A pair of heels clacked hard against the wood floor. Emily tensed and looked down at Miss Pickering. The woman swooped into the long, narrow space toting an armload of children's primers.

"…gave me her word she'd have everything cleared out, spotless. Humph," Miss Pickering grumbled. "She doesn't know the meaning of the word spotless."

Earlier, they had emptied the mound of disorderly piles from the closet and lined up the items along the long hallway, pushing them against the wainscoting.

Miss Pickering plunked the books onto a clean shelf and began stacking them meticulously into sets of twelve.

Emily gritted her teeth. Close quarters with the woman chafed. Nevertheless, she vowed to mind her p's and q's rather than give Miss Pickering further excuse to gossip about her.

Let the dust settle.

Emily's nose crinkled. Had the woman climbed into a vat of sandalwood cologne? The sweet, woodsy scent overpowered the narrow space.

Hearing the patter of feet, Emily peered over her shoulder.

Sarah's face poked through the doorway. "Miss Emily, make Jake help me! He left already."

Earlier, Emily had the children pick out the larger pieces of chalk from a bucket of dusty erasers.

"Where is he?"

"Outside, playing. Jake said he promised to teach Scoot and Chai Lin how to pitch washers. He's supposed to be working."

"Take it from me," Miss Pickering piped in. "If you want a job done right, do it yourself. I should have known better than to trust Ida. Why she insists on having her hands in *everything* is beyond me."

Emily's eyebrow shot up. She knew nothing about this Ida person, but how Miss Pickering failed to see her own glaring shortcomings boggled the mind.

Emily angled away from her and addressed Sarah. "I'll direct Jake back indoors in a bit."

Sarah let out a huff. "But why should I do all the work?"

"You may have play time, too."

"But I'm not done yet."

Emily turned on the stool, facing Sarah. "Well, aren't you the diligent one," she teased.

"Diligent?" Sarah's brows drew together.

"Very. It means you stick with a job until it's finished."

Sarah gave a smug little smile. "I am diligent. Too bad Jake only wants to play."

"Your brother loves nothing more than being in the thick of all those kids."

"Yeah, loafing."

"But isn't befriending orphans showing kindness?"

Sarah's mouth pulled to one side, her dusty fingers smudging chalk on her chin. "Well, yes, but it's nowhere near as good as being diligent."

Emily chewed the inside of her cheek to keep from smiling. "Hard work has its rewards," she reinforced. "I, for one, appreciate your help. There's plenty more to do."

Sarah beamed, appearing content with being the more helpful child. With her nose stuck in the air, she twirled in a spin and skipped back to sorting, her pinafore and dress swirling around her knees.

Needing a break from Miss Pickering, Emily treaded up the hallway and through the soaring central reception hall. She gained the front porch and squinted against the onslaught of sunlight, her eyes watering from the glare. She brushed off the dust and grime between her fingers and walked partway down the concrete stairs, lowering herself onto the steps. The gentle breeze cooled her skin, drying the layer of moisture coating her body.

From yards away, Jake raised his arm, flagging her. "Miss Emily, watch! Chai Lin almost sank the washer on the first try!"

Dimples dotted Chai Lin's cheeks. His gaze flicked toward her, then fastened on the concave bowl in the sand eight yards away. He took his time, studying the hole with single-focused intensity. He steadied his swing and pitched the washer through the air. It plopped right into the pit.

"Bravo," she cried, feeling her spirits lift.

She admired the boy's persistence. He refused to give up or settle for less. It took a unique child to rise above the expectations set by his station in life. He had grit and determination. The kind that pushed her years ago to finish her math in the glow of the oil lamp until her vision blurred. What might this boy accomplish if given the same opportunity she had? Somehow, putting up with Miss Pickering seemed a small price to pay for Chai Lin to be able to start school with the necessary supplies.

"Come on, Scoot. Now you do it," Jake coached.

Scoot poked out his tongue to one side. Scanning his audience, he flung the doughnut-shaped washer yards from the mark. His posture slumped. On the next try, he fared no better.

Jake scratched his cowlick and moaned. "Scoot, you've got to toss it easy-like. Remember how I showed you?"

As Jake trotted over to retrieve the washers, something shiny caught his eye, halting his steps. He stooped down and picked up a round object. Jake took a closer look, his chin dragging his chest. "Aw shucks … a bottle cap." He flipped the gold cap aside with his thumb.

Scoot cocked his head, curious. "So?"

"Thought a gold coin had washed up."

"We're blocks from the beach." Scoot scrunched up his face, missing the point.

From over near the wrought iron fence, a pimply-faced hulk of a kid cut loose with a snort. "There ain't gold in this yard or anywhere else."

"Oh, yeah?" Jake taunted. "Mr. Pitts said—"

"That addle-brained old man? He's older than Methuselah."

"Old enough to see pirates with his own eyes. Says there's a chest full of gold at Three Trees."

"You believe that old geezer?" the hulk barked a laugh. "Only fools go digging when there's nothing to show for it."

Jake stuck out his chest. "Oh yeah? Who's to say somebody didn't move it, like when Ben hid the treasure chest in a cave."

"Crazy Ben? That loon talked about gold in a ship's hull, not some cave."

Emily had heard about one of Lafitte's men paying for whiskey with gold doubloons.

Jake shook his head. "Not that Ben. Ben Gunn."

"Who?"

"You know … from *Treasure Island*."

The smirk slid off the kid's face, and he leveled a blank stare at Jake.

Jake hiked a cocky brow. "What? Don't you read?"

The hulk's silence unsettled Emily. She stole a glimpse at Jake, seeing his lip hitch to one side.

Leave it be, Jake.

"You do know how, right?"

The hulk balled his meaty hands into fists. He muttered a curse as he kicked up sand and tromped toward Jake.

Emily had an urge to step in and stop this nonsense, but what would Jake learn if she fought his battle—one he stirred up?

The orphans swarmed into a ring around the boys like coliseum spectators, eager to witness them coming to blows.

Warm fingers gripped Emily's hand. She peered down into dark, anxious eyes. Chai Lin had sidled up close to her, their bodies touching. She gave his hand a gentle squeeze.

"He'll be all right."

Her gaze sharpened on the bully, who circled Jake with his fists raised. The kid clearly enjoyed being the center of attention.

The muscles in Emily's legs tightened, ready to spring up if things got out of hand. How on earth would she explain a black eye, or worse, to Aunt Estelle?

The ring of orphans grew restless.

"Smack him, Reese, square between the—"

"Hard!"

"…got it coming."

"Yeah, knock him down a peg or two!"

Wagon wheels crunched on the road out front, and a horse neighed, the sound barely registering over the clamor. Emily kept her gaze locked on the bully Reese sneering down at Jake.

"Hey, why take his side?" Jake confronted the ring before sealing his fate. "It's not my fault he's ignorant."

Reese spat, "You best shut your mouth … you pint-sized—"

"Gentlemen," a familiar voice sliced through the commotion.

The wrought iron gate creaked on its hinges as heads swiveled toward the visitor. Reese spotted him before Jake and jerked back a step. He lowered his head.

Little Chai Lin leaned closer still. With reverence, he whispered, "They say I owe him my life. Someday I want to be a great man, like him."

Chapter 17

"You two strapping lads," Colin divided a look between Jake and Reese, "put your muscles to good use and help Jasper unload and pass out sodas. There're plenty of root beers for everyone."

Eagerness shone on the faces of the children around the ring, the fight forgotten. They fanned out and watched the delivery man stroll to the back of the wagon, whistling a tune.

Emily turned to the rustling beside her as little Chai Lin got up and scuttled down the steps to join the others.

Jake trooped ahead of Reese to the wagon, a look of relief washing any smugness from his face. Apparently the threat of a sound thrashing did wonders to adjust his attitude.

He and Reese gripped one side of the galvanized tub opposite Jasper and hoisted it to the ground on the count of three. It landed with a thud. The boys faced off and plunged their hands into the ice chips, jerking sodas in a race to see who passed them out the fastest. Reese grinned as he pulled out two for every one of Jake's.

"Boys," Emily muttered, giving her head a little shake.

She eyed Colin with new appreciation. He did more than preventing Jake from being punched. He did so in a way where both boys saved face in front of their peers. He even put their hands to work serving others.

Dressed in light gray trousers and waistcoat, a crisp white shirt, and tie, he weaved among the children, bending down to greet and chat with them.

When everyone had a drink, the minister strolled over to the steps toting two opened bottles. He handed her a beverage, slick and icy.

"I thought cold drinks would taste rather refreshing in this heat."

"That's mighty thoughtful and well-timed, as it turned out." Emily tilted her head toward Reese and Jake. "Those two are a mess."

"They put you in a most precarious spot. Had you stepped in, Jake would have been called a sissy for hiding behind his teacher's skirt. On the other hand, heaven help him if Reese had taken a swing."

"Ugh, my hands were tied," Emily groaned. That Colin understood her predicament steadied her.

She leaned forward, confiding, "I could have wrung both their necks, but you, I loved…"

Fumbling over the compliment, she noticed an odd glimmer flicker and fade in his gaze. Her mouth went dry. Of all places to leave a sentence dangling!

She fumbled for words, her ears burning. "T—that is, the way you handled them, well, it … it made me sit up and take notes."

"My pleasure."

A smile warmed his eyes, dispelling any lingering awkwardness.

His walnut hair, groomed neat and trim, looked as though he had just climbed out of the barber's chair. A whiff of lavender hair tonic confirmed as much.

Emily licked her lips and tipped back the bottle, swallowing half the liquid in one greedy gulp. The sassafras tasted smooth on her tongue though the fizz prickled. Out of the corner of her eye, she caught the amused look on Colin's face. She lowered the bottle and sipped the rest.

Across the yard, Jasper pulled out a coin from behind a shy little girl's ear. Above the oohs and aahs, a string of voices begged him to show them how he did the magic trick. He grinned from ear to ear and did it again, slowly this time.

"How is inventory progressing?" Colin inquired.

"I'll have it done by day's end."

"Splendid. May I offer further assistance?"

Her mouth twitched. "I'd be obliged if you'd take my place in the closet with Miss Pickering."

He took a swig of his drink, the glint in his eyes suggesting she asked too much, even for him.

She shrugged, not the least rueful. "You did step in and deprive me of the pleasure of giving that woman a piece of my mind."

He rubbed the scar along the top of his left eyebrow and said nothing for a moment. When he spoke, his voice dipped low and thoughtful. "I'm curious what offended you most: Miss Pickering's audacity to lecture you in front of the committee or that she spoke plainly, albeit without love."

Emily drew back and gave him a long look. "You agreed with her?"

"Miss Emily, want more soda pop?" Jake hollered.

Irritation flashed. "Not now, Jake!"

Tuning out the boy, she kept her eyes trained on the minister.

"In her timing and delivery, certainly not," Colin said. "However, there's wisdom in guarding your reputation." Lines pulled around his eyes in a tense crisscross.

"Too bad the message got lost between the barbs," Emily retorted.

Colin pressed his lips together and examined his polished wingtips, dredging a toe in the sand.

She blew out a gusty breath. "If you have something more to say, go ahead, say it."

Emily set the soda down on the step beside her. She folded her hands in her lap and appeared interested while her thoughts strayed to sorting through the list. It stood between her and a long soak in the tub.

The minister took a moment regarding her. "It is possible for one to mistake mere attraction for something … deeper."

How would he know the difference? The man lived with his sister, of all people.

Emily tucked in her chin. "You may think me naïve, but I'd wager we're attracted to those we love."

"Yet it is possible for one to believe that certain romantic feelings are enduring when they are not."

She had better things to do than listen to his brotherly lecture. She mustered enough patience to avoid sounding patronizing.

Almost.

"Thank you kindly, but I think I can sort this out for myself."

"Even if he breaks your heart?"

His words, though softly spoken, drew Emily up short. Her eyes narrowed. Though his expression was unreadable, color stained his cheeks.

"You know this firsthand." With sudden clarity, she sensed the truth of it.

Overhead, a seagull keened a lonesome cry. Emily lifted an eyebrow, waiting.

He lowered his gaze and studied the sand clinging to the tip of his shoe. "During seminary, I was betrothed to a young lady. If only someone had pulled me aside."

Intrigued, Emily fell silent.

"Luther Falls, Evangeline's father, awarded scholarships to seminary students. I earned the most prestigious. It paid my tuition for the first two years of school. During that time, Mr. Falls took a shine to me, and so my sister and I spent holidays and part of our summers at his estate outside London."

Emily nodded for him to continue.

"From the start, Evangeline and Gracie got on famously. For hours they rode bicycles and played croquet on the lawn. It eased my mind watching Gracie's face brighten after being solemn over losing Mum and Dad."

He gazed off with a distant, faraway look. "As for Evangeline and me, we were a mismatched pair. I cut my teeth on mission work while she grew up being coddled by maids and nannies. Moreover, the differences in our dreams spelled disaster."

"Well, something must have drawn you to her. Her faith, perhaps?"

"Nothing so noble. Evangeline's gaiety lifted my melancholy mood." He took a drink from the bottle. "You see, laughter floated around her like infectious bubbles wherever she went."

"She eased your sorrow. There's nothing ignoble about that."

"Right. But at the risk of sounding vain, Evangeline's attention flattered me. I felt manly, having her dainty hand draped on my arm. I paid no heed to how she turned coy whenever chaps fawned over her, believing her to be too innocent to trifle with my affection. If anything, their attention stirred my need to protect her."

"To the neglect of protecting yourself."

"The irony is not lost on me, I assure you," Colin grimaced. "Like all things counterfeit, attraction proved a heady assault. It twisted me inside out, wringing the very life from all objectivity. Suffice it to say, I limped away with my heart and dignity in tatters, though wiser, more cautious. I'm grateful I caught her with him before exchanging vows."

"Him?"

"Nigel, a neighbor and close friend of the family. The cad had used the element of surprise, not that that excused her behavior." His lips thinned in disapproval.

"Go on," Emily coaxed.

"Evangeline had gone chasing butterflies with a net while I studied in the library. I had stepped outside to clear my head when I heard laughter from the garden. I followed the sound, taking a shortcut between the taller rows of hedges.

"There I spied her reaching up on tiptoes, tugging at the net. It had snagged on a rose bush rambling over the stone fence, a rare monarch pinned inside.

"Before I had a chance to make my presence known, Nigel had come up from behind and circled her in his arms, loosening the net. When the butterfly flew out of reach, I heard her gasp. Supposing her to be upset over losing a fine specimen, I wasn't prepared—" Colin paused and cleared his throat. "He … he was planting kisses down the slope of her neck. Rather than scold him or pull away, Evangeline turned in his arms and swatted his chest playfully, her cheeks flushed with excitement." He said flatly, "It was not to be borne."

"How dreadful for you to witness that."

Colin nodded absently. "The price I paid for being an utter fool."

"What did you do?"

"I did the only honorable thing. I ended the sham courtship on the spot. As it turned out, that cost me my scholarship. Yet I considered myself spared a greater blow, for had I wed someone who lacked propriety, it would have been my ruin. If only I'd known then what I know now…" His voice trailed off.

Emily soaked in his story, reaching her conclusions. "You're still a bachelor because of her. You continue to sacrifice your happiness—"

"The ministry and raising Gracie take top priority."

"Yet I doubt either keeps you warm at night."

He set down the bottle and tugged at the bottom of his waistcoat. "I'm content," Colin's tone turned clipped. "Besides, endurance builds character. And what our choices say about our character is the heart of the matter."

Back to that, are we? Emily peered at him. "You think mine is lacking."

"I sense yours is being tested."

"To see if I pass or fail; is that it?" Emily hated the defensiveness edging her voice.

The corner of Colin's mouth curved gently. "Not everything in life is either pass or fail, Miss Cleburne. There are varying shades of grace, especially during trials. They can purify our hearts, even refine our character when we persevere."

The August sun beat down on her scalp, hot and relentless.

Colin crouched down and began scrolling letters in the sand. "A beloved professor once said, 'May your character be not a writing upon the sand, but an inscription upon the rock.' He went on to say, 'May your whole life be so settled, fixed and established, that all the blasts of hell and all the storms of earth shall never be able to remove you.'"

Colin smoothed out the letters with the palm of his hand. He looked up at her, his gaze intent. "May yours become so etched in stone that when others speak ill of you, your integrity silences them."

Emily shifted on the step, feeling ill at ease. Sidestepping his point, she landed on a safe topic. "You sat under Charles Spurgeon?"

Colin's brow rose. "You know of him?"

Emily lifted her shoulder, imagining what Grandpa would say if he knew that Colin had sat under the teaching of England's great pastor. "Grandpa used his benediction in sermons often enough. He called Spurgeon the mentor he never knew."

Not dissuaded by the tangent, Colin unfolded his tall frame and dusted off his hands. "Tell me … how is God using testing to refine you?"

His question stumped her. Must he be so fixated? She had Miss Pickering to thank for this grilling.

Emily opened her mouth to answer something trite, then pressed her lips together. For a full minute, she feigned mulling over the question while considering the most efficient way to record inventory.

At length, she shrugged. "I can't rightly say."

Mistaking the silence for self-reflection, Colin launched in. "Testing can drive us to seek faith. Even in matters of the heart—especially the heart—for out of the heart flow the issues of life."

For reasons she did not care to examine, his words burned going down.

She polished off the icy root beer and handed him the bottle. "That's all well and good, but the thing I need most is putting distance between me and Miss Pickering. To do so requires that I get back to work. So, if you'll excuse me."

Emily got up and turned to leave. She managed to brush him off without flinching, though his words pricked like stepping on a sticker burr.

"Miss Cleburne…"

Emily peered over her shoulder, bracing for a hint of disapproval. Instead, she watched his mouth pull down to one side and his eyes gleam with a familiar look.

A face floated before her. Brown eyes sunken with age, a glint of disappointment flashing. It worked every time. She had no defense against letting Grandpa down.

Emily blinked, seeing Colin's navy eyes blazing now.

Ministers! Did they perfect that look in seminary to induce guilty compliance? She loathed it. So what if she disappointed this man. She'd sought the respect of few people. Why should she give a hoot whether he esteemed her or not?

"Duty calls." Emily waved her hand, turning toward the door.

Colin cleared his throat. "Let me leave you with this." He waited until she twisted at the waist and met his gaze. "Beware of the lure of counterfeit treasure, for it can rob you of what is most priceless."

Her brow knit together. What did that even mean?

"Thanks for the soda."

With a nod, she waltzed toward the door, determined to attack inventory and finish it. As she pulled on the handle, she stole a backward glance, regretting it.

Off-key, Miss Pickering droned on humming the same tune repeatedly. At the same time, a dirt dauber batted along the ceiling, searching for a means of escape. Emily shot the woman a withering look, longing to do the same.

All afternoon Emily's mind strayed from the task of sorting, stacking, and counting items. She thought about Grandpa and missed him so much that her chest heaved. She pinched the bridge of her nose, squeezing her eyes shut.

Another face hovered before her, seeing a glint of disappointment flashing in his eyes. To her chagrin, it had the same effect now as it always did. Except for this time, those eyes were navy blue and pleading.

Chapter *18*

Miss Pickering bore down on the scrub brush. Down on her hands and knees, the woman crawled backward toward Emily's feet, dragging a bucket of sudsy water in tow.

Emily had returned from tracking down Jake again and overseeing the children's afternoon break. Fortunately for Jake, Reese had kept his distance. Then Lena stopped for a visit on her way downtown and offered to drop off the children at home. Emily couldn't refuse the gracious offer.

Now to forge ahead, uninterrupted.

Her stomach rumbled over the scouring Miss Pickering inflicted upon the floor. That morning, the aroma wafting from the Edwards' kitchen promised a hearty bowl of compensation. Chicken and flat-rolled dumplings made just the way she liked them. It gave her the push she needed to tackle the rest.

She picked up the clipboard and searched for the row where she had left off. Where was the…? Emily blinked and scanned the row once more. Her face twisted in confusion.

She slumped against the doorframe, cocking her head. What were the small chalkboards doing piled up high overhead? She had grouped the most used items within easy reach on the middle shelves, leaving plenty of room for new supplies to fit once they arrived.

She panned the long rows, taking in the cramped, rearranged jumble. Failing to make sense of it, she demanded, "What have you done?"

"Put everything in the right order," Miss Pickering sniffed.

Order? *What* order? Emily scanned the top shelf from left to right. Arithmetic books, chalk boxes, chalkboards, crayons, erasers. Her shoulders curled inward as the pattern emerged.

She did not!

Grinding her molars, Emily pushed off the doorframe. Alphabetical order. Her practical arrangement, gone.

If only she hadn't left to oversee Jake and Reese and then lingered visiting with Lena. Then everything would still be where it belonged.

She wanted nothing more than to rid herself of Miss Pickering, eat supper, and soak off the layer of grime and vexation that coated her from head to toe.

The list.

Emily blinked rapidly at the half-completed items marching down the page in neat columns. Realization struck. Now she had to recheck everything on the shelves against the list to figure out which supplies she needed to add. All that time, wasted.

Her fingernails dug into her palms, her nostrils flaring. Thanks to Miss Nitpicky, the workload had doubled. Emily saw no way around having to redo the entire closet. All of it.

Heat surged up Emily's chest and neck, flooding her face. "We'd be further ahead if you'd quit *rearranging* my work and scrubbing holes in the floor," she bit out, building up a head of steam. "Try looking to the ways of your own household and quit *poking* your nose in other people's business."

The brush had stilled. Miss Pickering craned her bony neck and stared up at Emily with bulging eyes, her surprise magnified by the spectacles sliding low on her nose.

Emily stared back hard without flinching.

"Humph," Miss Pickering tossed over her shoulder and resumed scouring the floor in vicious circles.

Emily pulled a face. So much for letting the dust settle. Stifling a sigh, she let her gaze drift up the hallway.

Behind the grand staircase, a woman toting a notebook stood before a door. She reached up on tiptoe, running her fingers along the top of the doorframe. Perhaps she was one of the lady managers who assisted in directing the home. The woman lifted a key, unlocked the door, and switched on the light. Before the door closed behind her, Emily glimpsed a desk and chair and a wooden file cabinet below a sloped ceiling. An office tucked under the staircase.

Heavy footfalls echoed through the great reception hall, drawing closer. A uniformed police officer rounded the corner. The floorboards creaked under his shuffling feet as he came alongside Emily. He removed his hat. She peered down into his round, ruddy face. The odor of sweat crusting his shirt crinkled her nose.

"Afternoon, ma'am," he dipped his chin in greeting. "Happen to know where I might find—"

"Roland," Miss Pickering brightened. She scrambled up off the floor and pushed past Emily.

"Hey, Auntie," the officer's voice sounded weary.

Miss Pickering pulled him in for a hug and patted his back. When she leaned back, she inspected the bags below his eyes.

Her face gentled. "You look positively haggard."

Emily stepped into the closet on a dry patch of flooring and swung the door partially shut. She peered up at the stack of arithmetic books on the top ledge, found it on the page, and scratched a pointy check mark beside the amount.

"Didn't get any shuteye," the officer yawned. "I pulled a double shift."

"Bless your heart. You work too hard."

"I know, but duty called, late as usual. Had to break up a disturbance at a variety show."

Variety show? Emily's gaze flicked off the page, her attention piqued. Wasn't that in the section of town where Nathan went late that night?

"Do tell," Miss Pickering murmured.

Emily peered through the crack between the door and the wall.

"You know I can't say much about what goes on in the precinct." The officer glanced away. "But all the other fellas have wives. Me? I'd be off my rocker if I didn't have you to confide in."

"You know I'm always willing to listen, but I admire your go-by-the-book attitude. More officers should be like you."

"Tell that to the Chief. I doubt he notices."

"Well, I notice. The Chief doesn't pay you enough to keep this island safe, especially in that part of town. You must deal with all manner of shady characters."

"Let's just say I don't get called to break up no tea parties."

"I can picture you busting through the doors demanding law and order."

"This isn't the Wild West, Auntie," the officer chuckled. "I broke up commotion in an alley, is all."

"A dark alley?"

"Relax. Just a guy harassing a dame."

"You always do look out for the ladies."

"This was no lady, if you catch my drift. A showgirl. Chinese at that," he added with heat.

Emily wondered if the recent news from China inflamed the officer's attitude toward the showgirl. The massacre of missionaries in the Boxer Rebellion had made national news.

"You risk your life for such riffraff," Miss Pickering's voice dripped with disdain. "In my book, that takes a hero."

The officer's chest expanded, straining the buttons on his uniform until gaps puckered his shirt. He drew himself up to his full, diminutive height.

Like fishing in a barrel. Emily saw no resistance as Miss Pickering reeled him in. The officer appeared eager to take the bait, as if his aunt's trolling for news eased his conscience over divulging it.

He cocked an eyebrow and leaned forward, with his tone pitched low and conspiratorial. "This was an odd case. When I got close enough to break it up, this guy froze like that statue on Broadway. Just stood there gripping the dame's shoulders, not even blinking. You'd have thought he'd seen a ghost."

"Well, I'd be scared stiff if you came at me with a nightstick."

"Nah, it had more to do with what she said."

"Don't sell yourself short, Roly."

"I'm telling you, I caught him shaking her like a rag doll just before. He might have kept his voice down, but voices, they echo off alley walls."

"I trust you were vigilant."

"Yes, ma'am. I stayed in the shadows with my back to the wall. As I closed in on them, I heard him demanding the whereabouts of some gal named Ying Su."

"Did she know this Ying Su person?"

"More than she let on at first. All she said was, 'She not here. Nobody see her now,'" he mimicked her broken English. "Poor guy didn't get what she meant."

"But I bet you did."

"Me? I had a hunch. It proved true. The guy, he kept firing questions, one after another, until the dame started squalling and told him outright, 'She dead!'"

Miss Pickering sucked in a breath.

"Yes, siree, that stopped him cold. You would have thought that little slip of a thing had hit him in the gut the way he choked out, 'How'd she die? Did *he* kill her?'"

The officer whistled thin and low. "Boy, that did it. She cut loose, shrieking, 'Your father kill me if I tell!'"

"Mercy!"

"That's when the guy froze. Went stiff and white as a starched shirt in a Chinese laundry," he snorted a laugh, amused by his own joke.

"Miss Pickering touched her throat. "What an ordeal. That would have rattled me, but not you. You keep your head when it counts. I'll bet you got more information from her, didn't you?"

"Indeed I did." He rocked back on his heels. "Pulled her aside afterward. I treated her like a real lady. Even called her by her name, Liang. Loosens the tongue every time."

"Well?"

"Found out Ying Su was her sister. Said she passed away five years ago. So," he shrugged, "I let her go."

"Did she say how her sister died?"

Officer Pickering cleared his throat. "No reason to dig deeper."

"But questioning people is part of what you do."

He grunted. "Some things are better left alone. The last time I went the extra mile on a case, the Chief, he chewed me out in front of the fellas. Made me look like a real dunce. Said I should have been out patrolling the district instead of wasting time. I've got to work with those guys."

"That's too bad," Miss Pickering murmured.

"Take it from me: you've got to deal with things the way they are, not how they should be."

"Hmm … I suppose you're right. But don't you wonder who Ying Su was to that fellow? An old flame, perhaps? But then, who courts those females."

The officer shifted his weight, scuffing the floorboards. "Say, are you planning on going to the Labor Day parade? I'll be working then."

"Did you arrest him for disturbing the peace?"

"Huh? Nah. Just ordered the guy to leave her alone or I'd book him next time."

"Just a warning?"

"Well … you don't tangle with some folks."

"So this fellow was someone important?"

At his silence, Emily peered closer through the crack in the door. The officer ran a finger inside the band of his collar.

He glanced up and down the hall and lowered his voice to a hoarse whisper. "Let's just say … his daddy ain't the sort you rile up without cause."

"Oh?"

"Not when he owns the place."

"The variety show?"

"That and some other shady joints, but that's between you, me, and the fencepost."

A chill spread into Emily's core.

"Do you recall the fellow's name?" Miss Pickering pressed.

"Can't say."

"It didn't happen to be … Chambers, did it?"

Emily swayed on her feet. She gripped the nearest ledge while the officer pulled out his handkerchief and mopped sweat from the back of his neck.

"Well, Auntie," he gave a nervous laugh, "as I said, some things are better left alone."

Miss Pickering clucked her tongue. "You reap what you sow, I always say."

"I'm starving," he said, a bit too heartily. "Haven't eaten all day."

"You must keep up your strength. Well, that I can fix. Come along, dear." Miss Pickering looped her hand through his arm, nudging him toward the kitchen. "I brought over a pot of pinto beans and sweet cornbread. Plus my coconut custard fried pies."

"Mmm. My favorite."

"I'll brew you a nice cup of hawthorn tea. After the night you had…" Her voice faded through the dining room.

Emily puffed out her cheeks and blew out a stream of air.

The news left her head spinning. Miss Pickering's speculation about Ying Su being an old flame was way off the mark. No doubt Nathan had come to press the showgirl for information concerning his father and learned more than he expected.

Still, questions swirled around like dust devils, picking up disturbing bits of debris in the churning. Why ask about Ying Su in the first place? Who was she, and how did she die? Clearly, the showgirl knew more about that than she was telling, but fear of Nathan's father silenced her tongue. Was Hayden Chambers capable of that degree of cruelty? Of murder?

It soured Emily's appetite that Miss Pickering had heard every word, to say nothing of the nephew's eagerness to tell her. Would the woman keep silent about what he shared in confidence? What might happen if she spread it around?

Emily shuddered. Nathan needed to know what Officer Pickering told the town gossip. Somehow she'd find a way to warn him.

Chapter 19

Emily sat at her desk, jotting the weekly arithmetic scores into the grade book. The lamplight shone on the numbers. Passing grades for both children. Not high marks, but improved scores nonetheless. A smile broadened around the lemon drop. Chomping down on the candy, she savored the sweetness of the moment. Patience, coupled with continued repetition, appeared to be paying off. Perhaps she might reward herself with reading another chapter in *Sense and Sensibility*.

Emily lifted the grade book and swept it in front of her face. The draft blew wisps of hair from her braid, tickling her neck. Despite the hour, the late August air remained thick and sultry. Even the parted curtains hung at the open window without the barest sway.

Across the way, she caught a glimpse of a tiny yellow flame. Through the window, she watched a thick stream of smoke blow out.

Nathan!

Not a creak on the floorboards had sounded for over an hour in the Edwards' home. Aunt Estelle had begged off from needlework in the parlor and retired early with a headache.

Emily pulled back the curtain and flagged Nathan's attention, pointing down. She slid out of the chair and crept out of the room into the darkened hallway. The remnants of stewed oysters from supper still lingered in the house. She paused, listening, but only the sound of muffled coughing came from Uncle Clayton's room.

"Shh—quick! Follow me," Emily whispered.

Nathan dropped from the trellis to the ground and plucked the cigar from between his teeth.

Emily grabbed his hand and ducked between the tall rows of oleanders. As they crouched out of sight, she breathed in the blossom's floral talcum scent mixed with the sweet tobacco.

"How forward of you," he drawled.

"Shh. It's not what you think," Emily whispered. "We can't be seen together."

He held onto her hand, drawing circles on her knuckles with his thumb.

In the shadows, a sly smile dimpled his cheek. "I'll take time with you anywhere I can get it."

He puffed on the cigar and blew out the smoke sideways.

The limbs of the bushes poked at her sides, prodding her. She cast a glance over her shoulder. Good. The Edwards' house remained dark and still.

"I can't stay long. If anyone notices… I can't risk it. My uncle insists that I avoid you."

"Why's that?"

"Shh! Keep your voice *down*. He's concerned that you're taking my reputation too lightly. Enough that it raised speculation with the orphanage committee."

Nathan pressed his mouth against the curve of her ear. "Darlin', there's nothing about you I take lightly."

Emily bit her lower lip and leaned back so she could see his face.

"Tell me about Ying Su," she whispered.

Nathan's fingers stiffened around her palm. He released his grip and dropped his hand. "Where'd you hear that name?"

"From a police officer."

"Explain," he said with an edge to his voice.

"The same officer who caught you with Ying Su's sister last week."

All at once, the streetlights beamed, shedding light through the pointy leaves. Nathan's eyes glittered round and hard as chipped glass.

Tension rippled off his shoulders in waves. "How do you know this?"

"He came by the orphanage Saturday to visit with his *Aunt Wilhelmina*." She gave him a moment to digest the news before adding, "I overheard them talking."

"So, he told his aunt."

"Afraid so."

"That woman spreads news faster than the paper. Who else heard?"

"No one. Just me. I'm sure of it."

Nathan bit his thumbnail. "Pickering … old Roly Poly. I didn't recognize him in the dark."

"Well, he recognized you."

He muttered a curse. "The way he hemmed and hawed, I have no confidence that he'll keep quiet." Nathan plowed his fingers through his hair, his face puckered in a scowl.

"That's why I came to warn you," she whispered.

He scrubbed a hand over his face, nodding. "You were right to risk it."

His approval flushed her with warmth. Still, her thoughts circled back around. "So … who was Ying Su?"

"Just one of my father's servant girls."

He shifted his weight from one leg to the other. He took a few puffs on his cigar and stared off over Emily's shoulder into the night.

Then his gaze sharpened and settled on her. "What did Pickering say? Tell me everything. Spare no details."

While Emily recounted the conversation, his shoulder bumped nervously against the sleeve of her shirtwaist.

"This raises the stakes, ups the timetable," he ground out, his eyes flicking from side to side. "There are things that must happen before the news goes to print."

Emily wondered what part the servant girl had played in his father's illegal activities. Activities Nathan would soon expose. That would explain why he looked like a sprinter poised on the mark, ready to dart.

"There's more," she put in. "After you left, Officer Pickering pulled the sister aside and pried more information out of her. It seems that Ying Su died five years ago."

Nathan's body stilled.

With her curiosity piqued, she tried an indirect approach to learn more. "Your father hires children to work for him?"

His gaze snapped to her. "What? No."

"You called Ying Su a servant *girl*."

"More like fourteen. Way too young to have been mixed up in that kind of business, but no child. Unfortunately, labor laws that protect youth don't apply to immigrants."

"Where were her folks in all this?"

"Among the poor in China. They discard daughters for a fraction of their worth. Sons, they honor."

"Discard…?"

"Sold for a price into the most degrading form of slave labor."

Goosebumps prickled her flesh. She tried to imagine being sold by her folks and forced into work that ate away at the soul.

Shaking her head, Emily wondered aloud, "What do you suppose happened to her?"

"I don't know, but I intend to get to the bottom of it."

At least someone planned to look into the young girl's death. Leave it to Nathan to step up to the plate when the Galveston police had dropped the ball.

"And you suspect your father might have harmed her?"

"He's capable, but to have proof…" Anguish sliced through his gaze before he glanced away.

She understood his alarm over the threat of word leaking. But the pained look haunting his eyes niggled at her. She found herself saying, "So … you knew her?"

He drew back. "Come again?"

"The officer said that you demanded her whereabouts. That you acted stunned that she had died." Emily lifted a shoulder. "I just assumed."

"Before I left for Harvard, I … I overheard her at the laundry in Chinatown. She charged a pile of mended silks to my father's account."

"Did you approach her?"

"I *followed* her back to the variety show. It sickened me that my father used girls so young."

Of course, exploiting young girls would bother him. "Was that the last you saw of her?"

He puffed on his cigar, slowly blowing out a long ribbon of smoke. "I uh … I ran into her later. Offered her a peppermint and got her talking."

With that smile and those dimples, Emily doubted he needed penny candy to charm information out of the girl.

"Go on."

Nathan narrowed his eyes. "As I said, she was a servant to the showgirls. She ran their errands while they slept."

"At least she wasn't doing … other things."

"Yet," he offered, his gaze clouding over. "The girls were grooming her to be the main attraction. That's how things work in the business. The most attractive girls are showcased and pull in the biggest crowds."

The most attractive girls. Emily swallowed the lump of insecurity rising. She refused to envy a dead servant girl.

"If your father was grooming her for that purpose, then I doubt he harmed her."

"He's more ruthless than you can imagine."

"Even so, why harm the girl who would bring in the greatest profits? He had the most to lose by her dying."

"Profits are short-lived. Men like them young. The younger, the better. After so many years, the girls become expendable."

Nathan looked away and drew on his cigar.

"Tell me you tried to help her," Emily whispered.

He breathed out a sigh. "For what it's worth, I did. I could've moved her somewhere safe. Not that she would've left without her sister. And Liang wouldn't leave out of fear of being caught and sent to the cribs—the worst shacks for those girls."

"Then you did all you could."

"I made matters worse."

"By giving her a way out?"

"By getting caught with her."

Emily drew back her head. "What do you mean?"

Nathan cleared his throat. "My father … he spotted us off Market Street talking. He blew his stack. He accused her of getting friendly with unpaying customers. Before I could stop him, he'd jerked her by the hair and drove his fist into her stomach. I stepped in and caught the next blow. By then, folks on the street had stopped and openly stared at us. It had to end, so I thrust a wad of cash at him. I told him I wanted her free. The man laughed in my face. He said the measly amount wouldn't pay for one night with her, much less buy the girl." Nathan shook his head in disgust.

"You offered help," she softened her tone, touching his arm. "You did more than most."

"Little good it did her."

Self-reproach carved furrows between his brows. The man wore blame like roughened sackcloth as if it were his place to correct the wrong his father caused the girl.

"You couldn't have changed how things turned out for her."

"He had the upper hand, all right," Nathan snorted. "He used his audience to shame her and humiliate me. He offered me this deal there on the street: when I returned from Harvard and my tour of Europe, he'd give her to me as a homecoming gift. Said that by then, she'd be worth nothing to him."

"He'd let her go?"

His tone soured. "With strings attached; only if I took Ying Su as my common-law wife."

Emily's brows shot up.

"He knew I wouldn't! No respectable man marries a girl who's no better than a prostitute. Besides, it's illegal to wed someone Chinese. He knew I'd never do it. That's why he made the offer."

His face hardened. Nathan puffed on his cigar while his gaze grew unfocused, as though the memory tugged him back into the past.

Emily chewed on her lower lip. If only Nathan said he felt no attraction or affection for Ying Su or that he'd never marry a girl he didn't love. But he said none of those things.

She found herself asking, "Were you … sweet on her?"

Insecurity gnawed at her until she lowered her gaze. She studied the creases forming in her tan skirt, her thighs burning from squatting.

He lifted her chin with his fingertips, forcing her to meet his gaze. "At that age, I was far more enamored with hunting rifles and sailboats than the fairer sex." His expression sobered. "Truth is … I felt sorry for her. Who wouldn't?"

Emily understood pity well enough. He had wanted the servant girl safe from his father's clutches, but his father tied his hands.

A stray fact she'd learned in school made her pause. Something didn't quite add up. Pursing her lips, Emily frowned.

"What is it?" he prompted.

"It's just that … if the folks in China sold their daughters, how'd they get here? The Chinese have been barred from immigrating to the States for nearly twenty years. What do you know about that?"

Slowly, the corner of his mouth curled up. With the tip of his forefinger, he traced the length of Emily's braid, draped off her shoulder. "You know, I admire your razor-sharp mind."

"What do you know?" she repeated, her cheeks growing warm.

He shot her a cryptic look and took one final puff of his cigar butt. "Suffice it to say," he replied, blowing out a thin stream of smoke, "you'll hear more soon enough."

There came the stamping of horse hooves out front. Emily parted the spiky leaves and watched a hack roll to a stop under the pooled streetlight directly in front of the Chambers' house.

She glanced at Nathan. His mouth flattened into a grim line. He dropped the cigar butt on the ground and crushed it with the toe of his half boot.

With mounting unease, Emily watched the lone occupant step down out of the hack onto the street.

Chapter 20

"Is that Mr. Chambers I spy across the way?"

Stalling in front of Emily, Grace Hensleigh's walnut curls bounced on her shoulders as she turned and pointed past the horse-drawn float rumbling down 20th Street.

Grace's gaze slid onto Colin, who stiffened beside her.

The minister leaned toward his sister. "It's not lady-like to point." His tone conveyed more displeasure than her lack of manners alone.

Grace widened her eyes innocently. "How else will she know where he is unless I point him out?"

As if Emily needed help singling out Nathan in the crowd. She had spotted him among the Labor Day spectators at once, jotting notes on a small notepad, his hair tossed in his eyes, his face furrowed in concentration.

Colin glanced at Emily and Lena. "Well, ladies," he touched the brim of his derby, "enjoy your day." He nudged Grace. "Do come along," he tilted his head. "Let us find a spot."

Grace, however, dug in her heels. Mischief flared in her eyes as she looked at Emily.

The crowd erupted in applause as a float rolled down the street past city hall, now coming into view.

Grace pitched her voice over the crowd. "Pity Mr. Chambers didn't escort you to the parade this time. Although, after yesterday, who could blame him."

"Grace, *please*," Colin warned.

Emily's mouth tightened. She focused on the eagle perched atop the float made of fancy tinwork in the shape of stars. Her gaze bounced onto Nathan, who watched the exchange twenty feet away. One eyelid drooped in a wink.

Grace clutched the long chain on the coin purse necklace. "Surely it didn't escape your notice how she behaved in church when he sat beside her. He may feel she no longer desires his company if she ignores him. Then what?"

Emily stared at Grace, a spurt of irritation surging. Why should the girl care?

Colin leaned within inches of his sister's face. "Not another word, young lady," he ground out. Above his starched collar, redness crept up into his cheeks.

He tugged the bottom of his waistcoat, facing Emily and Lena. "Ladies, do forgive my sister's prattle."

With a hand firm on Grace's elbow, Colin led her to the opposite end of the Lunch Room's long covered porch.

Emily muttered to Lena, "Where is a muzzle when you need one?"

Lena chuckled softly behind her fan. She looked lovely in the blue floral skirt and cream-colored shirtwaist. She smelled of lavender, the fragrance as fresh as their friendship.

Over the din of the folks huddled on the porch, Lena slid closer and lowered her voice so the children in front couldn't overhear. "Any casual observer might get the impression that you've lost interest in our Mr. Chambers, but your eyes tell a different story. If you don't mind my asking, what is going on?"

"More has happened since Miss Pickering pitched a hissy fit in front of the committee," Emily leaned in, whispering.

"Yet nothing has derailed his interest, or he wouldn't still claim a spot next to you in church. Tell me you aren't letting Wilhelmina dictate your choices."

"It's not her."

Lena fluttered her fan, stirring the muggy air. "Who then?"

"Uncle Clayton."

It took a beat before Lena's eyes lit with comprehension. They exchanged a look.

Emily's mouth drooped to one side. "Aunt Estelle said something to him after the committee meeting. He insists I avoid contact with Mr. Chambers. For the time being," she amended.

"Well, that explains a lot. Give it a while. Things have a way of unfolding in its time."

Emily watched the flags along the parade route ripple in the breeze, their stars and stripes flapping and waving. She dearly hoped Lena was right.

Lena swept her fan across her face with vigor. "So … how is the orphanage project coming along?"

At the mention of it, Emily's chest tightened. "Ugh, what was I thinking? It pains me to admit this, but I may have bitten off more than I can chew."

Lena tipped her head. "But Wilhelmina told the committee last week that she had the closet organized from top to bottom, the supplies ordered, and delivery on the way. According to her, she had everything well in hand."

Recalling the mid-August closet fiasco, Emily huffed. "More like she's had her hands in everything."

Lena's shoulders sagged. "Tell me she didn't overstate the progress. Were the supplies even delivered? School is due to start."

"Oh, I made certain she placed the order and checked myself about the delivery. It's slotted first on the list for this Saturday. But thanks to *her*," Emily made a face, "I had to haul out everything from the closet and start over. Then double-check it against the inventory list before she could even place the order."

"Mercy! Why didn't you say something? Call in recruits?"

"And risk being cooped up with that woman again?"

Lena gave her shoulder a nudge. "I only live a few blocks away. Saturday is washday, but…" She fanned the moisture beading her upper lip. "What needs to be done?"

"Aunt Estelle recommended that the shipment be checked against the order before we stock the shelves. That way, we can reorder what doesn't come in. It's a sizable order. Added to that, Jasper plans to deliver the rest of the donations at the same time. All those new clothes have already come in at the store."

Lena blinked and tapped her fan against her chin. She stared unfocused, looking a bit pale. "Don't worry. The committee will pitch in. We'll all meet Saturday … to finish."

For the first time in days, the tightness in Emily's chest eased enough that she drew air deep into her lungs. As she released it, she noticed Lena's dark lashes flutter, her eyes turning glassy just moments before they showed white and rolled back in her head.

Emily's mouth popped open as Lena swayed and collapsed in a heap onto the porch, her blue chintz skirt billowing around her.

"Mama?" shrieked Lacey, clutching Sarah and startling little Rachel.

Emily dropped to her knees beside Lena. She landed hard on the planks and winced.

A ring of shoes, their tips pointing inward, scrambled closer. Too close. The sticky heat instantly grew stifling.

Above the murmuring, a familiar voice rang out. "Step aside."

Nathan pushed through the press and crouched beside Emily, their shoulders touching. He gave off the scent of Bay Rum and confidence. His eyes roved over Lena's crumpled form. Peering over at Emily, their gazes locked momentarily.

Nathan turned and fired off to the crowd. "Everyone back up! Some-one—anyone—she needs water."

A pair of shoes clacked on the planks, scurrying into the Lunch Room. The ring expanded as feet shuffled back a few steps, the hems of skirts swaying.

Gently, Nathan lifted Lena's head onto his lap as Emily reached for the fan, splayed on the planks. She waved it in front of Lena's face, stirring the warm air.

Nathan patted her cheeks. "Mrs. Kesler…"

"Excuse me. Pardon me."

A pair of polished wingtips emerged into view, stepping into the inner circle. Colin knelt on one knee next to Lena, his expression sober. Behind him, Grace stooped forward, leaning on her knees.

Heavy clomping vibrated the planks. "What's all the commotion," a man barked at the crowd, clearing a path through to the front.

From under the brim of her straw turban, Emily's gaze traveled up the man's protruding belly to his ruddy, sweat-stained face.

Taking one look at the scene, Officer Pickering snorted. "All this fuss over a dame swooning?"

"A *lady*," Nathan countered, glowering up at him.

The officer's mouth puckered, ready to launch a retort. Emily caught the instant he recognized Nathan, for his eyes rounded like twin tarts. Blanching, he mopped the sheen off his forehead with his sleeve, scanning the crowd.

He gave a nervous laugh. "Well, there's nothing here that's front-page news. Readers don't care a fig about females swooning in the heat. Am I right?"

Nathan's nostrils flared. "Are you finished detaining us from helping this woman?"

Without thinking, Emily laid her hand on Nathan's forearm, trying to make him hush. The gesture was not lost on either Officer Pickering or Col-in, as two sets of eyes settled on the placement of her hand. Emily hastily dropped it to her side.

Officer Pickering looked around, bellowing, "Unless y'all want me to charge two bits for admission to this sideshow, break it up! Get back to the parade."

One by one, the circle of folks scuffled back to form a line facing the street. Only Grace and the children remained hunched over Lena, gawking.

Lena stirred and blinked. "W—what happened?"

"I'm afraid you fainted from the heat," offered Colin.

A lad thrust a glass of water under Lena's nose. The floating ice chips sloshed against the rim.

"Thank you," she murmured.

"Yes, ma'am." The lad stepped away.

Nathan lifted Lena to a sitting position, his arm supporting her back. She drank deeply from the cup.

Colin motioned to his sister. "Gracie, watch the children while we tend to Mrs. Kesler."

Grace, brightening at the prospect, lifted little Rachel onto her hip and spoke to Lacey. "Sweetie, your mama will be right as rain in no time," she reassured, turning the girls to face the street. She prodded Jake and Andrew to do the same.

Lena finished the water. "I might as well have taken out an advertisement in *The Daily News*," she whispered.

Emily glanced at Nathan and Colin. "Let's move her somewhere that's more private."

Colin lifted a brow. "Mrs. Kesler, do you feel well enough to stand?"

Lena slowly nodded. "Yes. Yes, I think so."

The men unfolded their legs and reached under Lena's arms, gently lifting her until she gained her feet. They led her over to a straight-back chair propped by the entrance to the Lunch Room and eased her down onto the rush seat.

Colin stayed by Lena while Nathan came alongside Emily. She'd gotten up, gathered Lena's fan, and brushed off the dust from her yellow dress.

He lowered his voice. "You've had your share of excitement today, hmm? Though I suspect not as much as our tryst in the bushes."

"Be-have," she whispered.

Emily felt her cheeks heat and cast a glance at Colin. The minister was leaning against the wall beside Lena, his hands tucked in his trousers pockets, watching. Taking in Nathan's gaze, warm and centered on her, noticing her flushed cheeks as she fingered the stray wisps under the brim of her turban, missing nothing.

So much for avoiding further speculation.

Emily was about to excuse herself when a young man trotted up to Nathan.

"I've been searching high and low for you," he panted. "The boss man needs you back at the office, on the double."

"What's this about, Scotty?"

"Two fellas are mighty anxious to speak with you."

"Did you get their names?"

His freckled nose wrinkled. "No. But they're from some office of the superintendent of something or another."

Nathan's eyes lit with intrigue. He clapped Scotty on the shoulder. "Good man. I owe you a tenderloin trout at Ritter's for hunting me down."

"I'll collect," Scotty grinned.

Nathan shot Emily a look before he dashed off with Scotty. She read the silent message he'd conveyed. Whoever the men were, this was no ordinary meeting.

Emily handed Lena the fan when she joined Lena and Colin. Lena murmured her thanks and flicked it open, stirring the air.

The aroma of rich coffee and chocolate flowed from the doorway, teasing Emily's nose.

Colin faced her, his expression unreadable. "Might I suggest you stay beside Mrs. Kesler until she's fully recovered while I assist Gracie with the children?"

"Thank you kindly."

Lena rubbed her forehead and stared at her lap the minute they were alone. "I should have stayed home. Peter will lecture me."

Emily bent and rested her hands on her knees, peering eye level at her friend. "I suspect he'll be mighty relieved that this was nothing more than too much heat."

Lena's face gained color, her olive skin flushing pink. She leaned toward Emily, whispering, "The thing is … it's not the heat."

Emily blinked and lowered her gaze to Lena's waist, where her friend had let out the hooks and eyelets. For the time being, the flare of her skirt hid the growing roundness of her belly. Emily peered up at her friend, a smile blooming.

Lena nodded. "I'm expecting, come early spring."

Emily crunched on a gingersnap as she made her way up the stairs to her room, carrying a glass of milk. Halfway up the rise, Dr. Ryker strolled past her, toting his black leather bag.

"Afternoon, ma'am," he drawled under his bristly mustache.

Downstairs, excitement buzzed as the children told Estelle about the Labor Day parade and Lena swooning in the heat.

The doctor joined the others, his baritone voice traveling up the stairs. "Clayton reports that he's feeling better overall. Less fatigued. He's even gained back a few pounds. All encouraging signs, though I cannot stress enough that he must continue to have adequate rest and…"

Emily smiled to herself, tuning out the doctor's instructions. Perhaps her uncle was on the mend. To top it off, a baby was forming in Lena's womb. The promise of new life and her uncle regaining some of what illness had stripped away. These things fostered hope in her.

As Emily's foot touched the top landing, hollering drowned out her aunt's soft-spoken reply. Emily tipped her head, curious. She opened her bedroom door.

The heat of raised voice sizzled through the open window. Emily tossed her hat on the bed, strode across the room, and sat on the edge of the desk chair. Pulling back the curtain, she peered across into Nathan's room.

The late afternoon sun slanted harsh and bright through the wall of open windows, illuminating father and son like boxers sparring in a ring. Emily leaned forward, unobserved, her gaze riveted.

Chapter 21

"What happened to her?"

"Come to collect on our deal?" Hayden Chambers raised an oval flask and took a swig. "I suspect your governess friend might object to sharing you."

"You know as well as I do she's dead!"

"Pity. That girl would have brought down the house with that face, those legs."

"Would have?"

"Never made her debut."

"Did you kill her to spite me?"

"Come now," Hayden chided. "She died of natural causes. All a matter of public record if you'd bothered to check. Any reporter worth his salt would have." His mouth slanted in a smirk. "You must be getting sloppy."

Nathan bristled. "Her name is not recorded in the county death registry. At least Ying Su lived long enough to tell me *everything*."

The scorn faded from Hayden's face. "Her tongue is silent in the grave, boy."

"She spelled it all out. Every detail."

"You know nothing."

"What I know will go to print."

"Careful," Hayden spoke, low and menacing. "You don't have what it takes to stand up against me."

"On the contrary, I have the law on my side."

"The law on this island has protected my shows since before you were born."

"I'm referring to *federal* law."

Hayden's face fell. "My records are tidy."

"Falsified papers won't hold up under close inspection."

"They'll find nothing," Hayden's voice boomed, waggling his jowls. "Nothing that'll stick."

"I came from accompanying inspectors on a raid at your variety show. As we speak, they're hauling your showgirls in for questioning," Nathan boasted. "They'll be deported back to China, with any luck, rather than sent to prison. They needn't suffer more so that justice has its day."

"Justice," Hayden spat. He tipped the flask for another pull. "Your meddling won't amount to a thing."

Nathan paused as if savoring the moment. "You have no idea the scope of my meddling." His lips spread in a wolfish grin, his teeth flashing.

"What have you done?" Hayden growled.

"I gave immigration enough dirt to bury your entire operation."

"You're not clever enough to bring down anything newsworthy."

"Agents located your safe house and swarmed it. Yesterday."

Hayden went rigid, his body stock-still. He glared at Nathan, as if appraising him with new respect.

"Your thugs, Bledsoe and Pike, squealed," Nathan went on. "According to them, you've fattened your wallet from misery for decades. That all stops today. The oppression—it's over."

"Don't think you can corner a rattler without getting bit."

Nathan's mouth twisted into a bitter scowl. "What will you do—*disinherit* me? You see how your threats backfired."

Nathan strutted to the bookcase against the back wall and picked up a leather sheath. Turning sideways, he slid out a foot-long Bowie knife. Sunlight glinted off the polished steel as he sauntered to within three feet of his father. Hayden's gaze never strayed from the knife that held him at bay.

Nathan jutted out his chin. "You'll need a lawyer by day's end."

Hayden's shoulders started to tremble and convulse. A belly laugh burst out, ricocheting off the walls like bullets.

Nathan stared unblinking at his father, his mouth slightly ajar.

Around a chuckle, Hayden wiped a hand over his straw-colored mustache. "What about your exploits, eh? Did you think you'd get off scot-free?"

"What are you talking about?"

"Months after you left for Harvard … your dirty little secret leaked out all over the floor."

Nathan tucked in his chin, confusion creasing his face.

"It's high time I knocked you down a peg or two."

"I've done nothing—"

"See, that's the amusing part. You don't even know."

"Know what, exactly?"

Hayden raised his bushy eyebrows for emphasis. "Ying Su's blood is on your hands, not mine."

"Nonsense!"

"Those narrow hips. The girl bled out."

Nathan's lips puckered, but no sound escaped. Clearly, he missed the point.

Unfortunately, Emily knew full well his meaning. How could she not, after watching a mare bleed out hours after delivering a foal? She pressed a clammy palm against her chest over the sharp twinge there.

"Nobody expected the little runt to live." Hayden gave a casual wave of the flask. "He proved himself a fighter, like his grandpa."

A dazed look stole over Nathan's face. As the meaning sank in, he jerked his head back. "That's a lie, straight from the pit of hell!"

"On the contrary, it's the honest truth. Again, all a matter of public record. The mother's name is on the birth certificate."

"You expect me to believe I had a son?"

"*Have*. The boy is alive and kicking."

"What? No! You're lying."

"Denying the truth never changed the facts. And the fact is Ying Su swore on her dying breath that you were the only one."

From beneath lowered brows, Nathan's eyes darkened like gathering thunderclouds. He fell silent.

"Oh, why so glum," his father taunted. "Cheer up. At least the boy's an American citizen."

Air sagged in the back of Emily's throat. She leaned in, willing Nathan to say something to set the record straight.

When Nathan spoke, his tone was flat. "If that's so … then where is he?"

"What…?" Emily whispered through parted lips.

She found no foothold in the quicksand of his question. The weight pressed down, heavy and oppressive, squeezing the air from her lungs, threatening to smother her.

It cannot be.

"Come now," Hayden mocked, "a fine sleuth like you ought to be able to figure out the whereabouts of a little boy."

Nathan glared at his father, shaking his head. "How do I know you didn't make up this whole story?"

Emily sucked in a dry breath. *Of course, he did!*

Hayden up-ended the glass flask and drank from it. "Prove me wrong. I dare you. I'll make it worth your while. Say, half-million, cash." Nathan went still, eyeing him. "On one condition: do right by the boy. Give him your name and a *proper* upbringing. Now, I'd bet you don't." He poked a beefy finger at Nathan's nose. "I know you won't because claiming the boy would tarnish the shiny image you portray to the fine folks of Galveston. You put on a fine show, but I know your true colors. You're too self-serving to do anything that'll cost you. Although, this potentially could cost you a fortune."

Emily shifted on the cushion. Why listen to such outlandish spew? *Forget the offer! Walk away!*

"Quite the dilemma for you," Hayden snorted. "To do the honorable thing would bring you dishonor. What better way, though, to prove your intentions? Of course … this could all go away. There's no need to broadcast your sowing a few wild oats. Neither should you have to settle for a mere half-million. I'm even willing to overlook your misguided zeal." Hayden spread his hands in a magnanimous gesture. "After all, you paid me a favor by exposing Bledsoe and Pike, the two-faced, liver-bellied cowards."

He stroked the lapels of his jacket with his thumbs as though he was considering his following words carefully. "When this inspection blows over in a few days, you will start managing the books for the business. Do them on the side, from home. You wouldn't want anything to tarnish your sterling reputation, now would you? No reason why anybody else should know about it … *or the boy.*"

The threat hung heavy in the air. A doorbell chimed faintly from downstairs.

"The inspectors," Nathan announced, his mouth drawn in a straight line.

Hayden spat a curse on his way to the door. He turned on the threshold. "I'll take care of this little problem," he bit out. "Meanwhile, you will print nothing about raids or federal inspectors. Nothing about me or our business, you hear me?"

Nathan gripped the knife handle and held his silence.

The doorbell chimed again. Hayden scowled fiercely and stalked through the door. His footfalls struck the hall floor with the force of a man used to bullying to get his way, either by force, threat, or bribery.

Nathan stared after him until the footsteps faded, his jaw clenched. Then in one fluid motion, he raised the Bowie knife over his shoulder and thrust it forward. The knife sliced through the air, right over where his father stood moments ago. The clip-point blade impaled the bust of the deer mounted on the wall; the blade stuck squarely between the eyes. Without a backward glance, Nathan spun on his heel and strode out of the room.

Emily stared wide-eyed at the emptied room. She puffed out her cheeks and blew out a shaky breath. Her fingers wove through the wisps of copper matted to her forehead from wearing the straw turban. She pressed her fingertips against the heat radiating from her temples. There, blood throbbed wildly under her touch. She lowered her arm and turned from the window.

Her gaze slid onto her lap. Her hands lay limp and heavy. Emily rubbed the yellow Swiss fabric of her skirt, squishing the nubby dots right above the knee. She stared until the pattern became a sea of dots. She blinked and tried to focus.

If only she had an eraser that could wipe clean that whole scene from her mind. She wished she'd never come upstairs. Never became privy to the sparring match that played out next door. Hayden Chambers had hit below the belt. What a pack of lies! Lies said to manipulate and threaten his son. The man gave no proof of anything. Not a blessed thing. Why should she give a liar any credence? If she had a lick of sense, she wouldn't give the word of the crook a second thought.

She got up and walked over to the bed. She lifted *Sense and Sensibility* off the top of her nightstand.

Without bothering to remove her shoes, she plunked down onto the snowy coverlet, heaving a sigh into the room. She stared at the ceiling for a long moment. She settled deeper onto the mattress, reached for her pillow, and tucked it under her head.

She fingered the bookmark and opened the book there, willing the story to soothe her, but she blinked at the words and gazed off through the open window.

If that's so, then where is he?

Nathan's admission rang in her ears. Only a fool would ignore the implication of that question.

If that's so...

With those three words, Nathan let slip an entanglement far deeper than pity. Far more profound than he let on to her. He all but admitted to the possibility of fathering a child. A son by Ying Su. A spasm quivered through her stomach.

Soon the news about his father's illegal operation would splash across the newspaper. She'd yearned for the truth to come to light, hoping it might redeem Nathan in his family's eyes. But what if there was a child out there somewhere? What if the truth about him came to light? How could that be redeemed?

A tangle of disappointment and unease had her insides twisted up like a figure-eight knot. No chance of slipping out of that loop. Not when Nathan hid a deep secret despite his determination to get to the truth. What would she do if it became public knowledge?

Above all, she had to protect her position as governess.

Emily turned onto her side and huddled on the coverlet, curling her legs close to her chest. She squeezed her eyes shut. A tear escaped and rolled down her temple, wetting her hair.

What a colossal mess. What could be worse than this tangle or the threat of being dragged down into the mire along with Nathan?

Chapter 22

"Walk the plank or die by my sword!" Andrew thrust the blunt end of a ruler at Jake's belly.

"Nay, mate," Jake snarled and puffed out his chest, his red bandana pushing his cowlick straight like a flaxen feather. "I'll fight you to the death!"

Emily glanced up at the boys from over the mound of donations heaped in the center of the orphanage's library. She reached for a white pinafore and folded it. Wooden rulers clacked in the duel. Bare feet squeaked on the hardwood floor as the boys skidded around the mound past Sarah and Lacey, seated opposite the pile from her.

Andrew jabbed at Jake with his makeshift sword. The boy curled his spine to sidestep the blow, then drew up straight and charged forward, hot on Andrew's heels.

"I'll feed you to the fish!" Jake's voice blared off the walls.

Emily gritted her teeth. "Simmer *down* Jake."

His rambunctiousness grated as an unusual pressure built in her ears. She'd never seen the boy so high-strung. Was it due to the change in weather?

On this eighth day of September, slate-gray clouds swept low and blustery while raindrops plinked on the windowpanes.

Of all days for it to rain. What gloomy weather for a workday.

Emily glanced up at the clock ticking on the library wall. A quarter till seven. She doubted anyone else would even show up.

Somehow, she had managed to put on a brave face and muddled through the week of school. By Friday, she'd given up on the pretense of having lessons, and they finished reading *Treasure Island*.

But not even Jake's obsession with pirate gold could keep her mind off of Nathan or the possibility that he had a son. Or what he might do if he found the boy, to say nothing of how she fit into the picture—if she fit at all. Would Nathan do the honorable thing and claim the child?

She studied the grooves in the wainscoting along the lower walls. What if answers were close at hand?

From beside her, Lena grimaced and rubbed her belly.

Emily leaned in and lowered her voice, catching a whiff of ginger candy on Lena's breath. "Upset tummy?"

"It's the sausage frying. It's making me queasy." Lena lifted her shoulder. "Usually passes by noon. Good thing. We have our work cut out for us."

Emily surveyed the mound the size of a wagon bed. She could barely see over the top of it. Beneath the pile of clothes, the school supplies lay buried. Had she been here when Jasper made the delivery, she would have instructed him to separate the school supplies from the clothes. Then she could focus on restocking the closet. But Emily had brought the children along. How could she not, after seeing the fatigue ringing her aunt's eyes over breakfast? There was no help for it. Might just as well—

A finger poked her ribs, gaining her attention. "Where's your mind this morning?" Lena teased as she scooted closer to talk over the din.

Emily gave herself a mental shake. "You were saying?"

Lena lowered her voice. "I said our Mr. Chambers created quite a stir with his news. Wonder what'll happen to his papa."

"No worse than he deserves, I suspect."

By midweek Emily had spied the headlines: *RAID EXPOSES SMUG-GLING THROUGH UNDERGROUND RAILROAD.* She'd snatched up the paper folded on Uncle Clayton's tray and read.

> *According to the Office of the Superintendent of Immigra-tion, showgirls from the variety show on Market Street confessed to having been smuggled into America through an Underground Railroad in El Paso, Texas.*
>
> *Inspectors located the safe house and found nine young Chi-nese females hidden on the border.*
>
> *In addition, they confiscated seventy pounds of opium. Hayden Chambers, the owner of the variety show, was arrested for immigrant smuggling and evading customs on opium ship-ments.*
>
> *Chambers' two accomplices, Harold Bledsoe and Bernard Pike, gave the names of brothels across Houston, Corpus Christi, and San Antonio, where Chambers supplied girls for prostitu-tion.*

Lena gazed at her with warm curiosity. "Folks applaud the stand he took, you know. I expected you to be bursting at the seams with pride."

After holding everything in for days, Emily was bursting at the seams all right, but not from pride.

Lena angled her head. "You're not, though. Why is that?"

Why indeed. Emily fingered the velvety ribbing on a pair of corduroy knickers. How could she explain overhearing news that overshadowed the headlines? News that held her future in a stranglehold, threatening to choke the very life out of her livelihood unless she kept her distance from Nathan. Sound judgment wagged its pointed finger at her, warning her to walk away without a backward glance before his personal affairs could become public knowledge.

Instead, she'd sat vigil each evening across from Nathan's room, devouring the pages of *Sense and Sensibility*. Two nights ago, what she'd witnessed in the moonlight made fresh tears well close to the surface. She lowered her head, batting her lashes dry.

"Ouch!" Andrew yelped across the mound, grabbing his stomach and giggling like a girl.

Jake hooted over the strike while Andrew tore off around the room. In an attempt to cut him off, Jake bounded over the edge of the pile. His hind leg hooked on clothes, flinging shirts and pants onto the folded stacks, toppling them.

"All right, *that's it*," Emily snapped at Jake. "Enough foolishness from you, young man."

Sarah chimed in. "Just wait until Mama hears—"

"Sarah, I'll handle this." Her tone brooked no argument. Emily pushed up on her knees, eye-level with Jake. She gripped his bony shoulders. "You either settle down this instant, or I'll separate you and Andrew for the rest of the day." His expression sobered. "Now go set the clothes right."

His shoulders drooped. "Yes, ma'am."

Jake had the sense to obey. As he finished straightening the stacks, the bell clanged. It sent a stampede of bare feet padding up and down the staircases and hallways.

The cook appeared directly behind Lena. She wiped her hands on a grease-soiled apron and jerked her thumb toward the dining room.

"Wash up and come and get it while it's hot. I cooked enough sausage and biscuits and gravy to feed an army."

With her shoulders squared and her posture straight as a wooden spoon, Etta Grimes gave orders like a military cook.

Jake tugged on Emily's sleeve. "I'm still hungry. Can I go, too?"

"May I," Emily corrected.

He bounced from foot to foot. "May I?"

Emily eyed him for a moment before waving him on. He and Andrew bustled out of the room and caught up with Sarah and Lacey.

As the cook turned to go, the pungent odor wafted from her apron. Below her, Lena wrinkled her nose. Her olive skin blanched pale. Scrambling to her feet, she clamped a hand over her mouth and fled to the lavatory.

Alone, Emily sat back on her heels. Now was her chance. The need for answers pushed her up off the floor. Her fingers itched with anticipation as she headed through the expansive central reception hall adjoining the library.

Behind the twenty-foot-wide grand staircase, she reached for the brass key set on top of the door frame where the lady manager kept it. Inserting the shaft into the lock, she opened the door. It creaked on its hinges. Emily threw a glance over her shoulder, wincing. From the dining room up the hallway, voices melded with the scraping of utensils against plates.

Silently, she stepped into the office and slid the door shut. Emily blew out a breath into the stale, muggy air. Dropping the key in the pocket of her calico dress, she patted it through the fabric and glanced around.

A lamp burned on the desk along the opposite wall, throwing shadows up the slanted ceiling. She eyed the wooden file cabinet to the right of the desk. Her gaze sharpened on its bottom drawer. A manila folder lay on top of the pulled-out drawer, askew. Pages stuck out in every direction. Had someone dropped it in haste?

She approached the file, her breathing shallow. Stooping, she gathered up the folder. She turned toward the light and opened it. A column of names marched down the top page, dated June 5th, 1900.

Orphan names.

She scrolled down, searching for one name: *Toy, Chai Lin.* Blood pounded in her ears. She ran her finger across the row of information. *Date of birth: January 1895. Place of birth: Texas. Place of birth of mother: China. Name of mother: Toy, Ying Su.* Emily sucked in a breath and held it. *Name of father: Unknown. Place of birth of father: Unknown.*

Emily spread her hand over her collarbone. "Unknown" didn't clear Nathan's name or give her the answers she craved. Would it always be this way?

She stared transfixed until the letters ran together on the page. Pushing the heaviness aside, Emily blinked and refocused.

At the end of the row, a familiar name caught her attention. How had *he* become involved? The man admitted the infant into the orphanage. *Reverend Colin Hensleigh.* Of course. It took an influential man to open doors. How else would a half-Chinese boy be admitted to a white Protestant home? But who dragged Colin into the middle of this ordeal? What if he knew the name of the child's father? If so, had he omitted it for some reason?

Her thoughts whirling, Emily straightened the pages back into the folder. Her gaze swept the office. A bronze box was upended on the desk blotter beside the typewriter, the sticks of sealing wax and wax seal spilling out. The middle desk drawer was left ajar. On the file cabinet, a key dangled from the lock.

No one had discovered the intruder yet. Without thinking, Emily acted on impulse. She squatted, inserted the file back with the folders, and then rolled the drawer shut.

Emily covered the man's tracks. That didn't sit well. Still, what harm did it do? He'd come for answers too. He took nothing more with him. Of that, she was certain.

Emily pushed to her feet and moved to the door. She pressed her ear against it, listening. Hearing no footfalls, Emily crept out into the hallway. As she pulled on the doorknob, a rustling came from behind her. Her stomach plummeted.

Emily spun and spotted Lena coming from the lavatory across the hall. A question creased her brow.

She approached Emily, careful to keep her voice low. "Spill it! What were you doing in there?"

Emily regarded her friend. For days, the weight of having no one to confide in had pressed heavily on her chest.

After a glance up the hallway, Emily whispered, "Checking orphan records. Nathan's father accused him of doing something scandalous."

"What does that have to do with records?"

Emily pressed her lips together. It pained her to say it. "A child was born … to one of his father's servant girls."

"And you think Nathan—"

"Had to find out."

"Well?"

"Records only verified the mother and son. Chai Lin."

Lena flattened a palm over her stomach. "Oh my."

"There's more." Emily tipped her head toward the door, still cracked open behind her. "Take a look."

Lena nudged the door open and peered in. "What happened here?" Their eyes locked. "You don't suppose—"

"Orphan records were left out. I—I filed the folder away."

Lena blew out a breath. "So no one has discovered this yet. I suspect—"

A wind gust blew open the front door. British accents lilted off the soaring ceiling in the central reception hall.

Lena met Emily's gaze. "The Hensleighs."

Through the calico fabric, Emily fingered the brass key. It weighed heavy against her thigh.

She gathered her wits about her. "Mind fetching the Reverend? I reckon he needs to know."

Lena gave Emily's arm a gentle squeeze. "Don't worry. We'll sort this all out."

Her friend was offering her a hand up out of the sinkhole she'd landed in days ago upon hearing the news. She laid her hand over Lena's, grateful for her support. "Thanks."

"Be right back," Lena murmured and stepped away.

Emily fished out the key from her pocket and set it above the doorframe seconds before the Hensleighs came into view.

Lena pulled Colin aside. The minister turned his ear and listened intently to Lena's lowered voice while Grace leaned in eavesdropping.

Colin straightened and strode over to Emily, his expression solemn. Above his striped shirt and navy jacket, tension reddened his neck and ears.

He dipped his chin in greeting. "Lena says you made a discovery."

Emily cleared her throat. "Afraid so. Have a look."

She pushed open the door and led the way into the room. Colin took a moment on the threshold, surveying the office.

His navy eyes sharpened on her. "Is this how you found everything?"

Emily swallowed. "Every bit the mess you see here."

The minister entered the room, peering past her. He spied the key dangling from the file cabinet lock. A question appeared poised on Colin's tongue, but he pressed his lips together.

Lena entered behind him and sank onto the armchair beside the door. "I'd gone to the lavatory, and Emily showed me the room the moment I came out."

Emily threw Lena a grateful look.

Grace edged her way into the office. "How *intriguing,* a burglary!"

Her eyes sparkled as she waltzed past Emily toward the desk. The scent of rose petals clung to her royal blue dress.

"Lower your voice, Gracie." Colin pushed the door shut with a grimace.

"Perhaps the villain stole cash." Grace rubbed her hands together, warming to the idea. She hunched over the contents of the dumped box. "Don't touch a thing. The police will check for fingerprinting."

Colin cast a tolerant gaze at his sister. "Not everyone collects fingerprints like in *Pudd'nhead Wilson,* dearest."

Emily's heartbeat sputtered at the reference to Mark Twain's novel, where fingerprinting was used to solve a murder.

"Some do check for fingerprints nowadays." Grace let out a contented sigh. "Here, I expected today would be as dull as dusting your books. Instead, we have a mystery afoot."

"One that is not ours to solve." Colin raised an eyebrow to stress his point.

Grace's mouth sagged in a pout as she fingered her butterfly broach. "Fine. Spoil my only amusement."

The minister peered at Emily and Lena, his manner brisk. "I must notify the Board of Lady Managers at once. I cannot imagine one of them leaving the room unkempt. They are most efficient and tidy."

Colin peered at Emily. His voice softened. "Since you discovered what may prove to be a break-in, the authorities will want to question you."

Not that! "O—of course. Whatever you need from me."

Emily's gaze trailed over to the file cabinet. At least she'd put up the orphan file. It hid the obvious reason behind the break-in.

"I'll make the call at once." Colin laid a hand on Grace's shoulder, meeting her gaze. "Go with Mrs. Kesler. There's work to be done. And don't breathe a word of this to anyone. Not a word. Understood?"

Grace nodded begrudgingly and allowed Lena to usher her toward the library.

Colin turned to Emily. "Miss Cleburne, I need you to step outside the office and wait for me until I return."

"Of course."

Colin followed her out, and shut the door. He strode up the hallway to use the telephone.

Alone, Emily sagged against the door. A police grilling. Any top-notch officer would be thorough. Tightness squeezed a band around her forehead. At least she knew how to maneuver around tense confrontations. Give quick, short answers. Nothing more. That's how she'd survived in the Cleburne household.

As the wall clock gave eight gongs, boisterous chatter streamed through the front door. It drew Emily to the end of the grand staircase. She peered through the railing across the great reception hall.

Chapter 23

"…threat of a gale ever kept me at home."

"Slowed you down a bit, though." A woman chuckled.

"More of a nuisance than anything."

"I'll say."

The women hovered around the hall tree, setting down their purses and dripping umbrellas. Lena and Grace joined them while they peeled off their gloves and hats. Their cheeks were rosy, their expressions merry, as if they gathered to celebrate a holiday rather than sort through donations.

Dressed in a spruce-striped frock, even Miss Pickering appeared agreeable. "Weren't the waves a sight to behold," she said.

"Oh, I adore waves," Grace pressed her palms together. "Do tell."

"Shooting up high as second-story windows."

"Truly? I caught a glimpse on the way. Oh, of all days to be stuck indoors," Grace cried. "What I wouldn't give to see them up close."

The children traipsed into the reception hall.

Jake grabbed Andrew's arm. "Hear that? Big waves! I bet they're churning up pirate gold. Maybe some that Crazy Ben hid, you reckon?"

Emily lifted her eyes to the ceiling. That boy had thought of little else since they finished reading *Treasure Island*.

Miss Pickering called out to Ida. A woman with a thick waist and a broad smile turned. So this was Ida, the woman who failed to clean out the supply closet. Her easy smile suggested a lighthearted temperament. In the crook of her elbow, she toted a covered basket. One corner of the dishtowel had flapped up, revealing a chocolate iced cake.

Shoes treaded on the floor beside Emily, gaining her attention. Colin came around and in front, blocking her view of the ladies.

He lowered his voice, his tone confidential. "The board chair contacted Chief Ketchum and summoned the lady manager over the books."

He paused, pinching the bridge of his nose.

The lady manager over the books. The muscles between her shoulder blades knotted. "Why involve her?"

"Earlier, I noticed the key left in the file cabinet."

Her breath caught. "And?" She waited, impatient for him to get to the point.

Colin rubbed his fingertips along the scar above his left eyebrow as if reluctant to impart the news. "As it turns out," he grimaced, "they keep cash for everyday expenses in that cabinet."

Now the police would examine the file cabinet with a fine-tooth comb. The dangling key insured as much.

She caught a whiff of sandalwood. Over Colin's shoulder, green and white stripes flashed. Too late, she lifted a hand to warn him.

"You'll need to make a statement once the officers—"

"Statement," Miss Pickering sniffed, coming alongside Colin. "About what?"

Colin shut his eyes briefly and faced her. "Madam, you needn't concern yourself."

"Police have been called?"

"Merely a precaution."

She touched her cheek. "The matron must be told—"

"There's no need to involve her. It's probably nothing more than a worker who failed to pick up at day's end."

"A worker, you say?" Miss Pickering peered over the rim of her spectacles at Emily. "And how does this involve Miss Cleburne?"

Emily's mouth tightened. Did her nosiness know no bounds? She bit the tip of her tongue. *Let the dust settle.*

Colin stiffened. "Miss Cleburne discovered the room."

"The office," Miss Pickering hazarded a guess, eyeing them.

Emily exchanged a look with Colin.

Miss Pickering set her mouth smugly, appearing pleased with her deduction.

It gave her greater boldness. "It's always neat as a pin. Let me have a look."

Colin held up a hand. "The fewer involved, the better."

A gust of moist air whooshed through the front door. Beyond the doorframe, wet leaves whirled in the air like confetti.

Jasper crossed the threshold dressed in an oilskin jacket, hefting a bag of oats on his shoulder. He wiped his wet boots on the mat and looked around. Spotting Emily across the great hall, his eyebrows sloped with relief.

He swerved around the group of women and came over to her. "Miss Emily, care to give me a hand putting up this food? I got deliveries coming out my ears, and I need to make them before worse weather cuts loose."

He glanced over his shoulder out the window to the swift rolling clouds, the skin beneath his dark eyes drawn. His grandmother had died in a hurricane. No wonder stormy weather made him antsy.

"Afraid not, Jasper."

Today was no day to be working in the pantry. She glanced at Miss Pickering. Her mouth twitched.

"However … I'm sure Miss Pickering would be more than willing to take charge and lend a hand." Keeping a straight face, she added with a note of gratification, "Take it from me—she'll do far more than you ask of her."

Miss Pickering shot her a look, unsure how to take the remark.

Yet never one to miss an opportunity to have her hands in everything, the woman gave Jasper a curt nod. "Very well. This way."

Pivoting on her heel, she trooped toward the pantry in the north wing while Jasper fell in step behind her.

Colin watched them leave and leaned in. Close enough that Emily breathed in a whiff of bergamot shaving soap. Was that approval gleaming in his navy eyes?

He lowered his voice to a murmur. "Until we know more, let's keep this between us, shall we? Donations to the orphanage must not suffer over what may be nothing more than conjecture. While I wait in the office, I need you to watch for the police. Promptly escort them back when they arrive, if you please."

Emily's pulse hitched. She didn't want to think about the police.

She mustered a casual tone. "Of course."

Emily leaned on the railing, watching him enter the office.

Time to get back to work. Perhaps the distraction would help while she waited on the police.

Jake skittered to a halt in front of her on her way to the library.

He laced his fingers together and thrust them upwards. "Can we go, Miss Emily, please?"

"Go where?"

"To see the waves—"

"We've come to *work*."

"I promise I'll be no trouble, no trouble at all. Can we go? Please, please?"

Jake's persistence spiked her annoyance. "You heard me."

"Just this one time? Please?"

"Absolutely not," Emily snapped. Jake drew his chin back. Sighing, she softened her voice. "Perhaps tomorrow, after church."

Jake walked off, muttering, "They'll be gone by then."

Pressure built behind her eyes. Emily wished the children had remained at home tucked in their rooms playing with marbles and paper dolls. She didn't need the added strain of them being underfoot, not with the police due to arrive at any moment to question her.

Lena approached, glancing over at Jake. "Everything okay?"

"I swear, that boy is pushing me toward mutiny," Emily muttered. She lowered her voice. "To top it off, I'm expected to give a statement to the police. Ugh! I'd rather walk the plank."

A faint smile touched Lena's lips. "You kept your poise with Reverend Hensleigh. You'll do just fine with the police."

As always, Lena's support bolstered her spirits. Emily returned the smile while a way out formed; a perfect plan if Lena would agree to it.

Emily cleared her throat. "I have an idea, one that may suit us both. Do you think… Would you mind taking the children on the streetcar to see the waves? Get some fresh air. Just for a little while." She thought of Lena's cottage nearby on Avenue O. "Then go home. Let the children play while you put your feet up for a spell, until your stomach settles."

"I don't know," Lena hedged, her face puckering with resistance. "There's so much work to do here."

Emily pressed her case. "I need the children out of here before the police arrive. They're due here any minute. You said your queasiness usually passes by noon, right? You can come back then and still have all afternoon to work."

Emily glanced over at the women folding. "Besides, you're the one who organized the work day. With all this help, we'll be home by supper."

Lena touched her forefinger to her pale lips, considering the idea. "All right, I'll go. But just til noon."

Emily released a sigh. "I'm obliged. More than I can say."

She waved Jake over. "You may go with Miss Lena to see the waves."

Jake's face lit with excitement. "Really?"

"But you best mind her, you hear?" Emily stooped down and wagged a finger in his face. "And no wading in the surf for anything shiny."

"Yes, Ma'am!" The boy bounced up and down on his toes. He turned to Andrew. "Hear that? I can go!"

"Go where?" Grace sidled over.

The girl had the hearing of a hawk.

"To see the waves with Andrew," Jake told her.

"Lucky you." Grace folded her arms, her tone flat.

Emily didn't trust Colin's sister to keep quiet about her notions of burglary or fingerprinting when the police showed up.

She addressed Grace. "Mrs. Kesler is feeling a bit under the weather this morning. Care to join them and help watch the children?"

"Oh, what a capital idea," Grace clapped her hands together, her eyes brightening.

"All right, then. I'll inform your brother of your whereabouts."

Emily spotted Sarah in the library, folding a pinafore. The girl had so little amusement since Uncle Clayton became ill.

"Sarah," Emily called, beckoning her over. The girl gained her feet and came over.

"Yes, ma'am?"

"How would you like to go with Lacey to see the waves?"

Sarah's eyes widened. "Are you sure? Because if you need me, I can stay."

My little helper. Sarah had a servant's heart. Shouldn't that be rewarded?

Emily pulled out the change purse from her pocket and dug for nickels, plinking four coins in Sarah's palm. "For the streetcar, for you and Jake. Go play. Enjoy the morning. The waves will make a great story to write your father on Monday."

Sarah circled her arms around Emily's waist and gave a squeeze. "Thanks, Miss Emily," she lisped before skipping over to Lacey.

By the door, Lena gathered Grace and the children. She secured her hat with a hat pin.

Emily strolled over. She motioned to the umbrella she'd borrowed from Estelle. "Take it. You'll need it before I do."

Her friend lifted a shoulder. "Who minds getting wet after the heat we've had? Come along, children," she shepherded them out the door, tossing over her shoulder, "See you in a little while."

The air moistened Emily's skin, smelling of wet sand and rain. Peering at the churning sky, she pushed the door closed. Through the window slats, she watched them trot down the stairs, the children waving their arms enthusiastically.

Her mouth tipped with satisfaction. Her plan had come together nicely. Better yet, everyone gained from it.

Still, her fingers trembled around the doorknob. Now to come up with a plausible reason why she had entered the locked office in the first place.

⌘

The scattered rain that had earlier plunked at the windows with fat drops now lashed at the panes.

The drumming nearly drowned out the orphans' chatter, echoing up from the playrooms in the basement.

Seated around the mound, Emily peered up at the clock for the tenth time that hour. Nine forty-two. She fingered the ribbing on a corduroy dress. What was keeping the police?

The ring of women chatted as they kept up a steady pace of sorting and folding clothes. At any other time, sitting with strangers would have made her stomach clench with tension. Not so today. Today she used being an outsider to her advantage. Tuning out their banal chatter gave her time to think. For once, she was too distracted to notice any awkwardness, much less care about relieving it.

The entry door flew open on a gust of wind. Emily turned at the waist as the lady manager over the books came into view. Below her knees, a watermark stained her blue dress. She set her wet umbrella over the drip pan on the hall tree and sailed through the reception hall back to the office.

A chill prickled up Emily's neck and scalp. She resisted the urge to follow behind the woman.

"From the looks of her," Ida observed from across the pile, "I'd say there's been another overflow."

Around the mound, the others murmured agreement.

"Overflow?" Emily's brows drew together.

"You're not from around these parts, are you?" Ida threw her a friendly, sage smile. "Well, Sugar, let me tell you, I awoke to the street gutters flooded in front of the house. It often rises from there."

"Come again?" Emily leaned back, not liking the sound of water rising.

"It's not uncommon for the tide to overflow and surround my place like a lake."

Emily's lips parted. "How far inland?"

"I live three blocks from the beach. Oh, you needn't worry." Ida swatted her hand dismissively. "Storms in the Gulf push the tide up. It happens on occasion. That's why we build homes on pilings, to keep the water out."

To keep the water out. Emily pictured herself treading through waist-deep tidewater into the Edwards' yard, the current dragging her feet. Her fingers tingled.

She plucked boxes of chalk from the bottom edge of the pile and formed a neat stack.

She moistened her lips, determined to sound calmer than she felt. "H—how high does the tide usually rise?"

A woman who'd introduced herself as Minnie chimed in from down the mound, her voice thin and reedy. "Deep enough for the little ones to paddle in washtub races. They have a grand time."

Emily relaxed her shoulders. How harmful were these overflows if parents allowed their children to play out in them?

Honestly, waist-deep water! She needed to rein in her imagination. She had enough to consider. Why borrow trouble?

The doorbell rang. Seated nearest the entrance, Emily sprang to her feet. When she reached the door, she wiped her sweat-dampened palms down the calico dress and turned the knob.

On the portico, the black canopy of an umbrella filled her view. A man stood on the portico wrestling with the broken ribs on the collapsible frame.

Chapter 24

The umbrella snapped shut. Emily stared into Nathan's face, disbelieving her eyes.

"Morning," he raised his voice to be heard over the rain pounding the balcony. The wind whipped strands of hair across his brow. "I'm here to speak to the lady manager."

Nathan tapped the tip of his umbrella on the porch. Water cascaded down the silk in rivulets. He fastened the tie closed, hooked the crook around his elbow, and peered at her expectantly.

Emily opened and shut her mouth, dumbfounded. What possessed Nathan to show up here, of all places?

She spun on her heel and led the way through the reception hall, her heartbeat sprinting ahead of her steps. Once she veered behind the grand staircase, she rounded on him.

"What are you doing here?" she hissed, lowering her voice. Was he *trying* to get caught?

A dimple hollowed his cheek, but his smile fell short of his eyes.

"I received a lead about the break-in when I dropped off apple fritters for Chief Ketchum's men," he leaned in, careful to keep his volume down.

His countenance was a sealed vault.

"A lead…" She swallowed the urge to laugh outright. That he hid behind a ruse threw her more than his presence did.

"Uh-huh." He propped the umbrella against the wainscoting. "I came for an interview without an appointment. Wish me luck."

Her gaze bore into him. What was he doing? Whatever the reason, it took a certain audacity to pry information under the guise of an interview. To poke around the scene Nathan fled hours ago, to say nothing of rubbing elbows with the police to learn what they knew. She might have applauded his nerve had she the stomach for pretext. Instead, it sickened her.

She ground her molars. "No need for luck. As it turns out, I filed the folder you dropped on the floor."

"*What?*" he rasped.

A look of alarm drained the color from his face.

"I know you broke in." She spoke with a firmness that belied her quivering stomach.

Nathan narrowed his eyes. "Who else knows?"

"Not the lady manager, if that's your concern," she murmured in a dry tone, unimpressed that covering his tracks was foremost on his mind.

He gripped her shoulders. "Good girl."

Emily stiffened under his touch. "Did you find what you came looking for?"

Clearing his throat, he dropped his arms to his sides. "I heard Ying Su had a son. That file verified it."

She lifted a brow. *How generous of you to share.*

"You could have gotten caught, you know."

"Almost did. The matron stirred." He tipped his head toward her room near the dormitory in the south wing. "When she got up and went to check on the boys, I dropped the folder and high-tailed it out the door."

That answered one question.

"You could have simply made proper inquiries rather than risk getting caught."

An elbow twitched at his side. "I doubt they would have told me anything since I'm no relation to the boy."

No relation. Emily's hope that Nathan would do the honorable thing hung tenuously in the balance. With it, disappointment loomed large, threatening to settle over her.

She somehow managed to sound matter-of-fact. "So … she had a son. What's that to you?"

He stuffed his hands into his trouser pockets. "I feared my father might have harmed him. I needed to see… I had to make sure her son was all right. That he was well-cared-for."

Emily took offence at the tidbits he tossed her. Had she not earned his trust?

"How *relieved* you must be to find him alive and well." Sarcasm put an edge to her words, and his eyes slanted on her.

"Yes, well … I had no idea he even existed until a few days ago."

His gaze roved her face as if he were trying to read her mood. As if her tone had thrown him off stride.

Emily itched to end this charade. Grandpa always said the best cure for trickery was a strong dose of truth.

"At what point," she bit out, careful to keep her voice down, "were you going to tell me the child might be yours? Were you ever?"

His Adam's apple bobbed up and down, his eyes widening. "Who knows who the father is," he countered.

Her lips turned down at the corners. "Have you ever laid eyes on the boy? He has your dimples, your persistence—"

He gave a firm shake, his mouth a flat seam of denial. "He is *nothing* to me."

"His *name* is Chai Lin, and I cannot abide your lack of honesty about your relationship with his mother. By your own admission, he may be your son."

"By my…? Who fed you these lies?" he scoffed, his ears reddening.

Emily folded her arms over her chest. "You forget my bird's eye view of your room."

Nathan grew still and stared straight ahead, his gaze unfocused. Was he reviewing the scene with his father?

At length, Nathan ran a hand down his mustache. "Meet me later," he sighed. "Allow me to explain."

"That may be a bit more difficult after Thursday night."

Nathan lowered his gaze. His fingers splayed on his hips, amusement crinkling his eyelids. "You are full of surprises," he murmured.

Emily shrugged a shoulder, her expression sober. "I watched you pitch your baggage off the balcony and disappear in the moonlight. I had no idea if I'd ever see you again."

"And if you hadn't … would you have missed me?"

After having forced his hand, Emily brushed aside the question. "Where are you staying?"

"On my sailboat. It's high time Mother took charge of her life and quit leaning on me to prop her up."

Emily gave a soft snort. "You can no more make a person stand on their own two feet than you can force someone to take responsibility for past mistakes."

He shot her a rueful look but said nothing.

Emily tipped her head toward the office. "The lady manager is with Colin Hensleigh. They're waiting on the police."

"What's he doing here? Did you tell him any of this?"

Emily bristled at his tone. "Odd that you should focus on him at such a time."

Nathan's lips thinned. He held up his forefinger and ordered, "Wait right here."

He walked over and rapped on the office door with his knuckles.

Emily stepped to the side of the staircase and craned her neck, keeping Nathan in her line of sight.

After a moment, the door creaked open.

"Yes?" a female voice inquired.

"Morning, ma'am," Nathan drawled. "Allow me to introduce myself. I'm Nathan Chambers from *The Daily News*. I just came from Chief Ketchum's office. He informed me that an incident occurred here during the night. A possible break-in? I'm sure you have pressing matters to attend to," he rushed to add, "but may I beg a minute of your time?"

"There's nothing to report."

"Someone did break in, correct?"

"Thus far, we have found nothing stolen."

"You suspect theft?" Nathan nodded, encouraging the woman to keep talking.

The lady manager let out a sigh. "We must be diligent in ruling it out. Now, if you'll excuse—"

"What do you suppose the person might have been after?" Nathan scratched his ear.

"It serves no purpose to speculate."

"Money?" he supplied.

"I assure you, we keep all cash under double lock and key."

"Folks want to be assured that you're meticulous with funds. That's good."

Nathan pulled a pencil and a small notepad from the pocket inside his seersucker jacket. He flipped open the pad and scratched down a few words.

"Please," she pleaded. "If nothing turns up missing, what is there to report? Consider the children. How they might be affected."

"Like you, my main concern is their welfare."

Her tone softened. "Then promise me you won't print a word unless the police verify theft. The least bit of bad publicity sticks in the minds of the public far more than a dozen good deeds."

"Fair enough." Nathan pulled open his jacket and tucked the pad and pencil away. "Mind if I stick around in case something turns up? I'll keep out of your way." He flashed his teeth in a smile.

She hesitated. "Today is a workday … with folks in and out. Your presence alone raises speculation."

He nodded. "I understand."

"Now, if you'll excuse me, I must finish."

"Ma'am," Nathan put in before she closed the door. "May I ask a favor of you in return?"

"What is it?"

"Will you keep me informed if evidence does turn up?"

The lady manager hesitated. "If anything is amiss, I will telephone you myself."

Emily stifled a groan. Nathan had led her straight to his objective: to be the first to hear should facts surface, which could pin him to the scene.

Nathan dipped his fingers in the breast pocket. He removed a business card and handed it to her.

"Thank you, Ma'am. I sincerely hope you have no reason to telephone me, and I have nothing to report."

What an understatement.

The door closed with a soft snick.

Nathan sauntered over. Smugness pulled his mouth to one side.

Nathan leaned in, his lips grazing her ear. "Come by my boat after church."

He drew back, studying her face.

Her mouth tightened. "I have lesson plans to prepare … laundry to do."

Even if she agreed, she couldn't slip away unnoticed.

"Monday evening then," he pressed. "You deserve an explanation."

Emily hugged her elbows in front of her waist, sorely tempted. "And what shall I tell my aunt?"

He gave a half-shrug. "Run an errand. Then go by the Mosquito Fleet at Pier 19." She knew of the immigrant fleet that swarmed the harbor on their treks in from the Gulf. "Pick up fresh shrimp or oysters off the boats and take them to the house. She'll never suspect a thing."

It bothered her that Nathan had kept things from her, again. But she needed answers, more than what she learned from the orphan files. His boat would offer privacy for their meeting, at least. Still, she couldn't help but wonder whether his sailboat had been where he'd met with Ying Su. The very idea made her stomach burn.

"Monday evening then," Nathan confirmed, taking her silence to mean consent.

From under lowered brows, Emily met his gaze. "Do not presume—"

The doorbell echoed through the reception hall.

"Ugh! The police," she grimaced. "Go out the side door."

As she spun toward the entrance, he caught hold of her hand.

"Monday," he persisted. He reached up and cupped her cheek with his calloused palm. "Don't give up on me."

Reaching for his umbrella, he grabbed it by the crook and headed up the hall.

Don't give up on me… The words were a barb to her heart. What was she supposed to do?

Emily marched briskly to the entrance, her mind whirling. She needed to find out what Colin knew about Chai Lin's father. Soon. Fortunately, people poured out their troubles to ministers every day. Maybe someone had confided in Colin the day Ying Su gave birth to her son.

Emily reached the door before anyone got up off the floor. Gripping the doorknob, she paused to gather her wits.

Nathan showing up unannounced had rattled her. She was in no frame of mind to make a formal statement, but what choice did she have?

Emily braced for a barrage of questions about to pelt her. Tucking her emotions behind a calm mask, she swung open the door.

The freshening wind gusts blew damp air and tossed wisps of hair in her eyes. She brushed them aside.

An officer shuffled his feet on the wide portico as he surveyed the sheets of rain, his back to her.

"Sir," she called out over the downpour hammering the balcony.

The man peered over his shoulder at her. Emily chewed on her upper lip to conceal the grin threatening to bloom. She couldn't believe her good fortune.

Chapter 25

Water dripped from the officer's nose onto his protruding belly. His uniform, soaking wet, stuck to his skin. He turned and faced Emily.

"I'm here about the burglary," Roland Pickering informed her.

Emily stepped aside as he shuffled over the threshold.

"Right this way," she lowered her voice to avoid the women eavesdropping.

Emily led the way through the reception hall, a smile strung wide across her face, lifting her cheeks. What providence that he had come alone. The man smelled of moldy socks, tobacco, and inferiority. Chief Ketchum's finest, he was not.

Behind the grand staircase, the man cleared his throat. "Say, ma'am, have you seen my aunt? She's in charge of this workday."

"She's occupied with stocking the pantry at the moment," Emily pointed up the hall to her left.

Through the office door, she heard Colin say her name. As she rapped on the door, the minister paused mid-sentence.

"Come in," the lady manager summoned.

Colin, seated in the armchair beside the door, rose to his feet as Emily entered with Officer Pickering. He reached over and closed the door. The officer strode to the center of the room while she hung back by Colin, her eyes fixed on the lady manager.

In the far corner, the woman crouched in front of the file cabinet, the bottom drawer pulled out.

The bottom drawer.

Emily's breath hitched in her throat.

The woman was leafing through files, her elbows angled at her sides, the wet hem of her blue dress mopping the wood floor. She glanced over her shoulder at them before her fingers returned to walking over the ridges of files.

"I'm here about the burglary," Officer Pickering announced.

"Thank you, officer." The woman didn't look up. "At this point, it's premature to call it one. I've found nothing missing, much less stolen."

"Nothing, huh?" The officer worked his jaw as his eyes drifted to the doorknob.

"Bear with me. I'm not finished, and I must be thorough."

The officer gave an impatient huff. "Any clues so far?"

"Whoever broke in picked the lock on the desk and found the key to the file drawers."

"What's in the cabinet?"

"Petty cash, among other things."

"Money all there?"

"Every cent," the woman said crisply.

"Anything else important?"

"Well, yes … orphan records."

Officer Pickering snorted, his belly jiggling over his belt. "No crook breaks in for those."

The woman peered over her shoulder. Her gray eyes appraised him behind her gold-rimmed glasses. "Are you ruling it out before I finish perusing the files?"

He dragged a hand down the stubble on his double chin and glanced at the door. "Ma'am, the east end, it's flooded. To top it off, we started the day short-handed. So unless you've got something worth swiping in those drawers, I'm needed back at the station."

Emily hoped that pressure from the chief made him careless enough to forget getting her statement altogether.

The woman pinned him with a stare. "I don't think you grasp the importance of orphan records. They contain personal information on each child admitted, on their family, where they're—"

"Listen, little lady," Officer Pickering said, "Nobody cares about your orphan files."

Emily sensed Colin's eyes settle on her. She glanced at him, spying an odd look creasing his face. What just went through his mind? Did he suspect Nathan of breaking in? Or was he remembering the day he admitted Chai Lin into the home?

Officer Pickering tapped his foot, now pointed toward the door. "Ma'am, we're short-handed," he repeated.

The lady manager's mouth flattened. "Were you even going to take this young lady's statement?"

Emily tensed. Her pulse kicked up.

"Forgive my manners," the woman addressed her. Unfolding her legs, she stood and gazed at Emily. "I'm Esther Dawson."

"Emily Cleburne, ma'am."

Esther peered down her nose at the officer, waiting.

Officer Pickering turned to Emily and scratched the stubble along his jaw. "What's your story, miss?"

Emily cleared her throat. "Like I told Mr. Hensleigh, I found the office in a mess. It appeared someone broke in."

"About what time was that?"

"Early. The children were eating breakfast."

"See anyone nosing around?"

"No, sir. Not a soul."

"Any idea of who might have done this?"

She kept her expression neutral. "I saw or heard no one acting suspicious."

Satisfied, the officer strode toward the door, jangling the handcuffs clipped to his belt. "Well, if you think of anything ... anything at all."

Esther's lips thinned. "If you're *finished*, I have a few questions."

Emily's chest sank. Must the woman be so meticulous?

Officer Pickering stalled by the door, his fingers drumming on the knob.

Esther walked over to the desk and leaned back against the edge. "I'm curious how you discovered the room had been disturbed," she began in a conversational tone.

Emily hid her trembling hands in the folds of her dress and willed herself to meet the woman's steady gaze. "I happened upon it."

"The door was left ajar? You saw inside?"

"No, ma'am, but I saw the light on."

"Did you find the room unlocked?"

"The intruder must have left in a hurry," Emily supplied.

Esther removed her spectacles and set them on the desktop. She weaved her fingers in front of her blue dress, her thumbs tapping together. "So, you found the door unlocked, the light on." She lifted a shoulder. "Why poke your head inside?"

"The folded clothes were piling," Emily said smoothly, just as she had rehearsed it. "I had no idea where to put them." All true. The clothes *were* piling before Jake toppled them, and she had no clue where the outfits belonged.

"Mr. Hensleigh tells me you're here for the workday."

"Yes, ma'am."

"Hmm. And did you knock?"

Emily blinked. "Pardon?"

"On the door. Did you knock?" Esther repeated.

Tension constricted the muscles around Emily's vocal cords. She swallowed. "Who enters a room without knocking?"

The woman's thumbs ceased their tapping and pressed together. "So you knocked but heard no answer yet barged into the room uninvited?"

Emily swallowed hard. "Well, I … I reckon I acted a tad impulsively."

The woman's eyes probed beneath her flimsy excuse. "That you did," Esther's mouth firmed with disapproval. "Are you in the habit of acting impulsively?"

Emily had trouble hearing due to the blood rushing in her ears. All at once, the walls pressed in. Her skin flushed hot. She glanced at the door, the urge to leave surging strong.

An elbow brushed her sleeve.

"Mrs. Dawson," Colin broke in, "I personally asked Miss Cleburne to assist the committee."

The lilting of her name steadied the tremor vibrating through her limbs. Emily leaned into the shelter of his strength, away from the glare of being exposed.

She noticed the gentle curve of his mouth as he spoke about her role as governess to the Edwards' children, of her sacrificing Saturdays to ready supplies for the school year. In doing so, he eloquently tucked her reputation behind his credibility. When he finished, he gave her a slight nod of encouragement.

Buoyed by his support, Emily flashed him a grateful look and pounced on his lead.

"Yes … well, I planned to finish restocking the closet today. But when I saw all those clothes dumped on top of the school supplies, I'm afraid it got the better of me. Not that that excuses my acting forward," Emily rushed to add. She mustered a look of remorse for good measure.

Esther pressed her palms on the desk's surface and continued to regard Emily until she fought the urge to squirm.

Esther tipped her head. "I thought you looked familiar." She waved a hand. "They go in the right-wing upstairs."

"Come again?" Emily's brows drew together, missing her meaning.

"The children's clothes. They go in the large room upstairs, off to the right."

Emily recovered. "Much obliged, ma'am."

Officer Pickering's hand tightened around the doorknob. "Well, I'm needed back at the station."

Without waiting for a reply, he ducked out of the room.

Emily cleared her throat, bent on following his lead. "Any more questions, ma'am?"

Esther Dawson brushed her blonde bangs out of her eyes as she studied Emily a moment longer. "No. No, you may go."

Emily and Colin exchanged a look before she walked out of the door.

Up the hallway, Officer Pickering clomped toward the pantry, searching for his aunt. He wasn't too concerned about the office being short-handed. The man probably earned every reprimand that the chief dished out.

The clock gonged at half past ten. Emily wandered across the hall, needing a moment of privacy. The fragrance of yeast filled the corridor. She licked her lips and looked forward to biting into the crusty sourdough, warm from the oven.

Stepping into the lavatory, she went to the sink and turned on the faucet. She leaned her elbows against the smooth porcelain and let the water gurgle through her fingers, cool and bubbly, sluicing down the drain.

At last, the dreaded ordeal was over. Officer Pickering had no concern over who broke in, only what the thief might have taken. And when no money turned up missing, his interest evaporated. In the end, Nathan and Chai Lin remained protected. She even managed to get through questioning with her dignity intact.

Thanks to Colin.

He'd acted like a true friend. By speaking up on her behalf, he'd tossed her a lifeline. He deserved more respect and admiration than she paid him. Perhaps she had been too hasty when she discarded earning his esteem.

Emily turned off the faucet and rolled her shoulders until the muscles around her neck began to loosen.

What next? Maybe she could finagle time to talk with Colin in private. Today, if possible. There had to be a way to discuss Chai Lin without raising suspicion.

She examined her reflection in the mirror above the sink. Color rose high in her cheeks. With dampened fingers, she smoothed the stray copper wisps back in place.

She recalled something Chai Lin had once told her. It was just the thing to coax the story out of Colin.

∞

As Emily strode through the reception hall toward the library, lightning flashed through the towering arched windows. She flinched as thunder boomed overhead and shook the panes.

Behind her, the bully, Reese, whooped from the stairs. "Water's coming up the road!"

His announcement sent arms and legs bending as the women scrambled to get up off the floor to have a look. Emily joined them, huddled around the windowpane, staring out front.

"Why, I declare," Minnie murmured. "Overflows nearly to Avenue M. Streetcars will shut down, sure as the world."

Through the rainfall, Emily stared past the iron fence. The tidewater foamed in choppy waves past the front door, lapping higher up the road.

"This far inland?" Her breath came in puffs, fogging the glass. How was that possible? The orphanage was a good six to eight blocks from the beach.

Ida's chocolate eyes peered sideways at her. "We may get the tail end of the tropical storm after all."

"*What* tropical storm?" Emily gaped at the others. How had she missed hearing the news? And why hadn't someone warned her before she sent the children with Lena? "Surely you don't mean a hurricane," her voice struck a terse note, despite efforts to keep it steady.

"Not all gales turn into one of *those*," Ida assured her in a tone reserved for folks not born on the island. Her tone suggested that Emily was blowing everything out of proportion.

A cluster of hazel, blue, and brown eyes peered askance at her. Emily scanned the other women's faces. Aside from Minnie, there were no opened-mouth stares or murmuring among them. Nothing to indicate the least startle over Ida's news.

Their subtle smirks reminded her of times when being a Cleburne barred her from fitting in. Emily ignored them and faced the window.

Rain slanted in streaks across the glass. Colin's horse whinnied. The chestnut mare pulled hard against the reins, tethering her to the hitching post. The tide splashed the horse's legs and covered a third of the buggy wheels.

The downpour was pounding the white caps until they flattened like hammered tin. Gulf water now swelled in the street and filled the gutters. It roiled with brown sediment between the fence slats and seeped into the yard, where the orphans had played sandball the previous Saturday.

A child's toy sailboat buffeted against the tide in the street, propelled by the wind. The mast had snapped in two, and the sails bent and flapped.

Every instinct warned Emily to leave before the tidewater barred the way home. But the children had not returned yet, and the closet remained unfinished.

If only she had read the weather forecast. The inch or two of the daily column only took a minute to scan. Instead, she'd combed the paper for news on Hayden Chambers all week.

The clock gonged eleven strokes.

Emily peered over her shoulder at the clicking of heels. Colin strode toward the entrance. By the door, the minister plucked his umbrella from the hall tree.

"Are you leaving, Reverend? I made your favorite. Chocolate cake," Ida called, coaxing him to stay.

Distracted, Colin peered out the oblong pane in the door at his mare neighing above the wind.

He turned to Ida. "I beg your pardon, but I must move my horse."

The minister ducked out onto the porch, letting in a blast of dampness that smelled of wet sand. Emily watched him battle his umbrella and lean into the stiffening wind.

Colin plowed through the gate and sloshed up to the mare. He untied the reins with one hand when lightning flared white-hot and veined across the sky. Thunder crackled like a flame to dry kindling. Wild-eyed, the horse brayed and reared up on its hind legs. The mare dropped to all fours, thrashing her mane from side to side, jerking hard on the leather straps until the reins slackened in Colin's grip.

Then the horse bolted straight into the wind after jerking free, racing up 21st Street. The buggy jostled behind her, away from Colin and the unbridled tide.

Chapter 26

Emily turned from the window as the minister came through the door. With his jaw clenched, he jerked the umbrella closed and plopped it down on the umbrella stand, stamping the water from his wingtips on the floor mat.

Colin tossed a wet thatch of hair off his forehead and peered at the women still pressed close to the window. His eyes lit on each face, searching. He frowned.

With forced restraint, he asked, "Where's Grace?"

Grace! Emily winced and pattered over to him. "I—I meant to tell you sooner. Grace went with Lena and the kids to see the waves. They're at the Keslers' home, just till noon."

Colin scrubbed a hand over his face. The skin glistening under his eyes tightened. Meeting her gaze, he let out a heavy sigh.

Her chin puckered with sympathy. "Too bad about your horse."

"Perhaps Sadie will turn up at the parsonage."

Emily glanced through the rectangular panes flanking the doorway. Charcoal clouds rolled like billowing soot, smudging the sky.

Colin eyed the scene as he flicked water off the sleeves of his blazer with the backs of his fingers. "I do hope they don't tarry. I don't like Gracie being out in this."

Emily compressed her lips. Why tell him that she sent Grace with Lena? In less than an hour, his sister would come strolling through the door with the others.

"She'll be back soon," Emily murmured.

Colin nodded absently. "Excuse me, but I must ring my neighbor about my horse and buggy."

He strode through the reception hall, his shoes squishing a wet trail of imprints behind him.

Emily rejoined the circle of women around the pile, where a quarter of the mound was now in neat stacks.

"…headed up the eastern coast," Minnie was saying. "Georgia or South Carolina, most likely."

"Not according to the morning paper. It's changed course," Ida informed them. "It's due to hit somewhere east of Texas. That storm has already caused no little damage in Mississippi and parts of Louisiana."

No little damage? Hair tingled at the back of Emily's neck. What if the storm veered further west? Minnie's eyes went out of focus while the others appeared unaffected by the news. What was wrong with these people? Colin's spooked mare showed more sense than they did!

Emily recalled hearing about the corpses strewn on the beach. She wanted to tell them about Mosey Pitts' mother dying in another storm but held her tongue. She didn't want to be viewed by the locals as prone to hysterics.

Minnie voiced aloud Emily's fears. "What if the storm reaches Texas?"

"I weathered the storms of '75 and '86," Ida boasted. "Now, *those* were hurricanes. I'd wager this is nothing more than an outer squall."

"I hope you're right," Minnie muttered without conviction. Her eyes roamed the ceiling. "I'd feel better, though, if this place hadn't been struck by lightning, twice. When building the home, lightning killed that worker, remember?"

Heads nodded around the pile.

"This orphanage is safer than our homes," Ida assured them.

"Still…" Minnie worried the corner of her lip. "Reckon we ought to leave while the streetcars are still running? I'm not walking home in this."

The women fell silent and kept their eyes trained on the top of the pile as they plucked out garments and folded them.

Miss Pickering treaded into the library, apparently finished with stocking the pantry.

Ida glanced up at her. "What brought Roland by?"

"Nothing of importance," Miss Pickering sniffed. "An utter waste of time, as it turned out. Of all days."

Miss Pickering peered down her nose at Emily as if the woman held her responsible for the weather soaking Roland to the skin.

Miss Pickering sat down beside Ida and reached for a shirt. "Roland said the water's rising on the east end. They'll send the patrol wagon to take folks to higher ground if this keeps up."

Higher ground? Emily's tongue stuck to the roof of her mouth. *What* higher ground? The island was nothing more than a sloping sandbar from the beach to Broadway Boulevard.

A prickling sensation crept over her scalp. Emily snatched up a gown, rubbing the bottom ruffle between her fingers. Images flashed of the toy sailboat pitching against the tidewater, of Colin's horse racing into the wind away from the encroaching overflow. What tide rose against the wind? Wouldn't a northerly wind push the tidewater out to sea, not flood the town? What did all this mean?

The clock gonged the twelfth hour, and the dinner bell clanged. One by one, the women drifted from the room.

Outside, the wind howled as rain poured down in torrents. Emily got up and went and stood by the window.

Where were Lena and the children? They should have returned by now. She pinched the skin at her throat and peered southward toward Lena's little cottage, watching a palm frond whisk past her view.

In the yard, oak trees shivered like paupers, yearning for a place to take shelter, the wind stripping leaves off their bony limbs. Closer still, patches of spindrift marbled the tidewater lapping at the bottom steps.

At last, a hack rattled to a stop out front. The leather sides trembled in the wind as the water rippled over the wheel hubs.

There they are. Emily let out a sigh of relief.

A full minute passed, but still, no one filed out.

The lady manager padded through the reception hall and out the front door, her umbrella bending in the wind. She waded to the hack with the back of her hem dragging the water.

Emily watched the wheels throw up the spray as the carriage rolled up the road.

The clock rang a quarter past twelve.

Emily entwined her hands and watched for the next street car, waiting for one to deposit Lena, Grace, and the children at the curb. Yet none trundled down the road. What on earth was keeping them?

Emily noticed an odd pressure building in her ears. It crinkled like tissue paper. She worked her jaw, but still, the pressure did not ease.

A tapping sound echoed through the reception hall, coming near. Emily threw a glance over one shoulder and watched Colin enter the library. Deep creases bracketed his mouth.

"Grace will be here soon," Emily forced a smile. It felt brittle.

"I'd rather she stay put until this passes."

He came alongside her. Colin peered out the window. He ran a finger inside the collar on his striped shirt as if the detachable band had him in a vise grip. His anxiety did nothing to ease the pressure building around her ribcage, where her stays felt too tight.

Emily tilted her head toward the windowpane. "You grew up by the sea. What sense do you make of overflows, given the direction of the wind?"

Colin scratched the scar above his eyebrow and studied the southeasterly winds now gusting at gale force. He shook his head. "It's unlike anything I've ever seen."

They lapsed into silence, their stiff postures mirroring rigid reflections in the pane of glass.

She sensed Colin eyeing her profile. She peered sideways and met his gaze. She saw his clear-eyed appraisal, like a pawnbroker examining a gold ring to determine its purity and worth.

"On a positive note," he watched her closely, "Mrs. Dawson found nothing missing from the office."

"That—that's good." Emily blinked and looked away.

What did Colin think as he gauged her reaction to the news? Did he suspect that she knew more than she revealed to Esther Dawson? Why cover for her in front of the lady manager if that were true?

Her insides quivered. Feeling trapped and vulnerable under his scrutiny, she watched the rainwater thrash the glass and bleed into horizontal rows like liquid barbed wire.

"Mr. Chambers came by earlier," he went on. "I couldn't help but overhear his conversation with Mrs. Dawson. It seems he already knew of the trespasser. It was most generous of him to refrain from reporting the news for the children's sake, since nothing turned up stolen. Rather self-sacrificing of the chap, wouldn't you agree?"

At his persistence, her right eyelid drooped.

Emily tried switching subjects. "Hmm… It's been a while since a trolley went by. Do you suppose they've quit running?"

"One would think that a reporter—"

"Isn't that Mr. Kesler?"

Suppressing a sigh, Emily pointed at the man treading down 21st Street.

Lena's husband leaned back into the wind with a hand pressed flat on top of his Boater. He slogged past the iron gate in knee-deep water and up the orphanage steps. Colin opened the door and let Peter in, releasing a blast of wet air inside.

Peter removed his raincoat and hooked his straw hat and coat on the hall tree pegs. "I've nearly sold out of bread, cinnamon sticks, and streusel. Given the steady flow of customers, I should have stayed put, but Lena insisted we dine together."

Colin paused. "We're expecting her momentarily."

Peter frowned. "She's not here?" He raked his fingers through his hair. "Let me ring the house," he muttered, heading through the reception hall.

Colin joined Emily at the window. "I suppose we ought to join the others before the food grows cold."

Emily allowed Colin to lead her into the dining hall, though hunger had faded to a dull ache.

Minutes later, Peter scooted the bow-back chair up to the table across from Emily.

"Lena can't get away," he announced over the hum of voices. He dropped a white napkin on his lap, lowering his head.

The morning sickness must have persisted.

With a fork, Emily pushed food around on her plate and carved a trench between the purple hull peas and the clump of sauerkraut. She nibbled on a slice of sourdough bread.

From down the table, Miss Pickering peered around Ida. "Mr. Kesler, your wife isn't feeling ill again, I pray. Roland mentioned she fainted during the parade."

Peter's gaze flicked up and fastened on Miss Pickering. "The boys merely dragged their feet coming indoors."

Emily chewed her bottom lip. "Surely Lena called them in when the storm worsened."

Peter ate a mouthful of sauerkraut and swallowed. "When she woke from her nap, they weren't in the yard or the street."

"Where do you suppose they scampered off to?" Colin asked.

"Who knows? Lena said something about a quest for some chest or some such nonsense."

That child! A vein throbbed down the middle of Emily's forehead. She drew her mouth into a flat seam. Jake better not have led Andrew out searching for a treasure chest in this weather. Undoubtedly the heavy rain ought to flush them indoors soon.

Colin dabbed his mouth with his napkin, observing Emily. "If I had my horse and buggy, I'd search for them."

"I'm sure they're fine." Peter dove into the bread basket for the crusty end of the sourdough. "Probably sitting on a neighbor's gallery, as drenched as alley cats but otherwise unscathed."

A tolerant smile pulled at his mouth, showing a gap between his front teeth.

At the far end of the table, Minnie spoke up. "Sir, what news have you heard of the storm?"

Everyone looked up expectantly from their plates.

Peter glanced around the table. "Bits and pieces have trickled in all morning." He shifted in his seat. "The waves tore up and twisted a railway trestle near the beach."

Emily stared open-mouthed at Peter. What kind of force ripped railings from the ground as though they weighed no more than the tracks from Jake's tin train set? She peered at the women. Their pinched faces mirrored their alarm.

"What about downtown," Minnie pressed.

Peter took a bite of bread, stalling, as though none of what he had to say made for pleasant dinner conversation.

"Water's rising on the Strand," he went on. "The weatherman poked his head in earlier and advised the merchants to put all staples onto higher shelves. Some of the shops are closing early."

Around the table, the women exchanged looks. It took more than hard rain and overflows to force men to quit work early.

Minnie twisted a piece of bread in her hands, her voice thin and tight. "What about the east side?"

"Refugees were pouring up Broadway from the east end when I crossed the boulevard." Peter looked at the group, gauging their reactions. "Aside from a few panic-stricken females," his eyes settled on Minnie, "folks were toting clothes and bedding, their children skipping ahead and playing in the rain."

He smiled stiffly, attempting to lighten the mood.

"You can't tell me it's safe to be out in this," Minnie countered, shredding her bread into doughy clumps.

Peter ran his tongue along his front teeth, looking as though he was reining in his impatience. "I dodged a bit of shattered glass falling from the upper windows along the Strand, but as you can see, I made it here without a scratch."

"Let the man eat," Ida chided, patting Minnie on the wrist. "There's a cake for dessert."

Around the table, the lull in conversation was broken only by the scrape of forks against plates.

Overhead, the lights flickered off and on, and then the dining hall plunged into murky shadows.

⸻

Candles burned in their globes around the tables, the food uneaten. The matron had managed to hush the children's squeals. She'd ordered them to finish eating, but only a few older children were feeding their younger siblings.

"Well, I'm off to the bakery," Peter announced, pushing to his feet. "I'm sure Lena will bring the kids by once the boys get in."

Emily rubbed her cheek. "What if the weather worsens?"

He lifted a shoulder. "They're welcome to spend the night. I'll drop them off at first light."

Emily watched Peter troop out of the room.

At the head of the table, Colin gained his feet. "Please excuse me. I must secure all the shutters. Then I plan to retire to the office and review my sermon. I do not wish to be disturbed except for when Grace arrives."

Emily slumped against the chair slats. There went her chance to talk with him about what he might know about Chai Lin's father.

One of the women had called for a hack. When the carriage finally arrived, they streamed out of the dining hall, except Miss Pickering, Ida, and Minnie. Minnie's mouth crimped with resentment when she learned that the hack lacked room for one more.

Emily's shoulders drooped as she watched her help bail out into the dusky hallway. More work now fell on the few who remained. How long would it take them to finish? She propped an elbow on the table, her chin heavy on her palm.

She may be a newcomer to the island, but the women's pattering feet confirmed this much: the storm was no mere overflow, no outer squall.

Miss Pickering reappeared in the doorway after slipping out into the hallway earlier. She stood on tiptoe and called to the line of women, ordering them to return to the dining hall. They shuffled back and formed a half-circle around Miss Pickering, murmuring behind their hands.

Emily got up from the table with Ida and Minnie and joined the others.

Miss Pickering clutched a globed light in one hand, her eyes gleaming. She raised a hand, hushing the group.

"I've just telephoned the police station," she informed them. "I'm afraid I have some rather disturbing news."

Chapter 27

Miss Pickering scanned the women's widening eyes, making sure that she had gained their full attention. "The bathhouses and shell houses are all breaking apart. All the lunchrooms along the shore—smashed to bits by the waves."

Emily's lips parted, her cold fingertips covering her mouth. It stood to reason why the covered bathhouses had shattered. They jutted out on pilings over the surf, but the other buildings edging the Gulf?

"And the trolleys," Miss Pickering reported, "they've all quit running."

"Oh, I knew it," Minnie moaned, wringing her hands. "Send the hack back for me. I won't walk home in this. I won't!"

Miss Pickering bristled at the outburst. She glared at Minnie until the woman lowered her eyes to the floorboards.

Lightning pierced through the gloom, flashing in the windows. The sky growled a low-throated rumble, causing the watercolor seascapes to quiver on the walls.

"There's more," Miss Pickering raised her voice to recapture the women's wandering gazes. "Even the trains to the mainland are canceled, all of them. Water's flowing too deep over the tracks across the bay."

All too vividly, Emily recalled gripping hold of the armrests as the train rattled over the bay bridge above the water. Water that now covered those very rails. A shudder ran through her body.

"Those poor people stranded on the east end," Miss Pickering clucked her tongue. "Their cottages are washing away."

Heat rose behind Emily's eyelids. This was *not* happening.

"I begged Roland to stay put at the station," Miss Pickering went on. "Let the younger men go. But would he listen to reason? He was first to volunteer to man the patrol wagon and rounded up those folks."

Miss Pickering fell silent, staring off with a watery gaze, her brow drawn together.

The semicircle of women closed in and formed a tight huddle, all talking at once.

Their voices grated on Emily. *Forget the work day. Hunt down Jake, grab Sarah, and get home while you still can!*

An image rose, of wading down the flooded streets calling Jake's name over the wind, the rain stinging her face.

Even if she knew where to look, a greater fear kept her frozen in place. If the overflow was knee-deep on Avenue M, how deep had the tide swelled down on Avenue O or beyond it to the beach?

A wail cut through her worrying. "There's no way off this island! We're all trapped!"

"Minnie Parker, pull yourself together," Ida scolded, her wattle jiggling under her chin. "There's no sense in blowing this thing out of proportion. Didn't Mr. Kesler tell us he saw entire families coming up Broadway? Why, during the storm of '75, folks were outside walking the streets by the hundreds, including me."

Shame silenced Minnie as she hunched her shoulders and retreated from view.

Emily rubbed her forehead. Ida had a point. Why blow things out of proportion? Despite the deteriorating conditions, refugees were out seeking dry shelter in the storm. At least the boys weren't out there alone. And neither the Edwards nor the Keslers lived on the far east end of town. Things could be worse.

"Let's ride out the storm here," Ida implored. "We can all finish what we started."

But Ida's encouragement failed to dissuade the rest of the women from filing out of the dining room, putting on their bonnets and gloves, and loading into the waiting carriage.

That afternoon the tide flooded the yard. It coiled on the bricks below the windows and washed over the bottom stairs.

Inside, the kerosene lamp and globed candles pushed the shadows into the corners of the library while the walls creaked and moaned.

The women pecked at the pile of clothing for hours, eroding deep dents in the mound while Emily filled and emptied a wooden box with items from the school supply shipment.

From time to time, Minnie ceased chattering about quilting patterns to crane her neck and listen for her ride, but no hack pulled up out front to take her home.

The clock gonged three times when a shutter wrenched from the window casing, banging against the brick before it blew off. Emily got up and went and peered out at the deepening sky. It had grown dark as twilight.

She squinted through the cascading rainfall as objects whizzed by. A baluster railing spun end over end like a flying baton. Deadly slates from roofs sliced through the air like meat cleavers. Her chest tightened.

Beyond the front gate, movement caught her eye. Like plucking up a weed, the wind tore the roots of a live oak from the sand and lobbed the tree onto its side.

In the street, barrels, crates, and other wreckage bumped and flowed in the river of debris. The brackish water had risen rapidly since the last time Emily looked.

The storm showed no sign of letting up, either. The stronger gusts rocked the walls and silenced the women's voices, except Minnie's. The woman kept up a string of ceaseless chatter.

The racket drove Emily from the room. She hoisted the box brimming with supplies and grabbed a globed candle on the way out. She set the box inside the supply closet and went to the telephone anchored to the wall.

Perhaps the boys had returned by now. Emily desperately needed to hear that Jake and Andrew were dry, sipping hot chocolate indoors, safe and sound. Then maybe her pulse would slow to its normal rhythm instead of skipping erratically.

Emily set the candle on the ledge, placed the trumpet-shaped earpiece up to her ear, and cranked the handle. She waited for the operator's voice to come on the line and direct the call.

Nothing. Nothing but dead silence.

The orphans romped up the stair from the basement, the older ones carrying globed candles. Over the squeaking of wet feet, their voices echoed up the stairwell. One by one, they bounded into the hallway.

"Be quick," the matron called from the rear. "You may finish your games in the attic where it's dry."

Single file, they tromped up the next flight. Chai Lin turned and waved before he fell in step with the others. From the sound of the children's slick feet, the tidewater must have gushed into the basement. None of them seemed the least bit concerned.

Emily's fingers tingled at the nail beds. If she knew how to swim, flooded rooms would be less daunting. She was thankful for the sturdy building that soared stories above her head.

Emily wet her lips and cranked the handle a second time. Squinting, she listened intently. She tapped her foot, waiting. Still, no operator's voice came on the line. Puzzled, she set the earpiece in the cradle and walked away.

If only she had called Lena earlier that afternoon. Now she had no way of knowing whether the boys were underfoot. Surely they would be by now. Wouldn't they?

Heaving a sigh, Emily entered the closet and set the brass candleholder on the ledge above her elbow. She peered down the long shelves and took a moment to soak in the closet's golden stillness. Last month, this closet had been a prison cell that she shared with Miss Pickering. Now its warmth and solitude calmed her over-stimulated senses. Here the sharp wind sounded muffled. She took a slow breath and collected herself, grateful to be away from Minnie's constant fretting.

The click-clicking of shoes passed by the door, left cracked open, but she paid no heed to who passed by.

Emily checked off the items in the box against the inventory list and filled the empty spaces on the shelves with the new supplies. On the lower middle shelf, someone had stowed an old cigar box. She lifted the lid. It contained odds and ends: pencil stubs, a rusty spinning top, and a wooden yo-yo with a broken string.

Emily pulled out the box, took a step back, and examined where to set it out of the way. There, the top left corner. She hefted the box over her head and shoved it onto the shelf.

A slight draft brushed the back of her neck. She caught a whiff of something sweet and buttery. Emily peered over her shoulder, curious about who shuffled in behind her.

Colin stood in the doorway holding two small dessert plates in his hands. Chocolate sliced cake, the cake that Ida baked.

"I noticed you ate very little earlier," he said casually. "I thought you might enjoy a slice, too."

Emily lowered her arms and turned to face him.

"Thanks," she gave a wan smile and took the plate. "I'm afraid I didn't have much appetite."

She still didn't, but the break gave them a chance to have a private conversation.

The bridge of Colin's nose crinkled. "In all honesty, I needed to eat something to get rid of the lingering taste of sauerkraut."

Colin leaned against the wall by the partly open door and crossed his feet.

The candlelight shadowed his cheekbones and the cleft in his clean-shaven chin.

He ate the cake while Emily sampled a decadent bite.

"It's a good thing I battened down the hatches earlier," he said, licking frosting off his lips. "I fear there's more to come." He lifted a brow, making clear his point.

Emily rocked slightly on her feet. "I tried calling Lena a few minutes ago. No operator. Perhaps they all went home early."

Colin shook his head. "I daresay the wind blew down the lines."

Now they had no way of hearing any further news or contacting loved ones. Those downed lines isolated them from the rest of the island. What was happening to her family?

Emily had difficulty swallowing the sticky morsel in her throat. She blinked and tried to refocus.

The minister regarded her for a long moment. "This has been quite a day for you, hasn't it?"

"Yes, well…" She pulled her head back a little, feeling the need to put more space between them. "Now to finish this closet."

In the soft light, his eyes appeared sober, clear of judgment. On his lips, another question puckered.

"The children just cleared out from the basement," Emily cut in. "Looks like water has leaked inside, not that it has dampened Chai Lin's spirits. That child is a trouper."

She pushed a cube of cake around on the plate with the fork tongs. "The day you brought sodas by the home, Chai Lin said something. Something about him owing you his life. What did he mean by that, exactly?"

Colin studied her for a long moment. He took another mouthful of cake while he seemed to mull over the question.

Emily's pulse hitched. She lifted a shoulder in a shrug. "It sounded like a good story, is all."

The minister turned so he could look her full in the face. Emily sensed that he not only measured her question but also wanted to see her reaction to his answer.

He lowered his voice. "The midwife who delivered the boy was our housekeeper's aunt. Flora often assisted her aunt with the more difficult deliveries. She did so on that night. When Flora feared his mother lay dying of hemorrhage, she called for me."

"Did you … arrive in time?"

He nodded grimly. "After we prayed, she begged me to take her son somewhere safe. So I brought him here."

Emily reached deep for a bland expression. "Didn't the mother have other kin who could have looked after him?"

Colin watched her from under lowered brows. "She had a sister. A showgirl, by the looks of her. Clearly not someone in any position to care for an infant."

A band of pressure squeezed Emily's temples. She cleared her dry throat. "What about the boy's father? Where was he?" she pressed.

Colin's eyes narrowed. He studied her with such single-focused intensity that she almost looked away. Instead, she held his gaze while he perused her face. She grew more unsettled the longer he scanned the stiff set of her mouth, the tightness underlining her eyes. Could he also read the turmoil beneath the surface or her motive for asking such a question?

His pinched expression suggested as much. Colin set the half-eaten cake on the shelf. He reached over, nudged the door shut, and leaned forward a little, keeping his feet crossed.

"I'm curious what you know about the father," Colin inquired, careful to keep his tone mild.

Chapter 28

Emily drew back until the shelf dug into her shoulder blade. She glanced at the brass knob. If only the closet were less narrow, the air less thick and close. What drove Colin to ignore propriety and shut the door?

"H-how would I know anything?" Emily stammered.

With the edge of her fork, she minced the chocolate wedge into bite-sized cubes.

"Of that, I'm uncertain," Colin kept his voice even, "but you have your suspicions. Am I correct?"

Emily speared a piece and stuffed it in her mouth. She barely tasted the bittersweet frosting or the moist cake.

Out of loyalty to Nathan, she said nothing.

"Do pardon my asking," Colin said with disarming gentleness, "but did you search for answers while you were in the office?"

Emily's eyes widened. How had he pieced that together?

"I presume you got wind of some rather disturbing hearsay," Colin went on. "Enough to merit searching for the name of Chai Lin's father."

Her elbow bumped the shelf, jiggling her plate. Emily tightened her grip on the china before it slipped from her hand. She gritted her teeth, hating how his probing affected her or that he noticed.

"But you found no such name in the boy's records," he probed.

It wasn't a question.

Emily squared her shoulders. "You cannot possibly think I broke into that file cabinet," she summoned enough heat in her tone to cover the desperation tightening her chest.

Colin lifted an eyebrow in challenge. "I'm merely suggesting that you gave in to the temptation of an already opened drawer and sought to verify the name."

A peal of thunder growled. Abruptly, the floor rumbled and quaked. Next to Emily's ear, a box of protractors jangled a tinny sound. It further rattled her.

Their eyes locked.

"Whose name?" she heard herself say, uncaring that it revealed the ulterior motive behind her being in the office. At this point, clearing Nathan's name was all that mattered.

"Upon my word," Colin vowed, "the mother refused to disclose the chap's name."

Ugh! He knew less than she hoped, probably less than she did. Emily glared at a glossy chocolate swirl and grazed off a fat glob. She stuffed it into her mouth, disgusted that she had let slip more than she had intended, disgusted with Colin for pressuring her.

"As it turned out," Colin continued evenly, "my housekeeper heard plenty."

Her eyes riveted on him. "Go on," she prompted, around the gooey mouthful.

"After I left, Flora and her aunt were down the hallway scrubbing towels when Hayden Chambers burst through the door. When he saw no sign of the babe, he demanded to know his whereabouts. Impossible, you see, since the mother wanted no part of hearing my plans. With Chai Lin out of reach, Hayden threatened to send the sister to the cribs unless the mother revealed the father's identity."

"Well?" Emily snapped, wincing at her impatience.

"To hear Flora tell it, the mother outwitted her boss. She named the one person he would not retaliate against, thus protecting her sister and her beau. At the time, my housekeeper's assumption seemed a plausible one." Colin hesitated. When he spoke, the cadence of his voice grew soothing and measured as if to soften the blow. "Nathan was indeed named the father."

"How convenient—the boss's son," Emily said dryly, giving nothing away.

Colin rubbed the back of his neck. "I cannot argue that it served the mother's purposes entirely."

"For a fact, it did! Who's to say there weren't other men," she offered, "men who were all too eager…"

The insinuation hung half-finished in the air. Emily's face heated to the roots of her hair. To regain composure, she averted her eyes to the shadows.

"Doubtful," Colin murmured, overlooking her discomfort. "If memory serves me, the mother was a mere servant, younger than Gracie's age. Too young to work in the variety show. Too young for a beau, more's the pity, but who can protect a young lady from her own heart once a gentleman charms her."

Emily plunked down her plate beside Colin's. She crossed her arms, unsettled by his remark and the evidence piling against Nathan. After all, she knew about Ying Su's beau, whereas Colin did not.

Grasping at straws, she lifted her chin and peered at him. "But not too young to be trained as a showgirl," she countered.

Colin's eyebrows lifted. "I take it you've heard more. From whom, may I ask?"

Emily folded her lips inward, debating how much to divulge.

"From whom?" he repeated.

"I overheard an argument next door after the parade."

Colin tilted an ear toward her, straining to hear over the surge of rainfall. He bent at the waist, leaning closer.

"Between father and son?" he asked.

Emily nodded.

"What was the gist?"

"A servant girl named Ying Su."

It took a moment before the spark of recognition flared in his eyes. "What about Chai Lin's mother?"

"Hayden Chambers accused Nathan of fathering her child before he went off to college. He offered Nathan money if he would claim the boy. The whole thing was beyond the pale."

"Claim the boy," his voice pitched. "As his son?"

"Yes."

Colin's navy eyes darted from left to right. "This most assuredly does not bode well." His gaze sharpened on Emily. "Did he give an amount to the bribe?"

"A ridiculous sum. Half a million dollars."

Colin whistled. "Quite a stack of enticement. Enough to flush out the real father." He scrubbed a hand over his face. "But why confront Nathan now and not when he returned from abroad?"

Shame bridled Emily's tongue, the rusty bit tasting cold and familiar. It kept her from disclosing that Nathan confronted his father about the girl, not the other way around, as Colin suspected. That single fact linked Nathan to Ying Su. As long as their connection stayed hidden, Nathan's reputation remained unspoiled. And she preserved what scraps of dignity she had left. Whether she liked it or not, the two were intertwined. It sealed her silence.

For once, the threat of dishonor had nothing to do with her being a Cleburne; it came from the smooth-talking charmer next door.

Colin pushed off from the wall. He started pacing down the length of the narrow closet, his wingtips scraping the wooden floor. Midway, he turned on his heel and ate up the distance between them.

The color drained from his face. "He must know where Chai Lin lives."

"Hmm?" Emily murmured, corralling her stray thoughts.

"Hayden Chambers must know it if he's bribed Nathan to claim him." He rubbed the back of his neck. "I shudder to think what his intentions were that night, had he gotten his hands on the boy. Flora hinted that the man had no qualms over disposing of infants to keep his girls working."

Emily shrugged off the unsettling remark. Her face twisted in skepticism. Chai Lin was safe even if the man knew where he lived. Wasn't he?

Reading her expression, Colin planted his hands on his hips. "I made a vow to that dying mother as she thrust her babe into my arms. I swore to do my utmost to protect him. To be his guardian, of sorts."

He shook his head. "A Chinese boy in an all-white orphanage… How hard would it be to spot him? After a few months with no inquiries, I naively thought he would be kept safe under my watchful eye. Protected. Now this. It would be most foolhardy to presume nothing has changed."

"Hayden Chambers is in jail," Emily pointed out. "The man is in no position to harm anyone."

"There's more," Colin ticked off on his fingers. "The orphanage was broken into with no cash missing, nothing but access to orphan records. This, after Hayden Chambers made headlines—reported by his son, who shows up early to get the story on the break-in. All coincidental? Perhaps. But what if they're somehow linked?"

"By what?" *Or rather, whom?* Had Colin figured out the intruder?

"What if Nathan's father ordered the break-in to learn what the records revealed? Remember, he not only demanded to know the father's identity the night Chai Lin was born but bribed Nathan days ago to learn it. What if Nathan caught wind of who broke in and came to gather info—"

"Whoa," Emily held up both hands. Colin's thinking was way off the tracks. "That's a lot of conjecture. Particularly since the police have no shred of evidence. The *truth* is," she stressed, spreading her palms, "anybody could have crept in for any number of reasons."

The truth. Emily's nose itched.

Colin shot her a skeptical look. "You sound rather emphatic. Is that everything you know?"

Emily pressed her lips together, thinking.

Outside, the wind howled. "The storm's getting worse by the minute," she observed. "It's turning into a hurricane, isn't it?"

"If it is, we're safe and dry here."

Emily swallowed hard. She peered up past the glow of the candlelight to the darkened ceiling.

Silently, Colin waited until her gaze lowered onto him. "I covered your blunder with Mrs. Dawson. Grant me all that you know. I beg you."

"I see," Emily's tone turned cool. "Your kindness has strings attached."

"I don't regret in the least standing up for you. Please, Miss Cleburne."

She loathed being obliged, especially when she had the power to cancel the indebtedness. Besides, how could she fault Colin for caring? He was concerned for Chai Lin's welfare. If only Nathan cared half as much for the boy.

Emily let out a sigh and shook off the pretense that weighed her down.

"Hayden Chambers sent no one to the orphanage," she began.

"You know that for a fact?"

Emily nodded. "His son broke in. I pried the news out of him this morning."

Colin's eyes sharpened as he took in the news, his expression clouding. He dipped his chin, encouraging her to continue.

"Nathan—Mr. Chambers, he came during the night to—"

"To disprove that the record listed him as the boy's father."

"More than likely," Emily admitted, annoyed that she had missed the obvious. "He came to save his reputation."

"Well, his name remains untarnished," Colin agreed.

Sadness twisted Emily's face.

Colin angled his head, reading her expression. "You don't still presume he's the boy's father, do you? Ying Su named Nathan under extreme duress. I sensed she withheld the father's identity to protect her true sweetheart."

Ying Su protected her true sweetheart, all right. By naming him. It had been one thing to overhear a man like Hayden Chambers accusing Nathan of fathering the child. But to hear Colin unknowingly affirm it clutched at her heart.

She clenched her teeth to keep her chin from crumpling. Could such a thing ever be put right?

Light pressure cupped her shoulders. She blinked at Colin through a moist sheen. Her eyes widened at the warmth of his touch.

"It appears that I have caused you further distress," he murmured, "when I had hoped to spare—"

A shriek split the air.

With a start, Colin squeezed her shoulders. He spun and wrenched open the door and dashed out of the closet.

Emily snatched the globed candle and fled up the hallway behind him. She nearly tripped over Colin's heels as they burst into the kitchen and halted abruptly.

Behind them, the ladies pattered through the doorway, huffing with exertion.

"Have mercy," cried Ida. "Etta, what is it?"

Etta Grimes stood frozen at the far window facing Avenue M. A hand pressed over her mouth. With eyes bulging, the cook stared out at the wrought iron fence.

They shouldered around the cook and peered through the heavy white rain, cutting horizontally.

Chapter 29

Emily made out a dark horse by the fence, battling the current. The tidewater coursed up to its haunches, careening as swift as arrows.

The horse nudged at a man's leg with its muzzle, neighing franticly.

Breath hissed between Emily's teeth.

Minnie moaned. "Oh, no!"

Rain thrashed the man's body, his coattails whipping upward in the gusting wind.

He lay slanted at an angle over the fence. His head bowed low.

"Poor soul," Ida cried. "Wind must've pitched him from the saddle."

The words sounded muffled in Emily's ears. She stared at his left arm dangling limply in the yard, the tips of his shoes dragging the river of debris. Her head pulsed in little shakes. She couldn't pry her eyes from the iron spikes impaling the man's torso.

Air moaned a dirge through the window sash, the relentless wind wailing between sharp blasts that shook the house. The pressure crinkled in Emily's ears.

"That half-witted hack driver," Minnie exclaimed, slapping the heel of her hand down hard on the nearest counter. "Now the water's too high to get me out of here!"

"Ladies," Colin addressed them gently, "let us all step away from the window, shall we?"

He coaxed the women into a huddle by the stove, where tart apples and cinnamon stewed in a copper pot, moistening the air.

"You've all suffered a most dreadful blow." The minister peered into their faces, his mouth set in a grim line. "A tragedy, that poor fellow. Moreover, the storm appears to be strengthening into a full-out hurricane. Though this building will weather the storm better than most, we must prepare for the worsening conditions. Let us all make use of what daylight remains."

He addressed the cook. "Fill every spare pot and basin with fresh water and cover them with cup towels, please, ma'am."

She gave a curt nod. The task appeared to steady her.

"When do you serve supper, Miss Etta?"

"Sundown. Six-thirty, sharp."

"The children need an early supper. Before dark, if possible."

"We can eat by six. Sandwiches, stewed fruit, and tea."

"That will suffice."

The cook began clanging pots as she hauled them over to the sink.

Colin raised his voice above the clamor. "The tide continues to swell. We must get everything off the floor if water washes under the doors. All the clothes and supplies. I'll inform the matron of the early supper and see what I can find to board up the exposed windows."

Colin stepped aside and motioned toward the door. "After you, ladies."

Miss Pickering snatched the globed candle from Emily's hand. She led the way, past the shadowy china closet and pantry, through the dining room, and into the great hall, her steps brisk with each stride.

As Emily trudged behind her, she pictured the tide water rising. Water slithering under doors. Darkness falling with no electricity. Emily pushed the harrowing images aside and braced for the hurricane bearing down on the island.

Mosey Pitts' deep voice came flooding back. *Dead bodies strewed every-where.*

It's already starting, just like before.

A sense of foreboding froze in her lungs, settling over her like hoarfrost in late autumn. She sensed more woes to come as surely as geese instinctively fled south to escape the cold winter's plight.

The women reached the library. Minnie skirted the folded clothes rimming the pile and went over to the window facing 21st Street.

"Look," Minnie threw over her shoulder. "Water's receding. Reckon that's a good sign?"

The ladies crowded at the windowpane. In the downpour, the flood tide flowed toward the beach rather than inland, as it had earlier.

Miss Pickering pushed her wireframes up on her nose and gazed out-doors. "Curious… It is curious. I don't know what to make of it with the water rising."

Later, they would learn that the brackish water from the bay had commixed with saltwater from the Gulf. Water now covered the city.

There came a wrenching snap.

"What's that?" Minnie shrieked, cringing at the ceiling.

"Part of the balcony tore off," Ida pointed out.

The wind and waves slammed the broken railing onto the concrete steps below the portico, the force plucking out spindles like broken teeth.

The clock gonged four o'clock.

"Time's a-wasting," Miss Pickering announced, setting down the candle. "We must buckle down if we're going to finish by dark."

Ida gathered up an armload of folded clothes. "Minnie, I need help putting these up."

Minnie left the window, plucked up a stack, and followed Ida up the grand staircase.

After retrieving the wooden box from the closet, Emily sat across the dwindling pile from Miss Pickering and set to work on filling the container.

Over the next hour, Ida and Minnie came and went, clearing the folded clothes from the floor.

Emily kept busy sorting and putting up supplies, but it didn't quell the restlessness tingling in her fingertips. Try as she might, she couldn't wipe clear the image of the man impaled on the fence.

Ida and Minnie padded into the library and took their places around the sunken pile. Behind them, Colin strode in without his jacket, with his striped shirt rolled up to his forearms. He held wood planks under one arm and gripped a hammer and a fistful of nails. At the window, he propped the boards against the wall.

Emily climbed up off the floor and went over to assist. "Here, I'll hold the board while you hammer."

Colin wiped his forehead on his sleeve. "I could have used your help upstairs. I started there and worked my way down. No need for little prying eyes getting a glimpse at that fence."

He threw her a meaningful look.

Colin turned and hefted a board, ready to place it flat against the exposed window when Emily stayed his hand.

There, across the street, she watched a tin roof peel up. It lifted off a cottage. The metal sailed over 21st Street and wedged itself against the orphanage fence.

Out fled a man and woman from their home into waist-deep water. In the downpour, a child clutched the man's neck, her legs locked around his waist. They inched along the iron fence toward the two-story home next door. Around them, deadly roof slates sliced through the air.

Emily jerked her gaze off the young family and held the board for Colin to hammer in the nails. Had Lena and the children left the Kesler's cottage for a sturdier home nearby? Were the boys with them, snug and dry?

Lord, let them be safe.

At least the Edwards lived in a two-story home further from the beach. That eased a measure of tightness in her chest. So did the soaring roof above her head. She had no cause to worry over having to flee the orphanage in rising water.

As Colin drove in the last of the nails, they heard knocking at the door. Refugees began trickling in from the neighborhood, seeking sturdier shelter. Ida dug out towels and passed them out while Colin directed Minnie to help Miss Etta prepare more sandwiches.

Once he secured the windows, the minister joined those milling about the reception hall, putting his arm around shoulders, praying with those who sought comfort.

A man stumbled in, shivering, his shirt ripped from his body. Colin took his navy jacket and draped it over his shoulders. He seated the man in a chair against the library wall near Emily. She was rolling up a set of maps when Colin brought him a cup of steaming tea and settled in a chair beside him.

"Our home went off its supports," the man explained flatly, his gaze fixed and vacant. "Afraid we'd be crushed, my wife…" he swallowed, "my wife … we crawled out the window, the water up to our armpits. Amelia never could swim a lick," he chuckled bleakly. "At Avenue N, she stepped in a gutter. I tried to pull her up, but the current… Her thin arms were so slippery," his voice caught, trailing off. He rocked back and forth in the chair, his gaze lost.

Colin sat there in silent support, knowing more than most that words were feeble comforters to one overtaken by grief.

At six o'clock, the dinner bell clanged over the howling wind and rain. Little feet swarmed the staircases. The refugees followed behind the children to the dining room.

Only Emily, Ida, and Miss Pickering stayed, picking up the pace. As darkness loomed near, they lowered the globed candles to the floor. The light cast shadows upon their faces. Miss Pickering kept eyeing the door over her gold rims, watching for her nephew, most likely.

Emily lifted bolts of calico and muslin. There, at the very bottom she found leather-bound books. Candlelight glowed on the titles: *Little Women, Heidi, Black Beauty, Tom Sawyer, The Adventures of Huckleberry Fin, Oliver Twist, Alice in Wonderland.* Like old companions, the characters between the pages had kept her company, had kept her sane, while growing up. With care, she stacked them into a straight column.

Fierce wind gusts shook the house like a coyote shaking a squirrel by its neck. Between the blows, awful crashing sounds boomed in the distance. Were those houses falling? So close? *Too close.*

Above the gusts, shrieks pierced the air. A boy screaming for his mama, a woman pleading for somebody to help her. Abruptly their cries died on the wind.

The front door flew open. Peter strode in. His wet clothes were plastered to his body, the shirt sleeves shredded.

"Where's Lena?" he hollered, his face twisted with alarm. "Is she here? The children?"

Emily got up and joined him. "They never made it back."

In the dim light, his blue eyes took on a crazed look. "I thought … I had hoped… Phone lines are down."

The glass shattered somewhere in the north wing. The high-pitched hissing blew in.

"It's gone," Peter moaned.

"What?" But Emily already knew. His eyes slammed shut, confirming the news.

"Our cottage—blown to pieces!"

Peter turned to go. "I must find them."

"Perhaps they're with your neighbor … the one Lena helps? Millie?"

Peter's shoulders sagged.

"You checked," she hazarded a guess.

"Their house is gone. Reduced to rubble."

What a nightmare.

Peter stalked to the door. Emily trailed behind him helplessly.

Lena leaving was all her doing. She'd told her friend to take the children and go home.

A cornice smashed through the library window, rain lashing the room. The wind growled through the opening.

"Hurry," Miss Pickering shouted, "grab what's left!"

A flurry of hands swept up great armloads. Miss Pickering clutched the candle off the floor and fled up the staircase with Ida, dropping a trail of stray socks.

Peter gripped the doorknob.

"Wait," Emily groped at possibilities. "Maybe Lena's with Aunt Estelle."

He plowed his fingers through his hair. "It's higher ground."

Peter threw open the door, leaning into the storm. Before he yanked the door shut, lightning flashed. Emily caught a glimpse over his shoulder. The homes looked like floating buoys attached by ropes to the seabed. The waves crested too high to resemble land.

Slamming the door, Emily leaned against the hard surface. No one knew the whereabouts of Peter's family, or Jake, Sarah, or Grace. Not a soul knew that she had sent them all away.

A string of globed lights bobbed into the great hall. The matron and teacher led the children, single file, through the east wing, up the staircase toward the south dormitory. Behind them, Colin shepherded the refugees with Minnie and Etta.

Later Emily would hear about the wind heaving chunks of posts through the dining room windows, cutting their meal short.

Colin paused toward the top of the dusky staircase. He hollered down. "Miss Cleburne, come! Leave the rest."

Later she would regret not going straight upstairs, but she spied the novels left on the floor.

Dampness seeped into her stocking feet, chilling her toes. Frowning, she glanced at her half boots. Her pulse leaped. Recoiling, she jerked back. The tidewater spurted through the vertical seam over the doorsill. Waves were now crashing upon the door. Inside, the water formed a pool, spreading outward.

She darted for the books. Squatting, she scooped up the grainy covers to her chest. Grabbing the candlestick, she sprang up.

On her way out of the library, she glanced at the clock. Half past six. But the roar ate up the gong.

She'd just set foot into the great hall when the floorboards lurched violently. She froze. The hairs on her neck bristled.

Everything happened at once. The beams hoisting the cupola from the top center roof burst. The roof thundered down on the east wing, crashing into the great hall, the weight crushing the grand staircase. The arched windowpanes exploded as bricks and debris reigned down.

The last thing Emily remembered before cringing in pain was the candlewick flare inside the globe then everything plunged into darkness.

Chapter 30

Pressure squeezed the length of her spine, down her legs and arms, pinning her in place.

Sharp twinges stabbed behind her ear and shot through her skull. Around her, the wind whipped wet with eerie, screeching sounds.

What happened?

Emily pried open her eyes. Bleary-eyed, she squinted into the watery gloom. Strips of shadow began to emerge. She craned out her neck for a closer look. Her forehead knocked against something hard, flat, inches from her face. She sniffed … pine sap?

Lightning speared the sky, illuminating the deathtrap encasing her. Her blood ran cold.

"Help!" she screamed.

Her fingers clawed wildly at her sides. She pawed the rough planks jammed against her back. Digging in an elbow, she pushed down hard. The board wobbled and twisted. An icy stream sluiced down her back and over her calves, pooling in her boots. She shivered violently.

"Help! I'm trapped," she hollered at the top of her lungs. "Get me out of here!"

No answer.

Had everyone perished? Who would pull her free?

Her heart thundered in her chest. Her body flushed hot, then cold.

She forced air through her windpipe in dry little puffs.

Overhead, a crack sent tremors vibrating down the timbers. Boards bent under the sliding weight, and she hunched her shoulders, bracing for impact. A post slammed into her upper arm.

Gasping, she held her breath. What if more debris fell?

A sudden light refracted through the slats, off to the right. Emily turned her head and peered through an opening. There, it flashed again.

"Help me," she cried. "I'm trapped!"

From a distance, the light hovered in one spot.

Above the driving rain, a shout rang out. "Miss Cleburne! Miss Cleburne!"

"Over here," she yelled. "I'm over here!"

"Hold on, I'm coming!"

She choked on a sob. Thank God, she wasn't alone.

From twelve yards away, she tracked the lantern's sway, dip, and rise. The glow inched behind the craggy piles. It crawled along the walls throughout the cavernous room on an uneven path over to her. Time and again, she called out, guiding the direction of the beam.

Great gusts ripped through the ruins. The force shook the planks, squeezing her ribs. She feared moving to relieve the pressure. Would it set timbers cascading down upon her head? If only she could loosen the corset cinching her waist. She panted through her mouth, frantic to be freed.

Time stalled as the minutes dragged out. Jittering in the cold, she kept her gaze trained on the lantern. At last, the light beamed up the boards encasing her.

"Right here," she called.

An outstretched arm held up the lantern. A few more steps and a face appeared through the slats. Walnut hair lay plastered on his forehead.

Colin.

"I'll get you out," he assured her.

Grooves dug between his brows as he assessed the situation. He hooked the lantern on a jutting beam and started hoisting the outer timbers.

With every layer he pried off, more of her surroundings grew visible. An avalanche of two-by-ten boards, thick beams, white patches of plaster, and roofing slid to her right. The boards pinning her were slanted against a massive wall, looming high behind her, tilting her backward.

Images flashed of the grand staircase, the soaring roof thundering down, crushing it.

Before she knew what was happening, cold water swirled around her kneecaps. In one rolling swell, the storm-tide had burst through the building. Her pulse lurched.

The water shifted the boards, lifting the post that jabbed her arm. Using the buoyancy, she dropped her shoulder and tucked in her elbow enough that the post loosened and fell, ripping her sleeve.

Without breaking his stride, Colin continued tossing off more layers of timber.

Emily eyed the rising floodwater with a growing alarm. Every minute the water inched higher up her thighs. Soon it swashed around her waist.

"Hurry," she pleaded through chattering teeth.

He grimaced and heaved off more beams.

Still, the cold saltwater slithered up her ribs, coiling onto her chest. She grew light-headed. Her pulse thrashed in her eardrums. She figured she had thirty minutes if the flood tide continued rising at this rate; thirty minutes until a watery grave, unless Colin could pry her loose.

All at once, a significant lull in the wind and rain settled in.

Emily sagged with relief. "Reckon it's over? The worst, at least?"

It had to be. Now the floodwaters would recede.

Colin paid no heed to the lull. If anything, he stepped up the pace. Sloshing in waist-deep water, he pitched hunks of plaster from the pile.

"Not yet," he hollered.

Had the wind shifted direction?

Emily squinted up at the clouds. "But the moon… I see the moon."

His mouth pulled in a grim line. "Prepare yourself."

Prepare? Not more water! The very idea turned her legs rubbery.

As Colin predicted, the wind and rain soon began to lash with renewed fierceness. The rain stung her skin like frozen pinpricks. The walls rocked violently under the onslaught, the boards pressing against her muscles and bones.

Water sloshed along her collarbone. It swelled over her shoulders and washed up the column of her neck. A wave rolled over her face. Saltwater stung her nostrils, sharp with brine.

Emily choked, gasping for air. "Get me out! *Now!*"

"I'm hurrying," he gritted out, heaving away planks frantically.

Minutes passed before a wedge between the slats widened. Emily tried to shoulder her way out. Not wide enough.

Her limbs quaked with terror. *Lord, help me!*

Her breaths grew shallow. She tilted her chin and pushed up on her tiptoes, straining to get air.

Saltwater seeped into her mouth, and she sputtered and clamped it shut. She drew in air through her nose. Water crept up the groove above her lip.

She sucked in one last breath and held it.

Let it be quick. Emily could open her mouth. Let the water fill her lungs. Go home to heaven.

The light quivered on the water, ringed with gray. It grew blurry, collapsing inward.

Her limbs went limp, heavy. Her lungs burned for air.

Fingers clamped her forearm and yanked. She plunged under the water, jerking upward, the boards scraping her belly and knees. She broke the water's surface, gulping mouthfuls of air, her arms flailing.

"I—I can't swim!" she shrieked.

"Here, I've got you." Colin's arm gripped around her ribs, pulling her to his side. "Hang on to me," Colin shouted. "Don't let go!"

Emily slung her arms around his slick neck, her weakened arm quivering.

Colin reached for the ring handle and thrust the lantern above his head. He treaded water back through the library.

Above the waterline, the light shined on the face of the clock. Eight forty-four.

He kicked his legs in a sidestroke and steered them over to the doorway leading to the back stairs.

Wind growled up the darkened staircase.

Emily gained the lower steps and drew upright. Her legs buckled underneath her. She slumped against the wall, reached for the railing, and hoisted herself. Her dress and petticoat hung like sopping weights about the hems. Colin climbed alongside her, his chest heaving.

"We must move up!" he yelled over the shrill wind.

He reached to cup her elbow and drew up short. "You're injured," he grimaced, peering below her shoulder.

He carefully wrapped his arm around her waist, supporting her weight. On wobbly legs, she leaned into him while they trudged up the steps.

Upstairs, water poured in under the blown-out eaves as rainwater sprayed down the darkened hallway. They stepped over sheets and blankets twisted in ropelike heaps on the floor, tossed from the linen shelves lining the hall.

They poked their heads into the front room. A toppled sewing machine blocked their path. Bolts of muslin lay upended on the cast iron base. Strewn glass littered the floor, bricks around the window frame broken loose.

Across the hall, in the back room, shutters banged at the windows. Water spattered on the floor from cracks in the plaster. Children's clothes lay on the shelves lining the room. The walls muffled some of the shrill.

Colin glanced around. "We'll stay here."

He helped ease her down onto the floor near the door. She winced, feeling a twinge below her right shoulder starting to throb. She leaned back against the wainscoting, shivering.

"Be right back." He took the lantern and disappeared into the hallway.

The room plunged into darkness. The shadows sharpened the eerie sounds, piercing as a doomed runaway locomotive barreling down the tracks. Emily shuddered, longing for light to relieve the gloom. What was taking him so long?

She heaved a sigh when the lantern shined into the room. Colin reappeared carrying a bolt of muslin, and a striped blanket slung over one shoulder.

"Found these fairly dry," he hollered.

Colin closed the door, set down the lamp, and emptied his arms. He gently draped the coarse blanket around her shoulders. The warmth soothed her. He slumped beside her and tipped his head back against the wall, shutting his eyes.

They rode out the gusts until their breathing slowed.

Emily peered sideways at Colin. "Where are the others?"

The lines on his face smoothed. "The south wing, upstairs."

"The children? Chai Lin?"

"All safe."

Emily nodded, recalling the string of lights moving through the great hall. They'd left the hall moments before the roof collapsed.

Colin shifted. "Let me tend that arm."

He slid the lantern close and knelt before her. Water dripped from the strands of his hair as he examined the puncture wound with gentle hands. Emily hazarded a look at the spike protruding from the jagged gash.

Colin met her gaze. "I must remove it, or it'll fester. I'll do my utmost to be gentle."

"Don't coddle me. Just … get it done."

"Hold still."

Emily pressed her lips flat while the wall quaked against her back. Colin waited until the tremors eased.

He gripped the splintered end and gave a firm tug. Emily hissed through her teeth. Pain stabbed at the gash as the wood slid from the raw flesh. Blood trickled warm down her arm.

An apology flashed in his eyes. "Almost done."

He pulled out a pocket knife and cut the muslin into long strips. With one, he cleaned off the blood. Then he gently wrapped the cloth strips around the wound, tying the ends.

He sat back on his heels. "It'll do for now."

Emily nodded, half-listening. Her head ached behind her left ear. She felt around and found a nasty knot swelling. She never saw whatever thwacked her on the head.

As far as she could tell, Colin suffered no apparent injuries from his heroics. The man had risked life and limb to pull her free.

The reality hit her fresh. She'd come close to drowning. Mere seconds.

Yet she survived, thanks to Colin.

Her throat tightened. "If not for you, I…" She swallowed hard and tried again. "Thanks for coming for me."

Inadequate words, but no less heartfelt.

"I heard your cries." Colin's eyes flashed brightly. He looked away, working his jaw. He took a moment to compose himself. "I could do nothing less."

How could she ever repay him?

"You're a true friend," she said with feeling.

A flicker of emotion lit his eyes. Colin shook it off and rubbed his hands together. Had what she said made him uncomfortable, or was he just chilled to the bone?

"Here." Emily lifted the edge of the blanket. "Scoot over."

He hesitated, eying her and the blanket. The floorboards quivered beneath them.

"Your chivalry is noted," she gave him a pointed look. "So is your shivering."

His mouth lifted to one side. He moved over, their shoulders touching. He rearranged the blanket until it wrapped them snugly. Though the wet clothes chafed, heat from his body warmed down her side.

They fell silent, bone-weary, and spent.

Though the storm would rage for several more hours until the wind would blow itself out, she drew comfort from having Colin near. From not being alone.

She sat swaddled in wool for a long while, willing her sore, tense muscles to ease.

When the hour grew late, exhaustion dulled the pulsating pain until heaviness pulled at her eyelids, and she drifted off to sleep.

Chapter 31

Emily let out a cry in the dark and bolted upright, gasping for air. Tears sprang to her eyes as a sob bubbled up. Tucking into a ball on the floor, she buried her face in her hands and wept.

The rising water… She shook off the dream as tremors coursed through her body.

Tears wet her palms. She let them flow.

She became aware of the hard floor biting into her knees, a hand warm on her back. She tensed but did not pull away.

"You needn't be brave any longer," Colin whispered. "Not for me."

It took no more coaxing for fresh tears to pool in her eyes and spill over, dripping off her cheeks and fingers until the pressure began to ease in her chest.

"You're safe now," he assured her.

Emily grew conscious of his tender touch, the boldness of his hand remaining between her shoulder blades. He was offering comfort, nothing more. Still, she mopped her face with the backs of her hands. She snuffled and inched up on her knees.

Colin leaned back against the wall and gathered the blanket off the floor from where her thrashing had wadded it.

"You're trembling. Come here."

Moving over, Colin tucked the blanket around her and then covered himself.

It had quit raining, finally. Moonlight peeked through the louvers.

Colin gazed at her in the silvery light. "It's over," he sighed.

They had survived.

The warmth from his body and the wool seeped through the layers of damp clothes. Her limbs grew heavy. Bone-weary and numb, her head drooped onto the hollow of his shoulder. Emily listened to the wind whistling through the cracks in the window and the rhythm of his heartbeat until her body ceased vibrating. Soon the pull of sleep lulled her.

Around dawn, Emily felt a stirring beside her. The weight of her body eased down onto the floor, and the scratchy blanket tucked under her chin.

⚬

The sound of church bells clanging in the distance woke Emily. Warm sunlight filtered into the room. She blinked and looked around at the clothes piled on the shelves, at the unfamiliar walls.

What happened last night came crashing back. The storm, the roof collapsing, Colin rescuing her. She wanted to block it all out, to curl up in a ball and fall back to sleep, but her aching body protested the hardwood floor. Yawning, she pushed off the floor into a sitting position. It took a moment for the walls to quit floating.

Colin had left. Had he gone to preach?

Emily took in her appearance. Pain throbbed at the wound, where dried blood stained the muslin. Touching the lump behind her ear confirmed its swelling and tenderness. Her scalp itched where the bun knotted at the nape of her neck. Her hair had dried stiff from the saltwater, as did her dress. She longed to soak in the tub.

Emily eased up off the floor and shuffled out the door. A bone-deep soreness stiffened the muscles all over her body. She wished she'd removed her shoes and stockings last night, but exhaustion had won out over the discomfort of being soaked to the skin.

She walked to the end of the hallway and peered into the cavernous reception hall. Large slabs of the roof, beams, two-by-twelve boards, and hunks of plaster sloped down into an avalanche, covering the rubble.

A brilliant sky domed the orphanage where the roof had once vaulted high at the middle of the building. Its splendor had no place above the ruins. How had that same atmosphere wreaked such havoc just yesterday?

Across the reception hall, the roof pitched above the south wing. Wedges of blue appeared through the eaves and sections of collapsed walls. No sound came from over there. No voices, no pattering of feet on the floors.

"Hello," she called out.

Her greeting echoed off the walls. Where were the others? Were they still safe? Needing to find out, she lumbered up the hallway and down the stairs, her muscles protesting.

The flood tide had drained out of the building, leaving a layer of black slime reeking of dead fish. Her shoes sank up to the laces in the muck. She squished around a fallen bookcase and over the spines of books. In the north entryway, she picked her way through chairs and plates that had washed in from the dining room. Slammed against the door lay a hall table tipped on its side, its legs sticking out like a bloated cow. With effort, she shoved it out of the way and pulled open the door.

A warm breeze brushed her face and blew strands of copper in her eyes. She tucked the hair behind her ear.

Glancing to her left, she stiffened, bracing for a glimpse of the man impaled on the fence. Mercifully, someone had taken down the body and carted it away for burial.

Emily tramped down the stairs, her nose crinkling. What was that smell? It reminded her of venison gone bad.

Scanning the yard, she spotted a barefoot orphan boy near the fence, lifting a sheet of tin with a stick.

"Excuse me," she called, steering around the debris to the boy. "Where are the others?"

He turned and pointed at a frame house by the orphanage. "Over yonder, where we spent the night."

"Y'all left during the storm?" Emily's eyebrows lifted.

"After the worst was over."

"Is everyone okay?"

He shrugged. "The young'uns bawled like babies, but they'll be all right."

Emily nodded, satisfied. "Have you seen Mr. Hensleigh?"

"The preacher?" He scratched his freckled neck and squinted up at her. "He left when the sun was coming up."

"Which direction?"

"That-a-way." He pointed south toward Avenue O.

"Thanks."

The boy went on his way, dragging the stick along the wrought iron posts. It sounded like the tatting of a drum.

Colin must have gone to find Grace. If only he'd woke her before he left. She could have spared him the trouble. The Kesler's cottage lay in pieces.

Emily peered past the cistern rolled on its side, down 21st Street. A house lay twisted in the middle of the road. But it wasn't the house that held her spellbound. Tipping her head, she stared beyond the homes, transfixed.

"What in the world," she murmured under her breath.

High as the rooflines, a ridge of wreckage formed a barricade that ran from east to west, as far as her eyes could see. What on earth caused the massive pile-up?

Her stomach pooled at her knees.

Last she knew, Lena and the children were in the vicinity of that wreckage.

No. No, they're fine. They were probably sitting around the Edwards' table eating bowls of steaming oatmeal and wondering what had happened to her. She pictured Grace pouting over having to wait on her brother to come to fetch her. All the same, Emily sorely needed to lay eyes on them.

That powerful urge pushed her out the gate and up 21st Street. She dodged ponds and drifts of debris in the street. Mangled in the wreckage, she spotted a drowned cat and her litter of kittens, two hens, a hound dog, and a twisted diamondback rattler. No wonder the stench.

Crossing Avenue L, she peered eastward, her steps stalling. Houses were blown to pieces as though dynamite had exploded. Fallen clapboard walls were piled with boards and ripped-out window casings.

From up the road, a gelding whinnied and trotted down to meet her. The poor thing was looking for its owner. Before Emily could grab the reins, the horse snorted air through its nostrils, tossed his mane, and loped away.

Emily plodded along several blocks when something caught her eye in the gutter. She turned and staggered back, gasping. A swollen corpse floated in the water. The woman's gray eyes stared sightlessly into the blue sky. Her pale hair fanned the water, the ends of her long braid tangled in the wrought iron fence. Is that how she had drowned? By getting her hair caught on the pickets? Had she lost her footing and gone under the water?

That could have been me.

Her legs quivering, Emily backed away and almost fled back to the orphanage, but she stumbled onward. Without thought of direction, she weaved down the streets full of splintered planks, tossed bricks, and past a house that lay upended. Another leaned sideways at a crazy angle.

Other folks were out roaming the streets, limping along, looking dazed. Is that how she looked?

A man in shredded long johns shouldered past her with a vacant stare. He smelled of whiskey and unwashed flesh. She turned as he hobbled on, oblivious to her nearness. One arm hung at a crooked angle below the elbow. With every step, the cuts on his feet left red imprints on the sand.

She drew in a deep breath and tried to gain her bearings. Pressing her palm to her forehead, she glanced around. Which way? What had happened to the orderly grid of streets? She was still heading toward Broadway, wasn't she?

A strangled sound rasped a few feet away. Emily scanned the skeletal remains of a house and moved closer, hearing the faint moan below her knees. She peered down and froze. A grizzled-haired arm covered in liver spots stuck out beneath the mound of two-by-fours.

Emily clutched her churning stomach as everything grew fuzzy, far away. Her breathing became shallow. *The pressure from the boards squeezed her lungs.*

"Ma'am. Ma'am," a voice sounded more insistent the second time. "You're not going to swoon or be sick, are you?"

Emily blinked at the man clomping toward her in boots, with his Stetson pushed back on his brow.

Groans came from under the rubble. The poor man was buried alive! She started grabbing the roughened planks and slinging them.

"Help me," she urged. "We've got to get him out. He's trapped!"

"Go on home." The man's tone held pity.

Emily shot him a look. Had the man lost his mind?

"Even if we could get him out in time," he drawled, "he won't live. Mr. Arnold's too old and frail."

"He's trapped! I can't leave him!"

"Ma'am, go on. Say a prayer for him on your way."

The old man lay buried six feet under the wreckage. She hated that she couldn't save him. That she survived, while Mr. Arnold would not. A wail bubbled up. She swallowed it behind gritted teeth and pressed on, the guilt pounding her with every step.

Further up the road, Emily passed by a knot of women huddled on a street corner.

"…with the clothes on our backs. We're staying with Mama for the time being. I've no right to complain. I still have a husband and my little ones."

"Anyone heard from the Simmons or Mr. Walters?"

"Saw Mr. Walters. He lost twelve of his kin."

"Bless his heart."

Twelve! Emily blocked out the rest of the news and kept moving until she reached Broadway Boulevard. She blew out a breath, relieved that she had her bearings. She glanced up and down the boulevard, her pulse climbing. Some larger homes and buildings lay in ruins, even on higher ground. What if the Edwards' home had fallen too? That possibility hadn't entered her mind. Until now.

On wooden legs, Emily crossed the esplanade. The need to get home pulled at her, despite the dread of what she might find when she got there.

At the corner of Sealy Avenue, Emily peered in both directions, scratching her head. How had she veered so far west? She turned and trudged eastward until she came across the ruins of First Baptist. The church steeples had toppled and crushed the building.

Coming out the parsonage side door, a woman tugged on a rope that she'd looped around a cow's neck.

"Come along, old girl. You're safe to live another day." The woman's thick Georgia accent held a note of humor.

She spotted Emily watching her. "I suppose it's not every day you see a cow tromping out of someone's kitchen. I pulled her in from the yard when she began treading water," she explained. "Mercy! That was some storm. It's a wonder any of us made it out alive when the tornado hit."

Emily cocked her head. "Tornado?"

"Appears so. Long about half past six. It blew down the steeples and damaged the upstairs bedroom."

An image flashed of the clock striking half past six moments before the roof fell in. Had a same tornado struck the orphanage and caused the roof to collapse?

"We crawled out the window and walked the plank to get out of the house," the minister's wife went on.

Walked the plank… Jake and Andrew had played pirates. Was that just yesterday?

"You take care now," the woman called, patting the cow's neck.

Emily treaded up the avenue. Nearing the block where the Edwards lived, she caught a glimpse further up the road. There, the ridge of wreckage loomed as it did south of the orphanage. What had happened to their thriving city?

When the Edwards' home finally came into view, the tension drained from her body. The house had weathered the storm, though the roof had dents and bricks crumbled on the chimney. The upstairs shutters gaped haggardly at the windows.

Voices flowed out from the house.

Next door at the Chambers' residence, a hefty branch had fallen and punctured the side of their house. The oak tree, the one Jake had climbed, had split in two and caused the damage.

Emily prayed Nathan was safe. Had he returned home and weathered the storm there? Surely he hadn't slept on his sailboat.

The gate creaked as she entered the Edwards' yard. She caught sight of a familiar patch of blue calico, tattered and mended, lodged between the iron fenceposts. Her eyes riveted on Miss Riggles, floating face down in a pool of water. She bent down and pulled Rachel's doll free, recalling Jake's words. *She wags that doll wherever she goes.*

Emily's blood ran cold. Where was Rachel? She bolted up the muddy steps onto the porch and through the door.

Refugees milled about the downstairs rooms, cradling cups of coffee.

"Rachel?" Emily called out.

The strangers turned their curious gazes upon her.

At hearing the padding of feet at the top of the stairs, Emily peered up.

Aunt Estelle came treading down the stairs with little Rachel on her heels, her golden ringlets bouncing.

Emily's arms went limp with relief.

The girl's mouth popped open. "Miss Riggles!"

Rachel pushed past Estelle and bounded down the stairs. She plucked the soggy doll from Emily's hand and squeezed it to her chest, soaking the bodice of her dress.

"Emily," Estelle said with a sigh. "Thank goodness, y'all are home. We've been so worried."

Rachel pulled at her sleeve and pointed up at the handrail. "I dropped Miss Riggles in the water from up there."

But Emily wasn't listening. She panned the house, searching each face, her stomach sinking.

Aunt Estelle drew her into a hug. The faint trace of lemon verbena barely registered.

Her aunt pulled away and craned her neck, listening as much as looking around the entryway and parlor.

"Where are the children?" Estelle ventured.

Chapter 32

Emily's throat tightened. "Lena hasn't brought them?"

"Why would Lena…? They aren't with *you*?" Estelle's face pinched in alarm.

This cannot be. A sudden coldness chilled Emily at her core. She wrapped her arms around her middle.

"Where are they?" Estelle pressed.

"They all … they went with Lena to see the waves. She felt unwell, so … so she took them home."

"But Peter came by looking for her. Their cottage…" Estelle pressed her hand over her mouth, her voice brittle enough to shatter. "Oh, where are my children?"

Emily glanced at the audience of slack faces, all staring at her. Feeling exposed, she tucked her chin to her chest. Her face burned with shame. What must they think of her, a governess who failed to keep watch over her charges?

She groped for a way to save face. "I expect them any moment."

Let it be so.

Emily caught the skeptical glances from the others while Aunt Estelle clutched the railing.

In the parlor, an infant let out a grating, high-pitched cry. The mother turned from view and put the babe to her breast.

"Your uncle had a horrid night," Estelle murmured. "I must go make him comfortable. Please watch Rachel until she's down for her nap."

"Of course," Emily replied.

"Make sure she *stays* indoors."

Her aunt's curt tone stung, but who could blame her? Without another word, Estelle mounted the stairs.

Emily felt a tug on her sleeve. "I'm hungry," Rachel whined.

"All right. Let's go see what Miss Inez has for us."

Keeping her head lowered, Emily clasped Rachel's hand and weaved them through the refugees, around the half-moon table turned on its side in the hallway, into the dining room. She stepped over a cracked blue and white platter that had fallen from the wall.

Her boots squished through the foul slime covering the floors. It coated the furniture as high up as her knees. The place reeked of rotting seaweed and fish.

In the dining room, Inez set a platter of peanut butter sandwiches on the table. Eyeing the houseful of folks, the cook drew close to Emily.

"Get enough for y'all," she muttered out of the side of her mouth. "Something told me to put the baked loaves up high. Otherwise, we'd all be eating crackers and peanut butter. The food in the ice box and lower pantry is ruined."

Emily gave a stiff nod. She picked up three halves and handed two to Rachel.

Inez left and returned with a coffee pot. She poured Emily a steaming cup. No milk or sugar. Emily scarcely tasted the bitter brew scalding her tongue or the sandwich wedge she choked down.

⁓ ∞ ⁓

Once Emily laid little Rachel down for a nap, she plodded into the bathroom and turned on the sink faucet. Not a trickle. She glanced at the tub brimming with water. It had to last until the city restored water. Her shoulders sagged. There would be no soaking in the tub to soothe her aching muscles.

Disheartened, she crossed the hall into her room. Part of the ceiling had caved in on the armoire opposite her bed. The clumped, wet plaster smelled like ammonia.

Emily wandered over to the window and pulled back the lace curtain. She peered next door. No movement inside Nathan's room or anywhere in the house. Where was he? She needed to find out if he was all right.

She chewed her bottom lip. She ought to be out searching for Lena and the children, but that ridge of debris barricaded the way south. Besides, Lena would bring the children by when she could. Peter hadn't found them, or he would have brought Jake and Sarah by at first light.

Emily heaved a sigh and let the curtain fall.

She let out a yawn. Her limbs grew heavy as the strength she had rallied to make it back to the house drained away. She removed her dirty half-boots and plopped down on the bed. Her body sank into the soft mattress. She reached below her nightstand for *Sense and Sensibility* and opened the pages. She found her place. For a little while, she wanted nothing more than to immerse herself in the troubles of Marianne and Elinor Dashwood rather than her own.

She read a few pages then rubbed the grit from her eyes. It was no use. She couldn't follow the plot. She set down the book and closed her eyes.

Sounds penetrated the walls. Muffled coughs came from the sick room, and voices flowed up the stairs. Apparently, some folks had nowhere else to go. At least the baby slept.

Emily shifted on the mattress, unable to get comfortable. Though she needed rest, her body vibrated with restlessness. She stared up at the shadows slanting across the ceiling before giving up. She got off the bed and brushed and braided her stiff hair. She gathered clothes and went and took a sponge bath. All over her body, bruises bloomed red and purple under the skin. No wonder she ached so.

Emily removed the strip of cloth from her arm. The tender wound looked swollen and clotted with dried blood. After squeezing water from a wet washcloth over the gash, she poured on iodine, wincing at the sting. She found clean bandages in the medicine cabinet. One-handed, she managed to wrap the wound and then put on dry clothes.

Glancing out the window, Emily spotted Colin coming up the road. On impulse, she dashed down the stairs.

Breathless, she gained the porch and waited while Colin squelched through the mud and mounted the stairs.

His steps were heavy and sluggish. He had changed clothes and shaved. However, muck caked the cuffs of his charcoal trousers.

"Miss Cleburne," he dipped his chin in greeting. "I'm glad you made it home safely. I regret not escorting you myself."

"Surely you had more pressing matters to attend to other than seeing me home."

He cleared his throat. "Is … is Grace here?" He looked pensive, hopeful.

Emily shook her head. She hated that her answer carved worry lines on his forehead. His gaze fell to his wingtips. He tried in vain to toe off the muck.

"I confess I hoped Lena had brought her here."

Emily gentled her voice. "Not yet. Why don't you come in and wait with us."

"I tried going by the Kesler's first thing," he went on, ignoring the invitation. "There's nothing…" His voice trailed off.

"I know. Peter came by looking for Lena. He said his house was gone. I'm sure Lena took Grace and the children to one of the neighbors."

Colin met her gaze with a stark stare. "I climbed the south stairs of the orphanage when I couldn't get past the wreckage. What I saw…" He shook his head as though he couldn't comprehend the scene. "There's nothing. Nothing left."

The minister's eyes watered.

Emily scratched her head. "*What*…?"

"There *are* no homes. Nothing's left."

Her mind whirled. "Surely it can't be that bad."

His mouth pulled into a grimace. "It's tenfold worse than you can imagine. Everything scraped bare, all the way to the beach. Not a slate roof, oleander, or live oak. Not even the grid of streets. *Nothing*. Not a single soul in sight. The loss of life must be staggering. How we managed to escape, only blocks away…" His voice faltered.

Colin stuffed his hands into his trouser pockets and looked away. He paused to regain his composure.

He went on as though he needed to unburden what troubled him. "We canceled services this morning. The sanctuary is damaged, the steeple and front of the roof. We'll need a temporary place to worship. The parsonage fared better. It's habitable, at least. My mare is still missing."

He massaged the side of his neck. "All morning, a steady stream of people came by. Most have lost family. I lost count of how many funerals I must perform. All those hurting people. One man can't possibly…"

"No one requires more of you than you can give."

The corner of his mouth lifted. "True enough." He let out a sigh. "Already the funeral homes are full, so the cotton warehouses on the Strand are being used as temporary morgues."

"Why, there must be hundreds."

"More like a thousand."

Her eyes widened. *Surely not!*

"I just came from accompanying an elderly widow. She searched the morgues in vain for her sister and grown children."

"How dreadful."

He nodded absently. "While the woman looked among the rows of bodies, I … searched as well."

His gaze touched upon Emily as though gauging her reaction. She tilted her head, missing his point.

"I was quite relieved," he explained, "that I did not find Gracie or Lena or the children among—"

"Why look *there*?" she snapped. "They're alive."

Heat surged up her neck, flooding her face.

Colin scrubbed a hand over one cheek, his expression pained. "Forgive me. I meant only to spare you the burden of searching for your cousins. I thought… I had hoped the news might bring you comfort."

Tears pricked behind her eyes. Emily blew out a shaky breath and rolled her lips inward, taking a moment to collect her emotions. "Forgive me. You didn't deserve my outburst. I don't know what came over me."

Her admission earned her a trace of a smile.

"You have been through no small ordeal," Colin told her. "I daresay we all are a bit on edge."

"It's just that … Lena could have taken Grace and the children anywhere." Emily spread her hands. "Perhaps they rode out the storm at a friend's house further inland."

"Perhaps," he allowed.

Another possibility came to mind. "Reckon they're at the hospital?" Why hadn't she thought of that sooner?

"Already checked St. Mary's and John Sealy. They're bulging with injured patients."

"Oh." She slumped against the porch railing.

Lord, where are they?

Colin rubbed the cleft of his chin. "It pains me to consider the worst, but we must brace ourselves for the possibility that all is not well with our loved ones."

She lifted her chin. "I must believe they're safe."

Colin gazed down the road with a faraway look in his eyes. "Whatever happens, may God's peace comfort us."

Emily hugged her midriff. She didn't want comfort. She wanted Lena to corral Grace and the children up the steps, safe and sound. Only then would her restlessness settle.

Colin motioned to her wound. "How's the arm?"

"It hurts, but I'll manage."

"You ought to see a doctor. You may need stitches."

"I suppose."

"The mayor called a meeting this afternoon," he reported. "I attended. They organized a Central Relief Committee to bring about order. They formed committees to assist with burials and to ease the suffering. With all the corpses, the most pressing concern is the spread of disease. There was talk of a mass burial, but the ground is still too saturated. All agreed we must act with haste."

Emily thought of Nathan. "Did you happen to see Mr. Chambers there?" she managed a casual tone.

Colin hesitated, regarding her from beneath lowered eyelids.

She tucked a wayward curl behind her ear. "I just wonder if he made it through the storm okay."

He straightened. "I don't know." He angled toward the street. "Well, I won't keep you." Though his manner was brisk, sadness clouded his eyes.

It clenched at her heart. The poor man not only longed to find his sister but also carried the weight of a grieving congregation upon his shoulders.

She touched his sleeve as he turned to go, stilling his steps. "At least come in and eat. Have some coffee."

"I must keep searching—"

"I'll wrap up a sandwich to take with you." Emily tipped her head toward the door. He appeared too weary or hungry to argue. Had he eaten anything since the slice of cake yesterday?

"Come," she insisted. "You must keep up your strength if you're going to minister to others."

Colin's expression softened. "Coffee, one cup, would be lovely, and whatever food I might eat as I go."

Colin entered the house behind Emily. He stepped into the parlor, where the Vercelli family sat huddled on the couch. Emily fetched him a steaming cup.

While the minister sipped coffee and visited with the young family, Emily wrapped a peanut butter sandwich in waxed paper. She carried it to him as Mr. Vercelli lamented the loss of their home on east Sealy Avenue and all the family heirlooms from Italy.

The mother dabbed at her eyes while clutching her wiggling babe. Emily caught a whiff of a wet diaper. Beside her lay cut squares of flannel for diapers made from Estelle's fabric bolt.

A toddler with dark curls and a cherub face peeked up at Emily from between the folds of his mother's skirt. What would become of this young family? Where would they go?

After Colin prayed with them, he thanked Emily for the food and slipped out the door.

The bread ran out by noon the next day. As Inez grumbled over what to feed everyone, Emily kept glancing over her shoulder, hoping to see Jake and Sarah trek into the yard.

A light rain had fallen earlier, thickening the air with moisture and sharpening the growing stench.

Feeling restless, Emily took a broom and started sweeping the front porch. The caked-on mud had dried. It would take a deep scouring to remove it. Water, she lacked.

Later that evening, she'd find a reason to go by Nathan's boat. She hadn't forgotten his plea for her to meet with him on Monday. The man had some explaining to do.

She finished brushing the loose clods from the front steps when she glanced up the road.

Emily's breath stalled in her throat. Her gaze sharpened on the lone figure headed in her direction, limping toward the house.

Chapter 33

The broom clattered at her feet. Emily flew down the steps and up the road, pushing against an urge to run in the other direction.

Emily called out his name on a dry breath.

What happened that shredded his britches up to his thighs? More significantly, why was he alone?

Dread blew through her.

Emily reached the boy. He wobbled on his feet and slumped into the circle of her arms. Then he buried his face into the folds of her shirtwaist. His bare arms, sun-browned and sticky, clutched her in a grip so tight that she struggled to catch her breath. She pulled back a little and kissed the top of his head. His stiff, dark hair smelled of saltwater and cedar.

"Where's Papa?" Andrew croaked. "He's not at the bakery."

"Out looking for you, I reckon. How'd you get here? Where's Jake?"

"A nice man carried me to town on his horse."

She leaned back and curled her fingers around Andrew's warm shoulders. She looked him square in the face.

"All by yourself? Where's Jake?" she repeated.

Lena's son swayed on his feet, saying nothing.

Emily's throat tightened.

"Where did the nice man find you?" she tried another approach, managing a tone far calmer than she felt.

Andrew's mouth pulled into a frown. "Not sure."

"Well, where were you headed?"

He stared down the road for a long while. At last, he whispered, "Three Trees."

Three Trees? Somewhere down the island? She recalled what Mosey Pitts said, and her mouth went dry. Never had she dreamed that exposing Jake to island history would result in *this*.

Her fingers dug in, squeezing Andrew's boney shoulders. "You and Jake went searching for pirate gold?"

Seeing him flinch, she eased the pressure on her grip.

Slowly, he nodded. "Yes, ma'am, but we … got lost."

She stifled a groan. What were they thinking, trekking down the island in the middle of a hurricane?

Her gaze bore into Andrew's. "I need you to tell me everything. Everything that happened." Her tone brooked no argument.

Andrew's body went still, his mouth a stitched seam. He said nothing for so long that Emily wondered if he would speak at all. The tears pooling in his dark eyes told her more than she wanted to know. So did the bleakness in his gaze.

Her insides quivered. Until now, she'd held out hope that somehow everything would turn out all right. That all her loved ones were safe, weary but whole. Yet what were the chances that they all came through the storm unscathed? Was Jake still out there somewhere, alone? What if he had broken bones and needed a doctor?

Andrew knew. Surely, he knew more than he was telling her. But she sensed that pressing him would gain her nothing. And given his fragile state, it might cause the boy harm.

Emily drew in a pained breath. She'd caused enough harm already. If only she hadn't sent Lena and the children away. Then the boys would have stayed underfoot. Then none of this would have happened.

Emily trussed up the expanding guilt and stroked Andrew's back. "Let's get you inside," she prompted.

He blinked and gave a slight nod but made no effort to move his feet. If Emily hadn't injured her arm, she would have scooped him up and carried him. Instead, she draped her arm over his shoulder and nudged him along into the house. There she put him straight to bed in Jake's room.

Inez managed to coax a few peanut butter crackers and a glass of water down the mute boy.

Once he'd changed into a pair of Jake's knee-length britches, Emily gave him a sponge bath. Only then did she notice the raised, nail-thin welts on his limbs. What had caused the red marks?

Emily noticed Andrew's eyes drift shut, his breathing even out. She tiptoed from the room and padded to the kitchen, where Inez and Estelle hovered around the work table. They sipped tea, anxiously waiting for her to join them.

"…little mite," Inez scratched her jaw. "I couldn't pry two words out of him."

Seeing Emily shuffle in, Inez tipped the teapot and poured her a cup.

"Well? What did he say?" Estelle's eyes pleaded for news on Jake and Sarah.

Using both hands, Emily took the cup from Inez and lifted it to her lips. While she took a bracing sip, she used the moment to gather her wits, debating how much to share.

"Very little," Emily decided, crossing her legs at her ankles. "He said a nice man carried him on horseback to the bakery, but his father wasn't there."

Estelle frowned. "He met up with this man … by himself?"

Emily uncrossed her legs. "I tried to get him to talk, but he looked ready to collapse in the road."

All true. A headache drilled at Emily's temples, throbbing behind the swollen knot.

"Then where is Jake? Those two are inseparable." Estelle blew on the surface of the tea and drank deeply.

Emily recalled what Peter told everyone at the table. Aunt Estelle would soon hear that the boys had taken off in the rain. Better the news came from her.

Emily swallowed a sip to ease the dryness in her throat. "Apparently, he and Andrew went off … exploring."

Estelle paled, rocking slightly on her feet. "Out in the storm?"

"Afraid so."

"Then *where* is my son?" Estelle's voice pitched with an edge. "And what were they doing outdoors in the first place?"

"Out playing in the overflow with the others. According to Peter, the boys left before Lena called the kids in."

Estelle's brows lifted. "When did y'all speak?"

"He came by the orphanage to eat lunch with Lena. When she didn't return, he called the house."

Estelle clicked a fingernail against the side of the cup, absorbing the news. The clicking ceased. The skin below her eyes tightened. "And you didn't see fit to mention this before now?"

Emily leaned away from the work table. "I—I've," she cleared her throat. "My mind has been a bit… fuzzy."

"We've all been through quite an ordeal," Estelle said, "but it's not like you to overlook such a thing."

Emily absently fingered the swollen knot and winced at the soreness. "Maybe the knock on the head has affected me more than I realized."

Estelle set down the teacup and came around the work table. Her expression softened. "Let me have a look."

Emily swiveled her head to give Estelle a better view.

Estelle made clicking noises with her tongue as she gently examined the knot. "It's nearly as big as a plum."

"The swelling will go down. I'll be all right."

"What hit you?"

"Best as I can recollect, something struck me when the roof fell in."

They stared open-mouthed at her.

"The roof," Estelle said, touching her throat, "on the orphanage?"

Emily nodded.

"Mercy! What happened?"

"The roof collapsed. I had… I'd just stepped into the great hall."

Emily's chest tightened. "Anyway … I—I'm fine. You needn't worry over me. I'm just thankful no one was hurt."

"All the same," Estelle's tone turned motherly, "we'll have Dr. Ryker examine you on his next visit. And that arm, too. I noticed it bandaged when you came in."

Emily wondered when the doctor would be free to visit, given all the injured people filling both hospitals.

"Where are the orphans?" Inez asked.

Emily swallowed the tea, missing cream and sugar. "Last I heard, they're staying in a frame house near the orphanage."

They lapsed into silence.

Estelle kneaded her forehead with her thumb and forefinger. "I had so hoped Andrew could tell us more."

Emily's mouth tightened, and she glanced away. She lacked the heart, or the nerve, to tell Estelle that Andrew had gone quiet when she pressed him about Jake's whereabouts. What would be the purpose of divulging that the boys went off down the island in search of buried treasure?

Estelle was murmuring, "We must get word to Peter. Perhaps leave a note at the bakery."

"I'll go," Emily volunteered.

The errand was her chance. Before long, it would be evening. Nathan moored his boat at the pier not far from Peter's shop.

"While you're out," Inez piped in, "mind going by the store and picking up some beans and rice, some canned beef and vegetables, condensed milk … and grits? We need grits."

At least the family in the parlor had found a room with the man's employer and moved out.

Emily drained her cup. "Make me out a list."

With a quick nod, Inez ducked into the pantry.

Emily's clothing stuck to her skin as she roamed the downtown Strand. The sultry temperature made the air more fetid, stinging her eyes and ripening into a full-out assault on her senses. Even though she breathed through a linen handkerchief, the stench stole her breath.

She left a note at Peter's bakery and threaded her way around piles of rubbish over to the mercantile store.

Some of the buildings, she noticed, had bricks and timber plucked off, leaving little more than the skeletal framework in place. They looked like the carcasses of old bones left in the sun to dry.

A crew of men hoisted long planks of timber, clearing the sidewalks. One man toted a gun up and down the road, discouraging looters.

A wagon rattled past her. Emily first noticed the stiffened legs poking out the back, jiggling. She gasped and shuffled back a few steps, sinking her half boots into the standing water that trenched both sides of the road. She paid no heed to her toes growing damp. Emily stared at the bodies heaped the width of the wagon bed. A shudder ran through her. She turned her face away and hurried across the street.

Sacks of coffee, onions, and persimmons flanked the mercantile store's entrance. The odor of rotting produce wafted with the stench building in the air.

Two men stood within earshot on the sidewalk in deep conversation. The older gentleman with a white, wiry beard inclined his ear to hear the other speak.

"…noble thing you're doing for our orphans, Dr. Buckner."

Emily eavesdropped at the mention of orphans while she peered through the window.

"It's my privilege. At present, I have room for a hundred children."

"It's unclear how many orphans are even left." The man dressed in a suit and bowler hat stroked the ends of his walrus mustache. "St. Mary's down the island washed away. Tragedy, that."

Emily pressed her palm to her collarbone. The orphanage down the way had nearly a hundred children living there. Had anyone survived?

"What about the orphans' home on 21st Street?" Dr. Buckner asked.

"The building collapsed, but all the orphans survived."

"That's marvelous! I must go see to their needs at once."

Emily stole a glance at Dr. Buckner. His eyes twinkled with exuberance. Of all things, the man appeared energized by the challenge rather than drained by it.

"Allow me to escort you." The businessman turned and led them down the walkway.

Emily pushed through the door, hearing the bell jangle. Miles, the store clerk, was stacking cans on a display table. Emily noticed the labels had washed off.

"Pardon the mess." Miles glanced up. "You're Miss Estelle's niece, aren't you?"

"Yes, sir."

"Well, what can I get for you?"

Emily handed him Inez's list.

Miles eyed the list. "Sold out of canned beef and condensed milk." He motioned to the stacked cans. "Help yourself. Your guess is as good as mine about what's in them. They're free pickings."

He pushed the rolling ladder over and climbed the rungs, pulling bags of beans, rice, and grits from the upper shelves and handing them down to Emily.

Below the watermark, the lower shelves lay bare.

Emily lifted a handful of grab bag cans off the table and dropped them in Inez's cotton sack.

Emily looked around. "Where's Jasper?"

"He's been rounded up to load the barges." His spindly shoulders trembled.

"Load what?"

"Corpses. They've given up on identifying the bodies. Too many. Too swollen. They're carrying them out to sea this evening. Looks like a watery burial for those poor souls."

Miles shook his head as though attempting to clear the image from his mind. The gesture caused the thinning hairs floating above his head to quiver.

A burial … at sea? Their families would have no proper place to lay their loved ones, no gathering with kinfolk around gravesides to say farewell. At least Lena and the children were not among them. Emily had Colin to thank for checking for her.

She glanced up at the wall clock. With a start, she wondered where the time had gone. She hefted the sack and thanked Miles before rushing out the door to meet Nathan.

The orange sun hung low over the water when she approached the deserted pier where he kept his sailboat.

Floating wreckage and barrels littered the harbor. Boats jammed together, some leaning toward the water with their masts bowed, the water slapping at the hulls. Other vessels were cast aground amid piles of debris.

Emily scanned the sailboats, searching. She vaguely recalled Nathan's boat was aptly named. She picked her way around dead fish and clumps of seaweed, a canvas sail, and a snapped-off wooden tiller.

In the sand, leaning to one side, she recognized the name painted on the side of the boat: Newsprint.

Her stomach fluttered with anticipation. Would the reporter in him tell her all that she wanted to know? Her mouth tightened. He'd better. Not that she relished hearing details about his relations with the young servant girl who gave birth to Chai Lin.

Emily lifted her chin and approached his boat. She peered into the sunken cockpit. Broken palm branches and wood planks littered the seats and floorboard.

Was he down in the cabin? She listened but heard no movement within.

"Nathan?" she called out.

Chapter 34

No sound stirred from within the cabin. Only the clacking of a pelican perched on the bent mast above.

"Nathan?" Emily tried again.

The bird squawked and flapped its wings over the intrusion.

She eyed the debris on the boat. Nothing suggested that Nathan had been near here since the storm. Neither had she seen light flickering in his room next door to indicate that he had returned home.

She fingered the watch pinned to her shirtwaist, noting the time. Quarter past five.

"He should be here by now," she muttered.

She lowered the loaded sack near her feet and slumped against the stern. Her stomach clenched. Was Nathan okay? Didn't he realize she'd worry unless he came as planned? He arranged this meeting, not her. He'd asked for a chance to explain about Ying Su.

She chewed on her bottom lip. She debated waiting a while, but the evening shadows lengthened on the Strand. She had to get back to the house before daylight faded.

Don't give up on me, he'd said.

She thrust out a sigh and pushed away from the boat. She had reached her fill of having no answers for one day. If Nathan was alive and well, let him get word to *her*.

As she stooped down for the sack, a cloud of mosquitoes swarmed about her head, buzzing and biting. She swatted at the air wildly and fled.

Arriving home, Emily found Andrew sitting cross-legged on Jake's bed, playing with toy soldiers and the sticks that Jake had gathered to build a fort. He sat still, his gaze riveted on two soldiers wedged in the shoots of two stems, propped against the headboard. Emily hung back by the door jamb and watched him unobserved.

With a whooshing sound, he flicked his finger and toppled one figure clinging to the stick. He dragged it over to the edge of the bedcover and let go.

Emily eyed the scene and the welts on Andrew's arms and legs. The back of her neck prickled. She went and knelt beside him. Lifting the hollowed lead figure from the rug, she cradled it in her palm.

She spoke softly. "During the storm, did you and Jake climb trees like good little soldiers?"

Andrew's eyes widened. He gave a faint nod.

She swallowed around the ache in her throat. "Was Jake hurt?"

Andrew plucked the pillow off the bed and hugged it across his stomach. He clamped his mouth shut.

Emily tried again. "Did Jake fall into the rushing water?"

His shoulders crept up to his ears.

"Did he grab hold of a branch ... and float away?"

Andrew peered off, his nose reddening. He sniffled, nodding.

"So last you saw ... he was alive?"

She caught the gleam in Andrew's eyes, and her heart lurched.

"Uh-huh," he whispered.

Relief blew through her in a swift current. She sagged against the side of the mattress. Thankfully, Jake could swim.

She peered over her shoulder at the shuffling by the door. Estelle leaned on the door jamb, her face stricken, having caught the tail end of Andrew's account.

A knock on the door sent Estelle flying down the stairs. A minute later, she reappeared with Peter. With watering eyes, Peter drew his son into a bear hug.

Estelle gave them a moment before asking, "Any news?"

Peter shook his head. "I keep searching." He set Andrew down and guided him to the door. "Bless you for caring for my boy."

"You're both welcome to stay here," Estelle offered.

"I've got cots set up above the bakery. Plenty of bread and water. We'll make do."

While Estelle walked them downstairs, Emily curled her fingers around the toy soldier. Jake was last seen alive. That buoyed her waning hope.

The following morning, Emily lingered at the breakfast table alone. She skimmed Tuesday's paper over a bowl of congealing grits. One caption made her sit up straight in the dining room chair.

"Leaving?" She frowned. "He can't leave!"

She read on. *No man has been busier comforting the grief-stricken people than Dr. R.C. Buckner of the Buckner Orphan's Home in Dallas County. He leaves Thursday morning for his institution with the homeless orphans of the Galveston Orphan's Home, which was wrecked by the storm.*

She breathed in the printing ink as she absorbed the news. Dr. Buckner was taking Chai Lin away.

From the moment she'd laid eyes on the little Chinese boy, he had crawled up onto the seat of her affections and nestled there. He'd been sitting by himself on the orphanage steps. She knew firsthand the loneliness of not fitting in, so she had taken hold of his hand and led him into the ring of orphans circling Colin. She'd stepped in and acted on his behalf.

She could do no less now.

Forget her wounded pride over Nathan failing to meet her at his boat. She needed to hunt him down today.

One way or another, she'd get word to him about Chai Lin leaving. The boy deserved that much. More was at stake than guarding her virtue or Nathan's reputation. Someone needed to consider Chai Lin's needs as well. Surely there had to be a way for Nathan to do right by him without losing the community's esteem.

Following breakfast, she set out for the *Daily News* on Mechanic Street. Nearing the building, she passed by a work crew clearing the street. She picked her way around a crashed telephone pole and downed wires. The door to the newspaper hung off its hinges, a derailed trolley car squatting near the entrance.

She recognized the young man exiting through the door. He had relayed a message to Nathan following the parade.

"Excuse me," she called. Scotty swung around and paused expectantly. "Do you know where Mr. Chambers might be?"

"Yes, ma'am. He took a break to check on his boat. Care to wait inside?"

"No thanks."

She turned and strode toward the pier, her tongue stuck to the roof of her mouth. What she wouldn't give for a tall glass of lemonade with ice. Or a long soak in the tub and clean clothes.

Nearing the water, she spotted Nathan standing beside his sailboat. He frowned up at the bent mast. His white shirt sleeves rolled up his forearms.

She came alongside him. "I went by the *Daily News* looking for you," she huffed, not attempting to mask her displeasure. "Where have you been?"

"Houston," he said, his eyes gleaming. "A reporter buddy and I crossed the bay with the messenger force on Sunday. We got word to the president and the governor about our widespread destruction. Having no telegraph or telephone service and our bridges down has completely cut us off from the rest of the world."

Her mouth twitched. "And you've made no effort to let me know you were alive and well all this time."

"Getting word out took priority over everything."

Everything. Even her?

"So … you thought of me," he quirked an eyebrow.

"You presume a lot for a man who failed to ease my fears." *Or show up.*

Nathan made his way over to the bow while he inspected the listing boat. Emily put her hands on her hips and followed him.

Did he even remember their Monday meeting? She waited for him to apologize for failing to show, but he said nothing. She refused to admit she made an effort. That he left the island without making sure she was safe hurt more than his slight.

"We have field rations, plus cots and tents coming," he went on, oblivious to the turmoil churning inside her. "Houston has sent over provisions and a hundred thousand gallons of fresh water. Hopefully, that'll last until our own system's restored."

He picked his way around planks over to the boat's port side. "More news," he said over his shoulder, "I'm part of the newly formed correspondence committee. Gathering and reporting on the city's needs will mean extra work, but an opportunity like this boosts a man's career."

"Good for you," she managed, though her tone lacked enthusiasm. She wished Nathan would quit checking the boat for one minute. "I have news of my own, none of it good."

He swung around, his expression sobering. "Go on."

"Jake and Sarah are missing. So are Lena and Lacey Kesler and Grace Hensleigh. They've not been seen since Saturday. And their names weren't listed in the paper among the dead." She swallowed, choking down the tears clogging her throat.

Grim lines creased his mouth. "I'm sorry they're missing."

"I found Andrew Kesler yesterday alone. He and Jake had gone off down the island during the storm. When the water rose, they shimmied up trees until Jake was… He was swept away, though Andrew saw him last floating on a tree branch."

Sympathy shone in his eyes. "Have you considered what you'll do if neither of your cousins survived?"

"Perish the thought," she snapped.

"The death count has climbed about five thousand. I'm merely being practical. It would be best if you were, too. Better to explore your options now, rather than—"

"No," she cut in. "I will not. Not unless there's proof that they're … gone."

He pressed his lips flat as though he had more to say but thought better of it.

In the distance, smoke rose in wraith-like plumes above the tattered line of funeral pyres. Ashes polluted the air with the stench of charred flesh. The corpses taken out to sea by the barges had washed ashore with the tides. At this point, burning the dead was the only recourse.

"I have other news," Emily pressed on. "Dr. Buckner is taking our orphans to his place in Dallas. They're leaving Thursday morning." She looked him full in the face. "He's taking Chai Lin."

His gaze strayed to the boat hull and focused on the gaping hole the size of a baseball. He muttered a curse and ran his hand around the splintered rim, inspecting the damage.

"The boy *should* leave," he put in casually. "Being locked up in a jail cell won't shorten my father's reach. He has men on the outside to do his bidding."

"How is his leaving best for Chai Lin?"

"He'll be in good hands. Buckner's a fine man, a minister. He runs a Christian orphanage if that's what concerns you." His tone suggested that he didn't share the same concern. "I should think you'd be happy about that."

She stiffened. "But what if … what if he's yours?"

Nathan glanced about, making sure no one overheard. He clenched his jaw. "What more do you expect from me?"

"Take responsibility! If anything, others would esteem you for taking in a displaced orphan of the storm."

His nostrils flared. "I've cleared my name. There're no records tying me to the boy. None."

"Does that absolve you of all responsibility when he may be yours by your own admission?"

"What would you have me do? Accept my father's bribe money," he shot back, lifting his chin.

"Forget the money. Do the right thing."

He snorted. "My father manipulates those closest to him. You have no idea the pain he's capable of inflicting. Believe me when I say a scandal would be the least of it. Surely you don't want that stigma on the boy. Anyway, I'll not give him ammunition to use against me."

"So Chai Lin pays the price and gets sent away to Dallas." She shook her head in dismay.

"It's the best thing for him. Rather providential, I'd say. Have you considered that this may be God's way of protecting him?"

"You're quick to claim His providence when it suits your purpose," she grumbled.

He turned away and resumed examining the boat. What a pity he cared more for his sailboat than he did for that precious boy. He considered the discussion closed.

Well, she had plenty more to say.

"Did you know," she informed him in a deceptively casual tone, "that Ying Su refused to tell who the father was?" Nathan shot a glance at her, his eyes narrowing. "She would have taken the secret to the grave, except your father threatened to harm her sister unless she confessed. Only then did Ying Su speak up." Emily paused and waited until their gazes locked. "She named *you*."

His mouth twisted in a scowl. "Says who?"

"Says the minister whom the midwife called in."

"Hensleigh." It wasn't a question. He spun around and faced her. "Another private chat, I see. Why go to him?"

"I needed answers."

Nathan's tone hardened. "Well, a forced deathbed confession is hardly that. It lacks credibility. There is no proof that the boy is mine. Let's not forget where Ying Su lived. She worked among unsavory men."

"If Ying Su depended on you, then surely you would have known, or suspected, if men were making unwanted advances or taking certain liberties."

His jaw clenched, but he held his tongue.

She dug her nails into her fists. "You pleaded with me to give you a chance to explain what happened. Well, I'm waiting."

He looked away, but not before emotion shadowed his eyes. He rubbed a hand over the stubble on his face and sighed.

"There was a bartender, Hal. He fancied younger girls. Ying Su was afraid of him. He'd corner her when her sister rehearsed or when my father or his goons weren't around. That's when Ying Su began slipping away to my sailboat. It was one place she could hide out from him.

"I'd be readying the boat to go sailing or washing down the decks. Meetings started innocent enough, me holding her until she quit shaking. I suppose she felt beholden and repaid my kindness with affection. I let things get … out of hand."

Emily absorbed the news. Hearing it did nothing to settle her quivering stomach. Images sprang to mind of Nathan with his arms entwined around a pretty Chinese girl, their bodies swaying with the boat's gentle rocking. She rubbed her fingers between her eyes, wishing she could wipe clean the image.

"Did Hal ever … touch her?" she asked, her cheeks flushing hot.

"She never said, but he was fool enough to break the house rule. He refused to leave the girls alone."

"If Hal or anyone else had laid a hand on Ying Su against her will, wouldn't she have exposed him to make him stop? Yet instead, she named *you* as the father. It begs the question: did you take advantage of her?"

Nathan stiffened. "Never. What happened was consensual."

"Then Ying Su was either certain you were the father, or she had another reason for pinning it on you. Maybe she was protecting someone else. Maybe her sweetheart."

"No," he swung his head adamantly. "If she had feelings for another fellow, I would never have touched her."

"Well, you gave her some reason to sully your good name."

"Hardly! I protected her from Hal. She wouldn't have—"

He looked away, working his jaw from side to side. "Rather clever, hemming me in, so I had no choice but to admit the boy was mine. And what if he is? Would you have me live with a constant reminder of that one indiscretion?"

Numbness seeped into her bones. She had hoped an explanation would help put right the past. Not this.

Nathan stepped closer. "I need you to let the matter drop, Emily. Trust me, it's for the best. As it is, I have repairs to make with your aunt and uncle before I can properly court you. It's for the best," he repeated.

She shook her head, the corners of her mouth pulled down. Turning her face away, she peered at the buildings lining the Strand.

Nathan lifted her chin with the pads of his fingers, forcing her to meet his gaze. "We need a clean slate to build on. A potential scandal would jeopardize our future together."

Emily went still. How could she let something this heavy rest when it caused so much unrest within her?

238

Chapter 35

Dry hacking echoed from down the hall and roused Emily from sleep. She stared at the faint light shadowing the ceiling, feeling the fatigue pull behind her eyelids. She was reluctant to crawl out of bed after being awakened throughout the night by her uncle's coughing spasms.

She lost track of how often she heard feet padding up and down the hall, the doors opening and shutting. Aunt Estelle was running herself ragged, nursing him.

Before the storm, the doctor had said Uncle Clayton was improving. Now, this.

Her uncle needed plenty of rest and fresh air. Sunshine. These days he breathed in smoke from the funeral pyres and mildew from the water damage.

She and Inez did what they could to clear out the irritants. They'd swept the sludge off the floors and pitched out chunks of wet plaster by the road. The house still needed a thorough scrubbing, but they had to wait until the city restored the water.

How could Uncle Clayton improve when the house he lived in and the air he breathed irritated his lungs?

Emily rubbed the grit from her eyes with the heels of her hands and yawned. These days, falling asleep was troublesome, with vivid dreams dragging her back into the rising tidewater.

The children. A flush of panic coursed through her veins. It often hit hard upon waking, that harrowing limbo of not knowing what happened to them. She could hardly believe they were still missing. The notion was too horrid and unreal to take in, let alone hold on to for any length of time.

A dull heaviness pooled in her chest. She twisted between the sheets and rolled over.

Little Chai Lin was leaving today. She pictured him standing off by himself, hesitant to leave behind every familiar comfort and move to a strange new place. A challenge for any orphan, but more so for a child of Chinese descent.

A shudder ran through her as she recalled the graphic picture on a July cover of *Harper's Weekly*. It illustrated the Chinese Boxers with heads of missionaries speared atop their bayonets. Such atrocities inflamed the nation. Would staff and children shun Chai Lin for being Chinese?

If only she had persuaded Nathan to provide a home for the boy. She couldn't shake the sense of failing yet another child, much less crimp the swelling discontent of Nathan failing to live up to her expectations of him. Did all females waver between esteeming those they set their hearts on and watching them fall from their lofty pedestals?

I need you to let this rest, Emily.

Did he truly believe she could set aside something of this magnitude as if it didn't change everything? And what did it say about his character that he refused to own up to what he did, let alone take responsibility for his improper behavior toward the young servant girl? How could she live with herself if she gave in to his plea and let the matter rest?

Impossible.

Emily stretched a foot from under the sheet and slowly drew circles with her toes.

We need a clean slate to build on.

To her way of thinking, Nathan needed to make things right before they could *build* anything. What the man needed was the clean slate that came from a changed heart. Her foot stilled. What if he were to seek forgiveness and take responsibility? Could she find it in her heart to extend grace to him?

Unsettled, she threw off the covers and climbed out of bed. Her worries sapped her strength and weighed down her feet as they touched the braided rug. She welcomed the coffee wafting from the kitchen.

That evening, Inez opened several unlabeled cans, and the family dined on hominy and beets for supper. While Emily choked down a forkful of the chewy hominy, little Rachel stabbed at the beets.

"I don't like beets," she fussed, her mouth forming a red-stained pout.

Tuning out her daughter's whining, Estelle gazed bleakly at the vacant seats across the table. The longer those chairs remained empty, the lower everyone's spirits sank.

Emily caught a flash of movement out the window seconds before the doorbell rang.

"I'll get it," she offered, eager for an excuse to leave the table.

She hurried out of her chair and went and opened the door. Her nose wrinkled at the horrid smell, more sickening by the hour.

On the porch, Nathan leaned against the railing with his ankles crossed. He held a can in one hand. Glancing over her shoulder, she slipped out the door.

A slow smile dimpled his right cheek. He acted as though they hadn't discussed weighty matters last evening. Or they were settled, at least to his satisfaction.

Her lips thinned. She had no intention of letting the matter rest. "About last evening…"

"For you." Nathan held out his offering. "Brown bread from the commissary. Food is pouring in from everywhere. At least now there's no threat of folks starving."

She had read about the city being divided into wards, each having a relief station to distribute these supplies.

"Thanks," she replied crisply, taking the proffered can. She studied Nathan. "I reckon we need to clear the—"

"I'm back at the house," he cut in, though tension pulsed between them. "I couldn't very well sleep on the boat."

He scratched his ear. "I hear the water is back on in parts of the city. I came by to offer the use of our cistern until we have running water. Use what you need."

Emily folded her arms across her chest. "Your mother won't mind?"

"She's gone." Nathan lifted a shoulder, his manner nonchalant. "Crossed over on the first ferry out. She has no stomach for disasters."

Emily glanced down at the hardened mud clumped on the porch. Her brows drew together. Ash flakes rained onto the planks. The house needed a good scrubbing for Uncle Clayton's sake.

She set her jaw. "We're obliged."

Emily begrudged how easily Nathan had turned the situation around so that she was indebted to him. It didn't set well after him side-stepping her attempts to discuss last evening.

"Still no word on your cousins?" his voice gentled.

She shook her head. "Not yet."

They lapsed into momentary silence.

"Bits of stimulating news came in throughout the day," he offered. "We're now under martial law since state militia's rolled in."

Emily tilted her head. She'd seen a gunman patrolling the Strand. Things seemed orderly enough when she was downtown.

Reading the question in her gaze, he explained. "It's short-lived. They're guarding the warehouses and commissaries. I suspect they'll also be put to work evacuating the women and children and setting up tents for those who've become homeless."

"Another thing," he had a gleam in his eye. "Western Union services are restored. We received a wire. A real shot in the arm for morale. Clara Barton and the Red Cross left today for Galveston. They're due to arrive on the 17th. With Miss Barton's connections, she'll attract national attention our way. Mark my word, the funds will follow."

Emily sighed and looked away. If she wanted to know the news, she'd read—

A wire! Estelle had been fretting over getting word to kin. The first mail arrived at the post office just yesterday. But a wire. A wire was short. Succinct.

Emily met his gaze. "Could you send a message for me?"

"For you, yes. But keep it brief. Just a few lines."

Nathan pulled out his small notepad and pencil and waited as she gathered her thoughts.

"Hmm… How's this: 'Alive. House standing. Conditions dire.'"

He scratched out the message with a pencil stub. Emily gave him Will's name and the address of the Chireno post office.

"That's fine. I'll send it first thing tomorrow."

Nathan turned to go. Pausing, he peered back around. "Be sure and tell your aunt I'm here if y'all need anything."

She arched a brow.

"Just repairing the damage." He gave her a wink.

Emily watched him trot down the steps before she pushed open the door and went inside. The man was flawed, but at least he took seriously his pledge to make repairs with her kin. That counted for something. What might he be like with a changed heart?

Just give him time.

As much as she hated to admit it, Nathan had been right about steering their conversation to safer ground. The front porch was no place to discuss weighty matters. That conversation would still take place. She'd make sure of it.

Estelle glanced up as Emily pulled out her chair and lowered herself onto the seat. "Who was it, dear?"

Emily schooled her expression as she set the can on the tabletop. "Mr. Chambers. He brought us brown bread for supper. Said to help ourselves to their cistern. Now Inez and I can give the house a thorough scrubbing."

"What a godsend," Estelle murmured.

Her aunt handed the can to Rachel. "Take this to Inez and have her slice it."

Rachel's face brightened as she scrambled off the chair and out of the room.

Estelle's brow furrowed. "I hope a deep cleaning eases Clayton's cough. It's worrisome."

It was that.

Emily forced a smile. "By the way … Mr. Chambers agreed to send a wire to Chireno for us."

Emily repeated the message. Estelle nodded her approval.

Emily nibbled on her bottom lip. "He uh … he also said he's available anytime … if you need a hand with anything. Just say the word, and he'd be more than happy to help," she embellished Nathan's message.

"That's rather neighborly of him."

Yet Estelle's cool tone suggested she required more of Nathan before her reserve thawed toward their neighbor.

During the next week, Emily made use of her restlessness. She and Inez hauled rugs and furniture into the backyard and scrubbed each piece, letting them air dry in the sun. Then they scoured the floorboards and lower walls with hot, sudsy water.

But no amount of scrubbing removed the fear shadowing Estelle's eyes. By Friday, Uncle Clayton's fever had spiked, along with night sweats and blood-stained handkerchiefs. That afternoon Dr. Ryker's carriage rattled up to the house.

While the doctor examined Uncle Clayton and talked with Estelle, Emily cuddled beside little Rachel on the parlor sofa and read *Alice's Adventures in Wonderland*. Twice Emily lost her place, her voice drifting off. Rachel didn't seem to notice. The child squirmed closer beside her and hugged Miss Riggles tightly.

Emily peered up at the mantle clock. What was taking the doctor so long? Would he still have time to examine her, too?

Shortly before suppertime, the doctor clomped down the staircase. Emily rose expectantly, but he walked past the parlor and out the door.

She shrugged off the oversight, for what were minor injuries compared to her uncle's failing health? At least the wound on her arm hadn't become infected. She'd keep it clean and bandaged.

When Aunt Estelle missed the evening meal, Emily took a tray loaded with steaming bowls of beans and rice and climbed the stairs. She tapped on her aunt's bedroom door.

Hearing murmuring, Emily cracked the door open and peered inside. Estelle knelt by the bed, her head bowed. At the interruption, her aunt turned at the waist and looked over her shoulder.

Emily drew up short, cringing. "I—I didn't mean to intrude. Inez sent up food."

"No ... no, come in." Estelle mopped her puffy, reddened eyes with a handkerchief. "Clayton needs his supper."

"There's a bowl for you too."

"Take mine back, please."

Cold pinpricks needled her stomach. The doctor's news must have hit her aunt hard if it drove her to fast and pray. The anguish pinching Estelle's face spoke volumes. But so did her closed expression. Now was not the time to ask questions.

Estelle sniffled and dabbed her nose. "Mind giving Rachel a bath and putting her to bed?"

"I'll get her bathed and tucked in."

Then a long soak in the tub now that water had been restored.

Emily set down the tray on the dresser and lifted Estelle's bowl, backed out of the room, and pulled the door shut.

The following morning Aunt Estelle stood hunched over the candlestick telephone in the hallway, speaking in hushed tones.

In the next room, Emily squatted on the library floor. She pulled out dampened books from the lower shelves, forming knee-high stacks lining the bookcases. The task did nothing to channel her spiraling thoughts, but at least it kept her busy. Over breakfast, her aunt had said nothing about the doctor's visit. How bad was the news if—

Emily heard a rustling at her elbow. She rocked back on her heels.

"Sorry," Estelle said. "I didn't mean to startle you."

Covering her self-consciousness, Emily motioned to the stacks. "It pains me to see books ruined. Two full rows. Reckon we might salvage some by drying them in the sun?"

Estelle fingered her collar and peered out the window, her gaze unfocused. At length, she spoke. "Once Rachel is down for the night, please join me in the parlor. We must talk."

Emily's mouth went dry. "O—of course."

Estelle's hollow tone unnerved her. Whatever the news must be, Emily dreaded hearing it.

⁂

The clock chimed on the hour as Emily lowered herself onto the chair beside Estelle. Shadows darkened the corners of the parlor, the feeble lamp casting a faint light around them.

Emily clutched her hands in her lap, pushing back her cuticle with her thumb. Her aunt's haunted eyes knotted the muscles in her neck, making it difficult to swallow.

The air grew thick and oppressive. She struggled to draw in a deep breath.

Estelle lifted the teapot off the side table. She poured the lavender tea, handing Emily a cup and saucer with a shaky hand.

Emily wrapped her stiff fingers around the blue and white china.

"Time grows short," Estelle began.

What did she mean? Did her uncle have but days to live? Is that what Aunt Estelle had to tell her?

Emily crossed and uncrossed her ankles.

Estelle cleared her throat. "I don't know how to soften this." Her voice sounded strained.

Emily shifted back on the brocade cushion, her pulse hammering.

"We must go. Every day we stay, Clayton deteriorates."

Go? Emily blinked. "You're going away … for a visit?"

"We must *leave* the island, Emily. Dr. Ryker said that if I don't get Clayton away now…" Her voice trailed off, the implication clear.

Estelle paused to compose herself.

Leave. "When? Where to?"

"Baytown." Estelle set down her cup, sloshing liquid onto the saucer. "Clayton's brother, Charlie, has a separate room for Clayton, if Rachel and I share. The news is all very abrupt, but it can't be helped."

They're leaving.

Emily strained to hear over the blood rushing in her ears. One thing sank in, though. There was no mention of room for her at Charlie's house.

She would be left on her own.

Chapter 36

"I've prayed for strength to leave," Estelle continued, her voice strangled. "It's terrible not knowing what's become of the children, but either we go, or I risk losing—"

"I'll stay here," Emily pushed the words past her dry throat. "I must … until we know more."

How else would she break free from the guilt shackling her?

Estelle's lips rolled inward. "I'm afraid that's out of the question. Clayton insists on closing up the house when we leave."

Did that decision have anything to do with Nathan living alone next door?

"Then I'll find another arrangement. Something suitable."

Emily swallowed a sip of tea, her mind whirling.

The suggestion seemed to mollify Estelle. "Clayton is too ill to go by ferry. We must find another way across the bay. Somehow God will provide."

She glanced over at the staircase. "I must go and try to coax more broth down him. Pray the fever breaks."

Emily nodded absently. Her heart thudded in her chest. She half-sensed the light pat on her shoulder or the fine muslin fabric swish past her. Above the mantle, the cottage scene with the hollyhocks and rambling roses swam before her eyes.

She slid out of the chair and wandered outdoors into the raining cinders. There the air pulsed with chirruping crickets.

Feeling weak-kneed, she plopped down hard onto the swing's seat, sending it swaying. Where had the cushion gone?

A mosquito whined near her ear. She shooed it away and stared off into the night.

She peered at the line of smoking pyres with their sickly orange glow for a long while. The stench of acrid smoke burned the back of her throat and nostrils.

The turn of events was uprooting everything: her role as a governess, living with kin, her sense of security. Gone.

Worse still, she had nowhere to go. What little cash her grandfather gave her would last a month, maybe two. Then what?

Emily swallowed hard, tasting the burnt ashes, or was that fear?

The flaring fires grew hazy as a wave of despair crashed and thundered through her, plucking her dreams and casting them adrift.

What would become of her?

***

The last hymn faded, and the sermon became a dull murmuring, though due to no lack of skill or inspiration on Colin's part.

With her head bowed, Emily's surroundings grew indistinct beyond the brim of her straw turban. Silent tears wet her cheeks. She could not stem the flow from rolling down and soaking the lapels of her brown suit.

She wrung her hands, feeling her palms dampen beneath her gloves. Where would she ever find a place to live? All the boarding homes left standing were crowded to capacity. Neither would her uncle consent to her living in the city of tents on the beach.

Even weakened on his sickbed, he guarded her reputation with strength and diligence. Though she respected him for it, Uncle Clayton eliminated one possibility.

What if no suitable living arrangements turned up? What then? Going home was no option, and none of her kin had extra room. She couldn't shake the oppressive image of her hunched over a bowl of gruel in a ratty poorhouse.

She grew lightheaded, swaying slightly on the pew.

Whatever will I do?

Emily sensed His presence. She had a Helper if she'd let Him be that for her. What other choice did she have?

For too long, she'd wanted nothing more than to set her course without Pa's interference. Admittedly, her grit and determination got in the way of her seeking faith. She'd been so focused on surviving the hailstorm of bickering and criticism that rained around her that she failed to notice her tender trust eroding, the doubts taking hold.

She pressed her eyelids closed. Was the Lord truly mindful of her misery, that He heard the cry of her heart before she uttered a single word?

Teardrops spilled past her lashes as inward groans gave way to feeble pleas.

Lord, what am I going to do? I've nowhere to go. No means to support myself. Please provide a way, a place for me to stay.

The strains of the doxology roused her. Emily blinked and sniffled. She kept her head bent over her drawstring pouch while she dug out a handkerchief and dabbed at her eyes and nose.

For the first time since Estelle shared the news of their leaving, Emily drew a full breath into her lungs.

Following the benediction, voices murmured as folks began shuffling up the aisle and out the doors.

Emily scanned the sanctuary where the congregation met on Sunday afternoons. The building had withstood the storm better than most, aside from the collapsed back classrooms, the toppled steeple, and broken stained glass windows.

She stood up and lingered at the back of the line while folks flowed out of the sanctuary. She spotted Colin by the door, his head bent toward Miss Pickering, listening intently. Shock registered on his face before compassion flooded his features. Miss Pickering straightened, lifted her chin, and walked on.

When Colin finished speaking with the last person ahead of her, he took in her eyes, swollen from crying.

He motioned to the back pew. "Care to sit?"

She went over and eased down onto the cushion. Dampness seeped through her skirt, cooling her thighs. She moved over to a dry spot on the seat. Colin sat several feet away and placed his Bible between them.

At the altar, a deacon poured the offering into a bag. The man strode up the aisle with a rangy gait, the coins jingling.

"Samuel," Colin called, "please keep open the doors and leave the lights on. We shan't be long."

The man dipped his bearded chin on his way out.

Colin's discretion did not go unnoticed by her. By keeping the doors open, the minister guarded them against speculation. That simple act moistened her eyes.

Emily struggled for composure while the sanctuary settled into stillness.

"What troubles you, Emily?"

Colin's gentleness lent comfort. So did his using her given name. It spoke of the deepening friendship they had forged since the storm.

She pressed a hand to her mouth and shook her head. "I can't... I need another place to stay. Immediately."

His brows drew together. "Why is that?"

"Uncle Clayton's condition has worsened. Doc says they must leave at once. They—they're going to his brother's over in Baytown."

"I doubt Clayton can cross over by ferry." Colin scratched his chin. "I know of someone. The man's boat is damaged but seaworthy. He may be able to take them across."

God will provide.

Patches of light shone through the bent lead and stained glass fragments clinging to the window frames.

"That would ease Aunt Estelle's mind considerably."

"I'll contact Ben. He's a good man."

Colin's brows drew together, his gaze pensive. "And what of you? Will you return home?"

"My kin has no room for me," the words spilled out with a rush.

Colin tipped his head. "Not even your folks?"

Emily grimaced, recalling her father's ultimatum. "Suffice it to say I've been kicked from the nest."

The clench in Colin's jaw registered his unease. "That's most unfortunate."

Emily gave a watery laugh. "It would be if I cared to go home, which I don't. Besides, I can't leave. Not now."

He shifted his tall frame and faced her. "Why is that?"

"I must find out what's become of Jake and Sarah. I'll have no peace until I do."

His navy eyes grew distant as if recalling a memory. "At such times, I've found God's peace is the only thing that guards our minds and hearts. The only thing."

He should know. He'd buried both parents days apart. Now his sister was missing. Even so, he remained unshakable.

His posture stiffened. "I'm curious ... does Mr. Chambers know of your situation?"

"Not yet. I only learned the news last night."

His tone remained neutral. "Do you hold ... any expectation that he may offer marriage?"

Where did *that* come from? Whatever prompted the forward question, Colin's expression gave nothing away.

Emily lifted a brow. "That's a bit premature. We have no understanding between us. Besides, Mr. Chambers has some decisions he must settle before I would consider him."

Was that a flicker of relief she saw in his eyes?

"I meant no offense," Colin's voice softened. "But being left with no chance of returning home puts you in a most precarious position. I would hate to see you act rashly. Promise me you'll say something should you feel desperate."

Emily was nearing desperate, but saying so out loud made it all the more unsettling.

She met his gaze. "I'm not prone to acting recklessly. Though I admit, I'm on pins and needles about finding a suitable place to live."

Colin steepled his fingertips and tapped them to his chin. "There is one possibility. It's only temporary, but it may give you time to explore other options. That is if you're willing to volunteer with the Red Cross. They've set up headquarters on the Strand."

Volunteer? Emily pressed her lips together. "I'll need a paying job."

"Workers are provided meals. Some have set up cots in the building. They may allow you to room there as well."

"What kind of work?"

"Relief work. Mostly sorting through shipments to distribute to the wards. They also set up a temporary orphanage."

Her pulse quickened. "Reckon they need a teacher?"

"It's worth pursuing. I spoke with one of the relief workers. Mr. Lewis, a fine chap. I suggested he check into borrowing the salvageable furniture from our orphanage. He's devoting one warehouse floor to those orphaned by the storm."

If anyone found Jake or Sarah wandering the street, wouldn't they be taken to the orphanage? If so, Emily needed to be there.

"It sounds promising," she said. "I'll go first thing tomorrow."

Colin leaned back on the seat and glanced out the doorway. "I've been in contact with Dr. Buckner," he told her.

Emily's brows lifted. "How's Chai Lin?"

Colin wiped a hand over his cheek. "From all accounts, I'm afraid he's not settling well. In class, the boy requires repeated prompting, even to complete assignments. And he's keeping to himself. I recommended that his teachers pair him with an older lad who might include him in activities. Buckner said he'd see about finding someone who's willing. I do hope it helps."

Emily's pressed her lips together. Nathan could have prevented this, the stubborn man. The boy needed the protection of a father and a stable home. At least Colin looked out for him. Chai Lin had that much in his favor.

She let out a sigh. "I hate that for him."

"Right. I'm concerned as well. I'll let you know what else I hear." Colin straightened and put his hands on his knees, glancing out the door. He reached for his Bible beside him and tucked it under his arm.

Talking helped clear her mind. Colin had listened. He cared. In so doing, a bit of trust had been restored to her; no small gift, that.

Gratitude welled up, filling some of the emptiness with warmth.

"Thank you," Emily said, meaning it. "You're a lifesaver on many fronts."

They stood to leave. On impulse, Emily reached over and pressed her lips to Colin's cheek. Traces of shaving soap clung to his skin, the scent crisp and clean.

At her nearness, Colin's chest expanded. He drew in a sharp breath, releasing it when she pulled away.

Emily gazed up at him, her brows puckered. She took in his parted lips, his eyes widening a fraction. His gaze bore into hers, his Adam's apple sliding up and down. Had he misconstrued her intentions? She'd meant nothing more of the gesture than to express gratitude for his kindness. Not only toward her, her kin, but Chai Lin.

The air thickened between them. Emily stepped back, the skin under her collar itching.

Did he think her a flirt or so desperate that she made unwanted advances toward him? It was bad enough having her reputation called into question by Miss Pickering, but she couldn't abide him thinking less of her.

The minister stuffed his hands into his trouser pockets and peered out the door, acting as though he had somewhere else he needed to be, or wanted to be.

He cleared his throat. "Right. Well, we must be off."

"I've kept you long enough," she murmured. Discomfort swelled in her chest.

"Once I have a word about the boat, I'll contact Estelle."

Emily lowered her head, hoping the brim of her hat hid the heat flaming her cheeks. "Much obliged."

"It's the least I can do. Your aunt and uncle are like dear family."

Her aunt and uncle. "Of course."

Just leave—now.

She cut her eyes to the door, her mind a blank slate.

Whirling around, she flew out the door, unconcerned whether Colin might think her flighty. Better that than him regarding her as being too forward or behaving in a manner beneath her dignity.

Chapter 37

"I'm interested in a teaching position with your orphanage." Emily cleared her throat and leaned forward on the balls of her feet, trying to gain the Red Cross worker's full attention. "I've served as a governess before."

"We already have a teacher," the woman replied without glancing up. She kept her head bent over a barrel of women's gowns and shirtwaists, busy sorting.

Emily licked her dry lips. "Have you an assistant?"

"No need. We expected hundreds of orphaned children from the storm. Presently, we have fifteen. Do you cook?"

"Cook," Emily repeated, buying time. She could shoot and field dress a deer, but preparing food had been her mother's domain. The few meals she cooked whenever Rosa took ill had been basic, simple food.

The worker kept her eyes trained on the task at hand. "Our most pressing need is a cook."

"I have … some experience," Emily hedged.

"Enough to prepare three square meals daily for all our workers and or-phans?"

"Uh … no, ma'am."

"Hmm, well…" The worker's tone suggested she had ruled out Emily for more than just kitchen duty.

Emily's shoulders slumped. It rankled that the woman had yet to look her in the eye or make proper introductions. Her impromptu interview was not going the way she expected. She had to secure work.

The thudding of horse hooves and the rumble of wheels echoed in the building.

The man seated at the desk by the open doorway called over his shoulder. "More wagons pulling up." He viewed the invoice thrust at him and let out a slow whistle. "Two thousand pounds of disinfectant."

"Our first concern is to protect the living," the woman informed Emily.

Emily scanned the deep warehouse that housed the Red Cross headquarters. The autumn light filtered through the windows at the front and down the sides of the building, where rows of crates and barrels lined the water-marked walls blooming with mold. Placed around the interior, workers bent over barrels sorting supplies for distribution to the newly formed wards.

Emily straightened her spine and tugged down the hem of her suit jacket. "Put me to work. I have experience organizing and stocking supplies for our orphanage. On the day of the storm, we sorted through a mound of donations."

"Well, this is more like a mountain, and there are more shipments on the way. We need volunteers who can tolerate standing on their feet from dawn til dark. Who don't run from monotony because it all starts over again the next morning."

Emily lifted her chin. What other choice did she have? She was no quitter. "I don't shy away from hard work."

"You do understand this is volunteer work—there's no pay."

"A cot and meals would be payment enough."

Emily needed it sooner than she'd expected. Last evening, Colin telephoned Estelle with news that a boat would be ready on Wednesday to take the Edwards across the bay.

"Our women are staying at the Tremont," the woman said.

Emily hesitated. "I—I can't afford a room. I was hoping I might stay here. My needs are simple."

The Red Cross worker peered up at Emily, her dark eyes probing, assessing. "You have experience working with children, you say? Grieving children?"

Emily considered her cousins. "Yes, ma'am. I served as governess to children who remained separated from their ill father. Both lagged in their studies, they missed him so."

"Can you provide two letters of reference?"

"I can provide one from my employer and my minister."

Was there another opening with the orphanage? Before she could ask, a familiar face appeared over the woman's shoulder, giving Emily a start.

She grimaced. *Not now!*

"Allow me to speak on behalf of Miss Cleburne," he drawled. I know her family and can vouch for her good character."

The Red Cross worker arched a brow. "And you are?"

"Nathan Chambers, a reporter for *The Daily News.* May I ask your name in return?"

"Mrs. Ward."

His eyes widened with recognition. "Mrs. Fannie B. Ward?"

"That's correct."

"Mrs. Ward, it's an honor to make your acquaintance. Your articles on the war in Cuba were superb. You inspired me to get out in the field where the stories are."

Nathan glanced at the men hauling in the barrels. "The Central Relief Committee has turned over distributing emergency aid to the Red Cross, but are these few workers equipped to meet the pressing needs here? You need more volunteers."

The woman studied Nathan with shrewd eyes, eyes that had seen too much to be easily discomposed, or flattered. "May I ask the nature of your business here, Mr. Chambers?"

"The relief committee has appointed me to report on the needs of the wards. I overheard you asking Miss Cleburne for references and thought I'd expedite matters. Every minute tied up interviewing worthy folks takes you away from the demands of your work."

Mrs. Ward's gaze swept the barrels stacked along the walls. "You make a strong point." She turned and faced Emily. "We'll need those references before you begin."

"Yes, ma'am. And I need a place to stay, come Wednesday. You mentioned the children. May I work with them?"

"In a supportive role, yes. At present, a teacher bunks with the orphans. She's up comforting those who awaken with nightmares, crying for their mothers. Another female would lend a calming presence for the children." Mrs. Ward rubbed her chin. "Let's say you start sorting shipments during the day and staying with the orphans at night. It'll be grueling work doing both. Do you have the stamina for it?"

Emily blew out a breath, letting relief drain her fears. "Ma'am, I grew up on a farm doing the workload of most men. I reckon that arrangement will be more than manageable."

Estelle carried little Rachel down the stairs, the child wailing, "But I don't want to wear socks!"

"She's tired, poor thing." Estelle glanced over her shoulder at Emily, who trailed behind them. "She's not used to being up so early. All this commotion. Pray she takes a nap on the boat."

At the bottom of the staircase, Rachel's bottom lip stuck out. She whimpered, "Socks are itchy … and hot."

Looking lost, Rachel folded her arms over Miss Riggles, pinning the limp doll to her chest.

The trunks and luggage were in the entryway beside the hall tree. Emily's suitcase, small trunk, and hat box were set off to the side. Separate. It drove home the point that she would soon become parted from kin. Alone for the first time. She pushed aside the ache gnawing under her ribs and followed Estelle into the parlor for the last time.

"Why isn't Emmy coming too?" Rachel fussed, climbing onto Emily's lap. Tears beaded the little girl's lashes.

"Remember," Estelle said, "we talked about this last night. Miss Emily is staying, and you, Papa, and I are going on a boat ride to see Uncle Charlie."

"Boat ride," Rachel giggled. "Uncle Charlie has a dog. His name is Nelson."

Emily forced a smile, savoring their remaining minutes together. "I bet you and Nelson will be friends in no time."

"Uh-huh." Rachel shifted her bony hips and turned, looking up, her big blue eyes searching Emily's. "Will Jake and Sarah be there?"

Emily's smile froze in place. Rachel's innocent question punched the air out of her lungs.

A horse-drawn carriage clattered to a stop out front, rescuing Emily from further questions. A rap at the door sent Estelle to open it. The taxi would take the Edwards to the pier while a smaller cab would take Emily to the Red Cross headquarters. It was due any minute.

Deep voices filled the entryway. One voice sent Emily's pulse climbing.

Colin and the driver appeared at the entrance. Colin shot Emily a brisk nod and followed Estelle up the stairs.

Emily had telephoned Colin after the interview. The call had been brief, stilted. When she had asked if he minded being a reference, he agreed to pen a letter and deliver it.

Emily had not seen him since she flew out of the church house on Sunday. What must he think of her? She regretted acting impulsively. Now awkwardness pulsed between them.

Hearing footfalls, Emily sent a sidelong glance toward the hallway. The men lumbered down the stairs, flanking Clayton.

"Papa," Rachel cried.

Clayton smiled faintly at Rachel. "Hi, Buttercup."

His arms draped the men's shoulders, the men supporting much of Clayton's weight. Dressed in street clothes, he appeared leaner than his earlier photographs depicted. A lock of straight, flaxen hair fell into his eyes. Jake's hair, the same hazel eyes. The resemblance speared Emily's heart.

Clayton met her gaze. "Emily."

He looked like he might say more but lacked the strength. Merely nodding, the men hauled him out the front door. Estelle followed behind with a pillow and blanket, telling Rachel to stay put. While her aunt made Uncle Clayton comfortable, the men went in and out, hoisting luggage onto the carriage.

"Don't be scared," little Rachel cuddled Miss Riggles, rocking the doll in her arms. "You're going with me."

Emily dreaded them leaving her behind. Her shoulders tensed as she considered what lay in store when she no longer had their familiarity to soothe her. Missing them already, Emily held Rachel tight and planted a kiss on the crown of her soft curls.

Estelle came through the front door. Emily helped Rachel down off her lap and stood up.

It was time.

She clasped hold of Rachel's hand and led her over to her mother. Estelle opened her arms, and Emily hugged her fiercely, absorbing the warmth and security of her nearness. Pressing her eyes closed, Emily breathed in the lemon-scent. Too quickly, Estelle pulled away.

Estelle reached for *Sense and Sensibility* off the hall tree shelf and handed the novel to Emily. "For you. Keep it."

Emily held it to her chest. "Thanks."

Estelle picked up her kid gloves and pushed her hands into them. She lifted her hat from the hook and pinned it with a hat pin. Turning, Estelle scooped up Rachel and shifted her, so she straddled one hip.

"You have our address and telephone number, should you need me or if you hear … anything."

"I promise I'll let you know the minute I do."

Estelle's blue eyes shone bleak with resignation.

"Well, your carriage will be along any minute." Her aunt planted a dry kiss on her cheek and bustled out the door with Rachel.

Emily leaned against the doorjamb for support. She watched them pass Colin on the walkway and climb into the carriage.

Colin trotted up the stairs. He removed an envelope from his coat pocket and stretched out his hand, holding the end of the envelope. "Miss Cleburne, I have that reference you requested."

Miss Cleburne, was it? Emily bit back a sigh, mindful that she had caused this formality. As she reached for the envelope, she noticed the tense set of Colin's shoulders.

"Thank you again," she murmured, "for everything."

"You're most welcome," he gave a stiff nod.

He stepped away, creating even more space than his cautious eyes reflected. It was Emily's undoing. Hurt and sadness, coupled with ever-thickening loneliness, closed in, swamping her. She needed a friend now more than ever. How would she cope with all the changes thrust upon her without one? Her inner turmoil must have flashed across her face unwittingly, for Colin stilled.

He leaned in, his voice softening. "Are you all right?"

Beyond him, she caught the movement of Rachel waving goodbye. Emily plastered on a smile and waved back.

"Not in the least," she murmured, choked with emotion. She willed herself not to cry. The last thing she wanted was Colin's pity. Much to her chagrin, tears wet her lashes.

"I don't suppose you are. I'm … well, Ben is waiting." Colin threw her an apologetic look, turned, and strode out to the carriage, climbing aboard.

Emily slumped against the doorframe and watched the covered carriage pull away and trundle around the corner, turning out of sight. Blurry-eyed, she stared off after them, feeling bereft. Pots clanging in the kitchen drew her gaze away.

Inez would lock up the house.

When Emily told the woman about the Red Cross being short a cook, she went there straightway and applied. It gave Emily stability knowing the crusty cook would be working nearby.

Emily trudged up the stairs and checked her bedroom one last time to ensure she had packed everything. With a sweeping gaze, Emily glanced inside the empty armoire and around the room. It bore no imprint of the months she had lived there. Breathing a sigh, she stepped out into the hallway.

Near her uncle's room, a paper lay on the floor. She picked it up. Water stains crinkled the thick paper, curling the edges. She flipped the square over and sucked in a breath.

Hearing the rattle of carriage wheels, Emily tucked the keepsake into her pocket, hurried down the stairs, and gathered her luggage.

Emily spent all of that Wednesday, the 25th of September, hunched over barrels of bright-colored shirtwaists. Did people not realize that Galveston women were in mourning? They wanted dark clothes to wear, not last season's gay castoffs. She tossed aside the uncharitable thought, knowing most folks gave what little they had.

At sundown, she ate a bowl of pinto beans and a chunk of cornbread without tasting the food. Her thoughts kept drifting to the Edwards. She wondered how her uncle fared on the trip across the bay and whether Rachel was settling in with the dog.

Her calves burned from standing when she hiked up the darkened stairwell to the second-floor orphanage. Her shoes clicked on the hardwood floor, announcing her arrival.

Her steps froze at the shuffling of bare feet. All the children turned at once, peering at her. Standing by their cots in the dim light of a kerosene lamp, they all wore the same blank stares.

What had they been through that their faces appeared deadened of expression? That they showed no reaction or even mild curiosity at seeing a new face?

A Red Cross nurse had found three more orphans that day. Pearl, their young teacher, had pulled them aside and showed them their beds. The two older boys hovered over their little sister.

Emily spied a young girl, not much older the Rachel, seated on a cot nearby. The girl tugged at her tawny hair. Emily went over and crouched beside her, observing the child's eyes held a vacant gaze.

"I'm Miss Emily. What's your name?"

The girl blinked. "Savannah," she answered.

"What a pretty name. May I comb your hair?"

"Mama braids it at bedtime."

Emily faltered, unsure of what to say. Did the girl realize that her mother would never braid her hair again?

"I'll braid it tonight if you like."

"I … I lost my brush."

"Then I'll use my fingers. Here, like this." Emily sat on the child's cot and turned the girl around, facing outward. She threaded her fingers through the thick hair, separating the strands into three ropes, and wove them into one long plait. She had no ribbon to tie it in place.

Savannah twisted around, bringing her face close. "I want my mama," she whispered so no one else could hear.

Emily's heart clenched. She longed to erase the fear and dullness clouding the child's eyes. Gathering Savannah onto her lap, Emily held the girl until she grew heavy and still, then eased her down onto the pillow and covered her with a sheet.

Later, when all the children were tucked in their beds, Emily sank onto her cot, her luggage stowed beneath it.

She pulled the folded paper from her pocket. Her eyes stung as the memories surfaced. Suppressing the dull ache in her throat, she fingered the scalloped ridges of shells. She outlined the practiced handwriting that water drops had blurred. She ran a fingertip over a hardened glob of glue where one of the seashells had peeled off the face of the card. The card Jake crafted for his father.

Oh, Jake, where are you?
Give us answers, Lord.

<h1 style="text-align:center">Chapter 38</h1>

"They're uncovering bodies by the hundreds along that three-mile ridge of debris," Nathan announced the following week.

Heads whipped up around the warehouse as the climbing death count caused murmurs to ripple among the workers.

Emily dragged her gaze over to the man who created the stir and found his eyes fixed on her.

"Who gave you this information?" Mrs. Ward inquired.

"The men who operate the pyres along Avenue O."

Avenue O. Something about the location niggled at the back of Emily's weary mind. But the smell of Inez's flaky biscuits baking and her grumbling stomach pushed her to finish. Only one more barrel stood between her and supper.

She pried open the lid on another crate. It bulged with crockery, wooden spoons, and rolling pins. The contents had to be sorted by suppertime for delivery to the wards.

"The workers have reduced the ridge by half," Nathan continued. Out of the corner of her eye, she tracked his movement between crates as he weaved toward her. "Who knows how many more they'll find buried beneath the rubble."

The hairs on the back of Emily's neck prickled. Her gaze flew to Nathan. "The Keslers live on Avenue O."

Lived. The storm had torn apart their house.

Nathan's boots scraped the floorboards beside her. "That's right. I found Peter and your minister sorting through the wreckage. All that's left of the neighborhood is a tangled heap."

A tangled heap full of bodies.

Emily's blood ran cold. What if Lena and the girls were in that tangled heap? Her chin trembled.

"What is it?" Concern laced Nathan's voice.

A bitter taste rose in the back of her throat. "That Saturday, Lena took the children and Grace Hensleigh to see the waves and then to the Kesler's to play. The boys took off in the rain, but everyone else ... stayed."

Nathan's eyes narrowed as her meaning became clear to him.

She'd sent them away. What would Nathan think of her if she were to admit the truth?

"Who saw them last?" he asked.

"They ... they didn't return to the orphanage like Lena had planned. She wouldn't leave without the boys, so Peter called home before the telephone lines went down."

Nathan rubbed a hand down his sand-colored mustache. "So, last you heard, the girls were still at the cottage." She nodded, seeing him grimace. "Did Sarah have on any jewelry or other items that might help the workers identify—"

Emily felt firm pressure cupping her elbow. "Need to sit?"

Emily's body flashed hot and clammy. She gripped the rim of the barrel and shook her head.

"This is difficult," his voice softened, "but important."

Emily's shoulders drooped. She shook her head. "Sarah only wore her delicate cross with the seed pearls to church."

"What about Jake?"

She pictured him that morning. "He had a red bandana tied around his head. The boys were playing pirates."

The grim set of Nathan's jaw did nothing to reassure her. A bleak reality took hold of her. With so little to go on, was it even possible to identify either missing child?

That Friday evening, Emily walked out the warehouse door and down the steps, intent on stretching her legs before supper. She started up the sidewalk on the Strand as dusk bled across the sky and stained the clouds crimson.

The first week of October brought a chill that bit through her shirtwaist and raised goosebumps on her skin. Why hadn't she thought to grab a shawl? Emily rubbed her palms up and down her arms.

A bell jingled. A man and woman exited a shop onto the sidewalk ahead of her, carting paper bags.

Across the street, Emily spied a familiar figure lumbering toward the bakery entrance.

"Mr. Kesler," Emily called, rushing past a horse pulling a wagon, its hooves thudding on the road.

Peter swung his head around. Lena's husband paused with his hand gripping the doorknob. In the waning light, he stared through Emily as if he didn't recognize her. It took a moment before his expression cleared, and he dipped his chin in acknowledgment.

One look at his watery eyes and drooping eyelids, and Emily knew. Her spine went rigid with apprehension.

"Tell me," Emily pleaded.

"We ah," Peter swallowed, "we found them." Peter's jaw wobbled. "Under the…" He drew in a ragged breath. "Lena and our sweet baby—" A guttural sob cut off the rest.

She waited, her breath caught in her throat.

Peter wiped his eyes on the cuff of his filthy sleeve. "They're with Jesus," he mumbled with a sniffle.

The news filtered through the haze fogging her brain one word at a time.

"But the bodies by now… How can you be sure?" Emily pressed.

"Her wedding ring. I found it."

Emily squeezed her eyelids shut. Oh, no! *Not Lena*. Not her sweet friend.

"…found Grace's broach," Peter was saying.

Grace. Oh, Colin.

Emily peered at Peter, dread balling up in her stomach. "What about Sarah and Lacey?"

He shook his head. "No sign of the girls."

"But they were *there*," she insisted.

Peter gave a helpless shrug, his eyes misting. "Perhaps they fell in the water. Who knows?"

Not another cousin lost in the waves.

Peter shuffled his feet, looking as though his grip on the knob was all that held him upright or tethered him to sanity.

Emily gave his arm a gentle squeeze. "You've suffered a shock. I'll," she swallowed hard, "I'll miss Lena dearly."

Peter clenched his jaw so tight his neck muscles corded. "I must see about Andrew. How am I going to tell him?" his voice cracked.

He turned away from Emily and entered through the door.

At least Peter still had his son. That was some comfort. More than she had.

Oh, Lena. Emily buried her face in her hands. How would she manage without her friend's warmth and support, especially now?

Emily lifted her head and stared at the darkened sky, the tears sliding down her throat.

***

The following evening, Emily watched Colin and Mr. Lewis hoisting another load of tables and chairs through the warehouse doorway and group them around the dining area. More furnishings they had borrowed from the wrecked orphanage on 21st Street.

Earlier in the week, the two men had carted over dressers and finished setting up the orphanage upstairs that now housed twenty-seven children.

Inez called from the back kitchen. "Suppertime!"

Emily finished emptying the last crate and plodded toward the dining room.

Since hearing of Lena's death, she shuffled about in a numbed haze, her limbs heavy. Her deep sighs did nothing to ease the soreness in her heart.

She spotted Colin and slowed her steps. He stood at the back of the line behind the orphans. Just as he'd stood behind formality in their brief encounters since the Edwards had departed. His hand rested on a boy's neck as he bent over to hear the child speaking.

Hearing her shuffle behind him, Colin glanced over his shoulder. He caught Emily's eye. She watched the briefest hesitation flit across his face.

"Good evening." He dipped his chin, his manner courteous.

Diverting her gaze, she mumbled, "Hey," then lifted a plate from the clean stack and gathered the utensils.

The silence stretched between them, filled in by clinking silverware and the voices drifting from the nearby tables.

Emily swallowed a groan. Were they reduced to nothing more than being polite? Only yesterday, the man had learned about his sister. She wanted to express her condolences, but not like this. Not here, in the presence of little ears.

The boy in front of him dug into his short corduroy pants pocket and pulled out a glass marble. He held it up for Colin's inspection, prattling over the swirled design.

Emily considered Colin's reserve toward her. Had it stemmed from his old fiancé's lack of propriety, from him being left feeling like a fool? Enough that he'd vowed ministry and raising Grace took priority, excluding marriage. Emily grew still. Did he view her as another unfit female he must avoid for his reputation? It made sense in the most bothersome way. Her mouth pursed. She refused to have him lump her into that category.

Colin reached the head of the line. As they stood side by side, their elbows brushed. Emily stepped clear from the warmth of his contact.

Steam curled up from the pans of fried chicken, mashed potatoes, gravy, and butter beans.

Inez glanced up from serving. "Care for gravy with your mashed potatoes, Reverend?"

"Please. Everything smells delectable, as always."

Satisfaction glinted in the cook's gray eyes, her cheeks flushing red and blotchy. She speared a crusty chicken breast and scooped out double portions of potatoes and beans for Colin before filling Emily's plate.

"Thanks, Inez," Emily said. "It's good having you here."

Inez bobbed her chin. "It's good to be needed."

Emily joined Colin over at the serving table against the wall. She sniffled. The blooming mold prickled her nose.

She peered out the corner of her eye at Colin, who dusted his vegetables with pepper. What to say…

Emily cleared her throat. "I heard the news about Grace. It pained me to hear it, for your sake."

More than you know. Guilt sliced through Emily. How would Colin react if he knew that she'd sent Grace to her death?

The tip of Colin's nose reddened. "You're most kind."

Colin let the conversation lag and sprinkled salt over the mashed potatoes.

"I—I can't imagine what it's like to outlive all your kin," Emily said, keeping her voice low.

"I'm not the only one. Miss Pickering informed me that Roland's body was found on the east end. He died rescuing people trapped in their flooded houses."

That must have been a blow, much as she disliked the woman.

"Still… It can't be easy," she put in.

"It's quite strange, really … now that it's just me."

Emily reached for the shaker and salted the butter beans swimming in their juices.

"I imagine your evenings are lonely without Grace."

He looked at her then, appearing relieved that she understood. "Evenings are the worst," he admitted. "I manage during the day as long as I stay occupied, but the nights… I do dread going home."

"Nights are hard for so many. Particularly the orphans."

"Indeed. I—I can't get St. Mary's off my mind. All but a few of their orphans drowned along with the nuns, tied together by ropes. What a tragedy."

She speckled black pepper over her mashed potatoes. "Who is ever prepared for the worst news?"

Colin picked up the pitcher and poured water into a glass, his expression sober. "I thought I had braced myself for the worst." A furrow deepened between his brows as he lapsed into silence, his gaze unfocused. "But finding my mother's broach pinned to Gracie's body was most dreadful."

An image flashed of the corpse floating in the gutter. Was Colin reliving finding his sister's remains?

"H—how awful for you," Emily murmured.

Colin blinked and shook his head as if to clear his mind. "This, on the heels of rather belated news. A fellow minister friend drowned under the waves, he and his family. Now his church is without a pastor."

Emily's voice softened. "And you are without a friend."

Unbidden, her last glimpse of Lena gathering her hat and gloves by the orphanage door lingered in her mind's eye. Tears stung behind the bridge of Emily's nose.

Dear Lena. If only I hadn't sent you away.

Never again would her friend flash a conspiratorial smile or lounge beside her on a quilt on the beach. Those days were gone, swept away by the tide.

Colin glanced sideways at her and lowered his head. "Forgive me," his tone held a note of chagrin. "Here I am unburdening my woes when you have your sorrow, and in no small measure. My heart ached when we found no trace of Sarah."

Emily's gaze fell to the row of empty glasses on the table. A dull pang thudded in her chest. She poured water into a glass.

"I've upset you," Colin's voice gentled. "I know it doesn't seem like it now, but suffering is…"

Emily gritted her teeth and tuned him out, studying the pattern of mold blooming on the wall.

Suffering, indeed. Had not even Job known the fate of his children? She was in no frame of mind to hear about enduring suffering, though Colin meant well.

If anything, he treated her with the utmost care and respect, as he did all his flock. How very *pastoral* of him. She wanted her friend back.

"…heaven seem all the sweeter," he paused, his voice growing hoarse with emotion, "and for that I'm most grateful."

Colin gave a watery smile and lifted his chin. With effort, he regained his composure as if there was virtue in bearing up under grief with a stiff upper lip.

His stoic reserve grated on her last nerve. Was there no time to mourn? Hadn't Jesus wept?

Her voice tightened. "Excuse me."

She marched away from Colin toward an empty table in the back, ignoring the teacher's lilting voice singing a song to cheer the children.

Emily pulled out a bow-back chair and plopped onto the hard seat, her back turned toward the others, blocking their dry-eyed faces from her view.

The greasy chicken thigh on her plate held no appeal. She lowered her head and said a silent prayer, more out of rote habit than heartfelt thanks. Unlike Colin, her gratitude waned under the weight of grief, despite God's provision.

She tunneled through the mashed potatoes with her fork, and the gravy leaked in rivulets from its fluffy mound onto the butter beans. She spooned in mouthfuls of mashed potatoes. Her body needed the nourishment.

A vein pulsed down her forehead, throbbing. It was bad enough that Lena and Grace would have no proper funerals, no heartfelt eulogies. But the indignity of having their bodies tossed into a pit and burned with unnamed corpses, dead cats, and chickens was more than she could stomach.

Emily hated the cinder flakes raining down and dusting every surface, permeating even the fibers of her clothing with its foul stench.

Above all else, she hated the word "missing" with no answers for her kin. Had Sarah been swept away in the tide like Jake? Or was her body among the unnamed burning in some pyre? Were they even alive? Worse yet, would she ever know for sure?

Emily's stomach soured. What if answers never came? What then? How would losses ever be resolved without them even being verified? How could she possibly move forward or have any sense of peace?

Only God knew the answers she sought. He knew, but He wasn't telling. And therein lay her distress.

Chapter 39

Emily jerked on the silk petticoat, ruffling its deep flounces, her jaw clenched. What halfwit packed these crates anyway? With a hard snap of the wrist, she wrenched the garment free from being intertwined in corsets and nightgowns, uncaring that a corset hook ripped a hole in the lace hem.

She let out a huff, her thoughts whirling like vultures circling the sky. *Lord, help us find the children. Give me something to tell Aunt Estelle.*

Emily found no shred of consolation the longer prayers went unanswered, when God remained silent. When days rolled into weeks without discovery and the hope of finding her cousins ebbed with the washing of the tide.

It would have been better for everyone involved if she'd never set foot on the island. Then Jake and Sarah would be across the bay chasing Nelson the dog with little Rachel. Then the Keslers would be bent over bowls of sauerbraten above their bakery, warmed by the closeness of family, though they had little else. Then Colin would be discussing the finer points of Mark Twain with Grace.

She wanted to rail at the unfairness of it all. The Karankawa Indians had the right idea. They gathered three times a day and mourned the loss of their children. For a solid year, they met and wept. To her way of thinking, the Indians were more civilized than most folks nowadays. They were nothing if not supportive and honest in their grief. No burying it under pleasantries or hard work.

Emily frowned into the sunken crate. Sorrow, anger, and guilt stirred together made a noxious brew. It burned in the belly, leaving a bitter taste in her mouth.

She sniffled, the musty air ripe with mold and ash irritating her nose.

Movement out of the corner of her eye caught her attention. Mrs. Ward appeared a few yards away beside an open barrel on her right. Without saying a word, she set her hands to work. The woman's dark eyes were red-rimmed. Her green dress reeked of smoke. Where had she gone? Not for the first time did Emily wonder what the journalist was doing organizing clothes for the Red Cross.

As the gathering clouds deepened the shadows in the warehouse, a current of excitement went up at the main door. Emily peered over her shoulder and squinted at the woman strolling through the entrance, nodding to the workers. They had all come to a complete standstill in her presence.

Though the woman was small in stature, her bearing commanded respect. She moved with a slowness that revealed her recent illness coupled with age, but that did not deter her from her mission. Her keen eyes panned the warehouse, spotting Mrs. Ward near Emily. She set a course in that direction and came alongside the writer.

"It's good to see you out and about," Mrs. Ward said.

"Humph," the woman muttered. "No sense in fueling the nonsense that I'm too frail to head the relief effort. To that end, an outing never hurts."

So this was the founder of the Red Cross.

Emily had heard talk that Clara Barton had become ill with the grip upon arrival in Galveston. The setback hadn't kept the seventy-eight-year-old woman from wielding her influence while confined to bed for several days.

Clara scanned the stacked crates of undergarments. "I see you have your hands full." Wry humor glinted in her eyes and deepened the wrinkles outlining her cheeks. The women exchanged looks, the kind shared by those who served together in the trenches.

"As Mistress of the Robes, I'm deep in the sea of unmentionables," Mrs. Ward quipped.

Emily envied their easy camaraderie. With a sharp pang, her thoughts turned toward Lena. Never again would they share their easy friendship.

Clara's hand curled at her ear, pulling on her lobe. Her expression sobered. "I am curious," she spoke with deliberation, "what you will write concerning this great tragedy once we finish here."

"I interviewed a man in charge of a crematory earlier today: a ghastly duty, that. While I stood by the pit, a golden curl blew out," Fannie recounted the incident, appearing caught up in the memory. The woman's eyes shimmered.

A golden curl. Emily sagged against the crate. Neither Sarah nor Lacey had blonde hair. It wasn't either of them. Relief battled with the frustration over having no answers.

Mrs. Ward dabbed at her eyes. "So, what's on your mind that sent you to sort things out?"

Worry wrinkled Clara's brow as she stroked it. "Re-establishing homes weighs heavy, with winter approaching. It won't do to leave eight thousand people displaced in tents. Louisiana is sending shipments of building supplies, but we still need bricks, tools, roofing materials. A building committee member is being sent to New York on a fundraising mission. In the meantime, I've sent the women out into the wards to assess household needs."

"All rather tedious work," Fannie put in, "but our women are up to the challenge. They know these families."

Emily had read about the prominent Galveston women's newly formed ladies' auxiliary. They and scores of women volunteers worked with the men in the relief shelters and wards.

Miss Pickering was listed among the names of volunteers. The woman was pouring her grief over losing her nephew into something constructive. At last, the woman had ceased interfering in Emily's life.

"Well, I mustn't tarry." Miss Barton turned to go. "We must make the most of what little time remains."

Emily's eyes snapped up. *What little time remains?* Pressure built in her chest in a spurt of panic. Feeling suddenly lightheaded, she pushed shallow breaths through her lips. What would she do when that time ran out?

Rain thickened the mid-October air. The downpour emptied the streets and drove the workers home early that evening, thus stalling further deliveries to the wards for the night.

Fat raindrops slapped the windowpanes while Emily and Pearl listened to the children say their prayers. They tucked them all in their beds, assuring them that the weather was nothing to worry over, that they would all be fine. No storm warning flagged the weather bureau today, after all.

Yet since the storm, reassurances were hard to say, even harder to believe. Would they ever truly feel safe again?

Emily sat on the edge of her bed, staring out a dark window. The ceaseless motion of her legs jiggled the cot, scratching the floorboards. How could anyone sleep in weather like this?

Her stomach clenched, remembering the penetrating cold of the tidewater. Dry-mouthed, she blinked hard and shook off the sensation, her pulse thrumming at her neck.

Pull yourself together. It's only rain.

Still, she hunched forward, hugging her elbows against her stomach, gently rocking.

Her restlessness drove her downstairs once all the children fell asleep. Wrapped in a wool shawl that she grabbed from a donation barrel, Emily strode through the warehouse, out the front door.

The air held a damp closeness that seeped into the fibers of her shirtwaist. She pulled the shawl snugly over her shoulders, warding off the chill.

Low light spilled through the side windows onto the narrow walkway between the door and steps. Beyond it, the hiss of rain fell in a curtain, obscuring all but the faintest outline of the road.

Emily started pacing back and forth along the short distance between the columns flanking the entryway, her muscles pulling taut with tension. She ran her fingers down the weave of her braid.

What was she going to do when the Red Cross left? The work had been temporary, a mere stepping stone. What about her future? What if she found no work on the island? What if she had to leave?

Emily had survived a collapsed roof, hadn't she? Yet things were breaking apart around her, the cracks in her plans widening, the mortar giving way, brick by brick. Things secured were peeling away like layers of plaster.

Yet one thing she knew with certainty: had she taken one more step into the great hall that night, she would have been crushed under the crashing beams. One step separated her from crossing over into eternity. The weight of that reality prickled up her spine.

The newspaper had called the sparing of the orphans on 21st Street a miracle since the children had passed through the east wing moments before the roof collapsed. Not one had been lost. For some reason, she was spared, too. Why her and not Lena?

Emily turned after three steps, her thoughts landing on Nathan. The man seemed more focused on reporting news about the relief effort and furthering his career than on her. He thrived from the chaos while she struggled under the weight of it.

The air stirred behind her. Emily whirled in the shadows and drew up short.

Colin walked through the door and gazed at the downpour, clearly debating the wisdom of venturing further without an umbrella. He crossed his arms over his chest, stalling. Only then did she step out of the shadows to make her presence known.

As if sensing her nearness, Colin glanced sidelong at her and took a step back. "Ah, Miss Cleburne, I … I didn't expect to find you out here at this hour."

Miss Cleburne. Emily ran her tongue over the front of her teeth. A month ago, she'd slept with her head on the man's shoulder. "I should think we'd be past such formality by now." She didn't care if irritation edged her tone.

Colin arched his brows and gave her a long look. "Does my showing you proper respect offend you?"

His directness threw her off balance. "No! Of course not. But I'd hoped that respect had fostered friendship between us."

Emily needed a friend. She turned and gazed toward the street, staring into the waterfall of rain.

At his silence, she cut her eyes at Colin. The minister stood regarding her.

She reined in her impatience. "It appears I presume too much," she said briskly.

He cleared his throat. "No. No, you do not."

Emily watched his stiff posture relax as he loosened his shoulders. The deep lines smoothed from his forehead.

At least he considered her a friend. That meant more than she could say. Standing side by side, they watched the rain striking the second step, beading a straight line where the water fell and spattered.

"I'm loath to leave just yet," he changed the subject to neutral ground.

She followed his cue. "You'll be soaked to the skin if you do."

Colin let out a sigh. "Gracie used to have the fireplace lit on chilly nights. I never appreciated how welcoming a crackling fireplace was until creature comforts no longer greet me."

Emily turned her head at his candor, taking in the weary slope of his shoulders. No wonder Colin made it a habit of eating supper with the orphans most days.

"You stayed past your usual time this evening," she noted.

"Yes. After the meal, a young woman hobbled in on crutches with four small children clinging to her skirt. A widow of the storm. Inez fed them leftovers while I listened to her story. Sadly, they'd lost everything. She couldn't work so she'd come to drop off her children at the orphanage."

"Must she lose her children too?" Emily said with dismay.

"Fortunately, the railroads are giving away free passage to storm victims. Her sister lives in Tenaha." He tipped his head toward the warehouse. "We set up cots in the back where they'll bunk for tonight. They leave in the morning to join family."

Was it wrong to envy the widow's good fortune? That she had kin who could take her in?

"At least the day ended on a cheerful note," he added, though his voice lacked cheer. "Especially after ringing Dr. Buckner."

Emily's jaw tensed. "How's Chai Lin?"

He rubbed his fingertips along the scar above his eyebrow. "I wish I could report improvement." Colin's mouth pressed in a grim line. "Chai Lin has fallen behind in his studies. We had hoped that pairing him with an older chap would encourage him, but," Colin shook his head. "It's more than the usual adjustment to a strange new place. More than missing the only home he's ever known or his old matron and teacher. His sadness is more … pronounced. Dr. Buckner fears he has fallen into quite a severe melancholy."

Her eyes burned with unshed tears. It was bad enough that Nathan rejected his son, but Chai Lin doing so poorly tore at Emily with a fierceness that startled her. Heat surged up her chest, demanding release. She shoved the shawl off her shoulders.

Behind the veil of rain that secluded them, she faced Colin squarely, her eyes blazing.

Chapter 40

"Hasn't that child lost enough already?" Emily cried.

Hadn't they all?

"He has no parent who claims him," she sliced a hand in the air. "No sense of belonging, when all he wants is to grow up to be a great man—like you! And what are his chances of excelling when he can't even concentrate? He's falling behind in school when he should lead the pack."

"At least he—"

"That child couldn't *wait* for school to start," Emily cut in. "Must he lose out on every opportunity because of that *wretched* storm?"

Emily's chin wobbled, her chest heaving. "I don't understand why the little ones are made to suffer. How can that be just or fair?" she challenged. "Why orphans and nuns and ministers perished while the privileged survived in their stone mansions—why *I* survived, and they didn't?" She shook her head wildly. "I don't understand. I don't understand at all."

Emily covered her face with her hands and sobbed. Warm hands cupped her elbows, lending support. She leaned against Colin's chest and buried her face into his shirt. "I prayed for answers. Oh God, where are the children? Where *are* they?"

Colin gently gathered her into his arms. Her shoulders heaved while teardrops splattered the shirt beneath his single-breasted jacket. Tears wet her cheeks, ending in a ragged breath.

"How can anything ever be put to rights?" Emily shuddered at the enormity of it all.

Colin's palm stroked her back, the pressure of his thumb tracing the braid resting along her spine.

"God will bring us through this," he murmured.

Emily pressed her cheek flat against the linen, inhaling the scent of starch and rain, feeling spent. The rhythmic beating of his heart soothed her.

What had come over her? She wasn't prone to outbursts. A real lady would have remained calm and self-possessed at all times. Yet her wailing resembled more the railing of a Karankawa mama than a modern lady.

Emily drew comfort from the warmth enveloping her. She peered into the faint lamplight at the shaven cleft of Colin's chin. A draft cooled her back as his arms loosened their hold around her.

Colin stooped and picked up the shawl puddled around her feet. Straightening, he draped the fabric over her shoulders.

"Thanks." Feeling overheated, she lowered the wrap and draped it around her elbows. "I—I'm … my behavior," she blew out a gusty breath.

"You were distraught. Understandably so," Colin offered.

The minister reached into his pocket and pulled out a handkerchief. Emily mopped the wetness off her face with the soft cotton square.

"What happens in this fallen world is far from fair," Colin said. "It brings great harm to many. To children in particular."

"But God allowed … the unthinkable to happen."

"That He did."

Emily looked up at him from under swollen lids. "If only we had answers," she whispered, her face crumpling. All the intensity had leaked from her tone and only confusion threaded the complaint. She chewed the inside of her cheek. "I struggle to hold on to faith when my prayers are met with stony silence."

Colin's eyes brimmed with understanding rather than judgment. He peered off into the rain. "I'm reminded of the teacher who cared for his pupils. Diligently, he taught them as much as their minds could grasp, answering all their questions until the hour of testing. But during the test, he remained silent, though ever-present, for the time to answer questions had passed."

Emily considered this new meaning behind the silence.

Colin leaned his back against the wall. "Such is the way of testing. We may not get the answers we seek in this life. And when we do not, we must learn to live with mystery and rely on what God has revealed about Himself through scripture."

A sigh eased from her throat as Emily mulled this over. Trust had always come hard for her. Trusting one who remained silent challenged her to the utmost. But was God's silence a test of whether she would still cling to Him in faith, even if her prayers went unanswered? Would she still follow in His steps even in the worst of times?

She fell silent and peered out onto the deserted Strand, drenched and glistening under the dome of streetlights.

"Now is my chance," he nodded to the scattering raindrops dripping in the puddles. "Better make a dash for home."

She handed Colin his soggy handkerchief. "Thank you … for listening."

"Sleep well, Emily." Colin nodded before he trotted down the steps and onto 25th Street.

It pleased her that he used her given name.

Emily lingered outside, looking up at the parting clouds. She sensed the need to reaffirm the road less traveled by, the one she had chosen in her youth. Except this time, she would choose it with eyes wide open, staring in the face the mystery of suffering. She hesitated. Was her commitment dependent upon getting the answers she craved? If so, how shallow and self-serving was her faith. Maybe God wanted her to desire knowing Him more than having answers. Maybe His silence didn't mean He had left her when she needed Him most. What if the Teacher stood silent during the test, yet ever-present and compassionate?

I will never leave thee nor forsake thee.

The verse settled deep in Emily's soul, wrapping her in comfort. She bowed her head, resolved to press on. *Lord, forgive my unbelief. Give me grace to trust You with what lies ahead.*

Having that settled, she wished more was settled within her heart. Far from it. Though releasing the brewing distress had eased the tightness in her chest, not so with her frustration with Nathan.

The following week, Emily popped the lid off a crate. Her nose puckered. "Oh dear," she murmured.

What was that rancid smell? Emily peered dubiously down into the container. She picked up a child's dress smeared with grease on the bodice, the hem having a three-inch rip in the seam. A yellowed infant gown beneath the dress smelled of sour milk. Who would send hand-me-downs that hadn't seen a washboard or the mending pile?

"These go out front," Emily muttered.

Not wishing to offend the islanders with unsuitable donations, the workers had begun setting a barrel out front. To Emily's surprise, no matter how pitiful the contents, she found the barrel empty each morning.

Her outburst with Colin on the warehouse steps still made her grimace. Though she grieved no less than before, Emily found herself dwelling less on questions that had no answers. Colin's counsel had made room for mystery, for things beyond her understanding.

She considered the question he posed to her months ago on the orphanage steps. How God was using testing to refine her. At the time, his question baffled her. Not so, now. Now she felt a greater need to seek faith. Like never before, she sought direction over her future, daring to trust that God would direct her on the right path and affirm her steps. In doing so, she depended heavily on His grace. Here was a well of strength and encouragement, of comfort, deep enough to sustain her through the long hours until she rested her head on her pillow, spent. Like tender mercies, there was an ample supply to draw from each morning. As for her character, she noticed a growing conviction to be true to the things she treasured most, no matter the cost. Even matters of the heart. She sensed further testing on the horizon on that front.

Emily hefted the crate and set it on the ground, a layer of grit registering on her hands. She lifted the lid off the next barrel and glanced up.

She spotted Nathan striding through the warehouse door. He drew a bead on Mrs. Ward, his aim focused. He trooped over to the woman standing less than ten feet away from her. Turned sideways, Emily averted her face but turned an ear, listening.

"I heard about the relief stations closing by October 25th," Nathan bypassed any greeting or small talk.

"See for yourself," Mrs. Ward waved her hand at the dwindling crates and barrels lining the walls, once stacked three high and two deep. It drove home the Red Cross's involvement was nearing an end.

"When do you expect headquarters to close?" he persisted.

"That's a question better answered by Clara Barton."

Paper rustled, then a scratching against a notepad. "So once the last donations are distributed, what else remains to be done here?"

"We must find suitable homes for our orphans. Good people willing to open their hearts and homes to them."

At hearing him shuffle, Emily pictured Nathan shifting his weight between his feet, the result of a guilty conscience, she suspected.

"How will you find homes for the children?" he asked.

"How about we start with *you*?"

Emily shot a glance at Nathan. Mrs. Ward peered pointedly at the reporter. He tucked in his chin, his eyes rounded like a cornered man.

"Beg your pardon?" Nathan drawled.

A part of Emily enjoyed his discomfort while she fingered the buttons and tucks on a white nightgown.

"It *is* your job to report on the needs of the relief effort," Mrs. Ward used a tone reserved for an apprentice rather than a seasoned reporter. "What better way than to spread the word? A well-written piece wields influence toward acts of charity. I suggest that you seize the opportunity. According to Mr. Lewis, we have twenty-seven children needing suitable homes. Time is of the essence. I urge you to write an appeal on their behalf."

"*That* I can do," Nathan said crisply. "Thanks for your time."

The sharp clicking of heels drew near and stopped. Nathan released a gust of air.

He appeared at her elbow. "I've been away at Hitchcock."

"Hmm." Without looking up, Emily dug down into the barrel. A week had cooled her frustration toward him.

Nathan came around the barrel, facing her. "You were the reason I went," he baited her.

Emily couldn't imagine why. She peered up at him, waiting for an explanation.

Nathan frowned at her. "What, no curiosity?"

She lifted a shoulder. "What does this have to do with me?"

"What if I were to tell you that a boy washed ashore on the mainland? On the night of the storm." His eyes roved her face. He waited until he saw her interest flare, then added, "I caught a lead on the story and went to investigate."

Emily's pulse hitched. The possibility that her cousins might have drifted to the mainland had never entered her mind.

"Well, go on! What did you discover?"

"After two days, I found the lad and interviewed him." His mouth pulled to one side. His voice softened. "I had hoped to find Jake for you."

Crushing disappointment pressed against her ribs.

That Nathan went to such lengths for her warred with his neglect over his son's needs. He may have gone in an attempt to make things right between them, but his efforts fell short of the mark. She needed more from him.

"Have you heard of others washing ashore on the mainland?" Emily asked.

"A few. None that fit the description of your cousins, though. You know I'll keep my ear to the ground."

Emily's face fell. "I'm obliged."

Nathan's mouth flattened. "The last thing I want from you is obligation,

Emily." He leaned in, crowding her over the barrel. "I went because I care about your happiness."

Emily lifted a single brow in challenge. She doubted that her well-being had been Nathan's sole mission for going.

"All is not lost," she offered. "I'm sure your readers will find the story both poignant and stirring."

Nathan whispered so that no one could eavesdrop. "Care to tell me what's gotten you all riled up?"

She studied him at length, before she lowered her voice to match his tone. "He is not doing well," she enunciated each syllable to drive home the point.

"Who?"

She pinned him with a stare. "Chai Lin."

Nathan glanced around the warehouse, searching the faces of every worker a safe distance away. For the benefit of any onlookers, he flashed a smile that did not reach his eyes.

He kept his voice even. "He has people watching over him. He'll manage."

Emily sniffed with disapproval. "He has severe melancholy and is lagging behind in school. Surely you wish better for him than that."

"Wishes are of little consequence."

"I'll not abide him doing poorly in school."

"You'll not abide…" Nathan worked his jaw from side to side as if to reign in the impatience flushing his skin. "It's far more important that he's safe," he murmured through tight lips. "And Dallas is where he'll remain."

His shuttered look discouraged her from further discussion. He'd made up his mind.

That left Emily only one choice.

Chapter *41*

"Have you read the news?" Inez asked.

The cook ladled grits swimming in melted butter onto a plate and poked a finger at the slices of bread. "How many?"

Emily put a hand over her mouth and yawned. "One, please. What news?" The fragrance of yeast whetted her appetite. "Make that two."

Inez gave nothing away as she stacked the warm bread by the grits. She peered up at Emily, clearly set on watching her reaction.

"The follow-up article your neighbor wrote." Inez explained.

Emily's pulse leaped, her eyes widening. She leaned closer. "What's the gist?"

"Let's just say … the father got his just desserts." The cook's bun quivered with a nod of approval.

Unease soured Emily's stomach.

Nathan's father had thought the federal inspection would blow over in a few days. Now he faced due penalties. The man must be seething.

Inez speared two sausage links dripping with grease and held them above her plate.

Emily held up her palm. "None for me."

"You sure? You need to keep up your strength."

"None this morning. Thanks for the news."

Inez lifted the plate and handed it to Emily. "What are your plans once the warehouse closes?"

"I," Emily shrugged vaguely, "I'm exploring possibilities." *Pitiful as they are*, she refrained from adding.

Although she checked the newspaper daily, no one advertised teaching positions. The schools that had just reopened had filled their vacant teacher positions already.

Last night, an idea came to mind and hovered; a possibility, but off the island. She hated leaving without knowing the fate of the children. The idea made her heartsick.

"Something will turn up." Inez's gray eyes filled with unexpected sympathy. "Always does."

"And you?"

"Ethel Harrington needs a cook."

"Excellent. Well…"

Emily peered over her shoulder at the line behind her. She threw them a look of apology and moved over to the serving table, pouring coffee.

Emily scanned the tables, spotting a folded newspaper on a center table. She weaved over and took a seat.

The *Daily News* was dated Sunday, October 21, 1900. She sat on the edge of her seat, turning the page. She found the article on page two. *VARIETY SHOW OWNER SENTENCED*. Emily peered over the cup's rim and read while the bitter taste awakened her senses.

> *Hayden Chambers, arrested on September 3rd for immigrant smuggling and customs evasion, received a two-year sentence on Friday to be served in Huntsville Prison, plus a fine of two hundred and fifty dollars.*
>
> *The Office of the Superintendent of Immigration Investigation revealed that the females smuggled into the country through Mexico were either put to work in Chambers' variety shows or sold to brothels in Beaumont, Brownsville, and Houston.*
>
> *The showgirls rounded up in the raid on September 3rd are awaiting deportation to China due to their illegal entry into the United States.*

Between bites of the thick bread, Emily considered Chai Lin. He would never know his aunt; yet another loss, unacknowledged.

But that bit of news dwarfed the more significant implication of Hayden's sentencing. Being fined might be a slap on the wrist to a wealthy man, but not two years in prison.

Emily's stomach clenched. What might the man do to strike back at Nathan? Send out men to do his dirty work while he sat in a prison cell, or wait and take revenge himself? Would he deliver physical blows or strike more subtly, hitting Nathan where it hurt worse?

Emily spooned a mouthful of grits, remembering what Hayden had said to Nathan after the parade; a veiled threat involving *the boy*. The remark had seemed ludicrous at the time, but now it fisted a knot in her stomach. Emily pushed away her plate. Would Hayden use Chai Lin to somehow punish Nathan? How safe was the child? Everyone knew that Dr. Buckner had moved the orphans to Dallas. What would stop someone from penetrating the orphanage and taking him? The Chinese boy certainly stood out among all the other fair-haired children.

Oh Lord, keep him safe!

The letters in the columns of newsprint blurred together. The workers sipping coffee faded from view, their voices growing distant. Emily stared off for a long while, her mind churning.

A hush fell over the group, pulling her gaze to the diners. Emily blinked and glanced at who stirred the silence.

Clara Barton was slowly picking her way between the tables. On her heels came Nathan trailing behind. Had he followed the woman from the Tremont Hotel? Nathan spotted Emily and sidled over. He shoved the empty chair beside her and lowered himself onto the seat.

His gaze slid onto the newspaper, noting what she read. They exchanged glances. Emily noticed a tic in his jaw. Did he dread his father's next move more than she?

"I've come for the big announcement," he whispered out of the corner of his mouth.

Miss Barton proceeded to the front of the dining room. Though feeble, she remained on her feet, using her petite height to her advantage. She folded her hands below her waist. Her direct gaze commanded attention and won it.

When Clara spoke, she chose her words with care, her diction beautiful in its delivery. "I'm pleased to find you assembled and with full stomachs." Smiles flickered around the room. "I have important news. We have learned that the towns on the mainland between Galveston and Houston received relief aid but no clothing. I'm sending Mr. Lewis and Mr. Marsh over to assess the situation fully. In the meantime, we must shift our last efforts to relieve their immediate need. Thus, the ward relief stations will close here by midweek."

Murmurs rippled among the men and women as Nathan dashed short lines on his notepad. Miss Barton held up a hand, silencing the group.

"The remaining donations will be sent by railcar to Houston, where I've arranged a temporary site for distribution. Therefore this warehouse will close by week's end on October 31st."

Voices rumbled as the workers leaned their heads together and whispered behind their hands.

So little time! Emily's nerves jangled. She rolled the edges of the newspaper between her fingers, smudging ink onto her fingertips. What was she going to do? Where would she go?

Make the call. The message rang clear in Emily's mind, resonating in her spirit with a sense of peace.

Beside her, Nathan's hand shot up. "Excuse me, Miss Barton, but what will be done with the orphans until they're placed in homes?"

"I've arranged for their supervision through the transition. And thanks to your appeal for their placement, Mr. Chambers, a number of the children's relatives have made contact this week. Plus, new families are eager to adopt the rest."

Emily peered at Nathan, who preened over Miss Barton's recognition. She wanted to shake the man. Why couldn't he do something for his son? Smugness pulled at Nathan's mustache. Her eyes narrowed. Had he raised the question to call attention to his article? The one Mrs. Ward had prodded him to write? And now he claimed full credit for his effort and the result. What audacity.

"Before we begin our workday," Miss Barton continued, "I wish to commend you all for your tireless service. You have distributed over fifteen-hundred cases of donations. Such diligence has eased much suffering here. Moreover, it allowed the good citizens of Galveston to get back on their feet. The impact has cast a ray of hope upon their future."

When Miss Barton dismissed the workers, Nathan followed her out of the warehouse, firing more questions at the woman as he jotted down her quotes.

Quit dragging your feet. Emily wiped her damp palms down the sides of her skirt and scanned the dining room. Now was the perfect time. The supper crowd had thinned until only Colin and a chubby-cheeked orphan boy was seated at one of the tables. A few stragglers were scraping their plates in the bin set by the kitchen door.

Steeling her resolve, Emily drew back her shoulders and hefted the coffee tray. She wended her way over to Colin.

Seated side by side, the boy was telling the minister about the time he brought a frog to church in his pocket, and it got loose. Amusement tugged at the corners of Colin's mouth as he polished off the last bites of fried fish.

Emily stepped up to the table, eyeing the slice of pecan pie by Colin's plate.

"Care for coffee with your pie?"

Colin glanced up at her. "That would be lovely."

"May I join you?"

Colin's smile faded as he noted the gravity in her tone. "Of course."

Emily set the tray on the table. Turning over two clean cups, she poured them coffee.

Colin laid a hand on the boy's shoulder. "Ned, be a good lad and scrape off our plates for Miss Inez. We'll chat later."

The boy's chin drooped a little, but he stacked the dishes obediently and carried them back to the kitchen.

"Sugar or cream?" Emily offered.

"A spot of cream, please."

Emily added a dollop to each cup and eased into the chair beside him. Colin sampled the pie as Emily sipped the rich coffee.

Meanwhile, Ned finished cleaning the plates and fell in step with an older boy. They moved toward the stairwell. The scrubbing of dishes clinked from the back kitchen.

"This day has been filled with news." Colin dragged his hand over his face.

"I'm fairly flooded with it," Emily agreed.

"Right. It's hard to imagine a time when the aftermath of crisis will no longer fill our days."

He picked at the flaky crust with the tines of the fork. A flicker of discomfort flashed in his eyes. "What will you do ... once the week is up?"

"I'm looking into one possibility. We'll see where it leads." It was too early to say anything more. "Fortunately, I have a little cash to fall back on."

She didn't want to spend the money her grandpa had pressed into her hand, but she might have to.

Colin lowered his voice. "Have you read today's paper?"

Emily nodded and matched his volume. "The sentence is worrisome. I'm concerned about Chai Lin."

Colin's mouth pulled in a thin line. "I must say I'm grateful the boy is away." He gave her a meaningful look. "But he won't be forever. Fundraising events are underway to rebuild the orphanage. And with backing from men like William Randolph Hearst, money will pour in. I foresee the home reopening within the next few years."

"About the time Hayden Chambers is released," Emily said, pulling her bottom lip between her teeth.

"Precisely. In the meantime, Dr. Buckner has assured me that they are working diligently to keep the boy from withdrawing into depression. Staff is keeping a close eye on him. Aside from that," Colin paused, dabbing his mouth with a napkin, "I'm not sure what else can be done for him."

Emily's mouth went dry. Matrons and teachers were inadequate protection against the men Hayden Chambers might employ. Moreover, the staff divided their attention among so many orphans. Their watchful eyes, however diligent, weren't enough to assuage her fears.

Just tell him and be done with it.

Emily squirmed on the hard seat, her pulse pounding. Still, she hesitated. Her silence had protected her dignity and reputation thus far. But what were they compared to a child's welfare? Too much was at stake for her to keep quiet.

Emily moistened her dry throat with a sip of coffee. "There's more you should know about Chai Lin. Something I've learned."

She fussed with the collar of her shirtwaist, wishing it was less snug against her throat.

Sensing her unease, Colin set down the fork. "Go on," he prompted.

"I, uh … I know who his father is."

Colin's brows lowered. "What have you learned?"

"It's as I feared."

"You're certain it's Nathan Chambers?"

"Suffice it to say … I cornered him into a confession."

Emily's mouth trembled. She pressed her lips together to curb her expanding disappointment with Nathan and with herself. She should have guarded her heart better.

Compassion softened Colin's tone. "Such a confession, however you obtained it, must have shaken you. I wonder," he paused, his shoulders stiffening, "if it's altered your impression of him."

How could it not? She let out a dry huff.

"I could sooner forgive the man's lapse in judgment than for what he has failed to do for his son. I won't settle for a man who lacks integrity. I know where that leads."

Admiration flared in Colin's eyes. "It takes character to stand firm and not be swayed."

Emily bowed her head to cover the heat flushing her cheeks. Instead of Colin thinking less of her, his respect had deepened. She very much wanted his regard.

Colin sat back in his chair, the legs creaking under the shifting weight. He let out a slow breath. "This news certainly compounds the current situation, does it not?"

She met his gaze. "More than you know. Before Hayden Chambers was arrested, I overheard him order Nathan to begin managing the books for his business on the sly. He said there was no need for anyone to know about it … *or the boy.* At the time, I thought the veiled threat was utter nonsense. But now? What if he uses Chai Lin to manipulate Nathan in some way?"

"Or to ruin his reputation," Colin put in.

"The thing he values most…" Emily's voice trailed off.

That Colin's train of thought was on the same track as hers flared the burning in her stomach.

Colin pushed the chair away from the table, standing. "Right. Well, I'll ring Dr. Buckner. I'll inform him of the news. I'll make clear my concern about the possible threat."

Emily nodded absently. "Thanks. I have a call of my own to make."

Chapter 42

Emily strode at a brisk pace before her purpose cooled. One way or another, something had to be resolved.

As she set off, she chewed on a chunk of cornbread she had snagged from the kitchen. The dry bread needed a pat of butter to moisten it, but there had been no time to spare.

The telegram had thrown her movements into a harried motion. With the slip of paper in hand, she had gone straight to Mrs. Ward and asked for the afternoon off. She had loose ends to tie up, she'd said. Loose ends, indeed. This meeting was her last chance.

Lord, give me grace.

As Emily devoured the last bite, yellow morsels dropped onto the high-necked lace inset of the dress she wore. She brushed the crumbs off with the backs of her fingers.

While sorting clothes yesterday, Emily had unfolded the gown and admired the lavender print and the delicate tucks that gathered at the waist. At a glance, she knew the dress would fit. On a whim, she asked Mrs. Ward if she might have it, and the woman said yes.

Emily felt feminine and pretty in it, something she had not thought about since the storm. And lavender added richness to her copper hair, now combed into a simple chignon. She had taken extra pains with grooming before she left, knowing it bolstered her confidence. She would need it.

By this time, the sun was sinking behind the tops of the buildings. With its descent, the nip in the air seeped through the sheer lace below the collar. She rearranged the folds of her shawl under the chin and tossed one end over her shoulder, blocking the chill. She had less than an hour before sunset. Emily quickened her pace until her shins burned, watching her reflection glide in the new windowpanes along the Strand.

At least her first stop had pointed her in the right direction. Emily shook her head. Her world was plucked up by the roots, and the man was repairing a sailboat. *A sailboat.* On his list of priorities, she rated below a vessel currently unfit to steer with a rudder or bend in the wind.

Half a block away, Nathan's pier came into view. The ringing of hammers had ceased for the day as hundreds of men who repaired the piers and wharves had headed home. Much of the debris littering the harbor had been cleared and burned. Along the dock, a row of boats bobbed on their moorings.

Nathan's boat was listing on the sand. The mast soared upward, now repaired. A rasping sound drew her around to the port side. There, Nathan vigorously rubbed a folded sheet of sandpaper over the spot in the hull that he had patched. A lock of sandy hair fell forward into his eyes.

"Inez said you dropped by headquarters while I stepped out," she told him.

"I came to see you."

He glanced at her and then dragged his gaze over her appearance, roaming her face and clothes. He set the sandpaper on the hull and dusted the grit off his hands.

"You look fetching. I'd say you made good use of your time off."

"I had things to do." She kept her manner brisk.

"With the warehouse closing, I'm surprised Mrs. Ward allowed it."

"She had no choice, really." Emily left the explanation at that for now. "We had no chance to discuss your father's sentencing the other day."

A scowl twisted his mouth. "It seems the penalty provoked quite a response. He's been busy."

Emily's breath caught. "What now?"

"A Houston reporter, Gus Holbrook, supposedly received an anonymous tip. He's known for writing lurid, sensational tripe. He was undoubtedly baited with a fistful of cash, though I can't prove it. He took the first train to Galveston on Monday. Came sniffing around for the rest of the story behind my father's arrest."

Nathan paused for effect. "He interviewed Liang."

Emily raised a quizzical brow, trying to recall the name.

"Ying Su's sister," he offered.

Emily pressed her fingertips to her mouth. It was happening.

"It seems that having my father behind bars has loosened her tongue," his tone tightened. "Liang told Gus the sordid tale about her sister dying in childbirth—with my child. She said I came looking for Ying Su months ago and tried shaking the truth out of her about her sister. Gus made much over

Liang being fearful for her safety. It appears the only information she withheld was the name and fate of her nephew.

"The story made the top of page two in yesterday's Houston *Post*," he glowered. "So now my name is linked with a fourteen-year-old servant girl."

It was just as Emily feared. Hidden things had come to light. A chill prickled up her neck that had nothing to do with the evening breeze ruffling the edges of her shawl.

"But Ol' Gus didn't stop there," Nathan curled his upper lip. "That angle lacked enough sensational edge for his taste. He claimed a more devious motive was afoot. He stated I exposed my father's deeds so Liang would be deported, thus preventing scandal from leaking over the child I fathered. Never mind that I stopped those girls from being subjected to further slave labor. He ended his sham of an article by posing the question, 'Was Mr. Chambers' reporting prompted by moral outrage and a sense of justice, or mere rage in an attempt to cover his indecent misconduct?'"

"My father must be crowing in his cell," Nathan clenched his fists. "That piece accomplished two things in one fell swoop: it questioned my credibility as a journalist and smeared my reputation. He knew just where to aim." He looked away, but not before a dark shadow clouded his eyes.

Emily rubbed her throat. "You must have expected he would strike back when you reported on his smuggling operation."

Nathan cut his eyes at her. His expression was rueful. "Ah, but I had no clue that he had anything to use against me. Certainly nothing scandalous. Learning the news of Ying Su dying in childbirth blindsided me."

A new impression began to form in Emily's mind, questioning the purity of his motives.

"I'm curious," she said evenly, "did you choose your career path to plot your father's ruin?"

Nathan kicked the toe of his boot in the sand. "Becoming a reporter provided a means to stop his illegal activity."

"That's rather … calculated."

He leveled his gaze at her, his right eyebrow lifting. "You think I'm cold and vengeful?"

"That knife embedded in the deer head mounted on your bedroom wall gave me pause."

"I've made no secret of loathing his ways. Nor do I regret putting my anger to good use. But that's a far cry from vengeance. I've vowed never to be like him."

The forcefulness in his tone flooded Emily with relief. "I understand your need to put distance between you and your kin. You did just that when you reported your father to the authorities. It also elevated you in the eyes of the public. So have your articles on the relief effort and having the ear of Clara Barton. You've gained respectability."

Emily paused, her expression grim. "Until now. Gus's article has thrown a wrench in your plans."

"How fortunate for me then," Nathan slanted a sly look at her, "that I have other plans."

Emily expelled a sharp breath. More surprises.

"You see," Nathan explained, "I have this chum over at the *Post*. Ethan warned me that Gus's article went to print.

"He also gave me a lead. There's smuggling reported in the border town of Nogales, Arizona. A new collector of customs came last year to stop the flow of Chinese crossing the border. From what he gathered, they suspect customs fraud and smuggling is happening among the inspectors." His eyes gleamed with intrigue. "Who knows how many are involved?"

Emily glanced at the horizon. The sun was sinking into the water while the fumes of cremation turned the sky a dull orange. Overhead, black-headed gulls wheeled and dived, crooning in search of a place to settle for the night.

With stiffened fingers, she pulled her shawl snugly around her shoulders, feeling chilled and heartsore. Did she even fit into Nathan's plans? Did she care to be included?

"Don't you see?" he recaptured her attention. "This is my chance to break free of my father's clutches, to be rid of all this speculation." He raked his fingers through his hair, shoving it off his forehead. "I could leave Galveston without anyone knowing my whereabouts. And it would give me time. Time to plan, to straighten things out so that we—"

"Well, time's a wasting," Emily cut in. "I'm leaving tomorrow."

"Leaving?" He drew in his chin. "Where to?"

"Dallas," she plunged in. "Buckner orphanage has an opening for a teacher. I have an interview on Friday. It's only for an assistant position but includes room and board. I learned that one of the main teachers will wed over the holidays, creating another opening."

Nathan leaned his head back and frowned. "You're going for the *possibility* of work? What if they offer the position to someone else? Where will that leave you?"

Nathan turned to the hull and rubbed a hand over the patchwork surface, examining it closely.

He wouldn't understand what prompted her to make the call. Or the peace that accompanied her stepping out in faith. She knew with certainty that she must go, even though she had nothing definite.

"I have another reason," Emily lifted her chin, throwing down the gauntlet. "I'm adopting your son."

Nathan's head turned sharply in surprise. His eyes were riveted on hers, bulging in disbelief.

"*Adopt?* Have you taken leave of your senses?" he snapped, spinning to face her. "What will people think of an unmarried woman with a Chinese boy? You'd be opening yourself and him to the worst kind of speculation."

An unmarried woman. That stung. Was Nathan implying that pursuing her would be out of the question if she went through with the adoption? If only he understood what compelled her to proceed with her plans, with or without him. Above all else, children needed to be nurtured and protected.

"No decent folks would frown upon a woman adopting a displaced orphan of the storm. Chai Lin needs a parent's stability," she pursed her lips, "and I aim to be that for him."

"So he'll have your skirt to hide behind when he faces the cold, cruel world, is that it?"

"Oh, I will protect him from your father if necessary."

"My father? Is this your way of forcing my hand?" He slid an index finger under his stiff collar and pulled it away from his neck. "Either I accept you and the boy or … or nothing?"

"You misunderstand your position. The issue is whether I will accept you or not. As it stands, I won't have a man who shuns responsibility for his child. Nor do I desire someone whose love of faith and family isn't genuine. And if that's not you, then—"

"Then what? You'll say farewell?" his voice pitched.

Emily stared off at the sinking sun, her voice void of inflection. "I've seen where mismatched unions lead. I don't wish that for either of us. Someday you'll thank me for sparing us both a lifetime of misery."

He reached for her then, clasping hold of her elbow, staying any movement.

"Don't go, Emily," he pleaded. "Don't leave me."

"Nothing has changed."

"Come away with me."

Come away? What was he proposing? Did he think her virtue meant so little to her?

"For a wordsmith, you can do better than that," she challenged.

He lifted his chin. "All right then. How's this? Marry me."

That she had not expected. Emily blinked rapidly as her arm stilled under his grip. She blew air through her parted lips. How often she had dreamed of this moment.

Marriage. The proposal was not what she envisioned, yet the possibilities tugged at her heart. Emily pictured them strolling down a tree-lined boulevard and climbing the steps to their home, their hands clasped with little Chai Lin walking between them.

Who, if anyone, would protest her marrying Nathan on a whim? Her folks no longer had any say, and the Edwards were over in Baytown. Colin? He'd cautioned her against acting rashly. He wanted to know if she ever became desperate, but what could he offer her?

A pang of unease expanded in her chest. What if her dream to teach had been just that—a fleeting dream? With life so uncertain, maybe she needed to take hold of a sure thing.

"Have I shocked you speechless?" His lips spread into a soft smile, dimpling one cheek. "I love you, Emily. Surely my persistence speaks that truth to you."

Her resolve teetered under the heat of his gaze.

Colin's words came flooding back. *May your character be not a writing upon the sand, but an inscription upon the rock.... May your whole life be so settled, fixed and established, that all the blasts of hell and all the storms of earth shall never be able to remove you.*

What was she to do? Was she strong enough to stand firm in her convictions, or would she allow circumstances to meld her character?

All at once, she sensed an inward strengthening of her will. Had she not prayed for grace? With it came clarity. *She knew.* Before she could accept his offer, she must see a change of heart, the kind born of faith. The kind that lasted.

Emily squared her shoulders. "I'm curious whether your proposal includes your son. Will he come away with us?"

Nathan pressed his lips into a tight seam. Emily studied him in the fading light, his face inscrutable, giving nothing away. He lowered his head until their foreheads touched, reaching for her hands, his grip firm.

"I'm asking for your hand, Emily." His fervency pinned her in place. "I love *you*. Say yes."

Yet he didn't answer her question. Was there no room in his heart for anyone else?

Emily drew in a shuddery breath and slowly disentangled herself from his arms until she stood at arm's length from him.

"Yet I desire more. And if you cannot give it," Emily's voice thickened with emotion, "then I have no peace in giving you my hand or my heart."

Emily watched the intensity in his gaze dim. He grew reflective as he peered out over the water. Clearly, he was not pleased with her answer, but when he settled his gaze upon her, she saw new respect glinting in his eyes.

"You're pressing me to change," Nathan challenged. "I hope you appreciate what that will cost me."

Will? Her pulse quickened.

She made no apology. "Whoever said commitment was without cost? Yet when we're willing, God does a work in our hearts. The rest will follow."

Nathan's raised brow said he doubted faith was that simple.

"Well," he drawled, "you've given me much to ponder. I need someone like you in my life, Emily. Always. You make me toe the mark. But decisions like this can't be rushed—or forced."

True words. Emily's heart squeezed.

Nathan gave no promises, but her heart was settled on where she stood. From that, she would not be moved.

"You know where to reach me," she managed to say, her voice wobbling as she turned to go.

"Until then," he murmured.

Without a backward glance, Emily faced the gloaming twilight and walked away.

Chapter 43

Emily's shoes rasped on the gritty steps of the warehouse as darkness set in. The light pooling below the streetlights shone on the men out front as they hoisted crates and barrels onto wagons headed for the railcars.

She plodded through the door toward the back of the warehouse. The dimly lit dining room had emptied already.

"Of all nights," she mumbled, her shoulders slumping under her shawl.

She'd hoped for time with Colin once she returned. He had no way of knowing she was leaving tomorrow. That she'd missed her last chance to say goodbye made her more out of sorts than she cared to examine.

As if walking away from Nathan hadn't left her in a low mood. Tears crowded close to the surface.

Her stomach growled. She headed into the kitchen, hunting for leftovers.

Inez stood hunched over the sink, washing a mound of silverware. The cook peered up at hearing the shuffling of feet.

She waved a sudsy hand. "There's a plate on the back of the stove. I saved you a pork chop and some skillet potatoes. There's also sweet tea in the ice box."

"Bless you," Emily said, inhaling the aroma of Southern fried comfort.

The cook's hands stopped their swishing as she eyed Emily. Her brow wrinkled. "You all right?"

Emily tucked a stray strand behind her ear, her skin overheated. Her meeting with Nathan had left her feeling wrung out.

"Not really," she admitted, "but I reckon I will be. Thanks for asking."

At least she knew where she stood and that gave her the foothold she needed to move forward.

Emily poured a glass of chilled tea, gathered the silverware and plate, and carried them to a table facing the wall. She plunked them down and sank into a chair. She bowed and gave thanks for the food and comfort Inez provided.

Emily downed the liquid until she slaked her thirst and dug into the fried pork and potatoes, moaning her approval.

She mulled over her exchange with Nathan as she licked the salt and grease off her lips. He'd said the words she longed to hear: love, marriage. Yet she'd walked away from him after he failed to acknowledge, let alone include, Chai Lin in his plans. Though it pained her to do it, oddly, she felt no pang of regret. Grace enabled her to stand firm in her convictions. She sensed the rightness of her choice, a profound peace from it; a sustaining strength and support welling up from within her.

Scraping clean the plate, she considered her next move. A letter would have to do.

Emily pushed up from the chair, went over, and dug around at the front desk and found a legal pad, an ink pen, and an envelope. Taking them back to the table, she sat down and set her plate aside. Pausing, she gathered her thoughts and then began to write.

October 29, 1900

Dear Colin,

I regret saying goodbye in this fashion, but I must. As it turned out, I'll be leaving on the first train out of Galveston tomorrow.

I have an interview with Buckner orphanage on Friday for an assistant teacher position. I felt a prompting to make the call. As it turned out, I spoke directly with Dr. Buckner.

Regardless of what happens, I will remain in Dallas with Chai Lin. He needs my care and protection. I plan to adopt him, and Dr. Buckner expressed his willingness to discuss the matter when we meet.

As for Nathan, who knows what he will decide concerning his son. I saw him this evening and shared my plans. He offered a marriage that didn't include Chai Lin. You needn't worry. I told him I wouldn't accept a man who shuns faith and family. That said, I left the door open. Either way, I will pursue my plans.

As for you, I thank God that He brought you into my life for such a time as this. He surely knew how much I needed your understanding and wise counsel. It's doubtful I would have survived this tragic ordeal without your compassion amid my railing. I drenched more than one of your handkerchiefs. Through it all, your acceptance and friendship have steadied me more than

I can say. As it turned out, you've earned more than my respect. You earned my trust.

I will sorely miss you. It would mean the world if I were to hear from you. Please don't lose touch. Whatever would I do in my next crisis if I couldn't reach you?

I wish you every blessing, for you have been that and more to me.

Fondly, Emily

Alone in the dim corner, she set down the pen. Crossing her forearms on the table, she lowered her head and wept.

<hr>

The following morning, Emily peered up from her plate of scrambled eggs and biscuits. She spotted Miss Pickering moving around the tables toward her. Since the relief stations had closed in the wards, their volunteers had come to help close the warehouse.

Emily ducked her chin, eyeing the fluffy eggs. "Walk on by," she murmured under her breath. To her chagrin, a plate plopped down on the table to her right.

"I heard from your aunt," Miss Pickering announced as she pulled out a chair and sat. With a fork, the woman shoved the mound of eggs away from a split-open biscuit covered with gravy. "They've settled in as best they can," she went on. "I'm pleased to say that Clayton's breathing has eased now that he's no longer inhaling ashes."

Emily swallowed a bite of jellied biscuit. "Good to hear."

She should have written Estelle. But how could she tell her aunt that she was leaving without answers?

"Estelle informed me," Miss Pickering added, "that you stayed at headquarters. The workload's not for the faint of heart. And yet you persisted. I must say, Miss Cleburne, you've exceeded my expectations."

Leave it to Miss Pickering to offer praise that felt more backhanded than complimentary.

Emily ran her tongue along the front of her teeth. "Sadly, most people fail to rise above the low expectations others set for them. But then, it's up to us to decide whether we allow their low opinions to dictate our choices or define our worth. I refuse to allow either."

A faint smile curled the corner of Emily's mouth as she realized the truth of that statement. No longer would she allow kin to determine her sense of worth.

"And what are your plans, pray tell," Miss Pickering asked over the rim of her coffee cup.

"I've applied with the Buckner orphanage for a teaching position." She had no intention of sharing more with the woman. My condolences," Emily offered, switching the subject, "on your nephew's passing. I know he meant the world to you."

Behind her spectacles, Miss Pickering's eyes were liquid. "He died rescuing folks on the east end. Other officers fell, too." She paused, working her throat. "Their poor families. Ida and I are taking over meals and watching the kids so their mothers can work. We'll all get by somehow."

"What a fine way to honor Roland's memory," Emily said, meaning it.

Miss Pickering gave Emily a long look. She allowed, "It comforts me to ease their suffering."

Emily pushed back her chair and rose. "Good day to you."

She went and retrieved her bags and hunted down Inez. Hugging the crusty cook goodbye, she handed her Colin's letter and rushed across the street to Union Station.

Emily sat on the oval passenger bench, facing outward. She glanced up from the pages of *Sense and Sensibility* for the third time in fifteen minutes and checked the clock. The pendulum swung with a slow heaviness that matched her heartbeat.

Her time here wasn't supposed to end like this. Nothing had turned out the way she had hoped. When she first set foot on the island, her future held such promise before the storm reduced her plans to rubble. Now the only sure thing was her commitment to Nathan's son. What if she had to raise him alone?

Emily gave her head a firm mental shake and peered again at the clock. Ten more minutes before she boarded the train. She lifted the lid on the small travel trunk and set the novel on the top tray, securing the latch.

Emily scanned the station. Her gaze flicked on a familiar face threading through the passengers.

Colin.

His eyes darted about the station, scanning the faces in the crowd, searching. In one hand, he clutched his derby and her letter in the other. His gaze landed on her. The determined set of his jaw competed with his slipping composure.

"There you are," Colin huffed, appearing out of breath, his brows lowered. "I dropped by across… Inez flagged me down. You're leaving." His tone held an edge of disbelief. He slid her letter into his blazer pocket. "I thought that… I feared I'd be too late."

From the look of him, her news had caught him off guard. Since receiving the telegram, there had been little time to absorb the sudden changes for her either. Colin's arrival drove home the reality of her departure. She was leaving. Permanently. Would she ever see him again? Her stomach twisted. To her chagrin, tears blurred his face.

Noting her discomfort, Colin offered, "Here, let's move over there, shall we?"

He tilted his head toward the outer wall beyond the row of columns. He picked up her bags and led the way, weaving among passengers toting luggage and dragging their children in tow. He found a place behind the potted plants with their jutting palm fronds. When Colin set down Emily's bags beside the wall, they both started talking at once.

"I hated saying goodbye in a letter."

"You have an interview?" Colin smiled with forced cheerfulness. "I pray it goes well."

"It'll all work out as it should." She hoped so, anyway.

Colin ran a hand over his hair, smoothing it. "So … you turned down Nathan's proposal, eh?" Something flickered in his eyes that she couldn't quite read.

"I wanted more than he offered."

"Who knows," Colin shrugged, watching her, "he may come around yet."

"Regardless, I'm firm on where I stand."

"And you're, ah, you're adopting Chai Lin. That's quite a big step, raising a child alone."

"There'll be plenty of challenges, as you well know."

"Right. True." He pressed his lips together. "I hope you're not doing this to win Nathan over to the boy."

Emily shook her head. "He must decide for himself what he plans to do. Regardless, Chai Lin needs me."

"You know," he paused, his tone gentling, "adopting Chai Lin won't bring back Jake or Sarah. It won't fill that void in your life."

Her mouth pursed. "I thought you, of all people, would understand. You practically raised your sister." She tugged at the hem of her brown suit jacket and lifted her chin. "Chai Lin has *no one*. He need not be alone. I sense the rightness of becoming his mother."

As he regarded her, the weary lines deepened around the corners of his eyes. With a sharp pang, she wondered what it had cost him to shoulder the grief of an entire congregation and lose Grace, too. How alone he must be. Who would be there to support *him*?

She placed her hand on his forearm and gave a squeeze. "You've given so much of yourself to so many. You've grieved your sister and friends, a whole church full of hurting people. You poured out comfort on them all, on me."

The whistle blared, signaling boarding time.

Longing flared in his navy eyes. Colin reached for Emily's gloved hand, his thumb rubbing over her knuckles.

"I've lost so many," his voice faltered. "Must I lose you too?"

Emily's breath caught in her throat. What was he saying?

"You have become … the dearest to me." He paused, struggling to control the tremor in his voice.

"And you, my closest friend," she admitted, swaying on shaky ground, unsure of where they stood.

His hand cupped her cheek.

"Would that you desired more, for I would give it."

Emily went perfectly still. Her pulse stuttered and lifted. She met his gaze, taking in the warmth and tenderness directed at her alone. That look rocked her back on her heels. She raised an eyebrow, encouraging him to speak.

"I confess I fought against my growing affection for you, so diligently have I guarded my heart. Yet you managed to slip behind my reserve."

Emily licked her dry lips, struggling to absorb what he was saying.

"My intentions are honorable, I assure you," he whispered, his face leaning closer. "I couldn't let you leave without telling you how … beloved you are to me."

Vulnerability softened his eyes as he sought permission. Emily favored him with a faint smile. He kissed her temple and then lowered his mouth to hers. Her throat ached at his nearness.

Colin eased back, his gaze taking in her dazed expression. She felt the gap keenly.

He chuckled. "I have more to say when you can bear it. But I daresay you've heard quite enough for now. Do let me know how the interview goes."

"Of-of course." She ducked her chin, her cheeks warming.

The second whistle wailed.

The conductor called all aboard.

She glanced at the train, dragging her heels.

Colin carried her bags to the passenger car and handed them to the conductor. He took her hand, and she mounted the steps. She glanced down for one final glimpse, her knees softening beneath her.

"Godspeed, Emily," he spoke in a gravelly voice. "I'll be in touch."

Then Colin dipped his chin and strode through the station.

Emily had no time to ponder their parting. All too soon, the train rumbled out over the bay waters. How had she blocked from her mind having to cross the repaired bridge?

Her muscles whipped tight as she gripped the wooden handles. She dug in until her knuckles ached. Emily kept her gaze trained straight ahead on the passenger seated in front of her, staring at the ostrich plumes trembling above the woman's hat. From the corner of her eye she glimpsed the expanse of water, her insides quaking.

The tidewater slithered cold up her neck and over her nose. She held her breath, her lungs burning for air.

Emily broke out in a sweat and shut her eyes, blocking the view. With great effort, she shook off the memory.

Pull yourself together. You must. Chai Lin needs you.

She had to somehow move forward, even though her cousins remained missing. Her chin quivered. But how could she do that knowing that she'd sent Jake, Sarah, Lacey, Grace, and Lena to their watery graves? Her face burned with shame.

No one must ever know.

She must bear that terrible weight alone. What other choice did she have?

But how would she ever manage? Emily went still, her spine rigid.

Forget the past. Leave what happened behind on the island. There was no other way. She'd banish the memory of sending the others away. How else would she bear up under the strain of keeping such a terrible secret?

She vowed never to speak of the storm again. She'd bury the memories deep. Lock them away.

And somehow go on.

Chapter 44

Galveston Island, 1926

On the deserted stretch of beach, Emily sat hugging her tented knees close to her body. Her shoulders curled over her chest as she buried her face in the folds of her yellow shift.

A low keening rose from deep within, wrenching her body with sobs. Bitter regret knotted her belly for what might have been if only Jake, Sarah, and Lacy had grown up and Grace had blossomed into a young woman. If only Lena had lived to raise her unborn child. Her shoulders heaved under the weight of the secret she'd kept hidden. To this day, no one else ever knew she sent them all away.

When her weeping weakened into snivels, she became aware of the wet cotton draping her knees, the moist sea air coating her skin. She listened for a long while to the gentle shush of the surf while her pulse slowed. She ran her palm over the powdery sand. Its coolness soothed her senses.

She lifted her head, peering from beneath the brim of her hat. She rested her chin on her forearms and stared distantly at the sea while tears crusted her cheeks.

Though she'd buried the memories deep, at times, pieces had bubbled up in flashes and dreams until coming here sluiced them to the surface.

No one must ever know.

Did she dare bring what she had kept hidden out into the light? Could she tell her husband her deepest secret and risk losing his esteem? How could she not and be free? Her stomach clutched with apprehension.

Lord, calm my fears. Give me favor in his eyes.

The footfalls crunching the sand didn't register until a shadow slanted over her body.

"I haven't slept so soundly in ages. Must be the sea air."

Her husband lowered himself beside her, squatting on his haunches. "Our son called. He wants to go sailing tomorrow after the luncheon. He wants you to join us." His tone was light, belying the heaviness of the request. "I explained that you have no use for sailing. I did my utmost to discourage the idea, but you know how persistent he can be."

At her silence, he held out his palm and presented her with a pair of angel wing shells.

She fingered their thin, brittle ribs. "How lovely."

Emily glanced sideways at him from beneath swollen eyelids. His smile faded when he saw the evidence of her crying jag.

"Oh, love." He set the shells down and settled beside her, wrapping his arm around her waist. The warmth from his body penetrated the cotton shift. "I shouldn't have brought you here," he murmured. "I thought … I had hoped…" His sigh brushed her ear. "Forgive me."

She rested her head on his shoulder. "No, you did nothing wrong. I needed… I have to put right the past."

Her pulse roared in her ears. She hugged her tented knees. *Give me courage, Lord. Rid me of this crippling shame.*

"I sent them away," she blurted out before she lost her nerve.

He stilled. "Who, love?"

"Lena and the kids, and Grace."

"On the day of the Storm?"

Emily nodded, staring off with an unfocused gaze. The cry of seagulls pierced the silence. What must he think of her? Did he consider her to be as wretched as she felt?

"That morning, I sent Lena home," she pressed on, her voice trembling with the confession. "I foisted Jake and Sarah off on her. I—I told Grace she could go see the waves if she'd watch the kids while Lena rested."

"You had no way of knowing—"

"If I hadn't, they would have *stayed*. They would have *lived*." How could he make excuses for her? "I didn't want the children around when the officer came and questioned me, so … so I sent them away," she buried her face in her hands, "and they never came back," her voice cracked.

Hot tears slid down her palms, dripping between her fingers. When she collected herself, she lowered her hands. A white handkerchief dangled under her nose. She took it and wiped her face.

"Thanks."

He softened his voice. "The truth is all our days are numbered, and we will live out every one. Those who died that day lived out their last. You did nothing to hasten their passing. But in taking on that load, you carried a burden for something out of your hands. These things aren't up to you and me."

She stared at a sandpiper drilling its beak down into the sand as the scene came flooding back. Lena tossing over her shoulder, "See you in a little while," as she shepherded the children out the door and down the stairs with Grace, eager to see the big waves up close. Emily's perfect plan had sent them to their deaths, Andrew alone being spared. She wanted to believe her husband, but the guilt lay squarely on her shoulders.

As if sensing the direction of her thoughts, he asked, "Wasn't it early morning when they all left?"

She blinked. "Yes."

"As I recall, children were still out playing in the overflow that morning. Had it been later in the day when the Storm worsened, would you have sent them on their way?"

"Of course not, but that doesn't change a blessed thing."

"Doesn't it? You would have never willingly put them in harm's way. Rather, it's your nature to sacrifice, as you did for our son."

He peered sideways at her. "It was your sacrificial love for him that proved my undoing. I could no more resist my growing attraction for you when you lifted that determined chin and announced your plans to adopt him. From the start, you believed in him. You nurtured and shaped the young man he's become.

"Despite everything, you didn't allow the Storm to hold you back from teaching or becoming his mother. Then you agreed to marry me. No small commitment, that." He reached for her hand and kissed it. "Your love has made me a better man, a better father."

She wanted to believe that she'd made a difference in the lives of those most dear to her. Still… She swallowed, frowning.

"What troubles you, love?"

"Guilt and shame are clingy bedfellows," she admitted. She wasn't sure she could shake them off.

"Do you feel that Mrs. Kesler would want you to blame yourself for what happened, much less *her* blame you?"

Emily ran her fingers through the powdery sand, considering this. *Would* Lena have blamed her? She stared out into the waves, picturing her friend leaning in with a conspiratorial glint in her eyes, the scent of lavender wafting between them.

The answer came instantly without conscious thought. "No. No, she would not. She'd want me to be grateful I survived." Emily gave a watery smile, sensing the truth of it. "And knowing her, she'd call me a silly goose for blaming myself over things that were out of my hands." She chewed her lip as a memory surfaced. "That morning … Lena refused even the protection of an umbrella. Said the rain was a relief from the heat." Her chin wobbled. "If only we'd known."

"None of us did. We had no way of knowing what would unfold. That dark chapter caught us all by surprise, but it's not the final page in our story. That has yet to be written."

Emily hugged her knees. Those words held such hope.

She examined the wet blotches on her yellow shift and gathered more courage. She pushed the words past the tightness in her throat. "Do you forgive me?"

He waited until she returned his gaze. "I cannot pardon what I do not hold against you."

She cuddled closer, her body sagging with relief. Emily remained still and quiet for a long while as the knot in her chest began to loosen. She leaned in, kissing the cleft of his chin, and settled her head on his shoulder. His bergamot shaving soap offered a familiar comfort.

She didn't deserve this man. Memories of their courtship still warmed her. He'd persisted in pursuing her for the better part of a year. He wooed her with long letters, brief calls, and rarer visits, making his leaving harder when the spark caught fire between them. But he couldn't join her yet. Work kept him away. Until the day he showed up unannounced on her doorstep at the Buckner home, where she advanced to a leading teacher role. Dressed in his finest suit, he bent down on one knee and proposed, good and proper.

Two months later, they'd married. Grandpa Dunne rode the train to Dallas with her brother, Will, and performed the ceremony. She cherished being with her grandpa one last time before he passed on to his reward.

She'd adopted Chai Lin soon after arriving in Dallas. Joy brimmed to overflowing the day she signed the papers, legally making him her son. She treasured being his mother. As it turned out, Chai Lin would be their only child.

That her husband chose to step up and be the boy's father beggared belief. It took a remarkable man to raise another man's child. Whether he did it out of love for her or to honor a dying girl's plea, it mattered little. Emily adored him for it.

She tilted her head and peered up at Colin. The sea breeze tousled his walnut hair, now threaded with silver strands. In hindsight, she saw that things had indeed worked together for good.

Emily glanced up at the sun, climbing higher in the sky. It was time.

She released a deep breath to slow her quickening pulse. "I have something I must do before we go."

"Take your time." Colin must have sensed the importance of what she had in mind.

Emily stuffed the handkerchief into her pocket and pushed off the sand to her feet. She picked up a piece of driftwood a stone's throw away and went over where high tide had packed the sand firm. Colin joined her.

With the pointed end of the wood, she etched in the sand a rectangle two feet long with a rounded dome. In the upper center, she drew a square cross. Beneath the cross, she scrolled:

In Loving Remembrance
September 8, 1900

Squatting, she scooped up the gathered shells and outlined the headstone, pressing each one firmly in place. Then she lightly pressed the angel wing shells over the face of the cross.

Her lips trembled. Jake had loved shells.

Emily unfolded her stiff legs and stood, peering down at the memorial in the sand. Colin dusted off his trousers and pressed her snugly to his side. He draped his arm over her shoulder. She paused, searching for words, while the breeze fluttered the hem of her shift around her calves.

As she spoke, her voice quavered with emotion. "We're here at last to honor those who passed on that Saturday in September so long ago. I cannot change what happened or the things I deeply regret. But I can choose to remember. And in doing so, I can mourn and honor each of you."

Tears welled up and heated her eyelids. "Jake, you were braver than you knew. You proved it by shimmying up that tree during the Storm. I wish you could have grown old as you wanted … but I must accept that these things were out of our hands."

She swallowed hard. "Sarah, my little helper. You truly were the diligent one. That day of the Storm, you offered to stay and work. How I wish that you had."

Emily sniffed and dug out the handkerchief, dabbing her eyes. Colin reached for her hand, interlocking their fingers.

"Lacey, you were a fine playmate for Sarah. I picture y'all hand-in-hand even now." That image brought her comfort.

Emily paused, rubbing the heel of her palm over the ache in her chest. "Dearest Lena. I miss your friendship still. From the day we met, I felt like I'd known you all my life. I've had few friends as rare or as treasured as you."

"And Grace…" Emily peered up at Colin expectantly. "Would you like to say a few words?"

Colin nodded, his eyes misting. "Ah, Gracie, I suspect you're unraveling the mysteries of heaven with Mum and Dad." The tip of his nose reddened. "For so long, it was just the two of us. You gave my life purpose during the bleak years. I don't know how I would've managed without you." He cleared his throat. "I do so miss our fireside chats, for now."

After a moment, he bowed his head. "Lord, we entrusted the lives of our loved ones into Your hands years ago, not knowing their fates, but You knew. And You know the number of our days, as well. So until that day when we join them in Your presence, may You comfort our hearts with peace."

He fell silent. Above the surf, the whiffling breeze stirred the air between them.

Emily released his hand. "If only I had told you sooner."

Colin's eyes brimmed with understanding. "We all cope with tragedy in our own way, love. Just as we all grieve losses in our own time—when we're ready. And when we are, we can call upon the Comforter to ease our sorrow."

"It pained me to watch you suffer." Colin's brow drew together. "I witnessed the first of many nightmares and watched your distress worsen when your cousins went missing. Then after you moved away, you dodged any mention of the Storm. I assumed you were grieving in your own way and wished to move on. But once we married, I sensed it was more than that. And when my attempts to encourage you to talk were shunned," his voice gentled, "I was at a loss on how to help you. So, I prayed whenever I noticed the things that troubled you."

Emily wiped her nose. "Like what?"

"Certain things … like the wind howling or the rain pounding the roof made you restless. You shut your eyes whenever we drove on bridges that crossed over water. Estelle's letters made you cry. The month of September made you moody. I knew to take the stairs because your breathing quickened in elevators. It took you hours to recover from panic spells, so you'd lie down."

She sniffed. "That you noticed these things makes me feel less alone in my troubles."

"I've always understood that you endured far more than I." Seeing the protest forming on her lips, Colin lifted a brow in challenge. "*You* were pinned in water and nearly drowned. Then your cousins' bodies were never found. Such burdens challenge our ability to bear up under hardship."

"But looking back," Emily countered, "I can see that I made matters worse by allowing guilt and shame to silence me. I buried the memory of sending them away so I could go on."

With a gentle tug, he pulled her close. "Well, that's behind us, hmm? Promise me you won't keep things that trouble you to yourself. You were never meant to shoulder those burdens alone." His eyes searched hers for assurance.

Accepting help had never come easy for her, but she sensed the rightness of his request. With grace, she'd continue to work through what pained her. She drew in a deep lungful of salt air, her mind settling.

She circled her arms around his neck. "We'll move forward, together." She sealed the promise with a kiss.

Releasing a sigh, Colin wrapped her in his arms, hugging her tight. She soaked up his warmth and comfort, feeling lighter.

"That is what partners do," he murmured into her ear, seeming in no hurry to release his hold on her. "How I bless the day you entered my life, Mrs. Hensleigh."

Emily's mouth twitched. "I doubt you thought so at the time. I recall glaring up at you from under my hat, annoyed that you were late."

He eased back and tugged on the hat's wide brim, chuckling. "Proof that we miss things on first impression."

Side by side, they faced the sea. The tide sparkled like crystals cast upon the water. She watched the gentle swells topple and roll to the shore, foaming and washing near their feet.

These Gulf waters had indeed left an indelible mark upon her life, but water also cleansed. She peered down at a runner wave washing smooth her tribute in the sand, softening the face of the cross on its way out to sea.

Emily absently rubbed the puckered scar below her shoulder. It bore witness to the pain she'd endured. But scars also bore witness that she'd lived through the Storm.

With the sun warming her shoulders, thankfulness bubbled up for having survived and built a meaningful life, despite everything. Lena would have wanted that for her.

She sensed a shift in her spirit, a mingling of hope and peace. And peace was worth the cost of returning to the island, even the pain of remembering.

Epilogue

Emily's stomach fluttered in anticipation as Colin lifted the door knocker and let it fall.

Estelle had planned this anniversary luncheon weeks ago.

They had dressed for the occasion. Emily smoothed the wrinkles from her navy silk dress and gazed at the gold thread embroidery trimming the hem, sleeves, and belt around her hips. She patted her waves below her cloche hat.

"Stop fidgeting," her husband murmured. "You look lovely."

"You look rather dashing yourself."

She admired him in his navy striped suit and paisley necktie. Colin removed his hat, his fingers tracing the crease down the middle of his fedora.

A little tyke opened the door. He had his father's dark eyes and his mother's curls, though a deeper shade of blonde.

"Hi there." Emily stooped down, eye level. "Are you our greeter?"

"Uh-huh." The boy poked his tongue into his cheek.

Emily tousled his soft hair. "You must be John Thomas."

"Yes, ma'am," he replied.

Aunt Estelle came bustling down the hallway, her satin gown swishing below her knees.

"Come in," she called, her smile crinkling her eyes with pleasure.

Sweet and savory aromas beckoned them forward.

Memories, sharp and wistful, came rushing back as Emily stepped over the threshold.

"Let me have a look at you two." Her aunt's eyes roved over their appearance. "Emily, your hair is so stylish." Her aunt gathered her into a warm hug. Emily whiffed the same lemon verbena cologne she always wore.

Footsteps came up behind them. Uncle Clayton approached. "I see our guests of honor have arrived." He grasped Colin's hand and gave Emily a side hug.

Emily swallowed around the sudden lump forming. Jake would have looked like his father. Tall. Lean. The same hazel eyes.

Rachel and Andrew came treading down the stairs, hand in hand. When the Edwards returned home from Baytown years ago, the two had become inseparable. The playmates comforted each other in the absence of their siblings until love took hold. Now married, they joined the circle.

"Emily and Colin," Rachel beamed. "It's been ages since we've seen you." Her wavy bob swayed around her cheeks, set off by finger curls.

Emily grinned. "Enough time for y'all to grow up, I see."

"Have you met our youngest, John Thomas?" Rachel asked.

"We did," Colin mentioned. "The lad answered the door."

"His older brother is upstairs. You may have to rescue your son," Andrew chuckled. "Jake got carried away with his first aid lesson. That boy is a live wire."

The couple had named him Jacob Nathaniel in memory of Jake.

Emily batted her eyes dry at hearing the boy's name said aloud. "Where are they?" She could wait no longer to see her son.

"In Lin's room," Rachel replied.

"I'll see what I can do." Anxious for a moment alone, Emily set down her clutch on the hall tree and padded up the stairs.

Chai Lin had begun his studies at Texas Medical College in Galveston after serving in the Great War. Estelle had persuaded him to move in with them.

Emily paused before entering the room she had once called her own, the one facing Nathan's old balcony.

Emily rarely thought of Nathan. For sure, any love he claimed for her lacked substance. She occasionally read his syndicated articles on the smuggling through the border towns of Nogales, Tijuana, and El Paso. He moved throughout the southwest, reporting on the injustice of slave labor.

His father had died in Huntsville prison, ending any threat to Chai Lin.

Through the door, Emily heard voices.

"That's a little too tight, Jake," her son complained. "Ease up on the pressure. Ouch!"

"Sorry," Jake mumbled.

She knocked on the door.

"Enter," Chai Lin called.

She swung open the door. Her son lay on the bed, his arm in a sling, with one leg bound in a splint. Jake wrapped a bandage around Chai Lin's head until he resembled a mummy.

Peter Kesler sat on the rocking chair in the corner, his mouth trembling with amusement.

Peter had never remarried after losing Lena. Emily felt a tender knot of connection with him.

Chai Lin broke into a lopsided smile. "Mom! I'd hug your neck, but, well… I'm tied up at the moment." Emily rolled her eyes. A dimple winked at her from between the strips of bandages. "I could use your help breaking free. Dr. Jake, here, cinched the bandages pret-ty tight."

Emily glanced at Peter. "So, what's your role in this?"

"Supervising," he quipped with a twinkle in his eye.

"So I see."

Turning to Jake, she remarked, "It looks like you've done a thorough job dressing the patient's wounds."

Jake grinned at her. Like his namesake, Emily took in those hazel eyes, sun-bleached hair, and lanky build. The resemblance made her heart clutch.

"I'm Miss Emily, your second cousin," she told him.

"Hello," Jake replied. "Mom told me all about you."

"Did she?"

"Yep. Said you lived with her here when she was little."

"I did."

"Said you knew Grandma."

Ah, Lena. "Your grandmother was a very special friend."

Emily's gaze flickered to Peter, noting his moist eyes.

Jake's voice dipped low. "I never got to meet her."

"Well," Emily reached to untie the knot in Chai Lin's sling, "you would have loved her. And knowing your grandmother, she would have fed you lots and lots of apple strudel."

"Grandpa makes apple strudel sometimes."

"I imagine he uses the very same recipe."

Jake's mouth pulled into a smile before slanting. "Mom said you found Pop after the Storm. That you brought him here to stay until Grandpa fetched him."

It blindsided her hearing Andrew's story retold. "That's right. I reckon he was about your age then."

"Golly. I'd be scared to climb a tree in a storm."

Emily blinked at the child. She wanted to say, "You talk about this?" Instead, she reaffirmed what she knew to be true. "Wasn't he brave?"

"Yes, ma'am. Mom thinks so."

Emily unwound the cloth strips from her son's head while he unbound the splint. His leg freed, Chai Lin swung it onto the floor and sat up. He slung his arm around her shoulder and gave a squeeze. "I'm glad you're here."

"Jake," Peter motioned to his grandson, "come along. Miss Elsa may need some help in the kitchen."

Peter gave the boy a nudge out the door.

Emily looked around her old room, still painted blue. Masculine plaid drapes and bedding replaced the lace.

"About sailing," Emily broached the subject. Her son deserved an explanation. "While I appreciate the invitation, I—I'm—"

"Come with us," he insisted, taking her hand. "It's been ages since we did anything as a family."

"It has, but the truth is … water scares me witless. I nearly drowned during the hurricane. When the roof collapsed on the orphanage, remember?" He nodded. "Your father pulled me from the rising tidewater just in time. So, I wouldn't enjoy sailing, although I'd love to join y'all for supper at Gaido's afterward."

"Gaido's it is, then. I didn't know that happened to you."

Emily smoothed down his mussed hair. "Parents… We think we must be strong for our children."

"Well," Chai Lin's face softened with affection, "I couldn't have asked for a better mom and dad."

Silence slid comfortably between them.

"So," Emily said, peering sideways, "tell me about your new friend, Lorena. Where did y'all meet?"

"We work together on the wards at John Sealy. She's a nursing student. She's skilled at treating wounds, so she's not the least squeamish over threading a worm on a hook."

"Hmm, you go fishing often together?"

Chai Lin groaned at her lack of subtlety. "We're just friends."

"You know … your father and I started out as friends."

Chai Lin chuckled. "Let's go join Dad."

Emily paused at the hall tree and opened her clutch. As she dug out the envelope, she heard the warm voices flowing from the parlor as father and son greeted one another.

She entered the room as they pulled apart from a hug. They sat on the sofa, and she chose the seat between them.

Uncle Clayton resumed telling Colin about the church's growth through the years. Colin stayed as pastor until the congregation repaired the sanctuary, and the summer days faded into the autumn of 1901.

Weeks before they married, he had accepted a rural pastorate near Waxahachie, away from the sea. The congregation had embraced their little family, and there they stayed.

When the conversation lulled, Emily handed Clayton the envelope. "This is yours. I—I found it on the floor the day I moved out."

Uncle Clayton broke the seal and pulled out the card. He sucked in a breath. The edges had curled over time, and the paper yellowed with age. He fingered the scalloped ridges of the shells and examined the glob of hardened glue where a shell had peeled off. He met her gaze with watery eyes.

His smile turned poignant at the edges. "When I received those cards from Jake and Sarah, it gladdened my heart more than I can say. Thank you for returning it," he said with feeling.

Too choked to speak, Emily gave a nod.

The doorbell chimed, interrupting the somber moment. John Thomas raced to the door. In hobbled a familiar woman leaning on a cane.

"I never did abide folks who held up meals," she grumbled, "and now these old bones have made me that person."

"Inez!" Emily exclaimed, popping up to embrace her.

Estelle greeted the old cook as she headed back to the kitchen.

Inez eased down into a chair. "Wilhelmina and Ida said to tell everyone hey."

"How's the living arrangement working out?" Clayton asked, explaining that Inez had moved in with the two women.

"Fine, fine, now that they've started the relief work for families of fallen officers. It keeps Wilhelmina out of my business and curbs her wagging tongue." She gave a sly grin. "At least now she's spreading the word about needy families."

Emily recalled that Miss Pickering and Ida had once helped the families of officers who died in the Storm.

Estelle stepped back into the room. "Food has been set on the table. Shall we eat?"

Emily and Colin joined the others heading toward the dining room. Colin leaned in and murmured, "These walls house a lot of memories. How are you holding up?"

"Better. Yesterday was a real turning point."

"Well, you handled giving Clayton his card with utmost poise. I couldn't be more proud of you." He pressed a soft kiss to her temple.

Emily clasped hold of his hand, needing the warmth of his touch. Together they made their way to the dining room.

Emily discovered new strength from sharing things she'd long avoided. To her relief, her taking steps that heal seemed less daunting now that she accepted support.

They joined the others gathered around the table, each standing behind their chairs. The blue and white china and goblets filled with sweet tea gleamed in the sunlight.

On the sideboard, there were serving bowls and platters filled with baked ham, chicken and cornbread dressing, crab cakes, sweet potato casserole, and black-eyed peas. A layered cream cake on a pedestal plate towered over pecan pies.

Clayton cleared his throat. "It's good to have you two with us," he began, his voice rough with emotion as he divided a look between Colin and Emily. "What a joy to gather as family and old friends to celebrate your silver anniversary. Before we say grace, let's take a moment to pause and remember those who have gone on before us."

Emily blinked, moisture forming behind her eyelids. What healing and comfort came from telling stories and from honoring the memory of their loved ones.

Estelle sniffled. Clayton handed her his handkerchief and she dabbed her eyes.

After giving Estelle a moment, Clayton asked, "Colin, will you offer thanks?"

Forming a close circle, they linked hands. As Emily twined her fingers with Colin and Chai Lin's, she drank in the golden moment. Thankfulness welled up for these greater treasures of family and friends. Each one had been placed in her life at that critical juncture years ago, just when she needed them most.

Though that dark time remained veiled in mystery, as was the way of trials, in hindsight, she could see a trail of goodness and mercy following throughout her days.

Looking back, she could see God's hand at work, picking up the fragments of her life and arranging them. Like a stained-glass mosaic, the darker, jagged edges of testing and hardship contrasted the richer, smoother pieces. Even the discarded shards He used. For with God, nothing was ever wasted.

Perhaps on that final day, she would gaze down upon her life once the veil lifted. Catch a fleeting glimpse of light streaming through the intricate design. Then she would better understand the refining work which forged her character and built up her faith. His handiwork no less radiant, though pieced together, for the Master Rebuilder of Souls was crafting beauty out of the rubble.

Author's Historical Notes

This book involved more than 20 years of research and writing. In fact, historical accounts fueled my imagination and often steered the plot.

The Great Storm gripped me the first time I arrived on the island in the late 80's and stood before a 1900 chromolithograph entitled, *1900 Galveston Hurricane and Tidal Wave*. I remembered staring, transfixed, at the image of waves the size of houses crashing, timber piling between toppled homes, people being pulled up on rooftops, bodies tossed by the waves. I took in the compelling scene and wondered how I had lived in Texas for more than a decade yet knew nothing about the deadliest hurricane in American history. I remember saying, "If I were to ever write a novel *that* would be the backdrop."

I wove actual people into the story, some merely mentioned, others showing up: Dr. Robert Cooke Buckner; Galveston's police chief Edwin Ketchum; the wife of the pastor of First Baptist Church, Jesse Wooten Harris; chief meteorologist Isaac Cline; Pirate Jean Lafitte and his deckhand, known to the locals as "Crazy Ben" Dollivar; Clara Barton, founder and president of the American National Red Cross; Fannie B. Ward, traveling writer with the Red Cross; Herbert W. Lewis with the Red Cross Orphanage; and Ray Marsh, assistant supervisor of the Red Cross warehouse.

Galveston excels on preserving its history. The Galveston and Texas History Center housed in the Rosenberg Library provided a wealth of information about island history, the Great Storm, and the Relief effort which followed.

I used the following books as references: *Through a Night of Horrors* by Casey Edward Greene and Shelly Henley Kelly; *A Weekend in September* by John Edward Weems; *Galveston and the 1900 Storm: Catastrophe and Catalyst* by Patricia Bellis Bixel and Elizabeth Hayes Turner; *Galveston: a History* by David McComb; and *Galveston: a History of the Island* by Gary Cartwright.

I hunted through *The Galveston Daily News* archives and found accounts on the Storm and the building and dedication of the Galveston Orphans Home. The original layout of the Galveston Orphans Home, reported in *The Galveston Daily News*, was built in 1895, and differs from the one that houses the Bryan Museum on 21st Street. I used the description of the building from the newspaper, dated September 1, 1895; and the layout on the Sanborn Map, 1899. Originally the home resembled a capital E shape and to my knowledge it had no office under the twenty-foot wide staircase or hallway closet. I created them as it suited the story.

I spoke with and wrote to individuals who referenced the Orphans Home online. Among them were those who had ancestors in the Orphans Home in 1900, like Darrell Marullo and Linda Groff, who each provided me copies of orphan records dated June 1, 1900. I included the records in my story and added a few fictitious columns. I also deviated from the historical timeline by adding an Asian boy. At the time, the home admitted only white, protestant children.

The *Texas Post Opera Glass* newspaper reported the lives spared at the Galveston Orphans Home on 21st Street was considered a miracle. The children had marched out of the east hall, which collapsed after they left that portion of the building. All the orphans and refugees who took shelter there survived, though the home had extensive damage. When the water receded, the children were moved to a nearby frame house, where they spent the night.

According to the *Baptist Standard*, dated September 4, 2000, sixty-seven-year-old R.C. Buckner rushed to Galveston after the storm and took more than a hundred orphans, including those of the Galveston Orphans Home, to his Dallas orphanage, where they remained until the Galveston home was rebuilt. Also included in my novel is *The Galveston Daily News* article regarding Buckner leaving the island with the orphans.

Fundraising events for the Orphans Home were backed by William Randolph Hearst and Mark Twain. The home was rebuilt and reopened by 1902.

The Red Cross Headquarters temporary orphanage used furnishings from the damaged Galveston Orphans Home.

According to library's vertical file on the Galveston Orphans Home, the home had been struck by lightning twice during construction. The second time one of the workers lost his life.

In John W. Harris's oral history, he told of a man impaled on the fence at the Orphans Home on 21st Street during the storm, and he was not allowed outside to play after the storm.

According to a staff member at the Galveston Children's Home, Hurricane Ike destroyed all the old orphan records.

The Galveston Orphans Home now houses The Bryan Museum. Check out this unique Texas museum, which highlights the building's history, the orphanage, and Texas and Western history. You may find the museum online at thebryanmuseum.org. It was quite a thrill to tour the museum and walk throughout the rebuilt orphanage.

I discovered a little known fact about the Storm, according to Mr. Casey Greene. The US Weather Bureau archives at the Rosenberg Library speculated that at 6:30 p.m. a satellite tornado took off the top of the Galveston Orphans Home and hit First Baptist Church, where it knocked off the steeples and the back upstairs bedroom of the parsonage.

First Baptist Church of Galveston graciously provided me with a copy of their historical records. According to the church's history, William Mercer Harris, pastor of First Baptist Church in 1900, reported that a tornado struck the church at 6:30 p.m. and blew a steeple into the parsonage. The family had brought their cow into the kitchen after the animal began treading water in the yard. The family later laid a plank out the window and walked the plank to safety.

I found no other survivors' accounts about a tornado spawning from the storm. However, Harris's grandson, Fletcher Harris, a survivor of Hurricane Ike in 2008, told *USA Today* that a tornado had destroyed his grandfather's church during the 1900 storm. Hence, it is clear the family passed down this story.

In his special report of the Galveston Hurricane of September 8, 1900, Dr. Isaac Cline, Local Forecast Official and Section Director, reported going around the Strand and advising merchants to put their goods on upper shelves, given the rising water. I used much about the details of the storm from his report and survivor stories.

Mrs. Fannie B. Ward, Special Assistant with the Red Cross wrote a poignant account of the Storm's aftermath in Clara Barton's Report of the Relief Effort, including an interview with a man in charge of a crematory. Miss Barton referred to Mrs. Ward as "the Mistress of the Robes," after putting Mrs. Ward in charge over women's and children's clothing.

In researching the Chinese Exclusion Act during 1900, I found accounts of customs fraud and smuggling the Chinese crossing the border through Nogales, Arizona, and young Chinese females through the Chinese Underground Railroad in El Paso, Texas, underscoring that human trafficking is an age-old problem.

Group Discussion Questions

1. What characters in the story did you relate with? Why?
2. Emily struggled with trust issues. How did that affect her relationships and her faith?
3. Treasure was a theme throughout *A Writing Upon the Sand*. What were some of the things that Emily treasured in her life? How did it affect her decisions? In chapter 17, Colin told Emily to beware of the lure of counterfeit treasure or it could rob her of what is most priceless. What do you think he meant by that? Have you ever been tempted by something that appeared real, but wasn't? What did you learn from it?
4. How was Emily's integrity and character tested? Were you ever tempted to do something that went against your conscience? How did you handle it?
5. Was there anything about the Great Storm of 1900 that surprised you?
6. All of Emily's plans were upended because of the Storm and its aftermath. Discuss a time when you went through a life-altering event. How have you grown from that experience?
7. Emily's faith was tested when God grew silent. How did it affect her? Have you ever had your faith tested in ways that stretched you or knew of someone who did? What advice would you give Emily?
8. Colin told Emily that we all cope with tragedy and losses in our own way and in our own time—when we're ready. Discuss the reasons Emily responded the way she did. How do you handle tragedy and losses in your life?
9. Emily dealt with harboring the shame of a tragic secret by forcing herself to forget what happened and go on with life. How would you have handled the situation if you were Emily?
10. In hindsight, Emily saw goodness and mercy throughout her days. Looking back on hard times, do you see goodness or mercy now that you may have missed then? How might that encourage you as you move forward?